# Cassie's Comet

## By Scotty Comegys

Edited by Nina P. Flournoy

**CASSIE'S COMET**

Cover by Dar Albert, Wicked Smart Designs
Copyright © 2023 NFES Publishing
All rights reserved.
ISBN: 979-8-9884688-0-6

## DEDICATION

In memory of my parents,
Jack and Marilyn Comegys, who
owned a 1960 Mercury Comet
they called Joy Green.

**CASSIE'S COMET**

# ACKNOWLEDGMENTS

My sincere thanks to the indefatigable Nina P. Flournoy, intrepid editor and multitasker who shepherded this novel—and me—through publication.

Long before the manuscript landed into Nina's Dropbox, I wrote a short story based on my experience at a Dutch border crossing in the 1970s. Converting that story into an 83,000-word novel required considerable assistance from a number of hardy souls. Sally Hamer and Liz Talley schooled me on craft. Critique partners, Phylis Caskey and Sandra Haynie, kept me on track through numerous subplots and drafts.

Cynthia Swanson, Kat Howard, and John Locke read early drafts and offered helpful advice and criticism. Julia Weber, freelance editor in Bremen, Germany, provided a German perspective.

Old friends and new acquaintances assisted with details and special insights. Cindy Dorfman and Cornell Flournoy reviewed drafts and helped to ease a bumpy path. And from World War II to Vietnam recollections, airport security, French vernacular, the Iranian revolution, and American military justice, sources generously shared first-hand knowledge. Caroline Ancelet, John Focht, Ali and Sanaz Hashempour, Don Huguley Jr., Ken Mattheyer Jr., Camille Meehan, and Jay Murrell contributed particulars I would not otherwise have been privy to. My apologies for inadvertent omissions, as many encouraged me along the way.

Finally, I am indebted to my children Clare and James, who offered unwavering support, and to my sisters Kennon and Johnette, who remember our family car, Joy Green the Comet, and agree that the book cover does the old car justice.

## CONTENTS

|   | Acknowledgments |   |
|---|---|---|
| 1 | Cassie Tate, Marshall, Texas, 1979 | 1 |
| 2 | Donny Ray Duggan, Bremerhaven | 5 |
| 3 | Cassie's Mercurial Comet | 8 |
| 4 | Donny Ray's German Autumn | 14 |
| 5 | One Silver Token | 20 |
| 6 | Bad News in Bremerhaven | 32 |
| 7 | Put the Blame on... | 37 |
| 8 | Donny in Disguise | 55 |
| 9 | Amsterdam, the Western Netherlands | 64 |
| 10 | Great Balls A'Fire | 74 |
| 11 | Dirt on Your Head | 79 |
| 12 | The Big Pitch | 81 |
| 13 | Schiphol Looming | 87 |
| 14 | Tinker Toy Man | 93 |
| 15 | High Beams, Bright Lights | 101 |
| 16 | Gaul Aboard | 107 |
| 17 | The Gambler | 115 |
| 18 | Hot Poker | 119 |
| 19 | Smoke on the Water | 125 |
| 20 | Up Against the Wall, Redneck | 129 |
| 21 | Spent Bombshells | 134 |
| 22 | Paladin, Paladin, Where Do You Roam? | 142 |

| | | |
|---|---|---|
| 23 | Swa-Swa-Swastika | 145 |
| 24 | Took No Prisoners | 149 |
| 25 | Staple Goods | 155 |
| 26 | And Made Them Cry | 163 |
| 27 | For What It's Worth | 168 |
| 28 | Papa Was A Rolling Stone | 173 |
| 29 | Too Much Talk | 177 |
| 30 | Tightening Screws | 182 |
| 31 | Slamming the Cradle | 188 |
| 32 | Genuine Pretense | 192 |
| 33 | Baby Needs New Shoes | 195 |
| 34 | Immigration Man | 198 |
| 35 | Paging Dr. Zhivago! | 205 |
| 36 | Black Velvet Chances | 214 |
| 37 | Caught Together, Hanged Together | 220 |
| 38 | Paper Tiger | 224 |
| 39 | Ramping Up | 229 |
| 40 | Luxembourg | 233 |
| 41 | Sugar Time | 235 |
| 42 | One Job | 239 |
| 43 | Love is Blue | 242 |
| 44 | Tired Tires and Fan Belts | 251 |
| 45 | Bubbling Bouillon | 258 |
| 46 | A Standup Couple | 267 |
| 47 | Hare Rama, Hare Rama | 272 |
| 48 | Ipana Fangs | 279 |

| | | |
|---|---|---|
| 49 | Dateline Schiphol: 11/03/1979 | 282 |
| 50 | Two Out of Three Ain't Bad | 284 |
| 51 | Braniff Stitched in Blue | 288 |
| 52 | Dateline Dallas: 11/04/1979 | 292 |
| 53 | All the Federales Say… | 296 |
| 54 | Culture Shock | 300 |
| 55 | All Spent | 305 |
| 56 | School of Hard Coughs, 1992 | 310 |
| 57 | Ribbon and Threads | 319 |

**CASSIE'S COMET**

# CHAPTER 1

## Cassie Tate

## *Marshall, Texas*

### *1979*

The empty eyes of half-melted mannequins gazed from the ruins of Gorgeous U, where glamour girls on billboards once soared through the heavens on swings tethered to the stars. Nearby, fire investigators in yellow hard hats worked through drenched black rubble. Smoldering wigs, airborne toxins, and broken dreams were all that remained of Gorgeous University—the area's premier cosmetology institute.

Cassie wiped tears from her ash-smudged cheeks and coughed through wisps of smoke. Gorgeous U should have been her alma mater, the ticket to high-paying hair styling careers with the ultimate job security. Whatever the economy, Texas women never missed their hair appointments—no matter how broke they were.

Sniffling, she kicked a charred placard, sending up little flecks of ash, rising like gnats from a dying philodendron. Grime blackened her sandals. All that time and money, student loans, and aggravation—now reduced to burnt curlicues on the ground. No pot of gold in the debris, no promises of the wherewithal to pay the electric bill on time. She used to have nice things, well some, before Donny Ray Duggan left town.

Dabbing her eyes with a soggy pink tissue, she shuffled back to her car—a 1960 Mercury Comet, the metallic turquoise relic shimmering in the August sun. When all else failed, she still had the Comet, like a trusted friend. Cassie reached into the driver's window to open the door from the inside and sat down hard on the cloth seat with its sleek vinyl trim.

A fat tear plopped on the steering wheel as she pulled out into local traffic on Highway 59 running through Marshall. She glanced around at the strip shopping center with grocery stores and a pizza joint, none offering better jobs than cosmetology—certainly not better than teaching, which had been her first choice.

To think she'd missed out on North Texas State's renowned College of Education. But money was scarce. Her father, Johnny Frank Tate, had died, then her mother, Della, checked out, and their death benefits didn't cover much. She couldn't swing the hefty student loans for four-year sleep away college just north of Dallas.

Moreover, to her dismay, she hadn't qualified for scholarships. She figured she wouldn't have gotten into the school anyway. Her grades had gone off the rails on account of Donny Ray, the absolute love of her life.

At the time her priorities made sense. He made her feel special. A football star who showered her with little gifts, he kept her all to himself. Truth be told, she didn't want to go off and leave him.

His spray-painted initials were still faintly visible on the viaduct up ahead. He hadn't seen the value of a college diploma. "Baby, you already know how to beautify," he'd said, softening his dark eyes. "Get paid for your natural talent here. We'll save money on family haircuts."

And that was it: her Donny Ray Forever Plan.

Unfortunately, the Army signed him before she did, but he wrote her mushy letters from basic training at Fort Benning.

"Someday we'll stand in front of a minister," he'd written, "and then we'll say I do." She kept the letter under her pillow at night. Her mother always said if you did that, it would come true. Cassie now doubted it.

Up ahead, as one lane of traffic opened, she seized the opportunity to switch lanes to make the light, saving maybe half a minute. Even small victories counted. Only 9:00 a.m. and the summer day would only get hotter. She was already thirsty. Might as well go home.

Her Comet's motor shook past Ward's restaurant—a Marshall landmark with picture windows looking out onto East Grand Avenue. She bet the folks in there knew what happened, but no sense in wasting breakfast money. She turned up the radio volume.

"Arson investigation continues," the reporter announced. "Police spokesmen suggest that acetone and cleaners overheated in a locked, windowless storage hut."

Frowning, Cassie tapped the steering wheel. Made sense, she thought—bleach and ammonia mixed with permanent wave solution, plus manicure glue. With all those fumes you'd have a regular nuke in there. Beauty school had taught her more about chemistry than high school science ever had.

KEEL 710 Radio returned to regular programming and music blared "I Will Survive." She wondered if she could.

At 22, she'd pinned all her hopes on Donny Ray, letting other husbandly prospects slide. Hardly any good material remained around town now. Her older brother Beecher was no help with introductions, either. All he'd come up with was a Vietnam War buddy with poor posture. She'd rather wait for Donny Ray.

Why hadn't she heard from him? Three months, six months? Well, it hadn't been a year, but it sure seemed that long. He used to write a lot from West Germany and even sent her a Heidi-style music box. In return, she kept him stocked with Jade East cologne and canned enchilada sauce.

She still had a couple of boxes waiting to send him, but he had to write first. She loved him, but she had her pride. Besides, all she had was his old address. Couldn't he at least send a postcard?

# CHAPTER 2

## Donny Ray Duggan
### *Bremerhaven, West Germany*

A Heineken clock glowed green through cigarette haze. Quarter to three: last round. "*Letzte Runde!*" The bartender, her face tense, dried down the beer taps, squinting into the shadows beyond the counter. Perched on a barstool, Donny Ray Duggan flicked ashes into a shot glass and watched her move. For a woman past 30, she still had the grooves.

"Bri-GEET-a!" He threw a parched peanut at her.

Her heavy eyebrows knitted a deep frown. Bulky and pale, Brigitta would not have been his type back home in Texas, but she'd rattled his headboard and stoked his adrenaline on the shores of the North Sea. Now he couldn't turn her loose.

Donny Ray wheedled. "Aw come on, stone face! Let's see a smile."

She jerked her head toward the last patron wobbling to the door, a pickled egg bulging from his lips. Streetlights shone into the tavern before the heavy oak slammed shut behind him. She handed Donny Ray her keys, but he didn't budge. She slapped his arm with a damp cloth. "Get your ass up and bolt the door."

"Nah, just keep talking." Her thick accent got him every time. Reflected in the mirror above the bar, the outline of her panties pressed against her jeans. He pinched his cigarette and took a final drag before sauntering over to the exit, where he keyed the deadbolts and secured a heavy steel brace to barricade entry.

Stiffening behind the counter, Brigitta motioned him to come back. Her widened eyes reflected the strain in her voice. "They know."

He toyed with his cigarette lighter. "Who?"

"*Bundeskriminalamt.*"

Hmmm, the West German feds, he thought. "And what do they know?"

Brigitta wiped the counter in hard circles. "They're tracking small arms." Her voice dropped to a whisper.

"And now I'm supposed to be a lip reader? Speak up. Jesus. Quit worrying."

"We leave the Continent now," Brigitta said, clutching his shoulder.

He brushed her hand away. "Cool your jets."

A hundred times he'd told her: his Army hitch wouldn't be up until next Spring. Then he'd be done—three years, that's all he was giving it. He'd never planned a military career; he only wanted out of Texas for a while, vowing to be home for his 26th birthday, and Brigitta thought she was going with him.

Too bad. He liked things as they were in Bremerhaven, but he didn't want to be responsible for a foreigner in the U.S., and good God, what if she got pregnant? Oldest trick in the book for a Permanent Resident Card—a green card—and a "green card marriage."

He threw back a fresh shot of Scotch. The burn ran down his throat, and warmth rushed through his veins—especially with Brigitta and her jugs-fest standing right there.

"What about Aldo and Jusef?" Thumping a cigarette pack, Donny Ray studied her face.

Brigitta said Aldo would probably go back to Berlin, which made sense; he'd been a mechanic in the Nazi bigwigs' motor pool during World War II. Still had friends and connections in the city. But as for Jusef, Brigitta reddened. "Dual loyalties. German and Iranian."

Both? An alarm buzzed in Donny Ray's brain.

Right. The two countries had a history of strange politics—odd bedfellows, with Muslims in the Nazi SS, and the German war machine running on Persian oil. Iranian oil. Jusef, born in Hamburg to Iranian parents, was among thousands of Iranians living in West Germany after the war. As a kid in the 1950s, he was shipped to England for school while his embittered family scattered. With underground connections, he was well positioned to assist the Islamic revolution, which had toppled the Shah of Iran in January 1979, only six months ago, with some help from stockpiled American-made armaments. And with the help of Donny Ray.

"My god is money," he'd once said, and looking back, he suspected Brigitta had seen "sucker" flashing in strobe lights over his head. Gitta gave him the impression she was doing him a big favor by introducing him to Aldo, a moon-faced old Mercedes-Benz mechanic who'd kept Hitler's bulletproof limo running right. His breath smacked of cigarettes and Schnapps, and with half-glasses perched on his vein-splashed nose, Aldo promised Mercedes expertise for someone with a strong back, closed mouth, and a premier skill set.

Check, check, and check. Brigitta had handed over her prize. Donny Ray saw it all now, like a mythical beast powering out of the North Sea, pulling him into the undertow of Gitta's dark world. Gun running had its own kind of beasts. Jusef. Aldo. And more. Who were they? It hadn't seemed to matter. He craved the excitement and the money—the big money he could only fantasize about back home.

## CHAPTER 3

### Cassie's Mercurial Comet

Brakes squealed as Cassie rounded a turn. The Comet had been her mother's car, passed on to Cassie, so it was old when she got it. Even so, it was the only thing her parents handed down that made a difference in her life—and at this point, the car was the only thing she had going for her. One of the only things that was hers alone. Her statement.

Way back, after she and Donny Ray went public, he spent a lot of time under the hood. "Let me at it," he'd said, "and we'll lay some bets on the quarter."

Everybody knew about the guys racing cars on an oilfield access road outside of town. They'd see who could clock the highest speed in just a quarter mile. Donny Ray had a Corvette, but he wanted the element of surprise in competition—so he pocketed a lot of green after converting the Comet's single-barrel Holley carburetor to a four-barrel. People couldn't believe such a small car had all that power. "It's a comet in the sky!" he bragged.

Cassie never raced, but Donny Ray showed her how to pop the clutch before stomping the accelerator, and whooee, a handsome black peel of rubber smoked the concrete, quad headlights gleaming. He liked that the car had no air-conditioning—less drag on the motor, though she wished he'd installed an after-market unit before he left town. And a working turn signal. She had to stick out her arm.

From her dreamscape, Cassie punched her left arm straight out towards Donny Ray, when a honk from two cars behind snapped her back to the present, dissolving the memory. She checked the rearview mirror, changed lanes again, and slowed the pace. She wanted to resuscitate the Donny Ray Forever Plan, but beauty school had been a bust. She'd clipped more ears than hair, and the dyes made her sneeze. Cassie—the former star pupil of St. Mary's Dominican—had failed.

Well, she hadn't exactly been the star at St. Mary's, but she did win first place in a French translation contest ("*Parlez Vous* and You") and even got her picture in the *Marshall News Messenger*. The nuns dubbed her a budding genius, but the bloom fell off when she transferred to public school. Grades became a tolerable nuisance, almost wholly eclipsed by Donny Ray's letter jacket.

Cassie massaged her brow. She shuddered at the thought of returning to work at the Piggly Wiggly cashier lane, but she didn't know what else to do. She'd spent most of her savings, and her brother was already leaning on her—him and his Army pal, a kind of nowhere man with an inordinate amount of animal magnetism. He sort of unnerved her, but Beecher said he owed his life to the guy, so he could at least give him a place to crash for a while.

It had been four years since North Vietnamese tanks rolled into Saigon, and American helicopters lifted desperate crowds from the chaos. Surrendering and raising the Viet Cong flag might have ended the war, but psychological horrors continued. Although Beecher and his buddy were now safe in Marshall, Cassie sometimes heard their cries at night.

She turned onto Burleson, a street of mostly older homes, with an occasional ranch style in the mix. Air conditioners hummed in the windows, and gray asbestos tiles peeped through tangled vines at the back of her house. It belonged to her and Beecher now, orphaned adults with double cemetery dues. Their dad died first—cardiac arrest—and three years later, their mother Della followed him into the Scottsville cemetery. Her brother called it the dirt motel.

Both parents had outlived their first child, a fact that Della wailed about for years until she couldn't stand it anymore. She went out clutching a gun and a picture of Baby Patsy drooling on a fur rug. Taking her own life was the last thing Cassie expected her mother to do. You just can't know what stirs inside a person's mind. That was Cassie's takeaway.

She slammed the car door and trudged up the back steps, a broken spring twanging on the screen door. Beecher looked up from the newspaper, his elbows on the maple table. Purple jelly smears and scrambled egg bits stuck on his breakfast plate.

"Man, you're screwed! Heard on the radio, it's a total loss. So, what's gonna happen now?"

Cassie leaned against the kitchen drainboard. "Probably leave us hanging. Take bankruptcy and leave town."

He put the newspaper down. "You better come up with something. You can't come looking to me for a handout."

"Didn't say I would!" She bit her lips on the inside and reached for a dented percolator. Hands trembling, she poured the last cup of coffee, padded to the table, and parked in a wooden captain's chair. Sipping the bitter sludge, she rotated the lazy-susan in silence. Crusty bottles of hot sauce and past-due utility bills crept past in a slow roll of yellows and reds.

For a second, Beecher lost his grip on the newspaper. "Where'd you get that?"

"The mug?" Cassie pursed her lips and met his stare. "Donny Ray sent it to me." She tipped it to show the embossed slogan, *Willkommen in Bremerhaven*. "It means welcome to Bremerhaven."

"I figured that much," Beecher said. "Thought I threw that out. Did he finish his hitch?"

"I don't think so." She outlined the raised letters on the mug with her finger.

"He never would've made it in Nam." Beecher snapped the newspaper. "Military's just a country club now they've got rid of the draft. They don't know how to fight."

"He used to fight plenty!" Cassie's voice rose, irritation tightening her lips.

"Yeah, in parking lots. Give me a break."

"You started it." She slid a copy of *Glamour* out from under a pile of mailbox circulars and opened it to the hairstyle feature. Little diagrams showed how to twist brush rollers to achieve the right effect, but she couldn't work them out on her beauty school mannequin. Her hair hung long and straight past her shoulders unless she used a curling iron, a cosmetic miracle by all accounts.

A shuffle on the patterned linoleum meant trouble. Cassie looked up. Chuck Denton slouched in the doorway, his sleepy eyes fixed on hers. He seemed to be looking into her soul and stealing her underwear.

Her brother clanged a spoon on his plate. "Hey Chuck," he said, "ask Cassie about Donny Ray's military service."

"Here we go again," she blurted.

"Thinks he's Elvis," Beecher said. "Tooling around Germany in an Army Jeep. But me and Chuck were heroes. Am I right, Chuck?"

Chuck grimaced, cracked his knuckles, and eyeballed Cassie. "What's cooking?"

"Nothing." Heat rose in her verges.

"What you got there?"

"Celebrity haircuts. Look here." Cassie licked her thumb and pinched the pages. "See, Charlie's Angels." She held the magazine upright for a moment. Chuck sidled over to the table and dropped into a chair between her and Beecher.

"Looks good." Chuck flicked through the pages. "I'll take one of everything."

"Uh, yeah." She closed the magazine, shoved it aside, and diverted her eyes to a vitamin bottle.

Six weeks had passed since Chuck first threw his stained duffel bag on the couch. Cassie thought he'd cleaned up real nice. Plus, his exciting stories of firefights and grenades reminded her of Steve McQueen in *Bullitt*—the dirty blond "King of Cool" with blue eyes and swagger. Chuck didn't have a badass Mustang GT, but he didn't need one.

She had resisted his charms, though, as her history with Donny Ray transcended all time and space. Without him, she had no real sense of herself. She lived for the day he'd reappear. Everything would go back to the way it used to be, with one difference: she'd be wiggling a Keepsake diamond on her finger. Not the kind of thing Chuck would do. You wouldn't catch him at the mall sorting through the Zales inventory.

Besides, he teased her and kept secrets. Chuck usually wore long sleeves, but the other day she'd caught a good look at him in a wife-beater shirt at the breakfast table. Pinkish, shiny skin snaked down his upper left arm, some of it jagged and glossy like silk thread, all the way to his elbow, and red dots peppered his forearms in tiny starbursts. He said he'd met the wrong end of a hatchet on the Ho Chi Minh Trail, which suggested a lot of manly testosterone in action but was probably the reason he went cuckoo for a while.

She figured none of that should matter to her anyway. Not the scars, not his smirk, not even that tight butt of his wrapped in faded Levi's. Chuck was frequently gone, a sure sign he was suit-casing—moving in with different women without the pretense of commitment.

Cassie wasn't falling for some lover-boy gadabout. She wanted permanence, with a wedding band gleaming on her finger when she reached for canned corn at the grocery store, to show she was worthy—a woman with a husband.

And babies, she wanted fat-fisted babies—the mark of real status. In this respect, she was her mother's daughter. Della had taught her that's what life is about. "You can talk all you want about Women's Lib and stuff," her mother used to say, "but it's a man's world, and honey don't you forget it." Della had never been wrong about such matters, and Cassie bought the whole package.

She did a slow blink as she reached for her coffee mug. It's true, Beecher had a fistful of medals, and he said Chuck did, too. Only now the war heroes were unemployed and hanging around the kitchen. Rising from the table, Beecher rolled up the classified section and popped it across the palm of his hand. "There's some openings down at the glass plant."

"I'm in." Chuck opened the back screen door.

Before it bounced closed behind him, Cassie twisted in her chair, taking one last look at Chuck's butt. Back-and-forth, back-and-forth. Donny Ray better hurry home.

# CHAPTER 4

## Donny Ray's German Autumn

Donny Ray leaned forward on the bar, locking his eyes on Brigitta's impassive countenance. With a sudden burst of paranoia, he had a bristling fear he was being played, being watched. Disposable. She was holding back on him. He faked a jab at the side of her face, pulling the punch at the last second. She didn't flinch.

"I need another drink," he growled. "And you need to tell me what's going on."

She wiped her hands and deposited a bottle of single malt Scotch with a fresh shot glass in front of him. "Here. Have fun." Fuming, she poured a glass of Spätburgunder, and slammed back a gulp, taking a deep breath. She said nothing.

He slapped the counter. "Turn the music down. I can't think with the goddamn Bee Gees yelling in my ears."

"I like the music loud." Brigitta gripped his collar and pulled him to her, cupping her hands over his ear. "Be still. Maybe microphones?" She scribbled on a bar napkin: *Rote Armee Fraktion.*

Donny Ray shrugged, narrowing his eyes. Her face tightened. She scribbled, scowling. "Red Army Faction—the RAF. West German militants. With Stasi support."

His throat tightened. Stasi! The East German security service—secret police, espionage, the whole ball of wax tied up with Soviet KGB string. "Damn, I always thought the RAF was the British air force," he muttered.

She grimaced, shaking her head, and scribbled again. "Baader-Meinhof Gang."

"Oh, those guys—yeah!" He'd seen the training films for the duty station here.

Far-left militants, they objected to former Nazis' presence in the West German government and the Americans' role in rebuilding the post-war economy. The RAF had signature moves—bomb attacks, hostages, assassinations. Kidnaping. Killing. Hijacking. The terrorist activities escalated into fury known as the German Autumn, from summer into fall of 1977. Then in mid-October, four of those sons-of-bitches died in Stammheim Prison, the supermax section. Police claimed they committed suicide with smuggled weapons. They called it Death Night.

He rubbed his forehead with the heel of his hand. "Thought the Red Army Faction had gone underground or run off to the Middle East."

"Listen to yourself," she hissed. "The Middle East. Of course. And a second generation moves forward." Brigitta bit the rim of the wineglass, and a thin stream of wine trickled down her chin. She wiped it with her dishcloth.

Sweat beaded across his forehead, and he gripped his glass. His mind raced, recalibrating what he knew or thought he knew. He was supposed to be with the good guys, the Iranians, power to the people. Back when the Iranian royal dynasty ruled, American-made weaponry shipped straight to Tehran, but after the Shah's recent overthrow in January, the new military had no way to maintain or repair it. Donny Ray thought he was helping Army to Army, to stabilize—how the hell did he get mixed up with the RAF? He leaned over the bar.

"Why would the Faction be involved?"

"Shhh. Transportation," she whispered. "In exchange for product."

Well, hell, he thought. Donny Ray had simply equipped the cars and packed stolen weapons. He never thought about who delivered them to Iran—although come to think of it, he'd been doing his gigs months before the Shah's dynasty fell.

Jusef always said don't worry about the details. And now—now Brigitta tells him it was about the Faction. Keeping some of the U.S. weaponry for themselves? Christ, the West German government might accuse him of complicity with urban terrorists.

"Why didn't anybody tell me about these bastards? Why didn't you?"

Sweeping his arm across the varnished countertop, he connected with a bar caddy that skittered across the wood and tumbled over the edge. Cocktail napkins, coasters, and skinny little straws rained onto the floor. "Fucking A, man!"

Grim-faced, Brigitta shredded the napkin, swallowing it, bit by bit, her eyes locked on his. Then she stretched a hand towel taut and pulled it to her throat.

"*Mitgefangen, mitgehangen.*"

"What does that mean?"

She yanked. "Caught together, hanged together."

Gitta twisted a fistful of her hair into a knot and then loosened it to unwind across her shoulders. But she said nothing. The clock buzzed overhead, and Donny Ray studied the bottle of Scotch. He couldn't think straight. "Let's go up."

She finished her wine, and he threw back one last shot before they stumbled upstairs to her flat. Neon signs lit the street outside and flickered through her thin plaid curtains. Donny Ray lay down on the iron bed and cast himself into an old Bogart movie, where lights flashed into cheap hotel rooms, and gangsters eyed the sidewalks below.

"What's your deal with the RAF?" He poked her arm. "And is it Red Army Faction or Fraction?"

"Both. A faction of the world revolution and a fraction of the Communist workers' movement. Depends who you ask."

"And you were–"

"Involved. With a lover." Brigitta's chest stuttered with short breaths. "I was at university. So much excitement! We wanted the same as in America, the riots, for social change."

"Name him."

"No matter. He's gone." Her voice quavered.

"How long were you together?"

"Through German Autumn and Death Night. And then some." Trembling, she combed her fingers through her hair. "We knew the truth: no suicides in Stammheim," she said. "Secret agent assassinations!"

Well yeah, Donny Ray thought he saw signs of a conspiracy there. "What about your boyfriend?"

"He died later. Shootout with police. And you know, it was a relief after all." She touched a jagged scar below her ear. "He cut me once when I tried to leave him."

"Did you ever kill anybody?"

Eyes glistening, Brigitta rubbed her cheeks with the back of her hand. "No. I trained, but I was just, you know–"

"His old lady? I get it." Too bad about her ear, he thought. He'd never noticed anyway.

Wrapped in Donny Ray's old football jersey, Brigitta buried her face in her arm. As she rotated into a fetal position, he pinched her ass.

She screamed into her pillow, "Don't touch me!"

So that didn't go well. "Hell, if that's how you want it–" He lay on his back and stared into the blurry light show projected onto the walls from outside.

Brigitta fell into a fretful sleep, but old memories and new fears held Donny Ray's brain hostage. He should have stayed in Marshall. Should have married Cassie and gone legit. Restless, he sat up, fumbling for a cigarette and lighter on the nightstand. He hit his marks. Smoke streamed out of his mouth and nose, rising to the ceiling fan circling above them.

The Germans couldn't hang charges on him for anything. He dealt U.S. property; none of the Krauts' business. Until tonight, he didn't know shit about the Red Army Faction being in on it. And Communists? Jusef and Aldo never said a word about them.

Donny Ray trembled. Communications specialists on the Army base manned headphones, spun dials, and controlled tape recorders on a 24-hour basis. They captured everything Soviet, from street-side conversations to Morse code from submarines in the North Sea.

Stroking a thin scar above his eye, he watched the cigarette smoke rise into the fan. He assured himself the Army liked him fine. He was a skilled mechanic when he enlisted, then trained as a small arms and artillery repairman posted at Bremerhaven Army Airfield. Specializing in infantry weapons and big artillery pieces, he had access to everything but rockets and missiles—even some electronics.

Good schedule, too—shift work, 50-60 hours a week, with overnights to repair artillery every month or two. He got most weekends off. Federal holidays and personal leave were super cool, spent with poker games and camp followers—those wide-eyed, mini-skirted American chicks who craved men in uniform and kept Donny Ray's buttons polished.

Even so, life became routine after a while, and he needed a new rush. He found it just beyond his post, with Brigitta in her harbor bar.

She'd poured him the good stuff for hours, and at closing she took him upstairs to the flat—where the bedposts vibrated to Earth, Wind & Fire. But now the bed was spinning, and he thrashed about, his cigarette's red sparks flittering in the dark.

Caught together, hanged together.

Donny Ray's vision went fuzzy, and he dreamed he saw them hanging from the ceiling fan blades, their legs dragging the flames of hell. Then in a sudden burst of light and heat, he lurched awake. "Goddamn sheets are on fire!" he yelled, grabbing his pillow to beat down the blaze. Brigitta leaped out of bed and ran down a hall, returning with a fire extinguisher.

Leaning back, she fired the foam like automatic weapon rounds, drenching the flames—and a good thing for that. The last thing they needed was firefighters and police descending on them. They yanked off the soggy sheets and lay on the wooden floor, pulling a quilt over them.

As daylight crept into the room, they clutched each other, and Donny Ray tensed. He moved his hips and nudged the small of her back. "Uh, Gitta, do you want to–"

"*Scheiße!*" That meant shit.

It wouldn't be the last time she cried it.

## CHAPTER FIVE

## One Silver Token

The radio warned of poor air quality in the vicinity of Gorgeous U, still smoldering hours after firemen had doused the flames. Cassie dropped her head on the kitchen table and bawled, her face heating up again, mascara drops dotting the cardboard placemat. Chuck and Beecher had left to see about jobs at the glass plant, but she had nowhere to go. Donny Ray had always managed her life, and she'd believed him about together forever and family haircuts. Now everything was ruined. Collectively, it culminated in a good cry.

She grabbed a paper napkin from the lazy-susan and patted her face, then paced the kitchen before stumbling into the den. Cassie pulled her dog-eared copy of *Le Silence de la Mer* (*The Silence of the Sea*) from the bookshelf and returned to the kitchen table. She blotted makeup splatter and opened the slim volume—a novel about the French Resistance published in German-occupied Paris during World War II.

That's how she'd won her ribbon in high school—translating heartbreaking passages about a young French woman who withheld expressing her love for a German officer. As a teenager, Cassie understood how it felt to hold back the L-word, though the book's heroine didn't talk to the man at all, being an enemy and so forth. Even so, the book still thrilled her.

As she riffled the pages of *Silence*, some of her father's old black and white Kodak prints slid out—now faded, the pictures captured young American infantrymen and French villagers, who couldn't possibly have known what lay beyond the next turn in 1944.

Methodically, she flipped each print to read captions, some in her father's thick handwriting and others inked in vertical cursive. She'd read them hundreds of times, but the black-lettered lines always brought back her daddy's voice narrating the scenes, as she hung over his shoulder in the den.

Her favorite photo showed him standing by a roadway marker in Ambronay, one arrow pointing toward Lyon, another to Bourg-en-Bresse. She held it up to the light. His smile brightened the muddy gray images of young, brave Johnny Frank Tate, now buried outside of Marshall, Texas, with a headstone proclaiming him a hero of the Allied forces.

Not only a war hero, but her daddy had also been a self-taught businessman with a pulpwood operation up near Jefferson. "Folks think I'm just a dumb country boy," he'd say, "but that's how I outsmart 'em." He taught Cassie to check the newspaper's market section for commodity prices—oil, timber, silver, and gold—in case she ever wanted to join his business and handle financials. He had confidence in her, and she would give anything for one last hug, one last sniff of grainy Falstaff beer on his breath.

Cassie fingered a chunky silver token dangling from a chain at her neck. More than ever, she wanted to go to that French road crossing and rediscover a lost part of him. He'd promised to take her there—despite Della's red-faced protests—but sadly, Johnny Frank's ticker quit before they could go.

She tucked the photos back into the book and eyed the Kit-Cat clock's black tail swishing on the wall. Ten o'clock already. She carried a wicker basket, nearly spilling over with freshly dried clothes, into the pine-paneled den. The hardwood floors shined warmly, still bearing the scratches of her kindergarten roller skates.

Settling in on the plaid Herculon sleeper couch, she batted the TV antenna and watched hundreds of hands clap for

*The Price is Right.* The announcer cried, "Come on down!" before natty host, Bob Barker, showed everyone the first item up for bids.

Cassie pulled socks from the basket and stuffed cotton knits into little pockets. She and Donny Ray used to watch that show on summer mornings after her mother left for work. Every secret rendezvous was a private thrill as they cranked up the air conditioning and lay together on a pallet, shivering happily beneath a cotton sheet. And whenever Cassie heard the words "come on down," she did.

Now the air conditioner rumbled in the window, and sorrow coiled her heart, as though a carnival balloon twister had wound it up and bit the ends with a snap. Whimpering, she dabbed her tears with the reinforced toe of an athletic sock. She missed him so much, the first man ever to see her as a woman—*In-A-Gadda-Da-Vida, baby*, in the orange glow of a mosquito repellant coil at the Capri Drive-In.

She would always miss her dad. Clenching a terrycloth rag, she maintained her resolve to go to Ambronay. She already had a passport—got it when she turned 18 and tucked it into a hidden compartment in her jewelry box, safe and secure from prying eyes and burglars. Good for 10 years.

But the journey would cost a lot of money. She could try beauty school again; surely Gorgeous U would find a way to reopen, if only in a vacant warehouse. She could make pretty good tips from walk-in customers, but even so, it would take her years to break even and pay for the trip to France. She needed a steady paycheck sooner than later.

She glanced at a wood-veneer shelf, where a bottle of Jade East cologne glowed green, its $5.50 price tag intact. Cassie planned to send it to Donny Ray whenever she heard from him again, although she was often tempted to open it for sentimental sniffs.

## 7-Eleven Rewind

Folding T-shirts, Cassie drifted back to 1972—a sticky June night in the 7-Eleven refrigerated section. She had just removed a carton of glass-bottled Cokes, condensation glistening on green glass curves when the store's automatic doors opened with a whir. A humid gust of heat and Jade East swept her way.

Donny Ray Duggan! The football sensation from Houston—Cassie's crush of all time—stood not 20 feet from her, sexy as hell in a Marshall Mustangs workout shirt. His brown hair hung in layers, and his dark sideburns set off a strong jaw.

"Pack of Marlboros," Donny Ray told the cashier.

"Everybody says you'll be high school All-American this year," the pimply clerk said. With a stiff nod and sheepish grin, he handed over a cigarette package.

"Wait'll you see what I do in the pros." Donny Ray lifted his chin. His half grin resembled someone with Bell's Palsy, but with a sort of movie star quality.

Okay, Cassie thought, time to make her move. She might not get another chance. She hurried to the counter, her boobs bouncing, the Cokes banging against her thigh. Donny Ray looked down as she hoisted the carton to the counter.

Deep voice. "Pretty woman!"

The heavens had opened! She batted her eyelashes. "Ahem, uh... I know you."

"Yeah?" He winked at her, and she was momentarily distracted by a thin scar that curved from his right eyebrow over his cheekbone. Very masculine, she thought. He probably got that in a fight.

"You've been to my house before." She straightened her shoulders. "You watched our color TV."

"Really?" He squinted. "Okay... you're uh... somebody's little sister."

"Beecher Tate, remember?" She held her breath a moment. "That's my brother. Y'all used to hang out some. I'd spy on you."

A flash of recognition crossed his face. He smiled broadly and looked her up and down. "Yeah, sure. Me and Beecher played ball together. But I don't remember you looking like this."

He motioned her away from the counter. "What's your name again?"

"Cassie Tate." A drop of sweat trickled in her cleavage. She had the sensation a bug was crawling around there, and she couldn't stand it. She pressed the spot, rubbing a little circle. She hoped he'd notice.

"Where've you been? Haven't seen you around school." He folded his arms, so the biceps bulged like the Arm & Hammer man.

"I was at St. Mary's Dominican. But I'm going to Marshall High in the Fall."

"I heard Beecher went to Vietnam. Heard he was a sniper." Donny Ray held her gaze.

"Yeah, he was over there for a while. He's an MP at Fort Hood now."

She shifted her hips to the right and toyed with her hair, recently styled thick and shaggy, with feathered bangs the same as public-school girls. But what did she think she was doing, trying to impress a famous football star? So what if he'd been to her house before? This was big-time flirtation. She hoped she was doing it right.

"Mm-hmmm, well Miss Cassie, let's step outside for a smoke." He thumped his cigarette pack in the palm of one hand, rolled it up in his sleeve, put his arm around her waist, and nudged her toward the exit. The height marks for robbers showed he was six-foot-two.

She looked back. "What about my Cokes?"

"Get them later."

"I don't know, uh..." She started to back away, but bright lights shone into her eyes. "Holy Mother, a Corvette convertible!" she squealed. Under the flashing neon 7-Eleven sign, it looked like a gleaming hammerhead shark. Cassie blinked, and Donny Ray goosed her butt. She skittered and giggled as he guided her to the phone booth's accordion door.

"Let's call Beecher," he said and closed them inside.

He moved his hands up her back, slid them under the straps of her 34D, and bub-bubbed her neck like a big goldfish. Maybe she should slap him, but how else could she get to be his girlfriend? He'd never give a prude a chance.

Every square inch of her tingled and swayed until someone honked the Corvette's horn and flicked the lights on high beam.

Donny Ray squeezed her ass again as he clattered open the door. "Where do you live?"

"Around the corner," she panted. "Burleson Street. Remember?" This was too good to be true—her idol, oh good Lord. And this was shaping up to be everything *Seventeen* magazine had ever promised with advice on how to kiss boys without smothering. Don't hold your breath. Close your eyes. She wanted to try.

"You got a car?" Donny Ray scanned the parking lot.

"I'm walking."

"We'll take you home." He grabbed her hand. "C'mon with me, baby!"

Her heart pounding, she wedged between the bucket seats with Donny Ray and a jug-eared guy in a baseball cap—who didn't even say hello, just puffed his cigarette.

"This here's Mark." Donny Ray jerked his thumb at the guy in the passenger seat. "Speak, Mark."

"Hey." Mark eyed her sideways. He didn't make room for her, and Donny Ray didn't ask him to—so she perched on the center console and gawked at the manual gear shift rising from a stitched plastic cover.

Donny Ray revved the engine. He made a big show of shifting gears, rubbing his forearm over her crotch. Schlitz beer caps littered the mats, and the radio blared "Mr. Big Stuff, who do you think you are…"

"Yeah, baby, that's ME!" he howled, squealing the radials out of the parking lot, with hundreds of horses pounding under that wide slick hood.

He roared into her driveway, parked, and kept the engine running. Mark and his ears disappeared down the sidewalk with a cigarette glowing orange in the dark.

Donny Ray traced a line up her thigh and touched her cheek. He eyed her closely. "How old are you?"

"Old enough." She lifted her hair and fanned the back of her neck.

"Old enough for what?"

"I don't know." Cassie had read or heard that line somewhere and hadn't thought it through. She wouldn't have read it in *Seventeen*.

He tossed the cigarette pack on the dashboard. "Maybe we need to find out."

And maybe she had over-hyped the merchandise. Better reverse course, she thought. She didn't want to be a slut. "I-I need to go in now."

"Already?"

She nodded.

"All right," he shrugged. "Your loss." He opened the door and helped her out. "Let me show you something first." He led her to the hood of the vehicle, its engine still humming warm.

Under the streetlight, the chrome Stingray logo sparkled against metallic red.

With his hands around her waist, he pressed her against the car. "It's a 2,000-pound vibrator, baby!" He draped Cassie's arms over his shoulders, gripped the small of her back, and nuzzled her neck. Her heart rate jumped off the charts.

"Cassie Jean Tate, get in this house!" Della stood at the front door in her flowered housecoat, its raveled sash hanging limp and uneven.

"Busted!" Donny Ray hooted.

"I've got to go." Giggling, she slid from between the two pulsating teasers, her white short-shorts streaked with dust. He brushed them off and laughed. So did she.

"My number's in the phone book. It's under Johnny Frank Tate." She knew she had to be a little forward to stay in contention with the other girls.

"Get the hell in here!" Della's bark was louder than the dog's next door.

Cassie ran up to the porch, turned, and waved at him. Slutty was fun, she decided.

"I'll call you!" he shouted, popping the clutch and burning rubber on the street.

The screen door slammed behind her as she lurched into the front room.

"Get in here, Cassie," her mother fussed. "And what happened to the Cokes?"

"Oh Mama, I'm so sorry, I'll go back."

"No, forget it. Dishes in the sink, crap all over the den. And don't ever let me see you with that piece of shit again. He's too old for you." Della tweaked her pink foam curlers and sank into the worn suede recliner.

"He's not too old. He's still in high school."

Della raised up on her elbows. "I don't give a damn. That boy has more mileage on him than a '49 Ford. What the devil you think he wants with a 15-year-old girl? As if I didn't know," she groaned.

"But he played ball with Beecher."

"I know he did. Used to come around the house. They held him back in ninth grade, so he'd be bigger for football." Della sipped from a short glass. "He's going on 19, I'm telling you. And he's a thug. Woman I work with knows for a fact he got in cahoots with a funeral operator over in Hallsville, smuggling dope in coffins and robbing graves."

Cassie pursed her lips. "Okay, then how come didn't he get arrested?"

"No telling, but he's common. Leave him alone."

Still, this didn't compute. If he'd broken laws, he wouldn't be playing high school football—he would have been expelled. She would fight this point all the way. "But Mama, he's got a Corvette!"

"So what?"

"Well, he must be rich then," Cassie nudged the chair's puffy headrest.

"No, he came up from Houston, those people always got a hustle. There's flocks of jailbirds roosting in the Channel."

Everybody knew about the Houston Ship Channel, where mysterious seafarers and burly longshoremen brought in barges and tankers from the Gulf of Mexico. Cassie couldn't imagine anyone leaving all that excitement for the East Texas piney woods. "I wonder what he's doing up here?"

Della shrugged. "I don't know, probably still robbing graves. Forget about the boy." She rattled the ice in her drink and returned her attention to the *M*A*S*H* episode on TV.

"Aw, man." Cassie dropped her arms and dragged into the kitchen. She wanted to have a big love affair like in *Dr. Zhivago* but without the Communists on horseback.

She frowned at the greasy plates soaking in the sink and breakfast toast crumbs floating in cold coffee cups—none of that mess was even hers. But she pulled on rubber gloves, ran hot water, and circled a tired old sponge around and around on the melamine plates.

The more she thought about Donny Ray, the cleaner the dishes got. She didn't care why he left Houston. He was hot as a two-dollar pistol, and that was oh-my-God fun. A vibrator! She tugged at her short shorts, unraveling a loose thread. She'd have to tell Sheree.

After she'd placed the last dish on the rack, Cassie emptied smoldering ashtrays and picked up the magazines in the den. She looked over at her mother, whose soft snores accompanied the late-night movie theme. Usually, Cassie woke her up and helped her to bed, but not tonight. Not yet.

She went to her bedroom, dialed Sheree on the Princess phone, and stammered her news.

"Are you talking about *the* Donny Ray Duggan?" Sheree's voice rose.

"Yes! The love of my life!" Cassie took a breath.

"I hope he calls you."

"He better, because it feels like somebody broke an egg in my panties."

## Della's Rules

Della might have read Donny Ray right, but Cassie didn't give him up. She saw him on the sly until she was pushing 17, the age of consent in Texas. By that time, Della was too tired to carry through on statutory rape threats and whatnot.

"Your daddy would've sent that boy to the penitentiary," she said, "which is where he belongs, but I'm too worn out to fight this alone." Whenever Della got emotional, she always veered to the topic of poor Baby Patsy in a little iron lung, and that would end the conversation for the night.

Nowadays, Cassie rarely thought about her much older—and long dead—sister Patsy, who would be in her 30s by now and might have had a lousy life packed with drugs, alcohol, and disappointment. If the angels hadn't called her up in 1947, maybe their parents would have doted on Patsy to the exclusion of Cassie and her brother. Maybe there would have been eight kids, not three minus one.

But she couldn't speculate. Cassie set aside the laundry basket and eyed the TV commercial break for Rinso-Blue. She held up a sock. Maybe she should try that? Just then, truck brakes screeched in the driveway. Beecher and Chuck had worked the third shift overtime, and she'd made lunch for them. After all, they were buying the groceries now.

With dust-smeared faces and sweat-slicked hair, they ambled into the house trailing the scent of sweltered Right Guard. She handed around pressed turkey sandwiches and glasses of iced tea, then straightened the wagon-wheel light fixture suspended over the kitchen table.

"When you going back to work, Cassie?" Beecher gestured at her with his sandwich. "You ain't getting Dad's benefits no more."

"I know, I know." She glared at him and slumped low in her chair.

"You could get a job at the plant," Chuck said. He licked a drop of mustard off the corner of his mouth. "There's women out there."

She batted the lazy-susan. "I'd rather go back to the Piggly Wiggly."

"Okay, fine. Three dollars an hour ain't nothing, but that's how you want it." Beecher rose from the table and put his plate in the sink. "See you later."

The screen door banged behind him.

"We need to fix that spring," she said.

"Yep." Chuck regarded the door, stroking his chin. Cassie rocked back in her chair, lacing and unlacing her fingers. "Here's the church, there's the steeple. Ever done that?"

"Nope."

"You probably did. You just forgot."

"I forgot a lot of things. On purpose," he said.

Cassie ran her thumbs under black bra straps at the edges of her aqua tank top. Her silver pendant lay cold at the notch below her throat, rising with each breath.

Come to think of it, Chuck was fine-looking. She resumed church-and-steeple fingers so as not to give herself away. Donny Ray always said she had the "Face of a Thousand Tells." And the look in Chuck's eyes indicated he could read a lot more than a poker face.

# CHAPTER SIX

## Bad News in Bremerhaven

Saturday customers jostled for rolls and pilsners, an afternoon snack to hold them until the evening meal. Brigitta slid platters of cheese, bratwurst, and potato salad down the counter. Suspicious of unfamiliar faces, Donny Ray glanced around the bar, watching for sudden movements, furtive glances, or anyone looking at him.

Brigitta had shaken him up with the Red Army Faction thing. He'd asked around on the Army base, and his sergeant explained that the RAF had gone quiet until Fall 1978, barely a year ago, with a shoot-out in a forest near Dortmund, followed by a gun battle on the German-Dutch border in December. Yeah, yeah, he remembered that.

More recently, in June 1979, the Faction tried to assassinate the Commander of NATO forces in Europe by setting a land mine under a bridge in Belgium. They missed the kill by seconds. Mere seconds. Donny Ray was keenly aware of that, especially since he and Brigitta had been in the area for a rock festival. It better have been a coincidence, he thought.

He lit a cigarette and observed the front door, sunlight knifing the dim interior of the bar. The Village People and "Y.M.C.A." blared from the speakers. Checking his watch, he reached for the clunky black phone. After three tries, nobody answered at Aldo's auto shop. With each successive ring, Donny Ray's guts jumped. Aldo had promised to meet him there to start a new project—so where was he?

Their partnership began easily enough in Aldo's garage, a cloak-and-dagger kind of place, where shadowy customers with nondescript sedans flashed cash and left their vehicles to him and his specialized skill set: trunk expansions, concealment boxes, and suspension adjustments. Donny Ray went by "Raymond" to avoid an identifiable American name. And that was fine with him; it was his father's name, and easy on his ears.

In exchange, Aldo paid him well and taught him the fine points of German car design and maintenance. Donny Ray even restored a 1963 Mercedes-Benz, 300SE coupe. Cherry red with chrome detailing—he loved it, even better than the old Corvette back home.

Once Jusef appeared at Aldo's, the rest was a blur. He upped the ante way high, tuning into Donny Ray's opportunism, the exhilaration of a score, and what he could have been in Texas if the drug cartels hadn't screwed him over. But this was even better, having hands-on combat weaponry, running it right off the Army base and into the garage, where he adapted it for special use and transport. Donny Ray couldn't say no to rock star money; he was meant for this business, and Jusef knew talent when he saw it.

But to Donny Ray's mind, the guns were supposed to be for the Iranians. Revolutions were good things; the Republic of Texas and the United States were built on them. But nobody said anything about the Red Army Faction, as Jusef brokered deals and Aldo played his codger card. Together with Donny Ray, they spun guns into gold. At least that's how Donny Ray saw it.

And now, no telling what was going down right in front of him. He beckoned Gitta with a nod. Bobby pins in her mouth, she turned, and swiping hair from her forehead she snapped the clips in place. "*Ja?*"

"Can't reach Aldo." He tapped his fingers on the bar to a rhythm in his head.

Gitta signaled the waiter to take over. Then she clasped Donny Ray's shoulders, faked a bite, and whispered in his ear. *"Toilette.* Go." They squeezed into the women's loo and locked the door.

"So, what the hell is going on?" He gripped her arms.

"All is good."

"How can you know that?"

"Usual way." She slid her fingers under his belt.

"How? I need to know."

A woman's voice, heavy, boomed outside the oak panels, juddering the water closet's doorknob. *"Sie sind verhaftet!* You're under arrest!"

The stockade flashed in Donny Ray's sights. Nowhere to run. Brigitta's hold on Donny Ray tightened.

"This is it," he huffed, embracing her. "I love you." He teased a crack in the door.

A stocky blonde stomped her platform boots and flashed a badge.

"What's that mean?" His heart raced.

Gitta peered at the badge and groaned. "Maritime agency. It's nothing."

The woman barged through the door. "Out of my way, you two—I have to piss!"

"Ah crap!" They cleared out, but that was a scary broad. She could have been working undercover or something. Donny Ray was in no mood for a joke—if that's what it was. He couldn't take anything at face value, not after Gitta's warnings.

And apparently, everyone in the tavern figured Brigitta had served him up a blowjob in there, so he acknowledged hoots and jeers as he made his way back to the bar. He parked on a stool, jiggled his foot, and lit another cigarette. This was getting out of hand. He wanted to keep a low profile.

"Gitta. Look here." Donny Ray kissed her, then he pressed his mouth over her ear. "Going to Aldo's. Catch you on the flip side."

He hauled ass across the Geeste River, the red Mercedes-Benz flashing chrome off rearview mirrors.

~~~

A "closed" sign hung from Aldo's front door. Donny Ray opened the lock with a heavy iron key, entered, and deactivated the alarm system within the requisite twenty seconds. Lights out, front office. That was odd, even for late afternoon. He cast around for signs of the old Nazi, but his car was gone, and his desk drawers hung open and empty. The motor oil calendar drooped askew. Apparently, Aldo had left in a hurry.

Donny Ray's stomach churned, and his head pounded. The guns, the guns, the guns—Perspiration pouring down his spine, he slid back the storage cabinet doors and panted with relief. M-16 rifles, MAC-10 machine guns, and shoulder-fired grenade launchers were still stacked in orderly rows with shotguns and mini-machine guns. Alongside were combat radio sets, receiver transmitters, and auxiliary receivers—specialized military issue for tactical control.

This shit was worth a fortune on the black market. Hell, Donny Ray *was* the black market. These weapons should have moved out weeks ago, he thought, reaching for his cigarette pack. All right, something had spooked Aldo, but it wasn't law enforcement—they would have seized the guns. Panic jetted through his core.

His heartbeat accelerated. He dropped to the floor, watching the doors for movement. His eyes darted to the windows, making certain they were locked tight and that no one lurked behind them.

Regardless of why Aldo left, the guns and electronics remained, and he had to get them into circulation before Army inventory control tracked the ammo back to him. But for now, he wouldn't touch the damn things. He was getting the hell out of there.

## CHAPTER SEVEN

### Put the Blame On...

Cassie pushed through the double doors of the Marshall post office, the heavy glass and metal swinging closed behind her. She wanted to buy some air mail letters, the one-page kind you simply folded it up, no need to put an extra stamp, and it went lightweight to anywhere. She planned to get the ball rolling on Ambronay, send a few feelers to tourism places in Paris and Lyon, maybe even the U.S. Ambassador if he was listed at the library.

She also planned to send a letter to Donny Ray at an Army Post Office, the last address she had for him. If he was still in Germany, he could take her to France. It was also the best way to avoid temptation with suit-caser Chuck, the patron saint of Samsonite.

Her mother's cigarette-laced voice crowded her brain: "It's a man's world." She needed a husband to look after her. Marry up, not down. Cassie had to find Donny Ray. As a military wife, she would never have to work. They'd have base housing, free medical, and exotic duty stations abroad. Everything came cheap at the PX, is what she'd always heard. And they'd have a good dog.

Shifting her feet, she stood in a line snaking through the lobby, cold air blasting from the water-stained ceiling. The smell of Johnson's wax mingled with markers, stamps, and slick magazines, and it slapped her back a few years, when she used to send Beecher care packages with hometown stuff he couldn't get in Vietnam. Her thoughts drifted to the boys "in country," land mines, newsreels, and to Walter Cronkite on the *CBS Nightly News*.

A hard pinch on her butt jolted her out of Southeast Asia. "Dang!" Cassie swiveled around. "You scared the crap out of me! What did you do that for?"

"To scare the crap out of you," Sheree laughed. "Oh, settle down."

"Well, it's not like I was expecting that." Cassie frowned and tilted her head. "Where've you been anyway?"

"Here and there. Sorry I haven't called."

Cassie had already heard about Sheree's latest romance, which crashed and burned, but you'd never know it from her conceited attitude. Swinging a plastic mail bin, Sheree bragged about working in the courthouse mailroom, where she was sure to meet a rich lawyer in a bow tie and seersucker suit. She scoffed at Cassie's travel plans.

"Still chasing Donny Ray? Good old D.R.—don't be such a chump." Tall and chesty, she looked down at Cassie—and on her, too, it seemed. Sheree didn't mind eating cheap tuna out of cans, but she got her auburn hair styled and glimmered at the priciest beauty parlor in town. She always said it paid to maintain a Hollywood front, because every day's a publicity tour. If Gorgeous U hadn't burned down, Cassie could have made a fortune off her.

"I'm not a chump," Cassie folded her arms. "I can go by myself, nearly have the money saved." Such a lie, but Sheree had a way of backing her into a corner. "Thought he could show me around over there."

"Okay, okay." Sheree slow-rolled her eyes. "Anyway, I heard you've got a sex god living with you, and I'm not talking about Beecher!"

Cassie caught her breath. Her heart stung, and she didn't know why. But Chuck really must be a suit-caser if Sheree had heard about him already—the girl had only just moved back to town after a short-lived stint with a rancher down near Austin.

Sheree persisted. "Anything between y'all?"

"If it was, would I be going to see Donny Ray?" Cassie pursed her lips.

"Just checking. So how about an intro? I'll drop by later." Sheree tossed her shaggy Farrah Fawcett hairdo and blew a kiss as she strolled away. Cassie's eyes narrowed. Pricey salon or not, Sheree's stylist must be ham-fisted. Her feathered bangs resembled bat wings flapping with an upstroke.

## Sock it to Me

Since last week's post office encounter, Cassie hadn't heard from Sheree, which was fine, sort of. They'd been friends since convent school, when redheaded Sheree was a Little Orphan Annie with second-hand school uniforms and a ten-cent allowance. She lived behind a plumbing shop with her crippled mother and ill-tempered granny, who peddled Sock-it-to-Me cakes in front of Woolworth's downtown.

Cassie's folks always told her be kind to Sheree, poor kid. They took her for ice cream and sometimes supper at Morrison's Cafeteria in Shreveport. At home, the girls went to the picture show, made scrapbooks using clips from movie magazines, and did sleepovers, but never at Sheree's, because guests had to walk around inventoried toilets and sinks to get to the living quarters.

But that was before Sheree's 12th birthday when her tits popped out bigger than Dallas. She started skipping class to meet older boys driving GTOs through the Sears parking lot.

After a while, the nuns had enough of Sheree's truancy and unbuttoned blouses, and when she dolled up like Rita

Hayworth and sang "Put the Blame on Mame"—with a strapless, skin-tight gown and bend-over wiggles—they rang down the curtain on the Diocesan talent show. Instamatic cameras flashed in a lightning storm when, on her way off the stage, she flung a long black glove into the audience. Even the Jesuit priests looked sweaty under their collars.

So off to public school she went, leaving Cassie to *Tiger Beat* magazine and "Adopt-a-Pagan-Baby" fundraisers to save the souls of unbaptized children in foreign lands. But Sheree kept coming around the Tates' house anyway, because she and Beecher couldn't keep their hands off each other.

At least she turned Cassie on to the Pill—obtainable to minors at a speakeasy kind of pharmacy on old Highway 80. Although the Church forbade it, Cassie reasoned it helped girls avoid other big sins. Vatican II didn't let you off light.

Now all the two women had in common was that they used to have something in common. Still, friends weren't easy to come by nowadays; seemed that all Cassie's old high school friends were married with babies, showing them off in strollers at the mall, like they had the only babies in the world. As though Cassie couldn't have one. And those girls quit using their husbands' real names, instead calling them hubby or hubs. Braggarts, Cassie scowled.

Frowning, she slumped across the room, adjusted the air conditioner control, and twisted the channel knob to a soap opera. In an anxious rhythm, her fingernails scritch-scratched a yellow throw pillow, as *All My Children* paraded its own Chuck around the town of Pine Valley. Why did it have to be that character now? Clearly, she reasoned, the TV was commanding her to address unwanted but burgeoning feelings for her Chuck, made more difficult by his chummy accounts of Vietnam days.

She twisted some strands of hair and rewound her memory tape to the day before; Chuck had been soaping dishes in the kitchen sink, and he recalled when Cassie sent Beecher a bottle of Halo shampoo in one of her care packages from home. He had lathered up the Halo in a bowl for the hell of it.

"The guys went smooth running nuts because it smelled like their girlfriends—hilarious," Chuck said, admitting that he had sniffed the suds, too—and with the fragrance still fresh, he studied her photograph until his eyesight went fuzzy. "Beecher had your picture taped by his bunk in the Quonset hut. And what were you? Thirteen?" He laughed. "I won't even tell you the rest of it."

Cassie didn't know whether to be thrilled or grossed out. However, if thirteen-year-olds were good enough for Jerry Lee Lewis and Edgar Allan Poe, she guessed it wasn't too creepy for Chuck to have thought about her that way. Anyhow, Priscilla Presley was only fourteen when she met Elvis, and everybody thought that was great.

A standup bass thumped inside her ribs, and Cassie felt her face flush. "Why did it take so long for you to tell me?"

"Bad juju. Had to get past it." He looked at her. "You've smelled firecrackers, right? With the smoke and the tinge in your nose?"

"Every Fourth of July. And after the beauty school fire." She puffed out her cheeks and whistled low. "All that smoke, it was bizarre—and the mannequins were staring into space. One of them was mine."

Chuck tipped back in his chair. "Hit you hard, didn't it?"

"Sure did." She rearranged cups and condiments on the kitchen table.

"Think about them being real bodies, laying in their own shit and piss and blood. Real faces frozen with their mouths wide open." Chuck's gaze went nowhere. "Killed for a fucking piece of ground."

Cassie had a hideous cringe in her stomach that ran up to her throat. "Thou shalt not kill," she mumbled. Chuck scrunched his face.

"How about rabbits? Would you let them mangle your garden?" He bumped his chair and folded his hands on the table. "And leave you to starve?"

"I never had a garden." She drew a clump of hair above her mouth to make a mustache and rubbed it between her thumb and index finger.

"Jesus! If you're poor and you want to eat, you kill Peter Rabbit, save your garden, and you get a rabbit stew."

She examined the tips of her hair for split ends. "Where'd you come up with that? Were y'all poor?"

"Not hardly," Chuck scowled. "But there've been times when all I wanted was to sleep indoors and get something in my belly. And that was *after* I got back from Nam." He snickered, staring at her.

Suddenly she burned to touch him, to hold him, to make everything all right. She could almost feel her fingertips on his cheek. But she certainly wouldn't reach for him. She needed a husband, not a lover. And she belonged to Donny Ray. He was fond of bunnies—not just the Playboy kind.

### Cashier's Lament

The Piggly Wiggly cashier stand was exactly as Cassie remembered it: morning shifts crazy, afternoons slow, and the six o'clock shoppers jammed in like a rodeo crowd. She got sick her first week at work, came down with a strep throat, and she blamed grimy daycare kids who piled off a bus for snacks and got their grubby hands all over her station. She even had to wipe one urchin's nose because Lord knows, he was dripping on the conveyor belt.

Piggly Wiggly sent her to a worker's comp doctor who gave her a ten-day pack of capsules and a shot of antibiotics big as a water cannon. "This'll even cure tuberculosis," the doc said, his eyes gleaming.

She felt fine right away, but the manager didn't want her spreading anything, and he sent her to the back of the store for a while. Cassie spent the next couple of days sloshing murky water and a cotton yarn mop that looked like dirty spaghetti floating in a bucket of gloom. Songs about love letters rang through her head, and a wave of heartbreak splashed into the pine cleaner. She rubbed her eyes. She was tired of waiting for Donny Ray.

No, mop that notion, Cassie chided herself. She checked the time, removed her apron, and clocked out. Tomorrow would be her parents' thirty-something wedding anniversary, and she always took flowers to the cemetery up at Scottsville. Beecher never cared about all that. He said they forgot about him when he came home on leave one time and stranded him at the Greyhound station.

## Dirt Motel

A light rain stippled the car windows, and Cassie regretted her cemetery plan when the car battery died in the florist's parking lot. The FTD cartoon man with a little pointy hat floated on a bright banner over Cassie's chirping car motor. She went back inside to borrow their phone and call home. Chuck answered.

"The dang car won't start," she said. "Can somebody come give me a jump?" She shuffled her feet. "I'm at the flower shop on North Crockett."

"Be right there." Chuck hung up the phone without even saying bye.

She studied the telephone receiver like a Magic 8-Ball and wondered if he was in a hurry to see her. Probably not, she sighed, just bad manners. Even so, he arrived fresh and combed, full of advice and rescue.

"Dead as a doornail," he confirmed, but a jumpstart got the Comet to a nearby service station. Chuck paid in advance for a new battery, but the guy still couldn't get to it for a while. "No problem," said Chuck. "Get your flowers, Cassie. Let's me and you go."

Wow, this was some kind of date, she thought—imagine, getting treated to a car battery! Those were expensive, more than dinner and a picture show for two. She felt regal, boosting herself into his truck, then directing him down an old farm-to-market road.

"I love the rain," she said. "My daddy used to take me riding on rainy days to look at pulpwood. There's nothing like a nice, stacked load on the flatcars."

"Uh, really? Want a beer?" Chuck jerked his thumb to the back seat where a Dallas Cowboys beer cooler rested among eight-track tapes, a pair of scuffed boots, and a tattered copy of the *Kama Sutra*. "Grab yourself a Tall Boy. We've got a break in the clouds."

Her eyes rested momentarily on the book; she'd heard of it, very racy, always with the Hindu people draped in gowns like the Hare Krishnas at airports. Chuck must have picked that up in Southeast Asia. Did he mean for her to see it? She wasn't about to ask him. Still, she had to wonder what he did with all that specialized knowledge.

Act normal, she told herself, and she popped the top of a Pabst. Resuming her place by the radio, she cranked up the volume and sang along with the Pointer Sisters, swelling up from her diaphragm to hit the high notes. He shifted in his seat and watched for the cemetery entrance.

"This is it! That's the turn!" Cassie pointed to the 12-foot bronze statue of Johnny Reb posed on a large granite pedestal. Wearing his signature wide-brimmed hat, he stood guard over the cemetery grounds with a long-barreled rifle. A stone chapel anchored the entrance, and a cyclone fence surrounded the well-tended gravesites.

Beneath a doused crepe myrtle, a double headstone showed Johnny Frank Tate on the left and beloved wife Della on the right. A smaller marker, splotched with discolored green in places, said "Patsy Gail Tate, beloved angel baby, departed for heaven in '47."

"Good rhyme," Chuck said. "Who's Patsy?"

"My sister."

"Beecher never mentioned her. That's a big spread in age between y'all."

"Yeah. But Mama was hardly 19 when she had her."

"What'd the baby die of?"

"Polio."

"Yeah, that was some bad shit back then. I had some cousins limping around." He brushed his hands. "Okay, that's enough of the dead folks. I'll wait over here." A weeping angel statue, one arm broken off, framed him in a modest landscape of iron fencing and wilted hydrangeas.

Cassie placed the flowers at her parents' headstone and stepped aside a spilled flowerpot covered in faded red foil. She returned to Chuck, a few paces ahead, his legs set apart and arms crossed over his chest.

"Step up here so I can see you good," he said.

He took her arm and helped her onto a short ledge, so they were facing each other at eye level. As he placed his hands on her waist, just above the hips, Cassie went into hormone overdrive, right there in front of her parents. And he was moving in a little closer.

Chuck squinted at her pendant. "You always wear that. Mind if I touch it?"

She elongated her neck and hoped for the best.

"Good for $10 in trade. Hemphill, Texas." He ran his fingers over the etched letters, gently replaced it, and stepped back. "It's pretty heavy. What's it for?"

"It's an old trade token from a lumber town—where Daddy stayed in the Depression. He won a couple of them in a poker game."

"Silver is worth a lot now. Do you ever take it off?"

"Sure, got to polish it—otherwise tarnish rubs off on my skin." She gripped the chain between her thumb and forefinger, wiggling the token with her pinky. "But Daddy told me don't ever lose it, because someday I might need to buy my way out of a jam. That's what he had to do."

"Yeah? What kind of jam?" He put his hands in his pockets and leaned in.

"Germans shot him in the eye on a prisoner march in France. A French lady rescued him and got him a glass eye. He paid her with a token." Pride welled up in her; the entire family had talked about it for years.

"Now that I heard about. You still got his medals?"

Cassie frowned. "He never got his. Clerical mistake, he said, everything all confused at the end of the war. And he didn't want to relive the misery simply to get some ribbon scraps to pin on the wall."

Drizzle began anew, and Chuck urged her down the walk. "Let's go back to the truck."

They made their way to the vehicle, stepping into uneven patches of sod that hid an inch or two of water. It ran over Cassie's ankles and into her squishing tennis shoes. She removed them in the cab and peeled off soggy cotton socks, enmeshed with blades of muddy grass. Rubbing her legs, she sat up, facing him. His eyes drifted to the pendant and below.

"You look cold," Chuck said.

"Yeah, I am. Can you turn on the heat?" She rubbed the gooseflesh on her arms.

"Uh, sure." He keyed the ignition, reached over, and tweaked the temperature controls. He rapped his fingers on the steering wheel. "What became of the French lady?"

"I don't know. But I want to go back to where she hid him, where he stayed—the fields of Ambronay. Daddy had promised to take me there someday."

"He never did?"

"No, but he took me to French movies." Cassie giggled. "He loved them."

Chuck looked straight ahead. "It must have killed him to leave her."

"No, Mama and Daddy were already married. He couldn't wait to come home."

"And you believe that?"

"Yes! The baby was dying, and he'd never even seen her. He got back in time for a couple of good looks, and that was it." Cassie sucked the tip of her thumb. "By the time I came along, you'd think everybody would've gotten over it—but almost every night, for as long as I can remember, Daddy lined up empty beer cans on the drainboard, smushed them in the middle, and wiped his eyes with a dish cloth."

"He never moved past the pain," Chuck said, "and God, do I know it, every single day of my life." He studied the windshield wipers, gliding back and forth in steady rhythm. "Chopper overhead. Nobody left alive but me and the sergeant. A single little tear come out of the corner of his eye—like this." Chuck put his fingertip up to Cassie's cheek to trace it. "He wiped it, looked at me, and all he said was the band plays on."

Chuck exhaled, blinked rapidly, and turned to her. "Agonizing. That was my life over there. But your eyes, your eyes empowered me on the other side of the world."

"Oh, my goodness." Cassie sensed trouble bubbling in her britches.

"I loved you then, and I love you now."

That did it. All this time she'd been quashing her lust, feeling guilty over a man who was across the ocean. But Chuck loved her. And he was here. Next to her. Reaching for her. And all she could think was, "Love the one you're with, honey!"

Chuck pulled her to him, stroking her hair and kissing her neck, finding her mouth and the pendant that hung above her breasts. His kiss deepened, and she swooned with visions of fire bursts and the steakhouse billboard on Highway 59. His hands slipped past her waistband and into her panties. Whoa, here's the church, and one hell of a steeple, she thought.

In a little while, she couldn't say exactly when, she looked up, dizzy, her eyes glazed. Wool upholstery itched her bare cheeks. Chuck gripped her tightly, and she didn't ever want to let him go. She was in graveyard heaven with Chuck. And Johnny Reb. Both of them heroes with mighty fine guns.

## Pot Pie Confessions

Cassie's graveyard ecstasy gave way to disappointment when Chuck passed out on top of her in the truck. No romantic glow, just some random snores, and her arm went pins and needles underneath him. When she nudged him awake, he half-smiled and muttered yes, it was good for him, too.

Even so, he seemed restless on the drive back and rummaged for sunglasses in the overhead bin; the rain had stopped, and the blacktop road steamed through glare. He dropped her off to get her car, waved bye, and hollered "see you later" before his truck rumbled away. Heartburn stung her chest at this lousy departure, but her friends at beauty school had been right—don't fall for the pretty ones, they're always on to the next thing.

She puttered home, where Banquet pot pie boxes littered the kitchen drainboard. Beecher was chowing down on his second chicken dish, and he offered Cassie the third.

Gripping a plastic fork, she jabbed the pie crust like a pirate with a dagger, making a blobby mess of the yellow gravy. She used plastic cutlery whenever she ate food from a metal container because her teeth always hurt whenever stainless utensils scraped the pan.

Eyeing her, Beecher speared a chunk of meat and peas. "Something wrong?"

"Kind of." She steadied her voice. "Little while ago, Chuck acted all hot and lovey-dovey, but he took off like a scalded dog."

"Ah, he's been in and out of rehab so many times, his brain is bent."

"You never needed rehab."

"Nope. I always stuck with pot and coca leaves in Nam. Chuck got into the hard stuff." He tapped his temple. "See, I'm smart." Beecher took a glug of Schlitz, held up the can, and grinned. "You don't change the feed on a winning horse."

Cassie gave a half-smile, but her shoulders drooped. "He said he loves me, but he dumped me at the service station and took off."

"His mind works different since he kicked the horse."

"You mean heroin?"

"Yeah. Couple of times a week he goes over to a little rehab place in Longview." Beecher shrugged. "At least he says he does."

"Rehab—thank God!" He hadn't been suit-casing after all, she thought. She chided herself for suspecting other women. What a relief.

Now she had to ask herself, "Donny Ray who?" He could keep his stupid music boxes, she thought. Chuck bought a battery for the Comet, a true expression of devotion. She could keep him happy. She *would* keep him happy. She'd let him sleep late on Sunday mornings while she dragged their little kids to Mass in their Tweety Bird pajamas.

"Say," Beecher looked up. "Guess who dropped by? Sheree! Said she saw you at the post office the other day."

She's stalking Chuck, Cassie surmised. She went rigid. "Sorry I missed her."

"I'm not." He beamed. "We kind of fired up our old—you know—relationship, if you want to call it that."

Cassie's blood pressure rose, pumping out the side of her neck. "Did you tell her about Chuck?" Her voice squeaked.

"Yeah. She thought that was cool, with the old war buddy thing."

"Don't trust her, Brother." Cassie pointed at him. "She already knew about him. Said she heard he was a sex god."

"Oh, you know how she is, always trying for the shock effect." Beecher laughed, scraping inside the little pie pan.

Cassie hated that sound, fork scraping pleated foil, like dragging a big nail across a washer board. "Quit doing that!" She pounded the table with her fist.

"What's wrong with you?" Wide-eyed, Beecher froze with his fork in the air.

"She wants whatever I've got. Even when y'all were together, she kept trying to snake Donny Ray away from me. I knew what they were up to, but I couldn't catch them at it."

"You should've let her have him. And anyway, she don't want Chuck. It's all about me and her now, kiddo."

Cassie rose from the table, stomped back to her room, and crumpled onto the chenille bedspread. Throwing aside the stuffed bears, she buried her face in the pillows and wagged her head side to side. She couldn't stand it. Sheree was always angling, and now she was using Beecher to get at Chuck, so what's that about? Well, Cassie would make sure that Sheree didn't find out.

## Moon Over Marshall

On Chuck's return that night, his hair was mussed up, and he reeked of room freshener—patchouli or something hippie style. Said he'd been visiting cousins in Shreveport; they'd invited him for a big supper, but they didn't have a phone, or he would've called. Honest to God, he would have.

He didn't wash his hands until she reminded him, but Cassie didn't care. He told her over and over that he loved her. For hours, euphoria saturated the sheets as he flew her to the moon the way Frank Sinatra sang it.

On breaks in the action, he smoked Chesterfields and talked particulars about Vietnam. She found most interesting the part about the French and the Nazis tangled up with the rubber plantations in World War II. Chuck said he knew all about it because he'd been a history major long time ago.

"You went to college?" She propped up on her elbow and tried to see him in the dark.

"Yep, the University of Oklahoma—OU." He paused. "I hated that place."

"Then why did you go there?"

"My parents were big donors. They made me try it for a while, but it just wasn't me. Football and fraternities, all that Oklahoma Sooners shit." His voice rose, and he got agitated. Flopping on his belly and twisting his feet, he tipped over a table fan with green blades oscillating and tangling the fringe on her bedspread. "Sorry. Sorry. Sorry."

Cassie rushed to pull the electric plug and disentangle the fringe. "That's all right. Can't see nothing in the dark—why can't we turn on the lamp?"

"Spoils the mood," he practically shouted, panicked that she might see him naked. Yet, she'd already seen much of his bare body anyway, and the moonlight through the blinds left little to the imagination. Inexplicably, he nodded off.

"I want to go to college," she whispered and stroked a scar glistening on his shoulder. She needed a college degree to be a teacher. But Chuck could rise in the ranks at the glass plant without one or be an electrician or plumber. She would have summers off with the children or maybe not work at all. He had a good last name: Denton. She'd be Cassie Denton. Excellent for monogramming. She planned to study various styles at the fabric store. She would steamroll Sheree all the way back to her granny's Sock-it-to-Me cakes.

### No-Tell Motel

Beecher decided Chuck had overstayed his welcome, what with all that bedspring noise. "If you want to bang my sister," Beecher insisted, "do it at your own damn place." That was all right, Cassie thought. What's fair is fair, even though Beecher was always running over to Sheree's place for their private Tilt-a-Whirl.

Down Highway 80 East, Chuck got a room by the week at the Moonrider Motel, where he and Cassie had the kind of courtship featured in steamy romance novels, and evidently in the *Kama Sutra*, though she never got a close look at the book that folks referenced in hushed tones.

She still lived at her house most of the time, though, and it worked out because she and Beecher agreed to keep noisy romancing off the premises whenever the other one was home. Wining and dining were permissible at the Tate house, and early September was ideal for the front porch swing and lazy toe-tapping in the late afternoon sun. A warm breeze stirred the ferns in hanging baskets.

"You want me to make some sangria?" she asked.

Chuck was clean and sober, and wine punch was harmless—not enough alcohol to count, in Cassie's opinion. She even knew some Baptists that drank it. "Give me a minute while I mix it," she said, "and then you can help me set up."

Assembling the wine punch in the kitchen, she sang along with "Blue Eyes Crying in the Rain" on the radio. Maybe Chuck would sing that about her if they ever broke up, inasmuch as her eyes were blue like his, and of course she'd sing that about him, too.

Sliced lemons and oranges bobbed along with ice cubes in a scratched-up smiley Kool-Aid pitcher, now slippery with condensation. Cassie balanced it on a tray with two striped glasses and willed herself not to drop it as she stopped at the front screen. Opening her mouth to ask for help, she clamped her jaw shut, unable to get a word out.

"Sheree," she grumbled. What was she doing there? Beecher wasn't even home, and she had to know it. With her wide brown eyes glistening Maybelline, and white jeans that looked spray painted on, Sheree laughed and lightly touched Chuck on the chest as he brushed back her hair, eyeing her like a soft-mouthed bird dog retrieving a winged drake mallard. Sheree's brass link choker flashed in the glare like a dog collar and lasered the temper controls in Cassie's brain.

"Need some help here!" Cassie screamed, stumbling out the door. The Kool-Aid man kicked up a red surf in time-altered slow motion before the glass pitcher crashed to the porch. She would never be sure if it was an accident or a childish impulse. Either way, she didn't mind the result. Sheree's white pants looked tie-dyed by the time the ice cubes slithered along the smooth concrete.

"You retard! Look what you've done!" Sheree held out her arms like a scarecrow, her sleeves dripping red wine.

"Hey look! Some got on me, too. See there, the pitcher slid right off the tray," Cassie insisted. "Let's rub ice on it. Got plenty here."

Chuck wheeled around and backed into the house, saying he'd get a broom and a dustpan. Yeah, you let me have the dustpan, Cassie thought, and I'll dump the broken glass in Sheree's bathtub.

## CHAPTER EIGHT

## Donny in Disguise

**B**rigitta refreshed a jar of cocktail olives against a background of mumbling afternoon drinkers and "Midnight Train to Georgia" playing on the tape deck. Donny Ray, his hands unsteady, stubbed out a cigarette in an overflowing ashtray and reached for another light. "Are you sure they didn't leave together?"

"Keep your voice down!" Thin white stripes of paste eyeliner highlighted the indigo lines across her eyelids with Cleopatra-looking wings. Scowling, she set off a line of crow's feet. Damn, she looked 35 after all, he thought. "No. They did not leave together."

How could she know that? His thoughts spun on a flywheel, whirrrrrr.

Gitta slid a wineglass on the oak rack suspended over the bar. "Aldo went on holiday."

"No way he'd run off and leave a small fortune–" he stopped. Frowned. "Something's wrong. He was a Nazi, and the RAF hates every Nazi ever walked. That's a fact."

Forearms resting on the counter, Gitta shot him a Martian death ray. "So, you know everything now?"

Donny Ray clenched his jaw. "Then forget Aldo. Where the hell is Jusef?"

"He is everywhere and nowhere. Maybe Antwerp." She rubbed her face, makeup filling in pockmarks like ivory spackling paste.

"Belgium? What's there?" Donny Ray frowned.

"Diamonds. Shhh."

Ice? Sure. Portability. Ease of concealment. And diamonds work when currency won't. People were all the time stitching diamonds into coat linings for dramatic escapes in turnip trucks across dusty Slavic borders. That wasn't the case here—Jusef had to be laundering money. Donny Ray bristled with new awareness of what a little widget he was in an immense machine.

The Zippo flame tapped the end of his cigarette, and he took a long drag. Exhaling, he removed it from his mouth with three fingertips and studied the orange hot box for a moment. Could Brigitta be trusted? Maybe she was a government informant, he thought. Maybe that's how she knew German intelligence was after them. Was she pushing disinformation? She could be wired. He had to find out. He tapped ashes, set the cigarette into the ashtray, and shoved it aside.

"Come here, you." Donny Ray stroked Gitta's hair and pulled it gently to move her face close to his. He kissed her lightly and paused. Then he shoved his hand down her cleavage and mashed everything real good. Nope, no wires, he thought with relief. A few bar patrons applauded.

"Oh!" Brigitta laughed, blushed, and tidied her blouse. "I love you forever."

"Yeah, me too, but don't tell anybody!" He showed thumbs-up to the onlookers, who whistled appreciatively as he made another playful grab.

She wouldn't sell him out—or would she? Sometimes he wondered how much she'd revealed of herself. He should have watched his step better.

Even apart from all that, he figured Jusef had to be coming back for the guns. Donny Ray sure as hell didn't know how to get them into Iran. All he knew was the payloads went to Switzerland, and somebody got them from there. He couldn't simply dump them in the river, or he'd have hell to pay with those crazy Faction fuckers. They trained with Palestinian militants. No wonder the RAF transported the stuff. They were going that way anyhow.

"Drinks on me! Everybody!" He held his shot glass aloft, while his thoughts rushed. He needed a van and new storage before somebody looted the place.

Donny Ray motioned Brigitta close. "Get me some beer crates," he whispered. "We got to get that shit out of Aldo's garage. Hide it somewhere. Anywhere but here."

Brigitta nodded. "It's you and me, baby!"

Caught together, hanged together. He couldn't get it out of his mind.

The next day, Donny Ray drove circuits around Aldo's neighborhood in a chilly September drizzle. He'd bragged to Army buddies about restoring the Mercedes-Benz sedan at the shop, but now he couldn't afford to be seen coming in or out on the street. He would be the only person, definitely the only G.I., associated with the place.

He'd read the espionage thrillers—street cleaners swinging pails, old men reading newspapers, and ladies pushing prams, all were spy candidates with cameras in ballpoint pens or fake bird nests across the street. Thank God, Brigitta knew another way in. Why hadn't she said so before? "Because you didn't need to know until now," she said. "This isn't Texas with your little drug ring."

She opened a notebook on the kitchen table, where drops of maple syrup glistened on sticky lined pages and an oilcloth table cover. With lacquered red fingernails, Gitta outlined paths with penciled lines and arrows.

"Sheet metal shop next to garage, right? In through their basement, back stairs to second floor. Storeroom with common doorway into Aldo's."

Donny Ray gulped a TUMS, a chalky coat on his tongue. "What is this, Man from U.N.C.L.E.?"

"Uncle?" She narrowed her eyes.

"Secret entrance through a tailor shop. Never mind. American TV." For over a year, he'd been in and out of Aldo's garage, and this was the first he'd known of the storeroom connection. Separate buildings, common wall. Another thing they didn't tell him.

"How do I get into their basement? Wouldn't they have an alarm?"

"Big keys for back door, small key for alarm. In a box outside, bolted to bricks. Paid privilege." She smirked and curled her fingers to make a gun with her hand. "Do you feel lucky? Well, do you, punk?"

"Your Dirty Harry sounds like Rudolph Hess." A thousand ways this could go wrong.

## Dogging the Collar

Adjusting his wool beanie, Donny Ray got off a tram near Aldo's and slouched at the entrance of a café, reviewing Gitta's notes under jittery neon. Simple. He hoofed it to the next block, hunching his shoulders, hanging close to buildings to avoid streetlights, mercifully dim in the breezeways.

Next door to Aldo's, a ribbon of frosted panes opened above a slab of red brick. Concrete steps descended from street level to a solid steel basement door, over which a yellow lamp glowed in dissipated light. Donny Ray scanned the area with a pocket flashlight. Two sets of locks and a sign meant "keep out"—*Zutritt verboten*.

Dogs barked inside the building as he worked the beam over the wall, twisted ivy and crusty paint cans partially obscuring the bricks. Stooping, bending, kneeling, he shook his head in frustration. Daylight had faded into murky gray, and he could not see a box of keys. No alarm panel was in sight, either—must be inside on a timer same as Aldo's, he thought.

He backed up and viewed the premises wide-angle. A rusty drainpipe ran down the wall at the corner. Bingo. Tucked neatly behind metal straps was a narrow black box containing the keys. He'd have to move fast and shut off the alarm blast as soon as he got in. "Are those dogs locked up in there or what?" he wondered.

His sweaty fingers worked the locks, gritty and unforgiving. Finally, the tumblers clicked, and he shoved open the door.

A siren wailed, lights flashed, and from somewhere emanated deep-throated barks. "Shit!" he yelped. He backed out, slammed the steel door shut, and stumbled over the first step. The noise stopped, thank God—but Donny Ray felt a cool metal pressure like a pipe jam into his back. He peed himself a little as he put his hands up and spun around.

"*Was machst du hier?*" A sturdy pale man urged him inside with a flick of his wrist and a .38 revolver.

Donny Ray's armpits flooded. "No speak German. *Ich spreche kein Deutsch.*" He jingled the keys, still in his right hand. "Aldo's friend."

"Ah. Aldo." The man's face was stony, but he relaxed his grip and patted Donny Ray down. Then, satisfied that he was not armed, nudged him back through the door and ordered him to kneel.

Hands clasped in front of him, Donny Ray submitted to the .38 and a pair of Doberman pinschers whining and pacing in a large kennel next to him, their toenails skittering across the plated steel.

The guy spoke English well, and he evidently had a history of heavy-duty interrogations. He worked Donny Ray hard, eliciting details about the Red Army Faction, Brigitta, and Aldo. Stasi, the son-of-a-bitch had to be Stasi, he thought.

"Listen man, I just want to rebuild an engine," Donny Ray said. "I can show you–"

"Not necessary. I know why you're here." The man flicked Donny Ray's chin. "Get up."

He struggled to his feet, his knees cracking. The Stasi landlord, or whoever he was, showed him the alarm box, just inside the door. The alarm's wiring was vulnerable to tampering, the man explained, so the two Dobermans had been added to the warning system. Instant alarm when he was on the premises; twenty seconds to disarm it otherwise. "Now I know to expect you until your business is done."

Donny Ray had to remain anonymous on the streets, the man told him. Unmemorable. Prostitutes grazed the alleys, and addicts crouched on street corners. Make sure not to give the police a reason to look his way. And it wasn't only for Donny Ray's security.

"It's my ass, too," the man said. "This building and these operations. Move in the dark. Blend in. This alley stays clear."

The next day, Donny Ray bought a Ford panel truck from a guy on base, and at nightfall, he drove it through drenching rain into Aldo's service bay. Thereafter, he took public transportation via oddball bus stops at all hours of the night, walking several blocks in zigzag patterns and varying his route, anything to avoid a tail.

He also needed a disguise, as by now surveillance was a given. Brigitta slicked his hair back and dressed him in black leather with safety pins, a spiked collar, and silver wrist cuffs. German punk rockers drew no attention after midnight, she said, especially in that area, with clubs dotting each block.

Initially, he felt like an ass, but nobody bothered him on the streets except to beg a smoke. He mostly came to enjoy the leather, plus, Brigitta got herself a matching set of everything. He was digging it.

Working through successive nights, blackout shades covering the windows, Donny Ray obliterated firearm registration numbers and modified the panel truck's suspension. He added a locking captain's bed, which concealed significant space underneath where he stocked the ammo in salvaged beer crates. Cubby shelves, a gas stove, and a large butane tank completed the look of a recreation vehicle, a standard-issue van.

Yet the question remained why the guns had been untouched in Aldo's shop –the Stasi guy next door almost certainly "arranged things." Donny Ray had been quickly schooled on the Soviet KGB and their East German pals. He was glad to have read *The Spy Who Came In from the Cold*, but the reality was grinding him down.

Nonetheless, joy surged through every pore when he finally drove the guns and the van out of Aldo's garage. He parked the vehicle near Brigitta's bar, and they moved it every day—up the block, into the alley, or the pay lot across the street—always where one of them could keep an eye on it. Or try to.

Off duty, he hung out in the tavern and waited for Jusef's order, knowing that when it came, they would have to run south to Bremen and await directives there. Brigitta's bar phone was likely bugged, so location info couldn't be revealed over that line. Instead, they had a number to call from Bremen and would move out accordingly. He'd drive the van and she'd follow at a safe distance in her old Audi. They planned some rendezvous points.

He merely needed sufficient notice to put in for leave or somehow finagle a couple of days off, enough time to drive the van wherever and leave it. Then he could go back to the base and forget that any of this ever happened. But this had dragged on too long. Where the hell was Jusef?

## Bremen or Bust

Dust motes flickered through beams of light in the tavern, and Brigitta closed the curtains on the west windows. Donny Ray lit a cigarette and blew a plume of smoke that floated into the Heineken clock. Most days after work, he sipped Scotch, joked with customers, and pawed Brigitta—until Jusef called.

She answered the phone behind the bar, gestured, wide-eyed, and handed it to him. Donny Ray pivoted and ground his cigarette underfoot.

"Move your ass!" Jusef shouted into the phone. "Now!" Then he hung up.

Donny Ray's stomach jumped. He slammed down the phone and faced her: "Bremen."

"Bag upstairs," she gestured and dropped a beer stein in sudsy water. She told her employee to take over, then wiped her hands on a towel and smacked it on the counter.

Donny Ray pantomimed, half whispering. "I'll get the van. Give me five minutes lead."

Gitta took a deep breath. He walked around the bar, gave her a tight hug, and touched her lips. Then, thrusting open the heavy-paned door, he stepped into the glare of the early autumn afternoon and adjusted his sunglasses. Jangling keys, he power-walked to the van a half-block away. He climbed into the vehicle, adjusted the mirrors, and eyed the perimeter.

Easing out of the parking spot, he stopped for cross traffic and edged into the roadway. As he pulled away, two white *Polizei* sedans crept into view, blue lights flashing. Terror stabbed him in the belly, and he slipped into a loading zone nearby. He hunched behind the wheel, watching the police as they raced into the bar.

Moments later, officers escorted a hysterical Brigitta, bucking and writhing, to the squad car. With a downward thrust of her shackles, she drew blood from an agent's neck as he shoved her into the back seat. "*Scheiße!*" she cried.

Sirens brayed and wailed. Pounding the steering wheel, Donny Ray wailed too. "Why did Jusef wait so long?" He howled, but no one heard him with his fist jammed in his mouth. He threw the vehicle into gear, and warily moved into an alley, the veins at his temples throbbing. His head was gonna roll right into the Army stockade, if he didn't land in Stammheim first.

## CHAPTER NINE

### Amsterdam, the Western Netherlands

Donny Ray pulled up the van to a two-story brick building with a single window in a sort of sketchy neighborhood mix of commercial, residential, and even some condemned properties. Instructions followed through random phone booths from Bremerhaven to Bremen, Oldenburg, and Groningen finally got him to Amsterdam, an unexpected destination. Normally a four-hour drive, it had taken eight with changing license plates, doubling back and forth, and now it was close to midnight.

His spirits had fallen headlong into a shithouse. The *Polizei* nabbed Brigitta and missed him by a hair. He figured he'd soon be AWOL unless he could dump those guns right away. Then he could reappear in Bremerhaven without risk, unless, of course, he was on German law enforcement's hit list already. In that case, they would have reached out to U.S. officials by now. "Ah Jesus," he sighed.

He couldn't stand to think about it. And the van, now thick with smoke and nicotine sludge, smelled worse than the meat packing plant where he worked one summer until somebody swung a meat hook at him. He had to dodge more than a meat hook now.

Rolling up to a steel door, Donny Ray honked three times. Slowly the door rumbled up on tracks, lights flashed, and a wiry-haired guy in coveralls with a shoulder holster motioned him in. A gray-beige Mercedes-Benz was parked alongside.

Man, that was a 1963 coupe, 300SE, he thought. The same as his. "Was that? What the?" he squinted.

The door panels closed behind them. Security cameras glowed green pinpoints of light. Donny Ray jumped out of the van and slammed the door, suddenly short of breath, hands trembling. "This way," the guy escorted him through an interior door with a drilled peephole and yellow warning decals.

"Where's Jusef?"

The guy shook his head, pulling a folded map from his pocket. "Meet him at the docks tomorrow. Noon."

"What the hell is this? And who are you?" Donny Ray wiped his sweaty palms on his jeans.

"Night guard," he said. "Food upstairs. Nothing hot, but good beer in a cooler."

"Is that my car parked out there?"

"Ask no questions." The guy eyed him, patting the holster.

### Truth in the Telling

A chill wind gusted across the Vlothaven harbor, a remnant of the September storm. As the sky cleared, Donny Ray and Jusef watched cargo freighters zigzag through loading zones, as seagulls circled, shrieking behind the noise of ships' engines. Quay cranes, running on elevated rails, lifted 20-foot containers two at a time, and stacked them like Rubik's Cubes.

Donny Ray tasted the bitter tang of nicotine in the back of his throat and coughed with raspy irritation. After all that rush out of Bremerhaven, he found that plans had changed in Amsterdam. Again. Another delay. This wrenched his gut.

"What happened to Brigitta?" he demanded.

"German intelligence. They connected the dots in Bremerhaven," Jusef said, stabbing imaginary dots in the air with his finger.

"But Gitta was never involved. Not in German Autumn." Hands in his pockets, Donny Ray focused on Hapag-Lloyd stevedores in bright orange coveralls.

Jusef stepped in front of him and met his stare. "Then why do you think she was arrested?"

"That's what I want to know, asshole."

"She stayed loyal to the cause." Jusef tossed his dark hair back from heavy eyebrows and winked. "She may provide useful information about you and Belgium."

"What about Belgium?"

"You tell me." Jusef smoothed his thick mustache.

Right, the summer music festival. "Yeah, Rock Werchter. Me and Brigitta went. Big deal."

Jusef stopped and put up his hand. "After that. Side trip. Brussels to Mons."

"So what?" Donny Ray winced to recall details.

"You dropped a hitchhiker near a bridge in Casteau."

How did Jusef know that? Anger and confusion simmered in Donny Ray's brain.

"And this bridge exploded." Jusef leaned in. "But the NATO commander survived."

In a mock show of sympathy, Jusef put his hand on Donny Ray's shoulder and spoke in soothing tones. "Seems your passenger did not place the mine in time—really, Raymond, your driving skills."

A terrible pressure in Donny Ray's forehead threatened to black him out. His mind reeled with recollections of cars and trunks and guns. Did Brigitta set him up? He didn't want to believe it.

"This way," Jusef gestured, and they turned their backs to the wind, stepping along loose gravel and cobblestones.

Donny Ray bowed his head, listening intently, watching the toes of his boots scrape the asphalt. "Me and Brigitta, we had something."

"Ice packs and stitches," Jusef laughed. "Come, come—your eyes advertise like an optician's sign. Are you so heartbroken? Brigitta vetted you. Drinking and boasting, you told her what we needed to know. It's not as though someone wakes up and says, 'Today I decide to be a gun runner.' And you hit on all cylinders, as the saying goes."

"But she sure as hell fucked me over." Donny Ray's memory wheel spun with flashes of insight. He shouldn't have ignored the signs; he cringed with thoughts of possibilities he'd denied. And in the end, she'd cold-cocked him. So why would he trust that Jusef was on the level?

Bells clanging, a tram arrived at their stop, and they swung onto the dimpled metal steps. Shortly thereafter, they descended the tram and stepped onto a well-scrubbed sidewalk. A small café-tavern beckoned from behind white windows nestled in aged brown brick. Aromas of brown bean soup, vegetable mash, and smoked pork sausage greeted them at the entrance.

They glanced around the room and went to the back where kitchen clatter raised the volume with the whap-whap of double swinging doors. They settled into a table with direct views into the cleaning stash of mops, buckets, and sponges.

Jusef steepled his hands. "You're in it now, you know. The Stasi, the RAF, big players. Allied undercover follows them and you will soon be in American sights—if not already. Your military ID photos are clean-shaven, yes? So, now you must grow a beard."

"For Christ's sake! I picked up a Belgian hitchhiker." Donny Ray folded his arms. "There's a thousand hitchhikers with their thumbs out this minute. I ain't kowtowing to nobody, and I sure as hell don't plan to grow a beard."

"Don't be stupid. You know the Faction bombed U.S. military bases." Clasping his hands to his chest, Jusef scowled. "And the NATO commander is an American general. Alexander

Haig. So yes, the United States would want very much to interrogate you."

Shaking his head, Donny Ray thumped his lighter on the table. "I didn't do nothing but rearrange Army inventory."

"And you refitted the autos for Aldo." Jusef shook a cigarette from his package. "Why?"

"Drugs and guns," he shrugged.

"The obvious, yes." Jusef fixed a hard stare. "Also, bodies. Live ones, dead ones, packed in the boots—the trunks, you say. All for the cause."

A smiling waitress arrived with a tray of sandwiches, pickles, and brews in stoneware steins. Foam trickled down the sides and puddled on the table. Jusef raised his beer in a toast. "Cheers to the profiteers."

"I can't eat," Donny Ray pushed away the plate. He glowered in resentment.

"What's your problem?" Jusef swiped his mustache with a checked napkin. "Look, you got what you wanted—the money, Brigitta, gambling in Monte Carlo, rocking in Montreux. Am I right?"

"But this is all messed up!"

"Doesn't matter. Brigitta's out of the picture for now. Irrelevant. Anyway, I have a new plan—operations in the U.S."

Donny Ray squinted into his beer. His temples throbbed—angry at Brigitta, for her betrayal, and at Jusef, a psychopath, like that *Clockwork Orange* guy. And now Jusef wanted him in on another deal. The man was disgusting, carrying on eating and slurping as though nothing was wrong. "I thought you hated the States."

"True, but the timing is right." Jusef glanced at the kitchen help visible through the swinging doors, wiping counters and stacking dishes. "We're talking big, big money. I promise you the Berlin Wall will fall—and with it, the Red Army

Faction. We will outlive our usefulness to them—and to Iran. You already have! So, we follow the money to the States." Jusef leaned in. "Cocaine."

Okay, Jusef must be delusional, Donny Ray thought. "No way," he said. "Pablo Escobar would chop our heads off."

Jusef pushed up his sleeves. "Escobar is good with it. He needs us. All we need is the Gulf of Mexico."

"You've been talking to Escobar?" Donny Ray was stunned: Escobar, the richest drug trafficker in the world with the Medellín Cartel—and now the King of Cocaine, running the Columbian drug trade through Central America into the United States. A renewed interest in hanging out with celebrity criminals tantalized Donny Ray's ego.

Jusef hunched his shoulders. "His lieutenants have been talking to me."

"What's the catch?" Donny Ray was on high alert.

"I need a green card."

Donny Ray flicked a crumb off the tabletop. There went the celebrity and power, he thought. "Look, I can't help you with that."

"Oh yes, you can." Jusef clasped his hands on the table. "Get me an American wife. Someone who won't talk."

"They all talk."

"Not if she has something to lose. Raise the stakes."

His brain buzzed, and Donny Ray felt his face redden. He lowered his voice. "You're out of your mind! I'm about AWOL, tangled up with jackoffs and we still need to unload the damn guns. Why would I even think about letting you rip me off again?"

"You owe me. I could have let you go with Brigitta."

"*You* could have let me go with Brigitta?" Donny Ray's stomach roiled.

Jusef eyed him. He felt in his jacket for cigarettes, pulling out some pocket litter. He sniggered, "Ah. My snoopy-loop."

Snoopy-loop? A rubber band. Some of Jusef's fancy Brit talk. Donny Ray drummed his fingers. "Let me get back to Texas and scout out some scenes, make a few calls."

Jusef twirled the rubber band on his index finger. "No. You bring her here first."

"I know you're shitting me." Donny Ray flattened his palms on the table and launched from his chair.

"No. Sit down."

"That's, that's," Donny Ray sputtered, "the most asinine thing I ever heard. It might work with the RAF, but—"

Jusef slammed his hand on the table, and their waitress scooted by, disappearing into a cloud of steam that poured out of the kitchen doors.

"Listen here," Donny Ray growled, "you want me to get a woman over here to marry your ass? Why can't we wait and hook you up in the States?"

"Simple." Jusef's tone deepened. "We must establish the relationship before we enter American airspace. Make her complicit. Best to get a needy one who yearns for affection. When our plane lands in New York, she must already feel she is part of me, married, loyal. I know these things, Raymond."

Donny Ray rubbed his jaw. God, this was making him crazy. "If you would just wait, I swear, I can find you a hundred women who'd marry you for the right price."

"Absolutely not. My American wife must have a vested interest, otherwise...." Jusef worked the rubber band through his fingers and shot it across the room. "Boom."

### Internal Combustion

The stubbly beard itched, and Donny Ray was chronically fatigued; he couldn't get a decent sleep with that overnight guard stalking around. His nerves played out with chest pain, stomach aches, and eczema flaring under his elbows. It was one thing to ship guns out to the Middle East, he thought. Those people were always rioting and carrying on, slapping their backs with cats-o'-nine tails. Nobody took them seriously, turbans and magic carpets, all that. But the fucking RAF? People jumped back.

Jusef had set up a good front in the Amsterdam building: another mechanic shop called *Vriendelijke Olie en Banden* (Friendly Oil and Tires), with a pay phone for incoming calls and signage for Esso and Michelin. A few legit customers came in for brake jobs and tune-ups, and Donny Ray kept his outside activities to a minimum, like *De Wallen* a few times. But hell, he couldn't find a poker game, his one obsession.

While Donny Ray yanked carburetors, Jusef left the building. A lot. Their mail came to a couple of suburban post office boxes, and for all Donny Ray knew, by controlled drops.

Turned out it was Donny Ray's Mercedes-Benz in the garage. Within hours of Brigitta's arrest, it reappeared in Amsterdam with a new VIN number, license plates, and color conversion from red to *graubeige*. "Because gray beige shows up light in black-and-white surveillance photos," Jusef had explained. "Anyone looking for your old vehicle will see nothing of interest. Anyway, witnesses always remember red, so we had to change it regardless."

Who were these people who could change that crap in eight hours? Must have been a lousy paint job, he thought—a good one takes days. Never mind, he had to keep his eye on the Escobar prize, quit worrying. At least he'd have his car back when the ammunition drop was done.

Yet, he had to abandon his carefully crafted van. "They'll be looking for your Ford," Jusef said. "Make, model—so you have a Volkswagen panel truck now. Make it a travel van. Strip it down and rebuild it as you did before."

"Aw, hell." True, Volkswagens were commonplace, virtually invisible to locals. But now he had to drag everything out of the Ford, redo the captain's bed, the storage, et cetera. "What are we going to do with the Ford?"

Jusef shrugged. "Sell it. Big market at American Express on Saturdays. People haggling, going about. I've got a Turk who'll handle it."

## Becoming Raymond

Weathered buildings with gabled roofs dominated the view from Donny Ray's second-floor kitchen window. He had unfurled half the blackout drape to let in some daylight. Given the mix of properties, high-powered photo lenses might be watching from anywhere.

Seated at a dinette table, Donny Ray flipped solitaire cards, not for the game, but for the tactile thrill of slick, glossy playing cards fresh out of the shrink wrap. Snap. Snap. "Fuck you, King of Clubs."

He tugged at his beard, a nice thick one now, he thought. Phony eyeglasses—large tortoiseshell affairs—dominated his face. And he had a false identity to get him through border crossings: an international driver's license and a U.S. passport with entry/exit stamps and signatures to match his alleged arrival here. His took his alias, "Raymond," from his dad's name, took his father's birthday, too, only jacked up 20 years so he wouldn't forget it under pressure at a checkpoint.

Everything fit, consistent with his appearance, all courtesy of "cobblers"—spy-guy techs in East Germany who fabricated stuff. With that talent at his disposal, Jusef should get his own damn green card, but he wouldn't hear of it. He said they invited extra scrutiny in the States, and he couldn't afford the risk. He insisted on a spouse to make it legit.

Donny Ray was taken aback when Jusef appeared in the kitchen. He hadn't made a sound coming up the stairs. How'd he manage that? Straddling a yellow vinyl chair, Jusef crossed his arms on the table. "Where's my American wife?"

"Still trying. No word yet." Donny Ray grimaced.

"Well, you must get the girl before we begin to move out the cargo."

"Why?"

"To lock her in. She accompanies you on the delivery, and now she's colluding. You have a mutual crime, much excitement, you see?" Jusef pressed his fingertips together. "This always works, especially with homely ones—look at Brigitta. Ha!"

"Well, that's pretty shitty." True, Gitta wasn't any Sheree, but not much difference in the dark. Seemed like Brigitta had worked a lot harder for his attention than Sheree ever did, between the sheets and in the kitchen. Damn, he missed Gitta—those tits and dumplings and wiener schnitzel.

"Raymond, it's all psychological. This woman will finally feel worthy of a man's attention, but she must be, uh, what's the word, malleable, easily influenced. Maybe even stupid. Of course, I'm fine with ugly on a professional basis."

Uh oh. Donny Ray didn't know any unattractive women in the States. He culled his flock specifically for their looks. But "needy" was a different issue. He knew one of those.

## CHAPTER TEN

## Great Balls A'Fire

Cassie finally understood what Jerry Lee Lewis and "Great Balls of Fire" was all about. She and Chuck had it going on, for as much as their uneven schedules would accommodate. His suite at the Moonrider Motel was right down the road from the Bobtail Bar and Grill—a real win-win for the time being.

And she was secure in the notion that when he wasn't with her, he was at work or the rehab place, where he volunteered to help other veterans with their mood disorders. Nobody but Sheree had gotten mad about the sangria incident. The guys laughed about it, and Cassie gave her a $20 bill for some new jeans. They were even.

It had been only weeks since the graveyard rapture, but when you're orbiting the Kama Sutra, time gets distorted. So, Donny Ray could stay wherever he was. She had moved on, and she was banking most of her salary for a potential wedding—and honeymoon in France. Adjusting her Piggly Wiggly nametag, she checked her reflection in the hallway mirror and smoothed her white uniform dress. Monogrammed towels would be easy, she thought, a single embroidered "C" for both of them, and for the Comet, which, come to think of it, had fired their true romance.

The telephone rang and interrupted her thoughts. Chuck must have quit work early.

"Hi-ya, handsome! I miss you!" She put her hand on her hip and tried to sound husky like Lauren Bacall.

"I've missed you too, baby!" A familiar voice emerged from the crackly line and struck a hard blow to her heart.

"Donny Ray? Is that you?" Cassie's pitch jumped—and so did her pulse.

"Who'd you think? How's my darlin'?"

"Okay, I mean...well, where are you?" Her legs went limp beneath polyester stitches, and she sank onto the couch. Lord, he still had a hold on her.

"Amsterdam. Everything okay?"

Cassie had a sudden desire to smell Jade East. "Are you still in the Army?"

"Nope. Left out of there. It's me and my buddy Jusef working on cars. Got a good little business going."

"Isn't this call costing you a ton?" She toyed with the coiled telephone cord, yellowed by a nicotine glaze.

"Nah, it's free. Jusef has a way to dial from phone booths, so you don't have to pay." His voice faded momentarily.

Cassie slapped the telephone receiver. "Donny Ray, are you there?"

"I've always been here for you. So, I want you with me."

"Over there? In Amsterdam?" Heartstrings yanked her like a marionette. Her voice broke.

"Cassie? Something the matter?"

"I'm seeing somebody now." She fell back on the cushions and flapped her knees. A runner in her pantyhose squiggled up her leg.

"Who's the lucky dickhead who'll get his ass kicked?"

"Chuck Denton is his name. He was Beecher's sniper buddy in Vietnam."

"A sniper? They're all psychopaths. And drug addicts. Those old Nam shots are contract hit men now."

"That's not true! My brother was a sniper, and–," she

began, fanning herself. Blue mascara dripped into a Picasso mess on her face.

"And your brother wanders the house at night rattling his medals in a Folger's can. You've told me that a hundred times. Cassie, lean on me. I'm strong. Just remember what we've had together."

Donny Ray's voice had a plaintive but formidable tone, even across the Atlantic Ocean. She could see him now, standing tall with a football in one hand and a pneumatic wrench in the other.

"I want to go to France," she blurted. "To Ambronay—and Lyon! Will you take me there?"

"Sure, wherever you want to go. Just get your pretty ass over here. I'll buy you a ticket—get you away from that psycho killer guy."

Psycho killer? Oh yeah, Chuck. Had Donny Ray hypnotized her? "I need to think about it."

"Think about being in my arms. I'm begging you. Come on, girl." His voice broke up. Cassie panicked, then the line went dead.

### Three's a Crowd

With Donny Ray uppermost in her mind, Cassie was a mess at work. His call haunted her, even at the cashier stand, where his face rolled down the conveyor belt in Chef Boyardee's hat. Chuck had loved her ever since he'd seen her picture in the Quonset hut. He'd said, "The First Time Ever I Saw Your Face" got it right. How could she walk away from love like that?

Simple answer: she couldn't.

After all, love stories were always fraught with difficulty, sometimes even tragedy. That's why loved-and-lost songs topped the Billboard charts. She had loved Donny Ray for a third of her life—but he never reciprocated the way Chuck did.

She had to make the best choice for herself now, and Donny Ray would have to understand and move on with his life, too.

When Cassie stepped inside the screen door that night, Beecher was slumped in the recliner staring at *Three's Company*. His face formed a tragedy mask from the high school drama club: bloodshot eyes swollen into slits, mouth turned down, jaws scrunched in pain. Empty beer cans lined the coffee table like Easter Island statues.

"Come here. Sit down," Beecher patted the sofa. "I've got real bad news about Chuck."

"Don't tell me he's dead!" Screeching, she put her hands over her ears and fell back on the cushions.

"Might as well be. He's gone, Cassie."

"Because you threw him out!" She flung a striped pillow across the room.

"He left town with Sheree."

"Sheree?" A platoon of tiny jealous troops, their torches blazing, marched through Cassie's heart, squeezing it like accordion bellows. She pulled her knees to her ribs and rocked. "Why would he do that to me?" Gasps punctuated each word.

Beecher grabbed her arm. "You don't need him. He's a junkie! You never saw the goddamn needle tracks?"

Yanking free, she shoved him with the flat of her hand. "He's clean! He's diabetic, you dumbass!"

"Diabetic?"

"Sure, I saw needles in the trash, so I asked him, okay? And he said Agent Orange gave him diabetes." She pounded her fist in her palm. "He shoots up insulin."

"That's a lie! Agent Orange messed him up all right, but it ain't diabetes—it's smack, and that's the truth. The rehab place kicked him out again." His face drooped. "I caught him trying to steal some of Mama's silver."

Silver? Mama's precious Buttercup pattern? Cassie spread her knees, bent over, and touched her palms to the floor.

Her chestnut hair puddled on the rug, and a whimper exploded into a full-fledged sob. "He wanted Daddy's silver token, too!"

"Listen to me, Cassie. Shhh, be quiet. Chuck was a mean motherfucker before he ever went in, and he can't handle it on the outside."

She jerked her head up from the floor, her hair covering half her face. "Donny Ray was right about him!" Her voice trembled. "And what's Sheree's excuse? Whore! Whore! Junkie, junkie whore!"

Beecher's nostrils flared. "Wait, how would Donny Ray know anything?"

"He called me today. He said things about Chuck." She took a deep breath and pinched the upholstery piping. Donny Ray had saved her from a loser, a druggie—how could she have betrayed him? All along, he cared about her, and she'd do anything to be with him. Safe and secure.

"I hope you told him to go to hell."

Cassie touched the pendant. "He wants me with him in Europe. Now I'm sure as hell going."

"You can't up and leave," Beecher clasped her shoulder.

"Wrong." She pulled away. "The band plays on, Brother, this band plays on."

## CHAPTER ELEVEN

### Dirt on Your Head

Hands full, Donny Ray lurched over the threshold into the shop, and the door clanged shut behind him. "Okay, think I've got us a mail-order bride." He set takeout pastries and mugs of strong Dutch *koffie* on a worktable.

"Great! Who?" Jusef looked up from a Hamburg newspaper, its pages spread out on a steel desktop.

"Old girlfriend from home. Name's Cassie. Sweet. Made to order. Should've thought of her first." Donny Ray pulled up a chair. "It would help a whole hell of a lot," he scowled, "if you'd get the phone going both ways. I've got cramps from dialing that outside code over and over." He clutched the warm cardboard mug to soothe his fingers as he sipped.

Jusef flapped his hand. "Forget about that. You told her you'd make arrangements?"

"I didn't get a chance yet. The line broke on me."

"So, call her back, tell her you've got a ticket booked for Thursday week."

What if Cassie says no? What about that sniper guy? Donny Ray scratched his elbow. "That's damn short notice."

"Tell her you got a swell deal on a one-way ticket. Big discount. Maybe first class."

"First class?"

"Say whatever it takes. But get the girl on the plane," Jusef flashed straight white teeth. "And then drive the last load to Switzerland." He tore a classified page from the paper and pushed it across the table. "Your orders."

Donny Ray smoothed out the page and scanned the personals section. He frowned. "What were you looking at?"

"These." He tapped four square adverts. "Railway station in Basel, Friday noon, passcode is tin drum. Buy *International Herald Tribune* at newsstand to signal your contact."

"You've got to be kidding." What a movie cliché, a newsstand—how many could there possibly be in that place? "I never signed up for spy shit."

"No spies here. We're careful entrepreneurs. We are independent businessmen. Which is why," Jusef thumped the table, "we're shifting our interests to the States and Escobar. Keep that uppermost in your mind, Raymond. But first, we complete this operation."

Crap, if Cassie had any hesitation at all, any loyalty to the sniper, this operation would crash and burn. His stomach knotted. "And how's this supposed to work?"

"Simple. You drive to Basel, park, unload. Your contact gives you a lockbox key and notifies me. We'll meet."

Coffee grounds settled at the bottom of Donny Ray's mug. He studied them with detached interest. "The timing really sucks."

Jusef's mouth moved, but his expression didn't change, "If you hadn't dicked around all this time…"

Donny Ray winced as little gremlins with tiny vacuum pumps flushed battery acid into his stomach. "I'll call her back tomorrow."

"Very good. I'm glad this will work out—because you know, Raymond, I wouldn't want to put dirt on your head."

"What?"

Jusef lifted his chin. "It's a Farsi expression—means to bury you or wish you dead."

Oh Jesus. Donny Ray clicked the cigarette lighter. "What if there's nothing in the lockbox? What if this guy is CIA?"

"What if you are CIA?" Ice-cold Jusef froze him out.

## CHAPTER TWELVE

## The Big Pitch

Dallas' impressive glass and steel skyline sparkled beneath the Delta jet, climbing skyward, piercing wispy clouds. Cassie smoothed her polyester slacks, pulled the shade, and sat upright with a death grip on the armrests. Was she the only one scared of a crash? Her elderly seatmate marked pages in a crochet book without so much as a glance up until the "no smoking" sign blinked off.

The old girl lit a Tareyton, bright red lipstick feathering the lines above her lips. Cassie adjusted the air vent catching a whiff of Marlboro smoke from one row over. Cassie would know Donny Ray's brand anywhere. Her insides tingled to imagine him right on the other side of the tray table.

A tiny yellow Dramamine, a mini bottle of rum, and several hours later, Cassie awoke with a jolt at JFK International Airport. Disembarking, she tightened her backstraps and reoriented to gravity. Her duffel bag had already been checked through, packed with her nifty red Adidas tracksuit, and running shoes bought on markdown in the Marshall Mall.

She would have been more comfortable flying in the warmups, and maybe she would have worn them if she were boarding a Freddie Laker airplane. Not appropriate attire for international travel, though. Flying name-brand airlines called for a tailored appearance.

Cassie glanced down at her tassel Weejuns with pride as she made her way into the international terminal.

Coming to an abrupt halt, she spied a swaying bald man patting a two-sided drum, his topknot keeping the beat. A sparkly female companion bobbed her head and chanted a familiar refrain.

Must be Hare Krishnas, she realized with a thrill. Both swirled in orange robes, which looked surprisingly like J.C. Penney sheets. Most travelers ignored them or stuck out their elbows to block the Krishnas' efforts to get in their space. However, a tip jar and a stack of publications drew Cassie's attention to a card table, where daisies bloomed from cloudy water in a Coke bottle.

The lady Krishna's beanie jewels jiggled as she swept her arms in free-form dance, circling Cassie and a startled onlooker. "I am Rasonnati," the woman trilled. "Welcome aboard our transcendental plane! And take a magazine, free for small donation." Little bells tinkled from her toes as the onlooker bolted for an escalator.

One magazine cover featured a cartoon of a man with blue-tinted skin and black ringlet hair, playing a flute for dancing chipmunks and women in gold-encrusted headgear. Cassie studied the title: *Back to Godhead*. Something about the stylized, colorful artwork, and the word Godhead, reminded her of Chuck's Kama Sutra book.

"Hey, what's this about?" Trembling slightly, she pointed at the cover.

Between thumps on the drum, the Krishna man sing-songed, "Our Bhagavad-Gita." Thump. Thump. "Sacred text. With special features to bind believers." Big thump.

Okay, she thought, the magazine was simply a promotional tool pretty much what the Catholic Digest did. Cassie inched closer to touch the man's drum, but he yanked it away, scowling. "No, no! This is a Mridanga, the incarnation of Lord Krishna's brother."

Lord Krishna's brother had a remarkable resemblance to Ricky Ricardo's conga drum, she thought. "Sorry, I didn't know," Cassie said. "But I can't join you. I'm on my way to Amsterdam." She stood straight, pulling her shoulders back.

"Wonderful!" Mr. Krishna smacked the Mridanga with renewed enthusiasm. "We have a divine temple there. We can marry your soul to the Godhead."

"Can you marry regular people, too?"

"Yes, of course!" Rasonnati stopped dancing to wipe her forehead and swig from a bottle of TAB cola. She had recently returned from Amsterdam, she said, where lovely weddings for the faithful were performed in the temple, with souvenirs available in an offsite tearoom.

Same as any other church gift shop, Cassie guessed. She fished a dollar bill and a Bic from her backpack and handed them over.

In exchange, Rasonnati scribbled her name and the Amsterdam addresses in the inside margin of an issue of *Back to Godhead*. She pocketed the dollar, returned the pen and magazine to Cassie, and handed her a flower, before turning to pitch new targets.

"Well, hello cosmopolitan life," Cassie said aloud, thinking maybe she would reinvent herself as a witty intellectual, moving in European circles of ex-pats clustering in major cities. However, she would have to keep in mind Beecher's warnings about Eastern Bloc prostitution rings operating in the West.

"Don't let your guard down," he'd warned. "There's men over there will play you for a fool—reel you in with a burlap bag tied over your head."

Cassie scanned the waiting area near her gate, where rows of thinly cushioned metal seats were hooked together by threes and fours, with aluminum armrests and square tables with ashtrays. A cigarette fog hung like a graveside canopy over the smokers. She found a seat at the back.

"Attention! Do not leave your baggage unattended." The airport intercom voice repeated the announcement in several languages. Cassie snapped to attention, placing a protective hand on her backpack. Shifting her sights to a nearby gate where a plane was boarding for Paris, she quietly repeated the French phrase on the intercom and smiled.

She had an authentic-sounding French accent, everyone said. That's the main reason her daddy sent her to convent school in the first place—to learn the language from a French order of Dominican sisters. Johnny Frank refused to put public-school teachers in charge of Cassie's linguistic development.

Come to think of it, he seemed to have a crush on France, collecting French coins and stamps. He even special-ordered records by Johnny Hallyday—the French Elvis. Her dad played them for her with great enjoyment. Cassie always had to leave the room for *"Que Je t'Aime,"* with its embarrassing sexy lyrics, but she listened at the door and found it remarkable that her dad had a Hallyday-style passionate side.

He had all kinds of contradictions, like his reverence for all things Catholic, despite his upbringing and Della's objections. She saw no reason to raise Cassie in a spooky church with Day-Glo statues and X-ray pictures of Jesus' flaming heart.

"We've belonged to First United Methodist our whole lives, even before it was United," Della bristled, always proud her family membership went back generations. "Cassie needs to stay grounded with us."

It wasn't just the Church's structure and stability he admired. Johnny Frank was fascinated with Catholic mystics, often remarking how faith and sacramental wine got the brave French through the war. He clung to the memory of those extraordinary years, which naturally annoyed Della because of the Baby Patsy thing. However, they worked out a compromise.

He tolerated certain Methodist hypocrites on the front row, and on major Holy Days of Obligation, he and Cassie knelt in pews to say rosaries in St. Joseph's on North Alamo Boulevard.

Despite feeling somewhat conflicted about the parental contest of wills, Cassie stacked the deck in her dad's favor by offering up prayers to St. Thomas Aquinas, patron saint of winning arguments.

His insistence that Cassie learn French paid off, and by the time she was in junior high, she could read simple French novels and watch movies without subtitles. Most memorable, however, was when they drove the new I-20 interstate highway to Shreveport to see *The Umbrellas of Cherbourg* (*Les Parapluies de Cherbourg*), a musical romance movie set in the northern French town of the same name.

Set in the 1950s and '60s, the movie featured a beautiful leading lady—Catherine Deneuve—and her lover the garage mechanic, who left for Army service abroad when she was unknowingly pregnant. But her letters didn't reach him, and they never married, so the snowy finale at an Esso service station was sadder than anything Bambi ever dished out.

During the *Cherbourg* showing, Johnny Frank wiped tears repeatedly, even out of the glass eye, scrunching a red bandanna handkerchief in his pocket. As the movie stars sang "I Will Wait for You," Cassie could hear his sniffing over the movie orchestra.

"For a thousand summers, I will wait for you..." He clenched his fist and swung his arm like a kid keeping time to "Good Ship Lollipop."

At least her parents were married, unlike the movie plot, so what's up with the waterworks, Cassie thought. She felt weird seeing her dad so upset. It wasn't until he died that she fully appreciated heartbreak and loss. Months after he passed, she walked around with a hole in her heart.

Love enough to hurt enough, that's the way of life and romance, right? Donny Ray had hurt her in the past, but he loved her, so Chuck could go to hell. Chuck used her, didn't he? He stole her mama's silver and would've taken her daddy's sawmill token too if Cassie had turned loose of it for a minute.

Well, Cassie used him, too, she reasoned. She walked on the dark side, the wild side, with a former sniper-killer-turned-junkie. All the thrilling crazy sex stuff, she'd done it. Now it was over. Donny Ray's more consistent qualities suited her fine. She could time a three-minute egg by that man, and she liked the predictable comfort. They were the romantic *Cherbourg* lovers, and she'd waited too many summers for him.

Flight monitors flashed. Her plane arrived ON TIME.

## CHAPTER THIRTEEN

## Schiphol Looming

Donny Ray pulled out of an Amsterdam petrol station and headed for the A10 motorway, a six-lane ring around the city. Cassie would arrive at Schiphol in about an hour. He glanced at his road map. Exit at Knooppunt De Nieuwe Meer.

Dutch names annoyed him. He was pissed anyway. He was nothing but a mule in this operation, but the promise of a big return—and Pablo Escobar—kept him going. He loved the adrenaline rush.

The first time is the best time, but still you keep looking, he mused.

Staring ahead at the A10 fast lane, Donny Ray's vision blurred for an instant, flushing out a buried image, like ducks under fire, flashing then gone. Poof! Dumpster. He remembered it right away—rusty green, dented, hunkered on damp grey cement. Just another back-alley garbage bin near the Houston port, and Donny Ray crouching beside his dad, heart pumping, scared, thrilled.

For years he'd wanted to reclaim the thrill of that first scam. He was about seven or eight when his dad took him on the run after a shell game gone wrong in Galena Park, near the Houston Ship Channel. They went tearing down Holland Avenue, hid out behind the Dairy Queen, and watched while their marks hunted them with pistols.

No telling what they could have done together if the old man—35 at the time—hadn't clocked out working on a Texaco drilling platform.

As it was, Mr. Raymond Richard Duggan had made news headlines: "Explosion, Three Dead in Gulf of Mexico." The Coast Guard arrived too late to save him, but Donny Ray got a big payout on a wrongful death claim. That's how he got the Corvette in high school, with money to spare. It couldn't make up for losing his father, but it gave him a fresh start.

Upon moving to Marshall to live with family, he tried to recapture the excitement with his cousin Mark; however, their attempted foray into funeral swindles imploded when a detective's auntie got a recycled coffin with marijuana residue. Luckily, only the undertaker took a rap.

Mark went quiet for a while, but Donny Ray still needed an adrenaline surge, so he turned to back-room poker and football. The girls adored his surly presentation, an angry young man who needed someone to love him tender like Elvis' movie girlfriends. In football terms, Sheree was the game-winning touchdown. Cassie was the whirlpool tub in the locker room—relaxing, warming, and soothing his pain.

Just like that, it ended with a busted Achilles tendon.

He hated the rehab center in Tyler—confinement in a wheelchair with his casted foot propped up. He remembered talking with jug-eared Mark on the rooftop pavilion, looking down on a loading dock, while sanitation workers emptied trash barrels nearby. Donny Ray had envied their mobility. "I guess this is how prison feels," he said, swigging a can of Pepsi.

Mark scoffed. "I've never seen a prison yard like this." He'd bent down to hand Donny Ray a cigarette and lighter. "It's a great view anyhow."

"Yep, another day in paradise." Atop an adjacent building, giant exhaust fans cranked whirring aluminum blades.

"Listen, man, you can piss and cry all you want but what's that going to change? Forget football—let's get our own mechanic shop. You've always been a gearhead anyhow." Mark hunched up, pulled a half pint of Scotch from his back pocket, and poured some into his empty soda can. "This'll grease your gears," he said, handing it to Donny Ray. "I can get us up and moving for twenty grand. Easy."

True, Donny Ray enjoyed messing with engines, but twenty grand was about all he had left from his daddy's settlement. Still, he trusted Mark. He was family, and smart. He'd already put in three years at a Chevy dealership.

"We can get us an operation down at the Channel," Donny Ray said. "Galena Park, like the old days. And a boat, I'll get a boat." A smile spread across his face.

"We'll keep it on Galveston Bay. Ain't nothing better than the open water." Mark nudged him. "Oh wait, I forgot. Cassie called. Said her mother killed herself. Sorry, man."

"Killed herself?" Donny Ray shook his head. "That's a hell of a bombshell to forget. What's the matter with you?"

Mark shrugged. "Didn't come to mind."

"As if I need something else to worry about."

"Well, help her through the funeralizing, anyway."

**Easy Money**

Even after rehab and private coaching, Donny Ray couldn't interest the college scouts; either they didn't return calls, or they said their rosters were full. In short, he was a football has-been, too slow for a starting lineup at Texas or LSU. He refused to be anybody's tackling dummy. Mark was right: time to move on.

They agreed to stay in Marshall to open shop. Donny Ray maintained some residual star power, and it should be easy to establish a customer base. After graduating high school, he got certified in auto mechanics same as Mark, and they got "Torque & Power" going on an I-20 service road halfway between Marshall and Longview.

Parts, bodywork, custom upgrades, they did it all for Detroit rides. Mexican ladies stitched fine leather into vertical channels for the seats—the tuck and roll they called it, as good as the Cadillac assembly line.

It wasn't only the fine-edged work that drew customers, though—a privileged few were also keen on the shifty side of business with a bookie in the back. And high stakes poker games were a big profit item, which frequently claimed Donny Ray's share of the day's receipts. To balance the books, he went all in for Mark's proposed expansion to a cocaine train running up Highway 59 from Houston.

"Got a plan." Mark had clicked a Jack of Diamonds across his bucked front teeth. "Right here," he said, gesturing at a state map. "That's us. Their boys drive in for service, we mark up the parts and stay legit on that side, but the main thing is, we got to get the coke into the seat covers and packed in the back. That's our value."

And from there it all rolled west on the interstate to Dallas. In only six months, they'd raked in so much cash, Donny Ray became Scrooge McDuck diving into a cartoon money vault. But the operation ground to a halt on a sunbaked afternoon in 1976, when a scraggly-haired guy, his snakeskin boots dragging the gravel, kicked up dust in the Torque & Power parking lot. He stopped his sputtering Suzuki and held tight to the shivering handlebars, twisting the right-hand grip and revving the engine.

Donny Ray stalked out. "What's the problem?"

Gesturing emphatically, the man looked around, delivering a threat in broken English. Donny Ray crammed a $100 bill into his hand and didn't even watch him go. Panicked, he dashed into the office and shouted to Mark. "Get in here, man! We've got to shut down!" Donny Ray's breath came in quick stutters.

Mark loped into the room holding a handful of colored push pins.

"You're lying!"

"No, I swear, we're in the middle of a big turf war—Mexican cartels." Donny Ray lit a cigarette, his hands trembling. "They're going to make examples of us. They'll dig out our skulls and post 'em on flagpoles."

"Fuck me." Mark threw the push pins into the air, raining reds and blues onto the gray linoleum floor.

Donny Ray dashed to the window and shut the blinds. "I'm out of here."

"And you're out of your mind." Mark smacked his fist into his palm. "We've still got the shop. All's we gotta do is drop the coke and stay out of their way."

"I ain't sticking around to see. You keep it."

Donny Ray emptied a box of timing belts, coiled like garden snakes in a tangled mess of plastic and rubber. Then he yanked open the desk drawers, shoving papers, notebooks, and a Yellow Cab souvenir ruler into the box. He hoisted it waist-high, and with his hands full, he rotated his shoulder to wipe some tickly sweat from his jaw.

Greeter bells jangled on the front door.

"Hey boys, am I interrupting?" Sheree poked her head inside, hair askew, a chunky silver necklace shining brightly on her chest.

"What are you doing here?" Donny Ray stuck out his foot to catch the door and darted past her. Sheree turned around, her necklace jangling, and chased him to his car.

"Got some news for you," she panted. Her hands in her back pockets, she angled her elbows and stuck out her boobs.

He chucked everything into the back seat and faced her. "Okay, out with it. Twenty-five words or less."

"The rabbit died." She poked his chest with her index finger. "Meet me at the preacher's or meet me in court."

"Tell the millwrights' union."

"I'm saying it's yours." She glared at him hard and cold in the summer heat.

"You ain't getting nothing from me." Donny Ray wanted out of town and out of state, while his head was still tied to his shoulders. And he sure as hell didn't want a little bastard calling him Daddy.

Time to run—and the Army needed a few good men.

So, bye-bye, Miss American Pie.

Donny Ray never heard another word from Sheree. He'd tried to reach her for this green card deal, but she froze him out. Probably there never was a baby. He'd heard of that con all his life, and he nearly fell for it.

Signs for Schiphol Airport loomed into view. He missed Brigitta, but he guessed she'd never really been his. Maybe she had already rolled on him. He was desperate to get the green card wife before Jusef turned on him, too.

## CHAPTER FOURTEEN

### Tinker Toy Man

Cassie stirred in her seat, eyelids heavy, as another yellow tablet and the smooth whirring of jet engines relaxed her into a Donny Ray dream state. When she stepped off the plane in Amsterdam, he would twirl her in the air, hug and kiss her, like he used to. She tingled with nostalgia, recalling his late-night phone calls to talk about mad things, sad things. He told it all. And Cassie had listened.

He didn't remember his mother—except for once as a little bitty guy in cotton undershorts, when his mama was crying, which got him crying. Then she left, and he never saw her again.

"Don't you miss her?" Lying on her bed, Cassie sank into the darkness, broken only by the amber glow of a streetlight near her window. An attic fan hummed and swirled the summer night air, billowing the short curtains and making shadow play on the walls.

"Nothing to miss."

"What if she comes back?"

His voice tightened. "She won't. She's dead to me."

So callous, Cassie thought. "You should honor your mother, no matter what," she said. "I honor my mother, and she's been a mess my whole life."

"That's you."

A little bubble of sorrow floated through Cassie's voice. "The day Daddy died, Mama fell apart, and I was crying, both of us chasing the stretcher into the front yard. As the men carried out his body, the sheet fell off his face." She sniffed. "Right then an ice cream truck pulled up, jingling 'Turkey in the Straw.' I hate that song."

"You didn't need me for this conversation." Donny Ray blew smoke across the receiver. She could hear it.

"Haven't you ever loved anybody?" She twirled strands of hair, staring into the murky shadows, hoping he'd say he loved her.

He grunted. "Loved my grandma and my dog. And lost 'em both."

A dog and his grandma? Not such a tough guy after all, she thought. Cupid's arrow struck her all over again. Donny Ray had a hard shell, but he was compassionate, and he could be tender, like Ernest Borgnine with the schoolteacher in *Marty*.

Donny Ray had lived with his Mamaw while his dad was working offshore. But his dad died, Mamaw fell, broke her hip, and had to move into a nursing home. Donny Ray got sent to Marshall to live with cousins.

"What about your dog?" Cassie glanced at the bedside clock radio, glowing 2:00 a.m. in green.

"Too many questions," he grumbled.

"Sorry."

"Don't ever say you're sorry," he shot back. "It sounds weak. And pay attention: I'm here to protect you from pricks like me."

## Continental Culture Shock

Double chimes and muffled flight announcements startled Cassie from a half-sleep as the plane circled over Amsterdam. She craned her neck to see out the window. Houses lined the canals like miniature Monopoly hotels.

Thrilled, she caught her breath. Big, strong Donny Ray waited below to take her in his arms.

Wobbling with excitement and swollen ankles, she stepped through the jet bridge and into corridors. Dang, it was cold —the time and temperature clock blinked 9º Centigrade, 49º Fahrenheit, without a sliver of sunshine to warm it up. Why did every checkpoint take forever? She shivered under her long-sleeved blouse, pulled a light sweater from her backpack, and crossed her arms to ward off the chill.

Donny Ray said he'd meet her at the luggage carousel, rather than wasting time threading the crowd and waiting in lines. That meant she'd have to navigate on her own, but he paid for the ticket, so she had to accommodate.

For over an hour, Cassie mindlessly moved like a cow among cattle, prodded through taped-off lanes, getting inspection stamps, and enduring luggage delays. Finally, gripping her duffel bag, Cassie paced the area, scanning faces, when a scary-looking bearded guy in glasses headed straight for her. A pimp from the Baltics maybe? A wave of panic washed over her. Where was Donny Ray? And the Krishnas?

"Cassie baby—it's your lover man!"

She gaped. "Donny Ray? Is that you?"

"In the flesh." He embraced her, rocked back, and put his hands on her shoulders. Beaming, he held her at arms' length. "Oh, I've missed you, baby."

My God in heaven, Cassie thought. Donny Ray had turned into a skinny Tinker Toy man. He used to beat up boys who looked like that. How could this be the same person? In tight leather pants! He didn't even smell the same.

"You dig the beard?" He rubbed his chin.

"It's different. I mean, it's a surprise." Indigestion burned her upper GI tract. "What's with the leather pants?"

"It's a European vibe," he said. "Very Continental." He vigorously rubbed her shoulders with the palms of his hands. "It's hip. You'll get used to it."

"Well, the glasses and all." She burst into tears and wanted to go home, but all she had was $200 in travelers' checks. She couldn't afford a return flight—Donny Ray had promised to handle that. At least his voice sounded the same, though, so maybe she should quit looking at him.

"What is it baby, why are you upset?" Donny Ray took her in his arms.

Sobbing, she put her head on his chest. He stroked her hair, saying "now, now," as though that could fix this train wreck. He still had his height, but he was too thin. A weenie-body had kidnaped her muscle man.

"It's okay," Donny Ray crooned. "Come on, you're tired. Please don't cry."

Pulling a tissue from her pocket, a Bobtail's matchbook fell out. She quickly stooped to pick it up, reading, "There's no match for Bobtail's" on the cover. Perfect example of the clash of two worlds, she thought.

Donny Ray dabbed her cheeks, held her for a moment, then he broke the hug, smiled, and brushed the hair from her forehead. "Time to hit the road."

"To Ambronay?" She wiped her cheeks.

"Nope. Switzerland. Come on, let's boogie."

"I thought–" She faltered, and he took her by the arm.

"We'll save all that other for later," he said. "Let's go. You got a jacket in your bag?"

"Thought I could get one here to save room in the luggage, but now I'm so cold! Even with this sweater, I'm m-m-miserable," she stammered.

"Aw hell—wear this." He removed his down vest and handed it over. "Told you it was cold over here. What's it, seventy-five degrees at home?"

"Yeah, about that."

Donny Ray had warned her about the weather, but only in a throwaway conversation. He had called her several times from street corner phone booths, always keeping it short, with minimal girlfriend-boyfriend chit-chat.

Cassie figured a new jacket labeled "made in France" would be a good souvenir. Besides, in a matter of moments they'd be cruising in his Mercedes-Benz, which would make the hike through those congested, multi-level parking mazes, with pee-smelling elevators mostly worth it.

Panting, they stopped before a Volkswagen panel truck. "Your chariot, my dear." Donny Ray gestured like a *maître d'* showing a fine table.

She let go of his arm, thrusting her head to eye him up close. "Is this a joke?" She examined the dented sides. "What happened to your Mercedes?"

Donny Ray's face reddened. "We'll see it later, but get a load of this—a real Volkswagen, from world headquarters in Germany! Isn't this great? It'll hold the road real good in the mountains." He slid back the loading doors to show the truck's interior, featuring a butane tank propped against a captain's bed with cabinets underneath.

He helped her aboard, guiding her head the way cops put criminals into squad cars. He pulled a red flannel shirt-jacket from the back, slid it on, and gave thumbs up.

What a mess. He'd oversold this trip, that's for sure, talking about Paris lights, luxury cars, and swanky hotels. And now this—a plumber's truck? Her trusty Comet looked better than this old thing.

As he squeezed her duffel bag into a cubbyhole, another wave of disappointment rushed over her. A cheapskate lot of nothing, she thought, barely masking her irritation.

"What if the butane explodes?" She shivered with memories of Gorgeous U.

"Nothing's going to explode." He ruffled her hair and pulled her close, stroking her back. "Baby, you've got to trust me here. I've got it all under control."

He clipped a pair of Foster Grants over his glasses, instantly improving his appearance. To her relief, he looked more like the old Donny Ray. Somehow, even the beard looked better—kind of distinguished. After all, they weren't in high school anymore.

As he piloted the vehicle onto the highway, Cassie felt slightly more at ease. She dug into her backpack for a faded Kodacolor print. "I've got an old picture of us. Want to see?"

"I'll look at it later," he said, checking his mirrors, and turning the heater on low.

"You had your arm around me." She raised her voice over the highway noise. Something about the panel truck made everything louder. Must be a lot of metal in there, bouncing all the sound waves. She'd seen a Coronet movie about that once in science class.

He gave her an air kiss, mwah. "You know I hate getting my picture taken."

She angled the picture and studied his chin. She'd always loved the way he worked her neck with it. He was beautiful then, and he was still handsome now, but in a different way. He could pose for the Sears automotive catalog. Those models always looked kind of weedy. She put the photo away. "Tell me about this guy you're working with now."

Frowning, Donny Ray scratched his elbow through layered fabric. "Jusef. He's in the import business."

Cassie fiddled with her backpack and retrieved a stick of gum. "I thought he was a mechanic."

"Yeah, well he gets car parts for mechanics. And things like ball bearings. Germans are big on those. We'll be meeting him in Switzerland."

She flinched. "Why?"

"I already told you. We're partners. And the Germans want us with a Swiss bank."

"Wait a minute, you're–"

Donny Ray grimaced. "Never mind. Give me a light." He grabbed an open Marlboro pack from the dashboard, shook it, and gripped a cigarette with his teeth. She leaned a Bobtail match into it as he puffed and watched the road. His voice now had a biting kind of stop-and-start that told her to step lightly on eggshells and go with something easier. "Where are we staying tonight?"

"In here. Good truck stops along this route."

Her face fell. "Hey, I didn't come all the way over here to sleep outdoors."

"Only for tonight, hopefully. Why waste this good bed?" He put his free arm around her shoulders.

"But we might get mugged or something."

"Nah, I look European. We're not targets."

Bells went off in her head. "Targets?"

"For street hustlers and Gypsies."

"You mean Gitans?"

"No, I mean Gypsies. Get used to it. We gotta blend in." He slowed for a turn and glanced her way. "You'd be surprised what bad guys will do. We need to stay on alert."

~~~

Donny Ray usually got high on tension, but this was an angle grinder stripping his nerves. He couldn't risk the superfast German highways, not with a bullseye on his back. And God, the guns—he even had his service revolver, a Colt .45 automatic, tucked under the front seat in a storage compartment. The Germans were strict about personal weapons—new laws had been passed a few years earlier because of the Red Army Faction.

Even if the border police never saw the ammo stash headed for Iran, possession of a firearm would be enough to get him into deep shit. He'd scraped the registration number off the barrel, just in case. He couldn't afford to get the weapon traced back to him.

By now, though, Brigitta might have ratted him out to interrogators—anything to drive a plea bargain. And military authorities had to be looking for him, if only about the AWOL problem. But once they got him, the rest of the rats would run out from the cupboard.

He glanced at Cassie. He couldn't tell if she was awake. "We're going into Belgium," he said, "and if we drive straight through, we'll be in Nancy by suppertime."

"What's the rush? I've been traveling since yesterday." Eyes half-mast, she braced against the window. "My face is greasy. Can't we stop for a little break?"

Donny Ray adjusted his glasses. "You're fine. I've got some snacks."

She frowned, sorted through the snack bag, and retrieved a spotted yellow pear.

"You'll like Nancy," he said. "Sweet little town."

"I damn sure better."

Donny Ray focused on the highway. She'd never been so bitchy before. Now, she was talking back to him. Not a good sign. If he couldn't make Cassie go along, his ass would be grass—with Jusef pushing the mower.

## CHAPTER FIFTEEN

## High Beams, Bright Lights

Cassie alternated sips of water with nibbles of pear. Donny Ray, his eyebrows drawn, gripped the steering wheel, reaching over to tweak the radio knob. News alternated with American pop music —a bit stale by her reckoning. She touched her silver sawmill token and remembered sticky-fingered Chuck. She'd never forget him, especially since Donny Ray resembled a bag of kindling sticks now. In leather pants, she sighed.

"What's that about?" Donny Ray glanced her way.

"Nothing."

Donny Ray held tight to the wheel, looking back and forth from the road to her face. "Sorry you came?"

"Why would you even ask that?" She added up the numbers on license plates passing them. "Anyway, I want you to help me find where Daddy was during the war. You know, he hid from the Germans in a beech grove. That's where he got Beecher's name."

"Yeah, that sounds great—we could see where Johnny Frank got shot in the eye." He put his arm around her and squeezed her shoulder. "I'm kidding."

She studied his face in profile, pleased to see the little scar still splashing across his cheekbone, a sweet reminder of his original 7-Eleven look and of the Corvette—a stark contrast to this heap of junk tooling down the road. Mr. Big Stuff and his cousin, she recalled. "Say, do you ever hear from your cousin Mark anymore?"

Donny Ray checked his side mirror before pulling over to pass. "We keep up some. He moved to Houston."

"Yeah, I remember he sold the old Torque shop."

"Right. Made us some money. And soon's we get back home I'll be moving down there."

"What for?"

"German car maintenance—the high rollers need their Beamers and Porsches worked on, Mercedes too. Been talking to Jusef about it, and he wants in. We'll make a mint with the ball bearings."

"Oh." Maybe she wasn't included in the plan.

He slowed the vehicle a bit, reached over, and patted her cheek. "You want to go to Houston with us?"

Ah, exactly what she needed to hear. She touched his hand, and he stroked it with one finger as he'd always done to show how deep the still waters ran. Even so, she wondered if he really wanted them to be together, or if he had some dead air to fill. He'd fooled her before.

## Lady and a Tramp

The highway looked the same as any other, all concrete and barriers; it might as well be the LBJ Freeway, except signage was in multiple languages and every other vehicle was a Peugeot or Mercedes-Benz. Lucky them. This bread box was a rugged ride, and Donny Ray chain-smoked, which had never bothered her before, but now the fumes nauseated her. He said it was a part of her jet lag, and he pried a candy cane from the dashboard. "This'll clear your head," he said. "It's clean."

She unwound the tacky plastic wrapper and cracked the window to ventilate. Turned out France wasn't such a big deal after all; it was only somewhere else to be. She yawned and rooted through her backpack, retrieving *Back to Godhead*. She examined Rasonnati's scribbles. "Hey, ever heard of Kerkstraat? It's a street in Amsterdam."

Donny Ray's head spun. "Where'd you ever come up with that?"

"It's where the Hare Krishna temple is. Or their coffee shop. Can't tell, exactly." She squinted at the page.

"Tell me you didn't give those assholes any money. You saw them in the airport, right?"

"They're not assholes, bigshot." She returned her attention to the magazine, pausing at "Bad Karma—There's More to It Than Stubbing Your Toe." The pictures showed a man's face, half tiger, and a woman's face, half bear. The article explained the Vedic "eternal traveler" viewpoint, which was interesting, not that she would ever buy into that. If it wasn't the Holy Trinity, she was out of there.

Violet hues of twilight descended over the landscape, and high mast luminaires lit up the signage. Donny Ray took the Nancy exit, wheeling through boulevards and side streets of travelogue fame, with their striped awnings, wooden shutters, boulangeries, and patisseries with signs assuring passers-by that they take American Express. Metal security curtains fastened the merchants' stores shut, but lamps glowed from within a bistro. Donny Ray parked in front.

Still a little unsteady, Cassie jumped down onto the brick pavement, sending shocks zinging up her legs. But the pain disappeared with the wonder of a chalkboard menu and fragrances of freshly baked bread and simmering cassoulets wafting from the entrance.

A little bell jingled over the door, which opened to a freshly scrubbed tile floor, red-checked tablecloths, and shelves lined with spices, liqueurs, and wine. Glass domed platters on the counter featured pastries and small cakes.

A dozen customers sat on stools and folding chairs, while a tiny man with a wooden leg played the *Lady and the Tramp* song on an accordion in the corner. "See now? Worth the wait," Donny Ray said, squeezing her shoulders and rubbing her neck.

A chubby brunette woman rose from her stool at the cash register and gestured to an open table. After a few false starts, Cassie eased into a French dialogue with the lady and guests seated nearby. "Ah, Americans!" Luckily the Yanks were in favor for the moment. Cigarette smoke curled through the room, and jugs of wine loosened everybody up. Several courses of meats and vegetables followed plates of ripe tomatoes and yellow cheeses.

The new acquaintances talked about Jerry Lewis movies and *The Umbrellas of Cherbourg*, prompting the accordion player to launch into "I Will Wait for You," which inspired the couples to smooch and sway. Cassie tuned up at the same parts of the song her daddy always liked. Flush with happiness, she embraced Donny Ray right there at the table. He clutched her and whispered that he loved her so, like the song said.

Café gourmand, with espresso and a caramel éclair, finished off the meal. Satisfied and grateful, Cassie bid adieu with cheek kisses and hand flutters, as Donny Ray maneuvered her back to the van. He hugged her tight, and she murmured "*Je t'aime*," believing she needed him always.

### Truck stop, truck go

A truck stop appeared outside of Nancy in a blaze of flashing signs and high beams. "See here, I promised you bright lights." Donny Ray poked Cassie's elbow and snickered. He parked next to big rigs, opened the door, and pulled her into his arms, as the wine had already inflicted its unique brand of cognitive impairment and scurvy-like incoordination.

"I want to wash up some," she said, leaning on him through the parking lot. As though peering at him through the bottom of a glass bottle, Cassie found Donny Ray looking better and better as he escorted her through the premises.

Still woozy, she knew she'd sturdy up, and she did immediately upon opening the washroom door, revealing the weirdest toilet she'd ever seen, with the bottom like a shower stall and a pull chain to flush. Nothing but a porcelain hole in the ground to squat over.

"Get me out of here!" She tried to edge past him. He gripped her flailing arms and kissed the top of her head. "Baby, you're not in Marshall anymore. Hey, they're not all this way. You'll get used to them."

"God almighty, it stinks like an outhouse. You could'a warned me."

"You want culture, don't you?" he grinned. "Come on, think positive. We're in love." He pulled her face to him, kissed her on the mouth, and headed for the men's room.

She locked the door behind her. "Love, my ass," she muttered, glaring at herself in the mirror. If she weren't so drunk and grungy, she would have flat-out nixed the truck stop operation. Was it too much to ask for a decent hotel room with curtains and a bathtub?

Prospects improved when she exited the washroom to find Donny Ray waiting with his glasses off. Throwing arms around each other, they moseyed through the mini mart, giggling and kissing between aisles of waffle cookies, Orangina, and car care products. When Donny Ray panted at her, she threw her arms around his neck. She'd started the trip off on the wrong foot. Donny Ray was no Tinker Toy man, she realized—just new and improved.

They swayed to the van, where he assisted Cassie onto the mattress. She let him undress her, first pulling off her shoes, then her bell bottoms, pausing with each little movement to kiss whatever he uncovered. Propping her left foot on the butane tank, she toed cool metal, grounding her in the moment. As the mattress stopped twirling, she time-traveled back home, to the football field, with Donny Ray splitting the uprights to score.

# CHAPTER SIXTEEN

## Gaul Aboard

Cassie sensed motion and heard the highway whine below her. Fragments of sunlight sneaked through her eyelids as she turned on her side. All she could make out was a large, red label marked "flammable gas" and a cartoon figure falling into a flame. Oh, yeah, that must be the butane tank. Boogie down, she thought.

Holy Mother, it was bright in there, and her head hurt. Her stomach didn't feel so good either. She tugged on the rumpled paisley sheet to wrap it around her, and sat up, bumping her head on the ceiling. Donny Ray's smiling eyes spoke to her from the rear-view mirror.

"Hey, big guy." She leaned over the driver's seat and put her hand on his shoulder, padded by woolens. "I'm your truck stop mama." Thank God, he'd shed the leathers, she thought. Gracious. She'd never been so happy to see him in jeans before.

He squeezed her hand briefly and turned loose to adjust the Michelin map. "I wanted to let you sleep in—you were a little shifty in the night. You feeling okay?"

"Got cotton mouth. Hey, anything in that thermos?"

"Coffee." Donny Ray handed it to her. "Here. And put some clothes on. We can take them off again later." He did a pretend leer.

She took shaky sips. "This van doesn't ride so good."

"Yeah, it's got a truck suspension."

"I think I'm going to throw up." She shuddered and cupped her hand over her mouth.

Donny Ray slowed the vehicle, exited the highway, and parked at a rest stop. With a pocketknife, he pried another peppermint loose from the dashboard and handed it to her. She wriggled into her Adidas pants, retrieved a hooded sweatshirt, and hurried to the women's restroom. Thank goodness, it was a regular sit-down commode—one of life's little miracles.

Three rusty sinks, three rusty mirrors—while washing her hands, she checked out her teeth. She rinsed with warm water and rewound the memory spool between her ears.

Despite her wino haze at the truck stop, she clearly remembered Donny Ray doing a lot of sexy stuff he'd never done before. She wanted more of those groceries—he must have been practicing with somebody else. But she had, too.

She climbed back into the passenger seat and beamed at him. She made the right call on this one. Chuck didn't matter. Only a fling. Everyone should have one before settling down. Now the little convent girl was a woman with a past.

"It's about three hours to Basel," Donny Ray said. "We can stop at the train station and get a hot shower."

"What about a hotel?"

He eyed the road signs, checking his watch. "Train station first. We can't check into the hotel until afternoon. Anyway, you need to get a jacket. I want my vest back."

Dang, what a cheapskate, she thought. They rode for several minutes before Cassie spoke. "I've never heard of taking a shower in a train station."

"You never got laid at a truck stop either." He looked at her. "Have you?"

"Maybe." She giggled, then shook her head.

"You better not have."

She hoped he wouldn't ask about graveyards.

Pulling a map from the visor, she studied it. "Why didn't we drive through Germany? It would have been shorter."

"I thought France would be more romantic."

"Oh, Donny Ray!" She touched his shoulder, lightly kissing his cheek. "Ever think about us getting married?"

He jerked the steering wheel but righted the vehicle before it crashed into a barrier. "Well, I think about you getting married."

"But I mean us. A family."

"If it's meant to be." He tugged her hair. "But we're not meant to know everything that's going to happen. That's the fun of surprises."

~~~

She asked too many questions, he thought. As if he wasn't already stressed. Abandon the van at the train station, Jusef had said, don't leave it out on the streets. Get a taxi to the Hotel Basel, Old Town. Jusef already booked rooms for them.

But which bank had the lockbox? The contact would tell him. Donny Ray and Jusef would sort it out, and tonight they'd introduce him to Cassie, let her get a bit familiar with him.

This was the first time he had ever intentionally set up another guy to steal his woman, but they both knew how to work it—the way Eric Clapton stole Beatle George Harrison's wife. Except Jusef had to move faster; no time to write a song like "Layla" to win her guilty heart.

Donny Ray stuck a cigarette behind his ear. He had to think positive. If Cassie bucked the marriage plan, he could persuade her. It didn't have to be forever. He'd tell her to think of all the money. She could go to college and buy a fancy car, new clothes, all the stuff she'd always wanted. They'd be a team.

Back when the Torque & Power stuffed his billfold, he'd taken her to some swanky restaurants in Dallas, where big-time oil guys and professional athletes threw money around. Donny Ray knew she wanted that again. He thumped the steering wheel and bobbed his head to the music. Yep, he'd charm her. It'd worked before. She'd do this for him. She'd climb on board with Jusef and ride him back home, he assured himself, momentarily diverting his attention to her. She sure as hell better.

Lower lip slightly askew, Cassie rested her boobs on a crumpled pillow, twirling strands of hair while reading the Hare Krishna magazine. Donny Ray knew she had a history of crushing on weird celebrities, like The Partridge Family, for example. But her interest in the Krishnas was way out there, even for her. He passed by their temple in Amsterdam once. A bunch of fruitcakes flailing around. He glanced over at her jugs again. Bigger than he remembered. Damn.

Dirty cotton clouds had absorbed the morning sun like a ratty sponge, now leaking light sprinkles on the windshield. The road better not get slick. All he needed was a vehicular pileup. He only had to make it to the train station, a little farther, a little more, and he could be rid of all this crap, including that captain's bed—nothing but a paper-thin mattress on a hard plank, no better than a jail bunk.

He reached down into the driver's side pocket and retrieved a large leather wallet stuffed with ID documents and Swiss francs. With one hand, he opened it and made a quick check while eyeing the road. His paperwork looked good, but the Army likely would be tracking him by now. Simple inventory would reveal how U.S. weapons made it from Bremerhaven to Tehran. And to the Red Army Faction.

The kilometers spun quickly as they approached Switzerland. Clock-ticking suspense was better in Western movies. Donny Ray chewed a cuticle, bit off a hangnail, and flicked it into the ashtray. Stung like a son-of-a-bitch.

Thank God, there was the border sign: Grenzwachtregion I – Basel. Donny Ray slowed the vehicle to a crawl. He nudged Cassie. "Passport, passport." He snapped his fingers.

She fumbled in her backpack. "Here."

Holding his breath, he presented their passports. No problem. Those Commie cobblers were good, he thought. The border guard simply gave the booklets a perfunctory glance, stamped them, and waved Donny Ray on into the drizzle.

"Show me your passport." Cassie stuck out her hand.

"Not now, let me concentrate here. Uh, what do you think about Switzerland?"

"I don't know. What happened to the Alps? This is all flat as a pancake."

"The mountains are a little way further. These are some pretty good hills, though." He exited at Basel-Wettstein and followed the signs for several miles, then he joined a stream of vehicles entering a multi-level parking garage.

"Wonder why it's so dark in here?" Cassie stretched and arched her back.

"Hell, I don't know. Maybe the electric timer broke. I'm thinking hard, so let's quit talking for a minute." On the second level, Donny Ray backed the van into a parking place sandwiched between two larger vehicles.

Cassie hugged herself against the chill as they approached the France-to-Switzerland connection. An elevator, then a winding hall, followed by huge sweeps of stone, marble, glass, and dark wood. Brass lanterns hung from the ceiling, and arched windows spanned the main wall. A huge round clock showed 12:00 noon. International travelers crowded the floor.

"Donny Ray, this is fabulous!" Cassie circled under the skylights, her arms outstretched to the cafés, gift shops, and jewelry stores that lined the wings. "I want to go shopping."

"Sure, hold on. Let's get us a paper first." He pointed at a newsstand nearby, where he bought an *International Herald Tribune*, a pack of cookies, and two bottles of mineral water. Keeping a sharp eye out, he walked her to a kiosk and arranged the snacks on a bar height table. He helped her with the chair

## CASSIE'S COMET

and unfolded the newspaper. He put it up to his face, snapping it the way Beecher always did.

"Tell me. What's it say?" Cassie tugged on his elbow, and he gently disengaged.

"Nothing special." Shifting his attention to the newsstand, he watched for a signal.

She munched a chocolate topped *Pépito*. "Aren't you going to read it?"

"Sure. It's the English language edition. I thought you'd like that, too."

"Aw, I could've read French." She smiled.

His grinding stomach cried for some TUMS. Motion caught his eye. That had to be his contact, staring straight at them, snapping a *Herald Tribune* against his palm.

Donny Ray rolled up his copy, saluted, and jammed it into Cassie's hand. "Take this, oh man, I've got the runs." He hurried her to the staircase leading to the lower level and McClean's shower facilities. She followed breathlessly behind him.

"That's happened to me before," Cassie said. "Distress in the lower tract."

"Right." He cast a glance backward. "Here's some money for the showers and buy a jacket when you're finished. I'll meet you here in half an hour."

"But–"

"I've got to go." He waved off the shower attendants, ran up the stone steps, and disappeared.

### Getting keyed

Hands in his pockets, shoulders relaxed, Donny Ray ambled across the lobby with a nonchalant air, concealing his racing heartbeat. His throat went dry as he joined a husky blond male, about mid-20s, leaning against the newspaper kiosk eyeing the *Herald Tribune* comics page. He dropped the paper when Donny Ray reached him. Both men knew the drill: firm handshakes, direct eye contact, and open grins to suggest old friends meeting. Nothing to see here, officer!

A red-bearded man joined them, his light wool jacket opened to a Swiss soccer jersey. They sauntered off, engaged in light conversation about sports teams, gradually accelerating to a brisk walk toward the parking garage. What if this is a sting? Donny Ray's pulse pounded even in his teeth. Stopping beside the panel truck, he reached for the handle.

The blond restrained Donny Ray. "First. Password."

"Drum."

The red beard guy shook his head. "No good. Let's go."

"Wait, no, it's–" Perspiration dotted his forehead as Donny Ray saw the outline of a revolver beneath his contact's jacket. "Tin drum."

Blond nodded, and Donny Ray's vaulting stomach regained its rightful place. He willed control of his wobbly hands, unlocked and slid open the side door. He inhaled deeply to soothe his tightening chest and climbed into the van, its odor reminiscent of a Dusseldorf cathouse with damp, rumpled sheets littering the floor. Hurriedly, he crammed them into Cassie's duffel bag.

Shoving aside the butane tank, Donny Ray helped the men into the van and clattered the door shut. He opened the storage bin for their inspection. Even in the chilled air, sweat soaked his armpits and dripped down his back.

The men pulled small flashlights from thin air and shined them over the boxes. "Sausage crates? Beer?" They frowned and met Donny Ray's eyes.

"Looks better than Property of the U.S. Government." He forced a shaky grin.

Hands-on, the buyers examined the contents, nodding, confirming that at least the top layer of ammo was legit. "And if it's not, you will hear from us," the red beard said.

The men stayed put while Donny Ray crawled into the driver's seat, somewhat confident that they wouldn't shoot him in the back while he was driving. But would they throw him off the roof? Unconsciously, he wagged his head and shifted gears with a lurch, holding his eyes on the next level until they reached the rooftop.

The men transferred the goods to a green transport vehicle with campground stickers and team slogans affixed to the bumpers. From outward appearances, they were harmless young holidaymakers stocking their camper with beer and sausages. Donny Ray wiped his brow and took a rest, sitting atop a Beerenburg bitters crate. "All done, right?"

"Finished. We got ours." The blond pulled a small white envelope out of an inside pocket. "Here's yours."

Still wary, Donny Ray unsnapped the envelope and tentatively removed a brass key engraved Credit Suisse 230825. He visualized stacks of fresh green cash cascading with the sweet smell of printer's ink.

"Now, out you go," Blond jerked his thumb at the door.

"Wait a minute, whose name is this under?" Donny Ray reexamined the envelope.

"Shhh! Secret." The man put his finger to his lips and cracked a smile. "Jusef knows. Name, access code. Now goodbye." He gave Donny Ray's butt a little kick.

Well goddamn, he thought, jumping out of their transport, his ankles smarting with a concrete jolt. "A numbered bank account," he muttered.

Donny Ray climbed into his van and crouched on the floor, raising his head little-by-little. Nothing. Elbows on his knees, he covered his eyes with the heels of his hands. Five hundred grand in high tech military equipment, and all he had to show for it was a lousy bank key.

## CHAPTER SEVENTEEN

## The Gambler

On a bench outside McClean's, Cassie sat with arms crossed over her backpack—a new down jacket and the water-spattered newspaper beside her. "Did your ass fall off? I've been waiting forever."

"So, so sorry, darlin'," Donny Ray smoothed her damp, chestnut hair, softly crooning the Velvet Underground's "linger on your pale blue eyes" line. Ordinarily, that band wasn't her taste, but he used to sing it to her back in the day, and now it cemented his European hip vibe. She was starting to warm up to him again.

"What do you think of my new coat?" She slipped her arms into it.

"Love that red on you! Goes with the pants." He kissed her cheeks. "When I came back you weren't here, so I went looking around upstairs. Sure wanted you with me, you know, like Elvis and Priscilla."

Cassie pulled a face. "They got divorced!"

"Then make it Johnny Cash and June Carter."

They laughed the same as characters in romance movies, locking eyes and ambling out of the tiled McClean's entrance. He smelled kind of rank, though—sweaty, but extra pungent. Rancid, maybe. What had he been doing? Not taking a hot shower, that's for sure. She shrugged. Possibly his bad stomach had stressed him out.

Anyway, she'd done some window shopping herself. Dozens of stores lined the open gallery. The showcase at Luxury Gemstone caught her attention with dazzling clusters of diamonds revolving on a motorized display. Maybe Donny Ray had sneaked off to buy her an engagement ring! That would make him sweat.

Yet, she couldn't disguise her annoyance when he wanted to get a taxi to the hotel. Lips pursed, Cassie yanked at his sleeve. "Why should we pay for a cab when we can drive the van for free?"

"It's bad security to park it on the street. Better if we leave it here."

"You goofball! My duffel bag's in the van."

His nostrils flared. "So's mine."

She checked her temper. Maybe he was planning a romantic proposal—maybe with a limousine ride to a mountain top. Her brow relaxed. Forever, she would remember the diamond ring glittering with stars over the Alps. "I'm sorry," she said, ducking her head into his chest.

"No, you're never sorry, remember? It's a sign of weakness. You're a warrior." He hugged her amid travelers swirling through the lobby.

A warrior? Where did that come from? He told her to sit down, don't move, and he'd take care of everything. Of course, he would, she thought. The gift wrap should be ready.

### Poker Faces

The plaza outside the train station was massive. Green trams punctuated the scene with tinkling bells and cat-howling whistles. Cassie regarded the building's façade—its expansive paned archways and limestone. Donny Ray ushered her into a taxicab and spoke in short bursts of German with the driver.

"What are y'all talking about?" she asked.

"There's a hot poker game in Old Town, but to get in on it, you gotta to know someone. Gambling isn't legal here."

The driver pulled up to a square, five-story building of polished concrete and glass; the Swiss flag flew from the top. Marble planters lined the sidewalk, and heat lamps warmed guests sitting at an outdoor café clinking beverage glasses and eating little weenies.

Donny Ray signed in at the front desk and yanked their luggage onto a rolling rack. Once in the hotel room, Cassie sat down on the bed, admired the green shag carpet, and kicked off her shoes.

Frowning, he emptied loose change onto the dresser, fingering coins two by two.

"Uh, don't you have something for me?" She crossed her feet at the ankles and swung them lightly. "Maybe ice or something?" She stuck out her left hand, and he looked up, wide-eyed but otherwise expressionless.

"The machine's right down the hall."

Cassie's neck went limp, and she squeezed a corner of the bedspread. Tears rolled off her chin and darkened her pants in little splotches.

"What the–?" He studied her. "I'll get you some damn ice, all right? But then take a nap."

The phone rang, loud and shrill. He jumped for it; his eyes tight. "Hey, yeah," he said, covered the receiver, mouthed "Jusef" to her, before returning to the brief conversation.

Turned out, Jusef couldn't make it to Basel until banks opened Monday. Something about the German ball bearings. Donny Ray kicked the nightstand then adjusted his grimace into a smile.

"Well, Cassie," he said, "now you can wear your new down jacket, wander around, see the markets and all. Get yourself something to eat."

"What are you going to do?" She twisted a little hank of hair into a pin curl, then let it fall into a lame corkscrew.

He patted her head. "Taxi driver gave me a contact for the card game. I'm going to show those Swiss boys how a Texan plays poker."

# CHAPTER EIGHTEEN

## Hot Poker

Slivers of artificial light trimmed the faded yellow curtains. Cassie stirred from a sweat-soaked sleep. She patted the bed in circles. Empty!

Flashes of panic powered her brain, and she bolted upright. Where was she? Switzerland. Hotel. Okay. She slithered off the bed, made her way around the furniture, and switched on a table lamp. The desk clock said 4:00 a.m.

"Where is he?" she wondered. Anxiety gripped her thoughts. Not that poker game!

Peeling off her T-shirt, damp with sweat, she stumbled to the bathroom and sat down on an ice-cold toilet seat. More than grateful for relief, within seconds she heard the room door open with a clack and rush of air.

"Donny Ray?" A terrible wave of fear clutched her, and she steadied herself by gripping a towel rack.

His face appeared at the bathroom door. "Shhh. We have to get out of here!"

"I'm on the pot!"

"I can see that. Where are your shoes?" He disappeared into the room.

"On the floor by the bed."

"Okay, grab whatever you've got."

She flushed the commode and stepped out. Donny Ray was a wild man, eyes wide, his hair sticking out everywhere. She wriggled into a dry shirt, her running shoes and jacket, then he helped her into the backpack and tugged the straps.

"What is going on?" She struggled with the new weight on her shoulders.

"Let's go, fast." He grasped the duffel handle.

"I've got to wash my hands!"

"No, you don't." He grabbed her wrist and pulled her through the hall to interior stairs.

He scared her. Bounding two steps at a time, they made it into the basement, where Donny Ray flattened himself against a brick wall. He flinched, peered into the boiler room, and motioned to her.

Cassie stuck to the wall, sneaking past electrical panels and a dozing janitor. "We have to make a run for it," he whispered. He opened the door to the alley, and a security alarm went off, screaming louder than a Civil Defense siren.

"This way!" Donny Ray shouted, pointing to another alley. They scrambled down narrow, sloping side streets, duffel bags banging against his legs. They didn't stop jogging until they hit Leonhardsstrasse, and Cassie's legs folded at a tram stop. Short-winded and quaking, she rocked back on a concrete bench and squeezed her eyes shut for a moment. Donny Ray bent over, panting.

A streetlamp lit them in harsh tones of black and white.

"Shit." She coughed. "Where are we going?"

"Train station. Less than a mile." He slouched beside her, his legs splayed. Occasional headlights illuminated his face and the bags at his feet.

"I told you it was dumb to leave the van there." Leaning forward, Cassie unleashed hot tears that sprinkled the tips of her shoes. With a quiet moan, she rubbed her legs with sweaty palms and swayed from left to right.

"Don't do that." Donny Ray gripped her upper arm. "I don't like this any more than you do."

"Want to bet? Again?" She wrestled her arm from his grasp and swiped her cheeks with the backs of her hands. "What in God's name is it with you and the poker?"

"I was winning, I swear, I was winning."

"And?"

"The cops raided it."

"You're not serious." Cassie sat up straight and curled her lips. "What happened to your money?"

"I lost it. I had to bolt. They would've arrested me."

"This is the damnedest deal I have ever seen in my life." Cassie pounded his chest, but he swept away her fists with a smooth stroke.

"Settle down. People'll think I'm trying to rape you." He grasped her shoulders.

"Does it matter what I think? I'm sound asleep up there, and you're out with God knows who."

"Your daddy played poker, and that was great with you, wasn't it? That's how he got you that silver thing—let me see it." He jabbed her arm with his index finger. She grabbed it and bit hard.

"Ow!" He sucked his finger and wiped it on his shirt. "You're crazy as hell."

Cassie mashed her nose against his, backed away, and cackled psycho-style, approximating Halloween sound effects at the dime store. "Yeah, I'm crazy, believing all your lies about dancing in Paris, skiing the Alps – whooo boy. Instead, we're running through alleys with sirens going off, Holy Mother."

Donny Ray clenched his jaw. "Sure, we should've stayed right there and made it real easy on the cops. And you could come visit me in prison."

"You're so paranoid. It was a poker game." She swiped his arm. "Something, something– is really wrong. What am I even doing here? I hadn't heard from you in forever, and now you're calling out of free phone booths, just had to have me."

"Wait, stop." He grabbed her hand. "Yeah, it was sudden, just a fireball in my brain saying my life is with you. I ain't lying. Couldn't stand thinking I'd lose you to the sniper."

She rolled her eyes. "Oh, come on now. You didn't know about Chuck till I told you. And you're dodging the point. Why the hell would a poker game–"

"Okay, you got me." He cleared his throat. "I'm not sure that's all it was."

"Please spare me, Jesus."

"So, I shouldn't be telling you this." He lowered his voice and pulled at his collar.

"What is it?" Cassie put her hand on his shoulder and searched his smudged-up glasses. He needed to polish them, she observed.

"Well." He regarded the slowly brightening sky. "I worked a secret mission with some East Germans."

"Oh brother, that is a big lie." She punched his bicep.

"Quiet. You never know who's listening." He turned and ruffled a shrub behind the bench.

"Why did we come to Switzerland?" Cassie raised her voice. "That Jusef character didn't even show, and I haven't seen a single mountain. Now I'm mad all over again."

An approaching tram whirred and glided down the tracks, silencing them with a swoosh of air and the screech of brakes. Triple headlights blanched their faces, and Cassie hid her eyes in Donny Ray's shoulder. They huddled in silence as the squeals and clicks faded down the line. He grasped her hand. "I'll make it up to you," he said.

Glowering, she studied his face, scanning left to right. "Let's go."

They said nothing as they puffed along the roadway. She cast a glance at him—loose-jointed and swift, his head moving out front like a racehorse. His German really was good. Still, the secret mission thing sounded weird, and it wouldn't be the first time he'd made up a story to get out of hot water with her. She didn't believe it for a minute.

They dragged into the station and made it back to the parking garage. "At least the van's still here." Cassie wriggled out of her backpack and climbed into the passenger seat. "I hope you kept some money to bail it out."

"I've got some francs," he said, "maybe forty dollars' worth. And your travelers' checks."

Cassie sat forward. "So, looking European didn't help after all. You got fleeced anyway, didn't you?" She pounded her fist on the dashboard.

"Don't want to hear it." He rested his cigarette hand on the steering wheel, and smoke curled into ghostlike designs on the windshield. He paid the parking lot attendant and eased the van out onto the street.

"They knew you were American. You had to tell that wooly-necked cab driver, didn't you?" She whacked the Michelin map. "You never were any spy, were you?"

"You heard what you wanted to hear."

"Wait a minute," she paused. "Is that why you took so long at the station yesterday?"

"Oh sure, I'm a world-class spy in a train station. Good one, Cassie."

"And I thought you'd gone to buy me a diamond ring!"

"A what?" He couldn't suppress a guffaw.

Cassie's eyelids drooped, along with her spirits. Dang, he thought it was funny.

"Baby, I don't have that kind of money. Not now." He tucked her hair around her ear. "Let's don't get ahead of ourselves. Just tell me what you want me to do right this minute." He stroked her cheek and kissed it.

"No more truck stops. Bottom line."

"Then we'll have to find something cheap until I can get some money wired in."

"Dang it, Donny Ray. Cheap stuff, everything cheap except that hotel, and we dodged the bill." She tightened her lips. "All of this, losing the vacation money, everything, because you won't stop gambling. And I bet your pal Mr. Scotch Bottle had something to do with that, too."

He groaned and pulled the van over to the curb. "You're right. I've been an ass." His chest rose and fell with each drag from the cigarette. "Tell you what, let's run in this shop and get some coffee, croissants, and then drive south. We'll get you some good mountains. Ever heard of Lake Geneva?"

## CHAPTER NINETEEN

## Smoke on the Water

The sun rose ever higher in the sky, reflecting off a distant snow-topped peak. Cassie lifted her sunglasses to view it—like a travel poster had been pasted on the windshield. She caught her breath with delight.

"Big enough for you?" Donny Ray winked.

"These are the real Alps!" She sprang forward in her seat for a better look at vineyards and Heidi cottages dotting the mountainsides. Warm drops streamed down her lips. She wiped them with the back of her hand. "Oooh, a nosebleed."

The altitude, Donny Ray told her. "Thin air. I'm used to it. But that's why the pro teams hate to play the Denver Broncos at home."

She snatched some tissues, stuffed them in her nostrils, and pinched the bridge of her nose. As they descended to the mountain base, chunky buildings, gingerbread houses, and modern high-rises stacked the slopes. "It's amazing these places stay put," she said.

"They've got it figured out." He turned to her. "Wonder how long you'll have that mess in your nose?"

"A few more minutes. Need to make sure it's cured." She wound the tissue trails.

He shook his head. Then he drove down, down to the edge of the water, lined with cafés and hotels. Young people on rollerblades joined strollers on the promenade.

"This, *Mademoiselle*, is Lake Geneva." He swept his hand to introduce it. "The quay of Montreux. Freddie Mercury's favorite place. And Deep Purple sang 'Smoke on the Water' about it."

"Wow, let's get out and see." Cassie crumpled the used tissues with some clean ones and stuffed them in her jacket pocket. She crept down from the van and planted her feet on the brick walkway.

She twirled around to hug him; he was finally good to his word. She was here. With him. She could practically feel that ring on her finger. Sooner or later, they'd be going to the chapel of love. Even if he didn't know it. *Yet.*

~~~

At an outdoor café, Donny Ray pushed aside a flower arrangement on a glass-topped table. Cassie studied the menu. Even in the off-season, Montreux was ridiculously expensive. He told a story about coming down for the summer jazz festival, hanging out with minor royals and rock stars. Freddie Mercury even bought a round of drinks at the fanciest bar in town, since Jusef had known him in London—way before Queen.

*Unh-uh*, no way, she thought. Didn't matter. She was tired, hungry, and had played out her temper already. "I'll have the granola stuff," she said. "With yogurt. And side sausage."

Their waiter brought a fresh carafe of coffee and took their order. Donny Ray clinked his spoon in a white porcelain cup, removed his glasses, and rubbed his eyes.

Cassie reached for the frames before he had a chance to stop her. "Hey, when did you start wearing glasses? You never did before."

"It's something the Army noticed. Give them back." He held out his hand.

She looked through them. "These are fake!"

"No, there's a little bit of correction." He rubbed his beard with his knuckles. "You know I was handling ammunition. I had to see *better* than 20/20."

"Now let me see your passport photo."

Donny Ray folded back the passport so that only his photo showed, his fingers obscuring his signature. Sure enough, he was wearing the glasses. She dropped the topic and turned her attention to a nearby hotel, known for terraces, fountains, and five-star amenities. Donny Ray said they couldn't afford to stay there.

Cassie put her hand on his and smiled brightly. "How about we just walk through the lobby?"

Nodding, Donny Ray paid the bill and rose to pull back her chair. Soon thereafter, he ushered Cassie through the busy hotel drive-up, where limousine drivers and uniformed personnel attended to well-heeled guests and their designer luggage. Twinkling chandeliers graced the high ceiling above the lobby, splendid with artwork, white marble floors, and stained-glass skylights.

She smoothed her tracksuit pants, aware that they were sorely underdressed. A uniformed hotel employee approached them to offer food in exchange for housekeeping duties. Donny Ray rose on his heels and moved his face in close. "Listen here, you son-of-a-bitch, last summer you were kissing my ass."

"No offense, sir. I told you with best intentions."

"Forget it." Donny Ray stood up straight, put his arm around Cassie, and guided them out to the portico. She fanned her face with the back of her hand as they stood in the shade of a yellow striped awning.

"We ain't got a pot to piss in," he grumbled, "or a window to throw it out."

Cassie stomped her foot. "So, wait, we still have to use *my* money?"

"Let's make the best of this, cut our losses, and drive back to France—head for your daddy's old stomping ground. That's what you wanted to begin with, right? We can light somewhere for a few days until I can get a hold of Jusef."

A uniformed officer motioned to shoo them away. "Please leave. No loitering."

"Yes, sir." Placing his hands on Cassie's shoulders, Donny Ray ushered her blubbing down the walk. "It's okay, Cassie. I promise you, baby, it won't be long, and you'll have everything—*everything*. We'll show those bastards."

# CHAPTER TWENTY

## Up Against the Wall, Red Neck

Beecher downshifted his truck off Highway 80 and pulled into the Bobtail parking lot, where outdoor speakers blasted "Up Against the Wall, Red Neck Mother." Beer and bourbon signs lit up the metal roof. He opened the roadhouse door to a gust of cold air laced with cigarette smoke.

Grabbing a barstool, he ordered a Busch and zoned out watching *Fantasy Island* on the TV behind the bar—until caterwauling, crashing wood, and a hollering female startled him out of the televised tropics. He'd know that scream anywhere. Sheree!

Slamming his beer on the counter, Beecher jumped off the stool and tramped into a mix of spilled tears, beers, and mushy French fries. Sheree's familiar gold hoop earrings caught flashes of light from a revolving liquor sign, as a paunchy guy in ostrich boots backed her up against the knotty pine wall. Bystanders stomped pointy-toed boots and howled.

"Hey, you shithead!" Skimming through cardboard coasters and peanut shells, Beecher thrust his forearm around the man's neck, twisted his arm behind him, and brought him to the floor. "More where that came from!" he shouted.

Beecher left him in a crumpled heap and grabbed Sheree's arm. She tried to wriggle free. "You're messing it all up!" She gasped, inhaling strands of her thick, long hair, shining rubellite red.

"Goddamn it, you're coming with me. Go on and get your purse."

Shouts of "Pimp! Pimp!" followed them out the door and into the still-warm October night air. Crickets chirped as big wheels rumbled on the nearby highway. Stumbling in her platform shoes, Sheree went into a full-scale bawl.

"Calm down," Beecher said. "Where's your car?"

"I didn't drive," she sputtered. "I had a date."

"With the ostrich boots?"

Sheree nodded, dabbing her face with a beer-soaked napkin. He shook her shoulders. "What happened to Chuck?"

"I left him." Blowing her nose on the napkin, she turned her face up to him. "I don't know what I'm going to do."

"Sounds like you've already done it."

"No, uh, we got married." An earring dangled from one ear. She pinched her other earlobe. "Where's my earring?" She stooped to search the ground. "These things are 14-karat gold."

"Married?" Beecher caught his breath but didn't have time to wonder as the Bobtail door opened, spilling rowdy goat-ropers into the parking lot. "Forget it. Let's get out of here." Clutching her elbow, he guided her toward his truck, visible in a swirl of moths and tungsten light. Sheree climbed into the passenger seat and slunk down, wiping her cheeks.

"Christ, Sheree, what were you thinking?" Beecher peeled out on the gravel and shifted gears. "You only knew the boy a couple of weeks."

She shrugged. "I got carried away, because you know, down at the courthouse, you don't have to wait or nothing. I didn't have time to think it through."

"And it's over already?"

Rummaging through her purse, she retrieved a lipstick. "Well, first thing was, he drove us way the hell over to Daingerfield. Turned out he's tight with some women there living with a pusher guy in a mobile home." She lowered the visor mirror, smeared pink on her lips, and smacked them.

Sheree scooted forward to meet his eyes. "Chuck wanted to trade me for a few hits of Black Tar, so that pissed me off. No way I was doing that, you know?" She waggled the lipstick tube for emphasis.

"Right." Beecher glanced at her mottled face, brightened by a passing truck.

"It was some crazy shit, so we came on back, and he said he was sorry about trying to pimp me, 'cause he was out of his head, and nobody knows the heart of a troubled man, so..."

"Give me the *Reader's Digest* version."

"Okay, he promised to clean up, but he didn't do no better." She took a breath. "And I hit my breaking point, so I kicked him out."

Beecher steered with his left hand and adjusted the rear-view mirror with his right. "So where is he now?"

She caught a teardrop with the back of her hand. "Moved back to the Moonrider."

Beecher watched the road while they merged onto Highway 59.

"And who was the moron in the bar?"

"Cattleman. The bulge in his pocket is a fat wad of cash." She frogged Beecher in the arm. "And you botched it for me. That man has money."

"Listen, Sheree, Chuck's got more, or he will have. You know that, right?"

"No." Her eyebrows squinched. "How?"

"Tell you what, his family's rich as all get out. He's even got a trust fund."

"A trust fund? He never mentioned one thing about that to me!"

Beecher backtracked, trying to tamp down her enthusiasm a bit. He needn't promote gold-digging here.

"Well, he won't get any money for maybe five years, and anyway, he can't get all of it at first—just a month-to-month deal for a while. So don't expect a million dollars raining in your yard all of a sudden."

She sucked her lip. "Maybe I need to fish my wedding ring out of the jewelry box."

"You run right over people, don't you?" Bright headlights on Beecher's tail blasted his side mirrors. "I remember you got to crying on my shoulder that time, and I even thought about marrying you. It could've been my baby."

"I already told you a hundred times. I didn't want to have it, that's all." She rubbed her arms. "Did Cassie ever find out?"

"God, no. She couldn't handle that—abortion, are you serious? And now she's in Europe with Donny Ray. I'm sure she told you that much."

Sheree squealed. "He called me a little while back!"

"Why didn't you say something before now?" Beecher slapped the wheel.

"I forgot. He talked to my stepmother. It was the only phone number he had, the old one. Anyway, she told him I had a boyfriend, go to hell or something."

"Son-of-a-bitch!"

"He's such a shit." Sheree's voice sounded brittle. "He talked my stepmom into taking his address—some Dutch town. I got so mad I wrote him a mean letter and mailed it before I could change my mind. Drove downtown to the post office and—pop! Into the drive-through slot." She swelled up. "Made me feel better, anyway."

"How long ago was that?"

"I don't know, last month some time."

"Wait a minute, he called you before he called Cassie. Said he had to have her with him."

"He must have missed Texas pussy."

Beecher glared at her. "I'm kicking you out of the truck if you say that again. You're talking about my sister."

"Well, I told her not to chase him."

"Bullshit."

They rode in silence back to Sheree's house, off the Indian Springs Road. Beecher pulled into the back and parked, the carport light barely illuminating their faces. A warm breeze stirred the leaves. A dog barked nearby, then two.

He squeezed the steering wheel. Sheree reached over to hug him. "Don't you want to come in for a little while?"

She didn't have to ask him twice. Brushing back her hair, he traced her neckline just as white light shone into the truck like an interrogator's lamp. They covered their eyes as a horn honked and brakes squealed.

"Caught you with my wife, man!" Chuck leaned out of the window of his truck and jerked his forearm with clenched fist, the middle finger proud. "Up yours, asshole!"

"You better get out of here, Beecher." Sheree steadied herself as she pulled the door handle and jumped down.

Beecher revved his engine. Sheree shielded her face from the light and yelled, "I'll miss you till I see you again."

Stomping the gas pedal, Beecher spun his wheels and made a violent U-turn in Sheree's yard, raking and crushing the daisies beneath his tires.

## CHAPTER TWENTY-ONE

## Spent Bombshells

The route from Montreux embraced Lake Geneva and skirted the Alps. Cassie's pulse quickened in the French landscape, and her muscles tensed. Wheezing, she clutched Donny Ray's arm.

"What's wrong with you?" He yanked the steering wheel and pulled over to stop. Random pebbles thunked the undercarriage as a sign marking Coutelieu rose from the roadside weeds. Two ladies, patterned bandannas tied under their chins, buzzed by on mopeds, loaves of bread jutting out of their baskets.

"Breathe. I can't." Cassie spread her fingers on her chest and winced in pain, doubling over on the seat.

"Hold on, let's get you a paper bag." He retrieved a small brown sack from the floor and dumped out candy wrappers and banana peels. He scrunched the top and held it to her face. "In and out. Big breaths, that's good. Keep going."

Her eyelids twitched. She stared first at the road, then at him. He kneaded the back of her neck and let her sniffle on his sleeve. "What's wrong with me?"

He kissed her forehead. "Bad nerves. It's like anything else—you want something forever, but you freak out when it really happens. I mean, a dog chases cars all day, but what would he do if he caught one? He don't really want that car."

His uncharacteristic empathy for car-chasing-dogs caught her off guard, relaxing the tension across her brow.

"I'm all right now." Her heart rate slowed, and she bent down to stuff the litter back into the bag. A little green Fiat buzzed by the window as Donny Ray put the van in gear. "Let's see what we've got here," he said, rolling into a hamlet of stone cottages, tiled roofs, and brightly colored shutters.

In the center of the village square, a tall ironwork crucifix adorned a granite fountain, now dry. Spent bombshells and artificial flowers rose from a mound of dirt packing the basin. "It's a war memorial," Cassie murmured, "in honor of– slow down, so I can read it–in honor of Pierre someone, arrested and deported *par les Nazis, mort a Buchenwald,* 1944." She felt a tingle of grief for someone she never knew.

She blew a sigh. Her dad gave it to Hitler on the chin, and good thing he did, or Johnny Frank's name would be on that fountain, too.

Stooped and bent, a white-haired man in a black beret added red poppies to the dirt, pressing them with care. "Let's ask him about a campground," Donny Ray said, braking, then rolling down his window. "Uh, sir?"

Raising his eyebrows, the man turned to regard them. He mustered a slight wave.

"Say there," Donny Ray began, "I wonder if you could–"

"No *anglais.*" He put up his hands.

"Okay, Cassie girl, this is your cue." Donny Ray screwed up his mouth at her. "The old boy don't speak English."

"Yeah, I got it." Smiling, she crawled over his lap, stuck her head out the window, and asked the old man for directions to the nearest campground. The gentleman's face brightened; his silver teeth glistened. He touched his cap and gestured to a fork in the road before waving them on. "*Le camping! De cette façon. Ambronay.*"

"*Ambronay! Merci!*" Cassie's enthusiasm spilled out of the car window—along with her torso. The man stepped aside, his eyes wide.

Donny Ray pulled her back into the car. "Damn it now, Cassie, you know I love you, but you're driving me nuts, girl." He gripped her arm. "Now tell me which way we go."

Cassie scooted back onto the seat. "Easy. Turn off this way. Three kilometers."

"Shoot, that won't take five minutes."

Canopies of trees lined the black top road. Cassie looked back and forth. "These are *déjà vu* from the pictures." She reached into her backpack and retrieved some snapshots. "See here? Don't they look the same as now?" She demonstrated with a flourish.

"Put those down. I can't see to drive," he snapped, waving the photos away.

She felt a twinge of nostalgia. "After Daddy died, Mama tore up most of his pictures. Threw a bunch into a window fan. Blades swirling, the pictures clacked like baseball cards in bicycle spokes. She said it wasn't any sense keeping old war crap around—just her crazy self. I wish she hadn't done it. I loved looking at them."

Donny Ray pinched some stray tobacco from his tongue and flicked the tobacco bits out of the window. "Maybe that gal was in the pictures, you know? The one that got him the glass eye and all."

"I've wondered that myself." Cassie turned in her seat as a sign disappeared behind them.

Donny Ray thumped the steering wheel. "Wait, up there–is that where we want to turn?" He pulled the van into a short stretch of gravel and paused at a closed gate. A large metal sign lettered in black and red hung from a nail. "What's that mean, Cassie?"

"Closed for the season."

"But there's some campers in there. Get out and open that gate."

She jumped down from the van and swung the gate wide. They drove in, stopping just inside the entrance.

"They don't look touristy." Donny Ray pointed to a circle of caravans parked some fifty yards away.

Small children played and squealed, the girls wearing flouncy dresses and sweaters, the boys in dungarees with knit tops. Nearby, women in long-sleeved, flowered caftans tended cast-iron skillets over camping stoves; all the ladies wore brightly colored scarves, knotted in the back. Large gold hoops swung from their ears.

"I think these here are old hippies," he said.

Cassie leaned over him to get a better view. "They're called Gitans."

"No, that's a cigarette brand. The one with a tambourine on the package." He mimicked rattling a tambourine. "You mean Gypsies."

"No, never mind." She wasn't going to argue Romany politics with him. He could be a real blockhead sometimes.

Donny Ray tugged his beard. A square granite structure with a red tiled roof caught their attention. "Must be the rental office. You got the travelers' checks? It's a loan, I swear."

She pulled the vinyl folder from her backpack, and they jumped from the vehicle. As they approached, Cassie noted a brick patio with chairs and a sleepy, spotted dog lounging nearby. "I hope that dog doesn't bite."

"The fleas would have to cart him over," Donny Ray smirked, stopping to pat the animal's head. "Hey ya, boy," he said. The old mutt wagged its tail but didn't get up.

"What if these people shoot trespassers?"

"This ain't Texas, Cassie. Guns are illegal here."

"Oh, okay." That's good, she thought. Guns made her nervous. Handguns did, anyway, ever since Della pulled her big stunt. What a shame. What a mess. Cassie flashed back to her mother's bloody housecoat.

They climbed stone steps to a closed-in porch and opened the door into a study nook. Lavender fragrance wafted from the boxy windows, and Cassie felt a clutch in her throat. Her head swam with cluttered memories of airmail letters and Johnny Frank.

"Well, go on." Donny Ray nudged the small of her back, and she stepped into a living room with an oak beamed ceiling and a black log-burning stove. Straight ahead was a wood paneled counter with a cash register and a hand-lettered sign that said *Bienvenue*.

Donny Ray tapped the bell, and a woman's voice called from the next room. "*Une minute!*"

Cassie stretched her neck to see what was behind the door: a gas cooker, refrigerator, and a breathless older lady wiping her hands on a flowered apron. "*Bonjour, je suis Madame LeNoir.*" Emerging from the open doorway, she lightly touched curly short bangs. Her amber eyes were bright behind slightly drooping eyelids.

Cassie didn't see a *Monsieur* anywhere around, unless it was that funny looking guy climbing down a wooden ladder from the ceiling. He had a feather duster in his back pocket. With unlined face and thick sandy hair, he looked too young to be her husband, though. Must be her son.

"Do you speak English?" Donny Ray put his elbows on the counter.

Mme. LeNoir flattened her hand and wobbled it. "*Hein*, not so good."

"Cassie here can speak French, can't you Cassie?" He put his arm around her. "Ask the lady if we can stay here a while."

"I understand that much," Mme. LeNoir said. "We are closed for the season."

Donny Ray forced a smile. "But there's other campers out there."

The funny looking feather duster guy came around the counter. "Problem?"

"We've got to get a place. Tell them, Cassie."

She explained they needed a couple of days there until meeting friends in Lyon. The man's gaze traveled as she spoke. Reflexively, she fingered her silver pendant, twisting it a turn.

He gave a little nod. "This time, we can accommodate for short term only. The others are permanent for the winter, you see."

Mme. LeNoir grimaced and shot the feather duster guy a look. He shrugged.

"Okay, forty francs a day," she grumbled. "In advance."

"Forty francs is fine." Donny Ray turned to Cassie, "It's a good deal, right?"

"I guess." She pulled out a check and signed Cassandra Jean Tate with an extra flourish on the J. She handed it to the woman. "Say, did y'all have any American servicemen around here during the war? I mean, staying here and hiding out?"

Putting his hands around Cassie's neck, Donny Ray mashed his thumbs into the soft spots behind her jaws. "Let the lady alone! She's trying to do us a favor here. Jesus."

Cassie squirmed.

Her passport matched the checks, and Mme. Lenoir pursed her lips in thought. "*Très bien*," she said. "See? *Americains.*" She showed it to the cleaning man, a small smile creeping across his face.

Donny Ray removed his glasses, wiping them on his shirt. "You better get some extra cash while you're at it."

"What for?" Cassie asked, returning her passport to the backpack. She suspected he took off his glasses to show Mme. LeNoir how handsome he is.

"We'll need food and gas."

Annoyance nipped her forehead. "Oh, that's great. I've got to buy the groceries, too."

"Cool it." Donny Ray put his arm around her. "You're embarrassing us," he whispered.

"Okay, okay," she replied. "But maybe you could tune up the old girl's car for credit or something."

He spoke low in Cassie's ear. "One more thing."

"Now what?"

"Ask if I can send a telegram to Amsterdam from here."

Mme. LeNoir brightened. *"Certainement!"* She retrieved a telegram pad. "You write. We call PTT. *Poste, Télécommunications et Télédiffusion.*"

Cassie's eyes met the feather duster man's. A red burn tiptoed up her neck.

"You have a nice place, Mme. LeNoir." Donny Ray reached for the pad and a ballpoint pen. "Do you live here?"

*"Oui.* And–"

The owner broke into a narrative, which Cassie translated for him in a kind of subtitle crawl. "She lives here. It used to be a farm, but they still have a garden. They added on the showers and a laundromat so customers could wash clothes. *La laverie.*"

"Yeah, all right, that's real good." Donny Ray bounced the pen like a drumstick.

While he filled out the telegram form, Cassie shuffled over to a settee, where a small magazine lay open on the coffee table. Skimming it, she figured out the publication was a romance comic—but instead of cartoons, it featured photographs of people posing dramatically with dialogue balloons over their heads.

"I've never seen this kind of thing before." She laughed. "These are soap opera stories, aren't they?"

"Pardon?" Mme. LeNoir blinked.

"You know, the soaps. Lover and killer mix-ups. May I take a few of these with me? I'll bring them back."

The *madame* frowned, but the guy stepped forward. "Yes, of course," he said. With two fingers, he tapped first his lips, then the magazine. "Very good stories for ladies."

"Thank you." Cassie thought he had an odd appearance somehow—built stocky and blond, but his face looked like he got it shut in a book. Long and narrow. He fingered a thin gold wedding band. She considered Mme. LeNoir, short and solid, with her hair in pin curls, dyed black with gray roots deployed. Cassie wished she could get a hold of that hair and do something with it.

And what about the woman's outfit? A flowered, calf-length skirt with turned down cotton socks and blue espadrilles. Wooden buttons on a bulky taupe cardigan with a big safety pin at the neck.

Goodness. Cassie thought fashion was supposed to be big in France.

After Mme. LeNoir called in the telegram, Donny Ray and Cassie moved the van to the closest camping space. Nice and convenient. Not far to run for a phone if a chainsaw-killer wandered out of the woods.

Also, it provided better access to the restroom, which she needed to use every five minutes, it seemed. She must have caught a plumbing infection from that truck stop bathroom. Great, she thought, out in the middle of nowhere France.

"See this is nice," Donny Ray said. "I'll get us some food. We can fire up a cook stove with the butane."

"That's fine."

But it wasn't. With Johnny Frank all in her head, the French vibes disturbed her. Of course, she'd never been there before, but something about the place stirred her soul. And the duster man seemed a little too interested.

## CHAPTER TWENTY-TWO

## Paladin, Paladin, Where Do You Roam?

That night the rains came, and a damp chill enveloped Cassie in the van along with odors of mildewed washrags and soggy cardboard. The smells puzzled and annoyed her. She'd never had that much of a nose, but now everything tipped her senses. Ever since she'd come over here, she often lay awake for hours in an olfactory assault. Donny Ray said that was the "B side" of jet lag.

She turned away from him, snoring and smacking next to her and buried her face in the sheets. She tried to relax, but she smelled something metallic. Inching over the mattress, she dropped her head, nosing around the cabinetry. Nothing. She ran her hand along a recessed shelf, fingering hand tools: flanges, screwdrivers, the usual mechanic stuff. But she also smelled WD-40 and bore cleaner under there, too. Sure enough, she spotted a bore snake—a cleaning cord she'd seen her dad pull through gun barrels.

A sense of loss clutched her again. The smell called up her daddy's pulpwood truck. Johnny Frank kept guns to shoot rattlers in the woods. "Donny Ray?" She nudged his arm.

"Uhhh...yeah?"

"Do you have guns in here?"

"Why would I?" He pulled the covers over his head.

~~~

Sunlight filtered through outdoor shrubs into *Madame's* campground office. Next to a stack of romance comics and *Elle* magazines, Cassie sorted her daddy's photos on the table in the sitting room. This is it, she thought. Her hands trembled slightly as goosebumps crossed her scalp. She thumbed a photo with a rectangular roadway sign, trimmed in black, listing two destinations: Lyon 59km, and Bourg-en-Bresse 26km.

Cassie rose from the couch, photos in hand, and ambled toward the kitchen. Scents of rosemary, wine, and onions wafted through the room. Poking her head around the door frame, she saw Mme. LeNoir and Donny Ray seated at a little table, a hunk of baguette in his left hand, a spoonful of gravy in his right.

"*Bonjour, Madame.*" Cassie approached the table, waving the photos. "Hey, Donny Ray."

Mme. LeNoir nodded, expressionless. With bread wedged in his cheeks, Donny Ray nudged a chair with his foot. "Sit down, baby, and have a bowl with us."

"I don't want to interrupt."

He winked. "Annette here says you're not interrupting."

First name basis, eh? Getting a little friendly here, Cassie thought. She sat down. "Thanks, Annette."

"I prefer *Madame*." She arched a brow.

Cassie winced. Oh, so that's how it is. She shot eyes at Donny Ray, who grinned broadly. "Annette's a widow-lady, aren't you, honey? But we're solid, am I right? Don't need no titles—those are for the Gypsies out back. Got to let them know who's boss."

Annette frowned but didn't argue. Cassie cleared her throat and counted out the photos, one by one. "May I ask you where that road sign is?" Cassie pointed to the print.

"Eh, no more of this," Annette said. "Gone. Very long time ago."

"Awww!" Cassie blinked. "I was so hoping–"

"Now, Cassie," Donny Ray patted her shoulder. "I warned you about getting your hopes up." Smiling at Annette, he pointed at his bowl, then at Cassie, and raised his hands in a questioning gesture.

Without comment, Annette rose, shuffled to the stove, and clunked a bowl on the table with a big spoon. Cassie tasted the rich dark meat, mingled with chopped garlic, thyme, and wild mushrooms.

"Delicious chicken," she said, smiling and nodding.

"Not chicken. Rabbit," Annette laughed, snorting on the inhale. "Thanks to him."

Oh no, bunny stew, she thought. Cassie stopped the spoon midway to her mouth. "So, uh, Donny Ray, how'd you kill a rabbit?"

"Got six of them. With her .22 rifle," he beamed. "And my X-ray vision."

Wavering, Cassie spilled some brown gravy on her shirt. "I thought you said guns are illegal here."

"Hunting rifles are okay if you got a license. A lot of country people have them."

"Oh." She set her spoon aside. "You have a license?"

"I'm ex-military. That's license enough." He cleared his throat. "Annette says it's good to have a hunting man around full-time, who can handle a gun. She's scared of the Gypsies."

Annette batted her eyelashes and pointed to his foot. Donny Ray hiked up his right pant leg, an automatic pistol strapped to his ankle. "That's my service revolver," he said. "Have gun, will travel."

## CHAPTER TWENTY-THREE

### Swa-Swa-Swastika

Wrapped in a blanket, sitting outside the van, Cassie watched some of the Gypsy kids singing in a circle, thumping tambourines and squeezing concertinas. Why weren't they in school? she wondered. A few brindle-looking dogs barked and chased, adding to the party.

Man, this was ridiculous—it sure wasn't what she'd expected. Her daddy had described olive groves and poppy fields, lavender and sunflowers layered upon rolling hills of green. But all she could see was dry grass, red clover, and jangling Gypsies.

A person didn't have to say Gitans to avoid offense. It had something to do with migration patterns. Just semantics. Anyway, they wouldn't care what Donny Ray called them. He cleared all gambling debts with engine repairs and tune-ups. He didn't want her coming over to mingle—although the men backed off from his Colt .45, the women still considered her a rival. "You know you're better looking than them," he said. "Don't want to make trouble here."

Seemed she and Donny Ray already had. He pulled out a smoke from his cigarette pack and cast a glance around. His eyes fell on a copy of *Jours de France*. "What's this junk?"

"Oh, that guy in the office loaned me some magazines and comics. What's his name, anyway?"

"Swa. It's short for Swastika. Annette's nephew. She said he was a war bastard, and that his father was a Nazi. Why do you care?"

"No reason." She frowned. "I'd just like to visit with somebody, that's all."

"I seen him looking at your jugs. Put your bra on." Taking a last drag from his cigarette, Donny Ray crushed it under his heel. He stood and ruffled her hair, before setting off for another card game.

Cassie did all right without Donny Ray underfoot. She borrowed more magazines from the office and did a little small talk with Swa. He'd seen *Dallas* on holiday in England and asked if she lived at Southfork Ranch. They laughed about the absurdity of that notion, and she talked about her actual background and her history with Donny Ray.

"Why do you call him that?" he asked. "He told Aunt Annette his name is Raymond."

She missed a beat.

"Raymond Richard." Swa pronounced it very Frenchy, like Ray-*mon* Ree-*shard*.

"Oh right, that was his dad's name—Raymond Richard Duggan." She laughed uneasily. "I guess he's gone all sophisticated on us, but his real name is Donny Ray Duggan. He just got out of the Army. He'd been up in Germany."

Glaring, Annette interrupted the conversation with housekeeping assignments before Cassie got the chance to connect with personal details. It was pretty clear that *Madame* didn't want any idle chit-chat on her watch. Swa didn't argue.

Cassie wandered back to the van, second-guessing herself about sharing so much personal information, which could be used for kidnapping and ransom. And why did Donny Ray lie about his name? This must be part of his new European vibe, like he was ashamed of his East Texas roots. Pretender! Very annoying, she thought.

Settling into her folding chair, she flipped through *Jours de France*, with John Travolta on the cover, and listened to the radio. The rest of her time she spent journaling and writing poems to sort out her feelings about Chuck and Sheree.

"Broken windows, Broken hearts, Glass and splinters, Icy chards," she penned. Or was that supposed to be icy *shards*? "Touch the glass, pierce your skin, Mercurochrome renews again." Fine, that was fine. Maybe she could have it set to music—if she ever got out of this joint.

She was tired of the whole escapade—not a bit fun, just creepy. She would set an ultimatum: if Donny Ray hadn't heard from that jackwagon Jusef by tomorrow noon, she'd demand that he sell the van and buy train tickets to somewhere, anywhere. "You can sell it to the Gypsies, or sell it down the road," she rehearsed, fists clenched.

Her ears perked up. Johnny Hallyday, her father's old favorite, boomed "Hey Joe" in French, but a Vietnam lyric came out of nowhere. That's not how Jimi Hendrix sang it, but the French had gotten tied up in Vietnam way before the Americans came and went.

Chuck and Beecher brought home more than battle scars, but so did Johnny Frank. Maybe that's why he cried at movies and stashed pictures in his desk drawer. Chuck was right about one thing: her father never moved past the pain.

Pebbles scattered, and she looked up, closing her journal. With a carrot in his mouth, Donny Ray sauntered toward her with a plate of sausage, potatoes, and cheese. He handed over the plate and pulled up a folding chair alongside. "What're you writing?"

"Nothing special."

He pitched the carrot into a trash container, then removed a blue cigarette box with a winged helmet on the front. "These here are Gauloises—the best in France."

Cassie stuck her fork into a sausage link and jammed it whole into her mouth.

Donny Ray patted her cheek. "What a talent. Let's take you on the road."

"I already am." She chewed and swallowed with a tight grin. "Say, Donny Ray, I'm laying down the law here now."

His head swiveled towards her like a ventriloquist's dummy. "Huh?"

"Tomorrow noon, *deadline*. If your big buddy hasn't called by then, we're leaving, and I don't mean maybe. You're going to sell this van–"

He reached for her with a glow in his eyes like the *Cherbourg* umbrella man. "We'll work it out. We always have, right? I only want to make you happy."

Oh! Well, that was easier than she'd anticipated. Smiling, she stabbed another sausage. "Now what's this about your name being Raymond now? That's what Swa said."

"We gotta be careful. Don't tell that Swa-boy *nothing*. He's half-Nazi, and they were always into breeding rights."

"Good grief, Donny Ray. You think everybody wants to get in my pants."

"Just stay where I can keep an eye on you." He kissed her hair and returned to the Gypsy camp.

Cassie watched him with troubled pride. Their complicated history had bound them together for a life sentence. She never would have thought that, years after the 7-Eleven phone booth, they'd still be together—at a campground in France, of all places. He'd pushed his luck with her as far as it would go. Tomorrow noon. That was the deadline. For real.

Putting down her book, she noticed the laundry room door bump open.

Swa stuck out his head and turned her way, then withdrew, a turtle in a shell. He gripped a small chain, its links barely visible in his fist.

## CHAPTER TWENTY-FOUR

### Took No Prisoners

Cassie awoke to a Kodak grayscale. Thick dark clouds blanketed the heavy, humid air. Two days at the campground felt like weeks. How long could it take for that Jusef guy to get a telegram? Donny Ray had already seemed nervous about it, chain-smoking by day, and kicking the sheets at night. But now that she'd set a time limit, and she meant to follow through.

Resting her chin in her palm, Cassie thought about the WWII monument down the way. Surely someone around there remembered the American prisoners of war.

She parted the striped pillowcase curtains to watch Donny Ray from the back window. His arms casually folded on a card table, and an old dog at his feet, he was talking to some Gypsy men moving around stacks of poker chips.

He wouldn't want her going out alone, but—she glanced at the table—he wouldn't be leaving that poker game, either. Especially if he was winning, but even if he wasn't. Stress drove him to bet scared money.

So, what was she waiting for? Better to beg forgiveness than to ask for permission. She pulled her track pants snug and tied her running shoes. She stuck a photo of Johnny Frank and his friends in her T-shirt pocket, slipped her Adidas jacket on, and meandered to the gate flanked by barbed wire.

Once outside, she walked briskly on the black-topped road, but another sense of *déjà vu* brought Cassie to a halt. Images from her daddy's photos appeared, like an old View-

Master had come alive. Her heart pulsed with excitement. Hands on her hips, she studied the cow pasture across the road, with beech trees and overgrown brush.

Cold chills claimed her scalp. Ever since she'd landed at the campground, she'd felt Johnny Frank's presence. And in her mind's eye, she saw him, a prisoner, marching through that very field. She imagined him escaping in the night and climbing one of those trees, right over there.

That scenario sort of made sense, but the landscape was open and flat. If the American troops were on a forced march, it was a thousand miracles that he got away with a single bullet in the eye, she thought. Surely, they would have mowed him down. That's what Nazis did.

Cassie removed her jacket and tied it around her waist; the sun had burned off the haze and sweat trickled down her back. Her fingers reddened and swelled. She clenched her hands. Ouch. Only three kilometers from here to the monument, and with a good pace, she'd make it in twenty minutes. Seemed farther than she remembered, but she welcomed a break from the cramped van.

Panting, Cassie rounded a curve, and a weathered signpost pointed the way to Coutelieu. Small commercial billboards advertised events in Lyon and Ambronay. A cluster of stone houses greeted her, with mission-style roofs overlapping red and brown clay tiles. A lazy ginger cat sunned itself at a front door stoop, mere feet from the roadway. Low concrete walls enclosed gardens, some scraggly in October, none being tended that morning.

A dark-haired woman in a fuzzy yellow robe stood outside her doorway, beating dust from a rug with a wire contraption. She paused to lean on the door frame and scratch red eczema scales on the back of one leg with a wooly-socked foot from the other. She looked up when Cassie called, "*Excusez-moi!*" and explained why she was there.

Avoiding eye contact, the lady shook her head, fingering plastic pink rollers that clamped over locks of gray-streaked hair. Then she called inside, and an older, feeble-looking woman appeared in the doorway. She had only vague memories of American soldiers. It had been so many years ago, she said, "*Il y a tant d'années.*" Then they hurried inside, dragging the rug, and slamming the door behind them.

Well, that was a disappointment. Were people's memories that dim? It had only been thirty years or so. Cassie had expected the ladies to thank her for the Americans' service, but they acted like she was a weirdo.

Yet, steps ahead, the war memorial's granite bulk supported the skyward bound crucifix, and Cassie's emotions swelled. She touched the low walls of the fountain basin and tracked her gaze up the ironwork. She crossed herself and then walked a circle around it.

"May I help you?" From a nearby house, a middle-aged Frenchwoman paused at her garden gate, bright blue shutters thrown open behind her.

Cassie whirled. "Oh my, *oui, Madame!*" Addressing her in French, she approached the lady's gate. "Two days ago, I saw a man here tending flowers. He wore a black beret." She mimicked the adjustment of a hat. "Do you know him?"

The woman studied her. "What is your business?"

"Well, this may sound crazy, but I came all the way from Texas to find where my dad was during the war. I'm staying at the campground, and I've been thinking about the memorial."

The woman's eyes remained wary.

Cassie was afraid her French vocab had sputtered out. And she had never been so thirsty in her life. "So anyway," Cassie said, "I thought they might have known each other?" Her voice rose to a squeaky question mark. That elicited a smile from the Frenchwoman, who might have taken pity on this sweaty American emerging from the roadway.

"You speak of my father, Raoul. He had mentioned you with amusement. He is napping, but I'll soon wake him for lunch. I am Lucienne." She opened the gate.

"Ah, may I trouble you for a glass of water?" Cassie's tongue made a popping sound against the roof of her mouth.

"Certainly, yes, come in." Lucienne fiddled with her bun, strands of hair coming loose.

Cassie followed her into the kitchen, where soup bubbled on the stove, and cold water flowed in plenty. She drank two glasses and splashed some on her face. "Were all of you here for the war?"

"Only Papa stayed. Before the war, we lived here happily, our little family. Then sadly—the Occupation." Lucienne knelt, running a finger over two wooden boards, one slightly raised.

"He dug a hole under the kitchen," she continued, "and stocked it with bread and wine and cheese. He sent us to Lyon to stay with relatives. Naïvely, he thought the war would go right by him. Papa believed he could stay and look after his chickens and cows and pigs." She sighed. "But the Germans ate his chickens and slaughtered the rest."

Footfalls descended the stairs, and Lucienne wiped her face with the edge of her apron. "Oh, he's ready for his lunch. You will join us?" She held out her hand. "Come."

Cassie caught her breath. Donny Ray would look for her soon, but she couldn't decline the lunch invitation. She'd been waiting years to find the missing link to her daddy's soul, and this was it. She followed her hostess through a swinging door into the dining room. The old man sat at the head of a long oak table, wearing a threadbare coat and a black beret.

Cassie smiled broadly, "Ah, *Monsieur*, hello again."

He peered at her and chuckled. "I remember you. Americans. In the van—you almost fell out of the window." He patted the seat beside him, inviting Cassie to sit.

Lucienne brought out the pot of soup, bread, a tray of sliced roast beef, mashed potatoes, and green beans. This same lunch was a daily special at the Coffee Cup Café back home, but it never tasted this good. Even the water was better.

She dunked bread in the gravies, dabbed her mouth, and subsequently diverted her attention to the Johnny Frank photo. Holding it out for their inspection, she asked, "Do these men look familiar?"

"Eh?" Lucienne frowned. "This was after the war, wasn't it, Papa?"

Raoul agreed and tapped the photo with the handle of his fork. "Yes, you see, it was right down the road."

Cassie's excitement registered in her voice. "Did you know the man in the middle? He was my father."

"All the Americans looked alike to me, big and strong with handsome uniforms." Lucienne nodded at Cassie and smiled. "But I was so young." She found a magnifying glass in the sideboard and handed it to her father, who brought his face close to the photo, tilting it toward the light.

His silver front teeth gleamed. "This man?" He rocked back in his chair and pointed. "Eye patch."

Cassie clasped her hands. "That's Daddy! He was shot in a prisoner march," she said, breathing rapidly. "And some farmers saved him. Do you remember anything about that?"

Raoul looked to the ceiling and tapped his fingers on the table. "Americans came here after German occupation. No prisoners. No marches."

That didn't make sense, she thought. "Then how did you know him?" Cassie took a bite of roast beef.

Lucienne cleared her throat and made a second pass with the breadbasket. "What was your father's name?"

"Johnny Frank Tate." Cassie sat erect. Yes indeed. An American hero.

Lucienne and Raoul exchanged glances. He began tapping his brow.

"We knew of your father, quite a hero, yes. When the war ended, he brought G.I.'s from Lyon to help rebuild our village and feed those in need—everyone was hungry. War widows and orphans, the disabled."

"I'm glad he helped," Cassie said, confused by the contradiction of her dad's war stories.

"You see, during Occupation, we did whatever we could to survive," Raoul said. He sipped a glass of wine. "Constant fear. Property taken, food, crops. And that was lucky compared to concentration camps and internment. So many died."

A clock chimed 1:00 p.m. With some anxiety, Cassie realized that she'd missed the noon cutoff she'd imposed on Donny Ray. And if he were out looking for her, she'd be in deep doo-doo. She thanked them for the meal and asked if they knew a shortcut through the pasture. She really must hurry back.

"Oh, you mustn't risk the pasture," Lucienne said. "Nettles and brush, angry animals, you know. I will drive you. Very easy."

Raoul nodded, and they said warm goodbyes as a little yellow Citroën warmed up outside. Lucienne dropped Cassie at the campground just as Donny Ray appeared at the gate.

## CHAPTER TWENTY-FIVE

### Staple Goods

Lucienne waved to Cassie and chugged on down the road. Cassie waved back and grinned at Donny Ray. She was not going to let him upset her. She'd already taken a punch to the gut with the new take on Johnny Frank's war years.

"Where the hell have you been?" His face drew up as if he'd eaten a green persimmon. He held the gate closed. "And who's that woman?"

"Nobody." She eyed him. "You going to open the gate, or do I need to climb the barbed wire?"

"Ain't opening nothing until you tell me what you were doing, running off and getting in somebody's car."

Cassie assessed the fence, pulled the jacket from her waist, and threw it over the top wire. Clutching the post with one hand, she grasped the unzipped jacket with the other and climbed the rungs like a ladder.

Then she jumped, landed on her bottom, and yanked the jacket free. Her early years in Texas timber stands and pastures with Johnny Frank had just paid dividends.

"Good God, Cassie, you can't be out running around on your own—rapists and thieves on these roads, hiding out in barns. Couldn't find you for nothing. You can't even imagine how pissed I am." He displayed a palm. "My hand is just itching to slap your face."

"I only wanted to walk around and see about the monument and stuff. You were busy. Then that lady offered me a ride, so I took it."

"Don't ever go nowhere without telling me. If something happened to you, Beecher would string me up." He pinched her cheek. "I'll see you later. Got you a lunch plate in the van."

"What about the deadline?" Cassie shouted, red-faced, as Donny Ray strode back to the Gypsy camp. She started to chase him, maybe to make a scene, but her feet were too heavy. Moreover, she didn't want to tell him about the lunchtime conversation. It felt like one tiny thread, pulled just right, had begun unraveling the whole tapestry of her daddy's heroics. Cassie suppressed waves of yearning for Johnny Frank, for their little house on Burleson, and Sunday dinners at Ward's Café. Had he really lied?

Maybe Raoul got it wrong. The picture showed her dad standing in the road with an eye patch on. He must have gotten shot somewhere in France, because she knew for a fact that he had both eyes when he'd left Marshall.

Cassie trudged to the van. Worn down, she alternated between being ravenous and nauseated—a bitch of a deal, and her breasts felt white-hot and tender. Pregnant? Nah, she never missed a birth control pill.

Maybe her thyroid was acting up again, part of her personal history of torment. A doctor once targeted it as the source of all her misery—mood swings, fatigue, and raging hormones. Fact was, nothing got straightened out until Sheree turned her on to the magic pills in a little plastic Dial-Pak. Foolproof, unless you forgot—which Sheree did sometimes, but never Cassie.

Although she was eager to get married and have a family, she wouldn't settle for a full-of-crap, loss leader like Chuck. He'd be a lousy absentee dad. Nothing but a meaningless fling.

Not like Donny Ray, who loved her, and she loved him right back. He only got mad because he wanted to protect her, she reasoned. They'd argued on this trip, sure, but that was just their way. He'd taught her early on how to bob and weave.

That's what you do when you're committed to someone. Like Marlon Brando and Stella Kowalski in *A Streetcar Named Desire*. Nobody ever said they didn't love each other.

Beyond tired after the day's adventure, Cassie fell asleep early in the evening. Just after midnight she awoke with urgency. She prodded Donny Ray, but he barely moved. She waggled his arm. "I've got to use it."

"The latrine is right outside." He pulled the sheet over his face.

"Come with me. I'm scared."

He raised himself on his elbows and lifted the curtain from the window. He squinted. "There's a light on in the laundry room. Go on. Ain't no killers out here."

"Will you watch me?"

"Sure."

She pulled on her jacket, slid open the panel door, and skidded out. Rocks on the driveway hurt her feet, even through her socks. On tiptoes, she hurried to the *laverie*, turned around, and waved to him. He waved back. She let the glass door whup closed behind her. Slipping past the washing machines, she headed straight to the *toilette*. Ah, that beautiful porcelain.

Relieved, she tidied up and peered out of the water closet door.

Seeing no one, she stepped into the service area. Those washing machines looked pretty good—she could run a load or two tomorrow. She studied the instructions: "*Preparez votre machine.*" Yeah, got it.

Cassie turned around. A scream froze in her throat. Swa blocked her, pointing a gun.

Shuddering, she blinked hard and felt a flush of adrenaline overloading her muscles. Her feet would not move. Was he going to tie a burlap bag over her head?

"*Dis donc! C'est toi!*" Swa flipped the lock on his pistol and stuck it in his waistband. "Sorry. Midnight, you know? I heard noise."

"Sure, it's okay." Cassie took a deep breath and scanned the room. She tried to nudge past him, but he gently gripped her arm.

"We must talk."

Cassie's heart stomped on the gas. "Let's do that tomorrow." She crossed her arms, rocking on her heels. "My boyfriend will be mad if I don't hurry up. He's got a gun, too."

"*Je comprends*. Come to the window. He can see you, not to worry. And other campers too, okay?"

"Uh, okay." She calculated the distance from Swa to the door. She needed to get close enough to bolt before he could trap her. Where the hell was Donny Ray? Perspiration coursed down the insides of her legs.

"Your silver necklace," Swa touched his chest. "I have the same. *Comme la tienne.*"

Got one like hers, does he? The hell he does, she thought. What's he trying to pull? Her breath came in short gasps, and she tried again to move past him. She never should have told him all those personal family things. He was going to stuff her in a fruit cellar and demand a ransom.

"Wait, wait," he said. "I show you." He pulled a silver disc and short chain from his pocket and held them out in the palm of his hand. "Same as you. *C'est la même chose.*"

Cassie stared at the polished disc, then she touched hers. Going weak in the knees, she caught herself on the detergent dispenser. "Where'd you get that? *Où avez-vous trouvé ça?*"

"*De ma mère.*"

From his mother? No way. It looked the same as Cassie's—with little raised letters boasting ten dollars and Hemphill, Texas. She stiffened and squeezed her eyes shut. When she opened them, Swa was still standing in front of her with the token on a keychain. "God, my head," she said. "I have to sit down."

Swa pulled out two folding chairs and helped her into one. She propped her elbow on a nearby table, its red paint chipped and topped with magazines.

"Did not want to say in front of Raymond. Had to be sure," he said. "I am waiting to tell you many things."

Cassie fanned herself. "Then tell me where your mother got that token."

"From my father," Swa said, his smile wavering. "Johnny Frank Tate."

"He's not your father!" Cassie's head swam like a bowl full of minnows.

"Truth. You must believe." Swa hooked the keychain around his forefinger, grasping the token in the palm of his hand.

"No." Her throat tightened. Cradling her head in her hands, she stared at her feet. Fluorescent lights buzzed above. "Where's your mother? What happened to her?"

Swa's face fell. "My mother Éliane is dead. Lost to the consumption."

Cassie looked into Swa's eyes and saw her daddy looking back. Those eyes—a mix of green over brown, with little flecks of gold. How had she not noticed that before? Goosebumps coursed through her scalp. "Did Éliane save him?"

"He saved her," Swa's eyes watered. "You cannot ever imagine how I wanted to know him."

The revelation sank in like a bag of wet concrete as he continued. He went on to explain that his mother had met Johnny Frank in Marseille, September 1944, some months after he came ashore in Operation Dragoon. He never hid from Germans at all.

"Mama was a nurse," Swa said. "She helped his eye."

"A Nazi shot him in the eye?"

"No. He hurt himself with *une agrafeuse*. You say maybe staple gun. He got a medal for the injury—service-connected. And American medics gave him the glass eye."

"Liar!" Cassie pounded her fist on the table, knocking the stack of magazines onto the floor. Rising from the chair, her foot slipped on the slick cover of *Télérama*. She sat back down, arms folded, anger pounding her temples.

"It is so," he said.

Cassie eyed him. "How old are you, anyway?"

"I have 32 years. Born September 1947," he sighed. "Johnny Frank never saw me except for photos. And we lived with the grief."

So Swa was born only two months after Patsy died, one life traded for another. Cassie's pulse rose. If he was telling the truth, their daddy didn't rock him and sing lullabies—but he didn't do much for Baby Patsy, either.

Cassie didn't know what to believe. Like the old Frenchman's story up the road, Swa's account of the facts contradicted Johnny Frank's version. But a staple gun? Who'd make that up? "I thought Éliane saved Daddy," she said.

"No, no. Wartime and after, very bad times for many French women. But Johnny Frank was a good man. He beat a bad guy who hurt Mama." Swa imitated fists in motion.

"I can't. I can't believe this," she stammered, shaking her head repeatedly.

He held up three fingers. "*Deux, presque trois ans*—two, almost three years together. Mama and Johnny Frank."

"Impossible. The war was over." Cassie's confusion turned to anger. "Daddy came home as soon as he could!"

"To your mother Della, yes? And a very sick little girl."

"How do you know about them?" She kicked, skittering the *Télérama* across the floor.

"I know many things. Please, be still." His tone was soothing. "He promised Mama he would get the baby well, and then we would be together. And you know the baby died—but even so, year after year, he said wait for him. So many excuses. But Catholic, no divorce. I cried for him. So did Mama," Swa shrugged. "At least I have his name."

"Swa-Swa-Swastika! That's your name." Cassie's head began throbbing.

"You misunderstand. My name is Çois—nickname for Jean François."

"Jean François?" French for Johnny Frank, she realized, with the power of a drilling rig collapse. Çois touched her arm. "Your middle name is Jean, so we share the same. But you know, he wanted you to be Françoise."

She did know that, but Della had said Françoise Tate was a ridiculous name, and she wouldn't stand for it. They named her after Cass County instead. "But what about Beecher?"

"Mama's family name, *de la Hêtraie*. It means from the beech grove." He nodded. "My name too, of course. *Jean François de la Hêtraie*."

Dizzying images of Johnny Frank swirled through stars and stripes and Esso signs, opening Cherbourg umbrellas to catch his babies' tears. A vise squeezed Cassie's chest. Everything went black.

~~~

Donny Ray awoke to a loud knock. An urgent voice at the van door shouted, "*Monsieur, Monsieur*—the lady is sick!"

"Ugh--what's going on?" Donny Ray sat up. What lady? Oh shit, Cassie! He pulled open the door. That goddamn Swa character was standing there.

"Sick lady. Laundrette," Çois pointed.

"What happened?" Donny Ray scrambled out of bed. "Christ." They ran to the laundry room, where Cassie sprawled on two chairs pushed together.

"Ammonia," Çois said, holding up a half-used jug of cleaning product.

"Well, wave it under her nose. Can't take my eyes off her two minutes." He brushed her hair back and watched Çois release the fumes.

Cassie's eyelids fluttered as Donny Ray's face came into focus. "What's going on?"

"You fainted."

"Çois is my brother," she murmured.

"What the fuck are you talking about?" Donny Ray lifted her left eyelid with his thumb.

"Ow!"

"Let's get you back to bed." He helped her into a sitting position and assisted her to stand.

"But he is," Cassie insisted. "Tell him, Çois."

"Quit playing." Donny Ray frowned at her. Then he nodded at Çois. "Appreciate you, man."

Çois shrugged. "You need more help?"

"Yeah, get the door, thanks. All I really need is a good night's sleep."

Donny Ray and Cassie hobbled out. She better not make a big deal about him falling back to sleep. He'd had enough of her complications. He managed to persuade her to extend the deadline one more day, inasmuch as she'd missed the first one while gallivanting with strangers. But if Jusef didn't get word to him soon, there'd be hell to pay.

# CHAPTER TWENTY-SIX

## And Made Them Cry

Cassie's thoughts raced through the night, Rockford spinning and fishtailing through her daddy's fictitious life: happy family man and war hero, loving simple pleasures and the Knights of Columbus. Outsiders never heard Della's loud accusations rattling thin walls with constant blame for Patsy Gail's death. If only Johnny Frank had been home, his little daughter would have survived, Della insisted.

Not everyone believed her mother's version, though, and Cassie had often wondered about the nature of Della's fits, which worsened over the years. Cassie suspected the baby's demise was a cover story for Della's jealousies. Other women openly flirted with Johnny Frank, by all accounts the most handsome man in Marshall. Waitresses, lady cab drivers, and the shoe clerk at the bowling alley had played their chances right in front of young Cassie. She'd been proud to be her good-looking daddy's sidekick, but as a little kid, she hadn't understood the dynamics.

"Johnny, Johnny, puddin' and pie, kissed the girls and made them cry."

She lay still, tears escaping the corners of her eyes, rolling into her ears, reminding her of warmed-up ear drops after swimming lessons at summer camp with her Brownie troop. Even Raoul and Lucienne in Ambronay had known the truth. They acted mighty peculiar about that photo of her dad—helping out war widows and orphans, indeed.

Her thoughts wandered. Must have been pretty warm in

Marseille when Johnny Frank misfired the staple gun. Yet, every time he told his version of the story, the snow got progressively deeper on the frozen ground where the Nazi soldier shot out his eye.

When Donny Ray finally stirred in the morning light, Cassie bolted upright like a corpse coming alive. "It's true," she said. "Çois is my half-brother."

"Where do you get this shit?" Donny Ray rose on his elbows. "You dreamed it. Period."

"I swear. He told me."

"Why didn't he tell me that?"

"He knew our names and everything. And his family calls him Çois, not Swa like swastika. I should have known from hearing it, but I'd locked in on S-W-A when you told me that."

"Cassie." Donny Ray touched her cheek. "You signed the travelers' checks. He saw your passport. Give it here."

She reached over the seat and retrieved it. He flipped several pages. "Here's your address, and what's this say, right here? In case of death or accident, notify Beecher Tate. Address. Phone number." He thrust it in her hand.

"Well, but Çois didn't check the passport. Annette did." Cassie clapped the booklet between her palms. "I mean, he saw it, but..."

"Maybe he goes through our stuff, you know. Wouldn't put it past him."

"No, listen, his real name is Jean François—French for Johnny Frank."

Donny Ray sighed and grasped his cigarette package. "Look it, Jean François is a common name here. Same as John Smith at home. Woods are full of 'em."

"So how did he get the sawmill token?"

"Goddamn, Cassie, he found it. Or stole it, Jesus, he could'a got it anywhere."

"He knew about Patsy Gail," she said, tugging on Donny Ray's undershirt.

"Oh, you like that idea? It means your daddy was whoring while your mama was home bawling and squalling. No wonder she killed herself."

"You're a mean son-of-a-bitch!" Cassie tried to hit him with both hands, but he grabbed them. She couldn't move.

"Now cut that out—what's got into you? And all that cussing, hell, I ain't ever heard that out of you."

"You were talking ugly about my mother." Cassie's voice vibrated like a steel guitar.

"She was crazy, and I swear to God you're starting to take after her."

Donny Ray rubbed her shoulders as she lay trembling on his chest. "You've got to be real here," he said. "This guy sees American travelers' checks and thinks he hit the jackpot. He's conning you. That's all."

"Ask Annette."

"Guess I just will." He slid out of the covers. "I'm going over to the office. Want me to bring you some breakfast?"

She nodded. "I guess so. Thanks."

"I'll be back in a little while." Donny Ray pulled on his shoes and left.

Cassie drifted off to an uncertain sleep, interrupted by a thump on the van. She bolted upright. Maybe the Gypsies threw an apple. Or was Çois breaking in? She held her breath and listened hard. Somebody was trying the door handle.

Suddenly, a cold breeze swept over her, and she was aware of a hand reaching toward her. She screamed, and the hand covered her mouth.

"What are you yelling about? I'm spilling the breakfast here." Donny Ray juggled the dishes.

"I'm sorry. I thought I heard something."

"That was me. What are you so scared about?"

"Everything."

"I can upset you a little more about Çois-boy if you want me to."

Donny Ray lifted a checked cloth revealing half a baguette with butter and cherry jam, sausage, and scrambled eggs. "Here, sit up, come around here now."

Cassie reached for the plate like a hungry lioness crouching over her kill. He handed her a bottle of mineral water and watched her for a moment.

"So, I asked Annette about your boy. Want to know what she said?"

Between bites of baguette, Cassie nodded. "Tell me."

"It's your call, but some rocks you don't want to turn over." He flicked her chin. "You ready?"

"Go."

"Now understand, her English ain't all that great, so a lot of this was jibber-jabber and hand jive. Know what I mean?"

She plonked the fork. "Tell me."

"First, Annette doesn't know anything about Johnny Frank. But Çois's mother got her head shaved for getting pregnant—so his father was German."

Cassie paused mid-bite. "Not necessarily."

Donny Ray paused. "Yeah, it was. The Frenchwomen who'd been sleeping with Occupation soldiers got their heads shaved to show they'd been screwing the enemy."

"But that doesn't mean a German was his father. Do the math, fool. Nazis surrendered way long before Çois's mother got pregnant. Americans were Allies." With a snap of her wrist, Cassie stuck her fork into the sausage like a totem pole. "That dimwit Annette got everything mixed up."

"Do you want me to tell you the rest or not?"

"Hell, yeah! How did Çois get Daddy's token?"

"It was worth a lot. And it would've bought a lot of time with his mother."

"What are you saying?"

"She was a whore. Worked soldier clubs in Marseille. Shamed the family, but they were poor as Job's turkey up here, so she banged them boys and sent her money home."

"Çois said she was a nurse."

"He wouldn't say his mama was a hooker!"

Cassie wilted. Her daddy had been cheating. She couldn't stand it. He'd lived a daily sin of adultery, all the while complaining about hypocrites in church. Well, she thought, he clearly knew his own tribe.

Donny Ray was right. No wonder Della killed herself; the truth had made her crazy. In her first attempt to commit suicide, she stuck a pencil in her ear to poke out her brains, but that just made her deaf on the right. It's why she kept the TV volume up high.

"Now you don't know," Donny Ray said, "it could've been somebody stole the token from Johnny Frank, or maybe he lost it somewhere. Could've been somebody else paid Çois' mama. She was sure spreading for the Yankee dollar, and I wouldn't claim that guy as family, if I was you."

## CHAPTER TWENTY-SEVEN

### For What It's Worth

Lying on a mechanic's creeper, Donny Ray scooted under the Madame's old Peugeot and barely cleared the engine. Feeling for a socket wrench, he shined a flashlight into the undercarriage. Finally, some peace and quiet to sort through his life's garbage dump.

Jusef had to be pissed off about the Basel mess, but Donny Ray hadn't known what else to do. The Swiss police were after him, and thanks to Interpol, the West Germans had to be on his trail too. He just knew it. And he could add the U.S. Army to the list. "Paranoia strikes deep," he muttered. Buffalo Springfield was right.

Anyway, it was Jusef's fault for canceling on him.

Cassie was getting on his nerves, too, carrying on about Çois—or François whoever—and she was a wreck over her father's deception. Çois probably was Cassie's half-brother, for as much as Annette could explain with hand-flapping and broken English. After the war, seems old Johnny Frank had basically moved in there for days at a time, being only a short train ride from Lyon.

Annette had shown Donny Ray some pictures, too, and he almost lost his lunch when he saw Cassie's dad sunbathing with Éliane by a cow pond. Annette had been just a kid, maybe 12 or 13, but she knew exactly what was going on, and she hated Johnny Frank for deserting her sister.

"No sense stirring all that up," Donny Ray had told Annette. And hearkening back to his grave-robbing days, he said, "Let the skeletons rest."

He didn't have time to waste with family reunions and sentimental shit. Cassie might want to stay or something, and he didn't want to deal with it. He sure didn't want to blow the deal with Jusef.

Meanwhile, Annette kept showing her petticoats to him. Under ordinary circumstances, he might have wanted her in a last-pussy-at-closing-time kind of way. But he couldn't bang that woman under Cassie's sniffing nose.

Sure, he'd given Annette some attention, his patented charm hustle because he needed that meal ticket. Still, she couldn't reasonably believe he would stay with her.

And those Gypsies—Donny Ray was campground security for himself.

He never intended to show his Colt, but Annette had bragged. Those sons-of-bitches put the fear in him after his straight beat their guy's full house. One of them pulled a knife and almost pinned his hand to the table. They'd reached an uneasy truce, but he stayed on alert and didn't beat them as badly as he could have.

Even now, as Donny Ray worked underneath the Peugeot, with the front end resting on a jack stand and a wooden block bracing the back wheel, he knew anyone could give it one swift kick, and boom!

He found the oil pan and loosened the plug with a socket wrench; then he moved out of the way and left the oil to drip into the drain pan. As the caster wheels swiveled, they tore little holes in the paper covering the workspace. What a total mess, he thought.

He sat up, elbows on his knees, and dangled the wrench like a hypnotist's pocket watch. The smell of motor oil reminded him of Aldo's place—and of Brigitta. He flinched.

Maybe her arrest was merely for questioning. The handcuffs could have been for show. Just because she was arrested didn't mean she'd flipped on him. Jusef would know how to find her.

Donny Ray had called her that morning from the campsite and got a line pretty fast but had to disconnect when that numb-nuts Çois showed up with a white rag and a spray can of furniture polish, wiping the same shelf over and over. The chick who answered the phone at the Bremerhaven bar said she'd never heard of Gitta—maybe code for tracers on the line.

No big deal. By the time the cops found this joint, he'd be long gone. And he sure as hell wouldn't dare cross the German border.

Donny Ray reached for a round white filter. He could do an oil change in his sleep—the first mechanic skill his cousin Mark ever taught him. Fast-talking Mark with his big ideas, a wannabe. But Donny Ray had moved beyond I-20 and small-time dealers.

Now he was in with real power players. Red Army Faction, Iranian revolutionaries, Palestinian terrorists, and now Escobar—hot damn! Cassie would tie it all up with a bow. He had to keep her happy. No Cassie, no Jusef, no Escobar. If Cassie don't play, Jusef is out, and Donny Ray could forget about being an Escobar man.

In the campground parlor, Cassie told Çois what Donny Ray said about Éliane during the war. Çois slammed a shoebox on the table. "Mama was not a whore!" Red-faced, he shouted in his aunt's direction. "*Tante Annette, tu raconteur des mensonges?*" He lapsed into a frenzy of French curse words Cassie could barely understand. Basically, he called his aunt a lying, old mad cow. That pretty much settled it.

"Mama lived alone; a nurse in Marseille," he said. "Germans lodged at her house. No choice. Nothing else she could do."

True. Cassie remembered reading about that in *The Silence of the Sea*. Once the Nazis decided to take your house, you were cooked.

François became agitated, his voice wavering. "*Oui*, Mama was mistress to German officer. *Une collaborator horizontale*. He gave her rations, chocolate, stockings. She sent them home with money. Aunt Annette ate chocolates, didn't she? Fruit and meats, while villagers starved, their goods plundered to supply the German front line."

Cassie hesitated, then asked, "So, did your mother really get her head shaved?"

He nodded; eyes wide. "Shaved and marked with the swastika. Pulled her clothes. They shamed her," he said. "But you know, they could have shot her instead."

"Daddy helped your mother, though."

"Yes." Çois nodded.

"And he won medals." Cassie brightened.

"Yes. Operation Dragoon, he came ashore, but he–" Çois thumped his chest.

"Heart attack? He always had a bad heart. That's what killed him." She felt a pang of regret and recalled "Turkey in the Straw" and the sheet falling from Johnny Frank's face.

"Yes. So, no more fighting."

Oh geez, Johnny Frank should've been 4-F, she thought. What did he do for all that time?

Çois pantomimed typing. "Telegraph. Very important job." His eyes gleamed. "And after war was over, he stationed in Lyon for post-war cleanup, you know. He stayed with Mama many times here."

"Your aunt said she didn't know anything about him."

Çois blinked. "Not true!"

So, either Donny Ray lied about that, or Annette did. Or maybe they couldn't understand each other. But one thing seemed clear: her daddy wasn't any hero. He didn't even bring back some of those participation medals. Cassie wrung her hands. "Even Eisenhower left Europe before Daddy did. He just wanted Éliane."

"And she wanted him. But your sister fell ill, and he chose her." Çois clenched his fists. "I hated him for leaving us. And I hated Beecher for taking my place as son. Bitter for years, but *la vie continue*. Life goes on, you know."

Cassie shook her head in dismay. Johnny Frank had let down the whole family. Two families. In a kaleidoscopic twist, he emerged with a French mistress and a love child, while his wife rolled bandages, donated blood, and cried over a toddler in a baby iron lung.

"Letters, so many letters." Çois thumped the shoebox, untied the string, and lifted the lid.

# CHAPTER TWENTY-EIGHT

## Papa Was a Rolling Stone

From the box marked *Maman et Papa*, Çois removed a packet of envelopes, each with a US Airmail stamp and postmark streaks. He pointed to Johnny Frank's printing in the upper left corner of each envelope: a post office box, his business address. A sudden pain tightened Cassie's forehead. Seems like her daddy had been signing more than freight invoices in his pulpwood office.

Cassie slowly twirled strands of hair as she watched Çois deal a half-inch stack of black and white photos from a deck, like the ones she had at home. He had pictures of Johnny Frank and Éliane together, smiling and hugging with unfiltered cigarettes and bottles of wine.

"Oh." A flush crept up Cassie's neck.

"Another." He handed over a picture of Éliane, smiling with a slight twist to her lips, accented with dark lipstick. Upswept hair with fluffy curls framed large eyes and heavily penciled brows.

"Is *vrai*, true. You see now," he said, wiping both eyes with one sleeve.

A dead weight sank on Cassie's heart. Her father, her idol, had been a philandering jerk. She'd never seen him treat Della as tenderly as he treated Éliane—at least in those photos. But the camera doesn't lie.

"More. *Comme ça*." He handed her the shoebox, and she riffled packs of photos bound with ribbons. And on the backs, the same handwriting: her father's angular lines and Éliane's cursive elegance.

One photo showed Johnny Frank and Éliane breaking bread with family groups, and even Annette smiled for the camera and raised a glass of cheer. Cassie looked closer, recognizing a younger Raoul, sporting a black beret even then. "Damn," she mumbled. "That hurts."

Ribboned separately, a tiny blonde girl in an Easter bonnet, festooned with bows and flowers, gazed into her father's eyes. He wore a Sunday suit and tie, his thatch of fair hair wet-combed into place. He held her on his knee, her lacy dress and crinoline petticoats blooming like magnolias. Butterflies tumbled through her stomach as Cassie regarded the familiar setting and date stamped on the margin. "This is me," she whispered. "Where did that little girl go?"

The faded color photograph told a story of small-town America 15 years removed from foreign wars—a handsome Army veteran and his sweet Baby Boomer, safe and well in a muted green front yard. On the back, she read Johnny Frank's familiar script: "Easter Sunday, 1960."

"Why did he send your mother these?" she asked. "They'd make me want to cry if I was her."

Çois opened his palms. "Mama wanted to see, to know. In her heart, she was the true wife. She did cry, but she believed you and Beecher were hers, too. Merely a fantasy with Johnny Frank. Neither would give it up."

Through the years, he said, Johnny Frank sent money to help them. A nice gesture, Cassie thought, but that's why Della had to work when all the other moms got to stay home and collect S&H Green Stamps. She'd come back to the house frazzled and tired after being on her feet all day at a soda fountain, making milkshakes for kids who blew drinking straw wrappers at her. Meanwhile, Johnny Frank kept a paramour stash of pictures and letters that Della must have found after his death.

"Last one." Çois pulled a creased picture from the box.

"Aw, that's the Methodist church picnic. Daddy died a couple weeks later." She brushed away a tear.

Çois exhaled. "Della wrote *une méchante lettre*—a very mean letter—to Mama after his death, called her a whore with a bastard, and do not ever write to Johnny Frank again, he's dead! Most angry, Della was."

"Oh no," Cassie gasped. "What did your mother do?"

"She never saw the letter. I burned it."

"Then how did she find out about Daddy dying?"

Çois frowned. "Eventually, her letters were returned. Stamped 'deceased.' I felt guilty to see her so hurt, but–"

"Sorry, Çois, that was a blockhead thing to do, letting Éliane get clobbered that way." Cassie sniffled into a Kleenex.

"I couldn't think another way. Your mother…" He threw his hands in the air.

"Yeah, yeah, I know." Guilt tiptoed through Cassie's ears and tumped over a loaded china cabinet—just like her poem said, glass and splinters, icy shards.

So, after Johnny Frank's death, Della had confirmed an awful truth—that her husband had always loved and mourned Éliane and the little son he couldn't see. That he wouldn't have returned to Della if King Polio hadn't beaten down the defenses.

Cassie took a deep breath. "Couple years after Daddy died, Mama killed herself. Knelt beside the bed and put a gun in her mouth."

Çois touched her shoulder. "Oh, I am sorry—so many hearts broken."

"Yeah, guess our Papa was a rolling stone, wasn't he?" She winced.

"You say?" Çois knitted his eyebrows.

175

"Never mind. Motown. An American thing."

Cassie held her feet still, but she kneaded the edges of the shoebox top. Prisoner marches and heroism—none of it was true. Her father was a clerk-typist who put his eye out with a damn staple gun. No wonder he got upset when Beecher tried to untangle a shoelace with an ice pick—one wrong move, and there would've been two eye patches in the house.

Poor Della. Cassie's heart hurt for her—stubborn and apparently in denial, but still a brave woman who would not let her husband's duplicity tarnish the family's image of him. No way she would have divorced their daddy and left the kids to flail their arms in the backyard on Burleson Street.

Like a curtain parting, Cassie suddenly saw her mother's truth: she sacrificed out of pride and to spare her babies the pain. She muddled along, drinking and pushing through it until she couldn't do it anymore.

Della could have been a country music hit.

Cassie returned to the photos of her daddy and Éliane. One picture showed her sitting on his lap, kissing him on the cheek. The war was over in France. Their faces showed it, reflecting their happiness even in her daddy's glass eye.

## CHAPTER TWENTY-NINE

## Too Much Talk

To Cassie's surprise, Çois didn't run around dusting for Annette all the time. He had a technician's certificate in construction and roofing and ran his own business. Years before, he worked as a military policeman after the draft sent him to the French West Indies—Guadeloupe, a French colonial commitment. "An overseas department," he explained. "Or state, you would say."

"Military police?" She frowned. Annette didn't need Donny Ray for security. Çois could keep the Gypsies in line by himself, she thought, reaching for a warm mug of tea. The cozy sitting room at the campground easily accommodated her and Çois, now exchanging stories, both more relaxed, if still a mite awkward. The default topic hovered around Çois's wife Michaëlle and their young son.

"It was very complicated, so you may say I am much like my father." He tilted his head, smiling broadly. "I fell in love abroad, but Michaëlle's family did not want to lose their beautiful daughter to a foreigner."

Tiny wheels spun in Cassie's head. Love and war, the complications: Johnny Frank and Éliane, Çois, Michaëlle, and how many others? No wonder there was a market for movies like *Cherbourg*.

"But you're married now," Cassie eyed the gold wedding ring on his finger.

"Yes. I made it happen because I loved her enough."

Okay, that sounded like a dig at Johnny Frank, she thought. Things might get testy here.

From Guadeloupe, Çois explained, he returned to France alone, completed military service, and worked briefly as a police officer in Lyon. He and Michaëlle missed each other terribly, but she wouldn't leave her family without assurance of regular visits home. Çois couldn't make that promise until he inherited his mother's share of the property.

Cassie didn't see how, though. Owning half a dumpy campground didn't seem lucrative. But Çois said he had some land sales and rentals and had started a construction company. Building projects had slowed with the approach of winter, so he had time to maintain the house and grounds.

He reached a framed photo from a collection on a tall shelf. "You see?" He dusted the glass with his sleeve and handed it to her.

"Your wife is beautiful," Cassie said. The camera caught Michaëlle's almond-shaped eyes and exquisite brows peering from thick natural hair and ringlets past her shoulders. Their cute little boy had a button nose and baby teeth.

"Your son's name?" Cassie tilted the picture, viewing it right and left, trying to find some evidence of her family.

"Jean-Jacques." He replaced the photo on the shelf.

Cassie took the last sip of her chamomile tea and set the mug on a frilly lace doily. "It's great everything worked out for y'all. A lot of people get dumped."

"*L'amour est bleu*, you know!" Rising from the settee, Çois picked up his feather duster from a low cabinet. "Some hearts never heal, never love again—the same as Aunt Annette, widowed many years. Her husband was killed in Vietnam when France controlled."

Well, if Aunt Annette had always dressed in those frumpy get-ups, Cassie could understand how she blew some chances to remarry.

Çois moved closer and lowered his voice almost to a whisper. "I heard your boyfriend on the phone, speaking English and German, mixing up words so I won't know. Very strange. Tries to find a man named Jusef."

"That's his business partner."

"Common name in Middle East." He glanced around. "Anyway, he also called a woman long-distance."

"A woman?" Cassie's eyes widened.

"Shhh. I think so. Big mystery."

Cassie's heart kicked up a notch. Who the hell did Donny Ray think he was, calling another woman from this jackass trip? "He told me he was a spy for the East Germans."

Çois frowned. "Not a spy. He talks too much. But something else."

"Like what?"

"Eh, from Lyon to Montpellier, a good route for drugs and guns. Then off into the seas, to Syria for carry over land to Iran. The Interpol tracks them—you know, the international police. Europe, United Kingdom, the U.S., and so forth."

Cassie gripped the bridge of her nose as she tried to make sense of this. Had Donny Ray been trying to outrun Interpol? Why'd he changed his name to Raymond? She'd thought that whole Switzerland thing was mighty peculiar—he'd run them out faster than Hot Wheels.

"What is it?" François gently tapped the feather duster on her shoulder.

Cassie sank deep into the sofa cushions. "Donny Ray got into some kind of mess in Basel. That's how we wound up down here. Broke."

"Oh?" Çois sat beside her. "A chase?"

"He thought it was, but I didn't see anybody. He said police raided a poker game he got into, and he was afraid of getting locked up."

Çois dangled the duster on his work boots. "Poker games are tourist traps, and they're illegal, that's true. But the raids are usually staged. Actors portray police, who scare the players into giving up their money."

"Donny Ray didn't stay around to find out."

"Too much reaction. He fears police for other reasons." Çois eyed her. "Leave him. I'll put you on a plane in Lyon. *Très facile.* Very easy."

Whenever Cassie heard something was supposed to be easy, that was a red flag. Doubts plagued her. Beecher and Donny Ray had always told her not to be gullible. What if, after all this, Çois was a maniac? Maybe he and Aunt Annette had killed Éliane to get her property. Maybe Annette was really his mother. Cassie hedged.

"Anyway, you must call if you get into trouble." He tore off a blank invoice from the tablet at the desk. "This name, this number—and this is the address of course. *Le voici.*"

She repeated the name "*Jean François de la Hêtraie.* Johnny Frank from the Beech Grove." Cassie tucked the paper into her pocket.

"Wait, who's that?" She pointed out the window. A uniformed man was riding up on a bicycle outside. He parked the bike, climbed the steps, and rang the bell. Çois answered the door.

"*Télégramme pour Mssr. Richard.*"

Annette appeared, wiping her floured hands on her apron. "I take it. *Merci.*" She fished in her apron for a franc and handed it to him.

He tipped his hat and left the way he came. Wrinkling her forehead, she turned off the stovetop burners and went out the kitchen door.

"I got to get back to the van," Cassie said. "Something's up." She dashed out. Annette was hurrying down the path to the Gypsy camp, waving the yellow envelope excitedly.

Donny Ray stood up from his card game, and she handed it over with a flourish. He unfolded a thin piece of paper with ticker-tape ribbons running its width, and his face broke into a big show of teeth.

Even from a distance, Cassie could tell it was good news for Donny Ray and bad news for Annette. Well, what did she think it would be? Cassie watched her turn and walk away, kicking pebbles with her blue espadrilles. Her flowered skirt billowed in the breeze.

Moving closer, Cassie watched Donny Ray put his cards down on the table and shove his chips to the center. It looked to her like some wheeling and dealing, with wide gestures and a mixed vibe. He trotted back to the van.

"What's going on?" she asked.

Donny Ray dangled the telegram in front of her. "See, see, see? That's all there is to see." All she could make out was "Sofitel Bellecour" before he yanked it away.

"But what does it mean?"

"Okay, Miss Nosy. Jusef is wiring money, thank God. American Express in Lyon. And we've got a hotel. Let's move."

"Now?"

"Sure, unless you and Çois-boy have a party going on."

She scowled. She wanted more time with Çois. On the other hand, a hotel sounded wonderful, and maybe she could call Beecher from the American Express office. Donny Ray said she would have to wait for an overseas line.

"Remember when I used to call you from Amsterdam? It takes a while to get through."

"I don't mind waiting," she said. "I miss him."

She also had $300 tucked under the shelf liner in her closet. Maybe he could wire her the money so she wouldn't have to beg off Donny Ray—or Çois. She'd catch a flight out of Lyon.

## CHAPTER THIRTY

## Tightening Screws

Donny Ray started packing and fooling with the butane tank. "You go on in the office and say bye to Çois-boy if you want. I need to organize here for a minute."

"What happened to the big hurry?" she asked without waiting for a reply. That's all right, she wanted to see Çois anyway. On her way to find him, she turned around to see Donny Ray turning screws on the license plates.

She shrugged and entered the office, the lavender fragrances enveloping her once more. She thanked a flush-faced *Madame*, her eyes bloodshot, for the hospitality and saw Çois in the next room. Cassie told him what the telegram said, including the words Sofitel Bellecour.

"Ah yes, a luxury hotel in Lyon—very lucky for you. Farewell," he said. "But not *adieu!*"

"I won't tell him what we talked about," she said. "Donny Ray still doesn't believe you're my half-brother anyway."

"Good. Better. Call me. You have the number, yes?"

She felt her pockets. "I guess I put it in the backpack."

"Take *une autre.*"

"I'll write you soon. And Çois? Think you could get me copies of those pictures of Éliane with Daddy?"

"I will."

"What's the hold up here?" Donny Ray marched into the

room. "Come on now." He put his hand on Cassie's shoulder and drove her out. She waved her hand and twisted her neck to get one last look at Çois. "À bientôt mon frère!"

"Okay, that's enough." Donny Ray swatted her butt. "The van's ready."

As they pulled out of the gravel driveway, Cassie noticed the curtains flutter at the office window. Annette's painted fingernails swayed, and Cassie waved back. Donny Ray didn't turn his head.

"Bye, bitch," he muttered and headed south toward the Rue François.

Dang. That bitch was her aunt. Sort of.

Motoring back the way they came, Cassie sensed a dream unfolding—a troubled one, the kind where she runs naked in a True Value hardware store. She glanced at the war monument, knowing Raoul had done a soft sell to spare her feelings. All those villagers knew what was going on with Éliane and Johnny Frank.

However, how could she be certain Çois was his son? True, he had her daddy's eyes, and he had a treasure trove of memorabilia, proving only that he believed Johnny Frank was his father. Not only did Çois believe it, but her father had, too.

Cassie pulled out a map and studied the highway markings. As they approached Lyon, traffic increased along with the noise.

"Which way, Cassie?"

"Right at the next light."

The roadway took them through a commercial industrial section, followed by rows of modern high-rise apartments and impressive 17$^{th}$ Century buildings. "Lyon is bigger than I thought."

"Almost as big as Paris with the suburbs and all," Donny Ray said, watching the side mirrors.

She glanced out the window and spied a policeman on a motorcycle. "Çois used to be a cop."

"He was? Where?" Slowing the vehicle, Donny Ray invited horn honks as he looked back and forth from Cassie to the road.

"Military policeman. In Guadeloupe."

Donny Ray sighed and returned his view to the highway. "Aw hell, that's in Mexico."

"No, it's the French Caribbean. And he was one here, too, for a while."

"He is so full of shit. Jesus." Donny Ray bit his cuticles, staring hard at the road, weaving in and out of traffic. He was crabbier than ever and scowled at her. "I said, which way?"

"Wait a second." She rustled the map. "Keep going, slight turn, straight ahead. All right. We're here." She looked up. "Aren't we?"

Wow. She figured American Express would be a small office. Instead, it sat inside a fancy hotel and office complex. Although they had to walk a block because Donny Ray didn't want to pay for the indoor garage, the lobby was the big payoff—marble entryway, ornamental woven rugs, and antique tables mixed with sleek furnishings and tall windows. Heavy drapes fell from scalloped toppers. Must be a name for those, she thought.

Cassie nudged him. "They know how to do it up."

Even the clerks dressed in spiffy uniforms. Feeling out of place, she hovered by the potted palms. Donny Ray approached a service counter, checked his watch, and shifted his weight from foot to foot. She could tell by his stiff shoulders there wasn't any money for him.

Still, the process looked easy enough. Cassie approached a different service counter and tore two travelers' checks from her folder. She signed and presented them to the clerk, along with her passport. "Can I make an overseas call from here?"

"No, you go to PTT, that's the post office. Not far." The clerk scribbled an address for her. "Ask for an overseas line. You make a reservation for it. A hotel switchboard can do the same." He eyed her wrinkled clothes. "But very expensive that way."

Donny Ray came up from behind, squeezing her shoulder a little too hard. "Thank you for your courtesies."

Cassie frowned, jerking her head. Donny Ray probably worried she'd tell the man a secret or run off with him.

The clerk pressed his lips. "*De rien.* Enjoy Lyon. Next."

Donny Ray guided Cassie to a seating area ringed by ceramic urns, tall lamps, and birdbath-style fountains that spilled blue water into tile tubs. "I've told you before, don't go getting friendly with strangers. Can't believe you went off with that Ambronay woman. Let me do all the talking, or you could wind up without your kidneys in a bathtub full of ice."

"Actually, I've been thinking a lot about my kidneys," she winced. "I may need to see a doctor."

"Is your pee red?"

"No."

"Then forget about it." Donny Ray pulled out a cigarette and his lighter.

She slouched and sighed, "Did Jusef send the money?"

"Not yet. We've still got a wait." He crinkled the cellophane from the cigarette packet and stuck it into a terracotta crock.

"Can we go to the post office? I want to call Beecher."

"All right," he shrugged. "I'm giving you five minutes to get all your talking done. We've got time limits here."

The receptionist gave them directions, and they returned to the van. Cassie's heart pounded. It was Tuesday morning in Marshall, and Beecher would've worked the second shift. She had a window of opportunity to reach him.

Donny Ray headed the vehicle to the Rue Grolée and soon crossed le Rhône. Lyon streets ranged from multi-lanes to narrow, twisting alleys and fine old buildings made of smooth concrete and large blocks of masonry. Balustrades hugged upper windows, and decorative columns projected from walls and doors with ornamental scrollwork.

Even the post office had wrought iron balconies, massive windows lined with pansies, and bright yellow postboxes mounted on pedestals. With Cassie alongside, Donny Ray swung open a heavy, brass-trimmed door to *"La Banque Postale."* Misstepping, she nearly ran into a sign. As he squeezed her neck, she reserved an overseas phone line.

"One hour," the clerk said. "You are next in the queue."

"Yay!" Cassie clapped. "I thought it took all day."

"Midday is good." The stern clerk pointed to a large bronze clock hanging from ornamental ironwork. "Come back at one o'clock."

T-shirt dresses fluttered from short clotheslines strung under small tents, alongside stands of fruits and vegetables, and tables of souvenir sunglasses. Market day. The pavement was breezy and active, with office workers on lunch breaks and pedestrians milling about. Cassie and Donny Ray stepped into the nearby *tabac*, where he bought a *Time* magazine and cigarettes. She got an *International Herald Tribune*, a pack of Hollywood chewing gum, and a *Paris Match*.

Cassie was glad Donny Ray wouldn't be able to read the *Match*. She wanted to show off a bit, so he'd come off his high horse and quit bossing her. She still loved him, though.

The old Donny Ray was still in there. If he would just be the way he was when they were in high school, she thought. Back then, he couldn't keep his hands off her and said he loved her all the time. She savored visions of being barefoot in the kitchen, while he fixed cars, ambling inside for lunch with a sweaty brow, taking her in his arms even as she peeled apples over the kitchen sink. They would recover from this fiasco, she was confident.

Locating a coffee shop, Cassie welcomed the sun's warmth and sipped an Orangina at an outside table. A server brought ham croissants and fresh fruit, which looked like a country club lunch she'd seen in a movie. She still had light bouts of nausea. Nothing a few peppermints couldn't cure.

Flipping the pages of *Match* made her feel so French, and yet some of that original gloss had darkened. The whole point of coming here was to celebrate Johnny Frank's heroism, but he turned out to be a goldbricker. She checked her watch—the overseas line would open in 15 minutes. She nudged Donny Ray, "*Vite!* Come on, let's get moving."

He retrieved cash and coins from his pocket, sorting and examining them before placing them on the table. "Stop pushing me. We have plenty of time." He stood, stretched, and gestured to the server.

"You're going slow on purpose!" Cassie popped a stick of gum into her mouth and chomped with fury. She hurried up the sidewalk, pausing every few feet to make sure he was still with her. By the time the post office door closed behind them, the clock on the wall said one o'clock. Sharp.

The clerk pointed to an empty telephone booth. "You see, *cabine téléphonique*." He explained that she should answer when the telephone rang. "*Vite, vite*."

## CHAPTER THIRTY-ONE

## Slamming the Cradle

Even her fingertips felt sweaty. Cassie opened the phone booth door, only to be hit by a disagreeable waxy smell with pungent hints of pine cleaners.

"Ugh!" She held her nose, fighting a wave of nausea.

"Darlin,' you okay? Come on out," Donny Ray said. "You need fresh air."

"No!"

He stood, unmoving, with his foot propping open the door. Cassie sank to the stool, her head in her hands, leaving the phone jangling. Donny Ray yanked the receiver before she could reach it.

"You are not going to hijack my call!" Revitalized, she sat up straight, wrenched the receiver from him, and cradled it to her ear. She told the operator to reverse the charges: *"Post due payable par la reception."*

The line rang five times. A sleepy voice answered, but perked up, to accept the charges. "Cassie!"

A wave of homesickness crashed into Cassie's heart. "Yeah, it's me. Can you believe it? I'm in France! How are you?"

"Well, I'm fine. You caught me off guard."

"How's everyone?" She spoke quietly. Donny Ray's presence pissed her off—leaning into the booth, scratching a match on the rough side of the phone. She elbowed him.

"Well, Chuck and Sheree got married. They've moved over to–" Beecher's voice disappeared inside muddled clicks and dial tones.

"What the...?" Stunned, she struck Donny Ray's arm with the telephone receiver. "You hung up the call!"

Grabbing the receiver, Donny Ray held it outside the booth. "It's your fault! If you hadn't frogged me–"

"I tapped you with my elbow to get you out of my face! You flipped that button there." Cassie pointed to the telephone cradle and pressed the switch up and down. A single franc clinked in the coin return slot. She dissolved into the phone booth with the varnish and the wood panels.

She didn't get a chance to ask about the money, and damn it to hell, Chuck married Sheree. Cassie felt a pie knife scooping out pieces of her heart like bleeding cherries. She pounded her fists on the phone booth wall.

A security officer intervened, his mustache twitching. "Excuse me, please vacate the booth."

Busy lighting his cigarette, Donny Ray looked up. "She'll get over it."

"*Monsieur,* another party waits."

Cassie staggered out. She had lost Chuck forever, not that she ever needed a junkie man anyway, but she sure wanted to finish that call and get her money wired over.

## Super Snooper

Glowering, Donny Ray hustled her into the van. No question he hung up that call. She might have asked Beecher for money, so maybe she could bolt. He grimaced and glanced her way. Cassie tipped her head against the window and cried in plosive puffs of wet misery until her eyes shut and her mouth fell into a lopsided frown.

Well, that was quick, he thought, reaching for a cigarette. She ought to be over jet lag by now, but there she lay, sound asleep in the middle of the day, with a little dribble at the corner of her mouth. She resembled an old granny napping without her dentures. Her fatigue, the weight gain, the hormone crazies—she had to be pregnant. He knew the signs. One surefire way to find out.

Checking for snoops, he gently unzipped her light jacket and pulled apart the fabric panels. Cassie's T-shirt put everything out there, and he touched her lightly. She awoke with a squeal and a slap. Then she glared at him, zipped her jacket, and wriggled back to position against the window.

"Bingo," he whispered.

He cranked the engine and swelled with pride. He wasn't simply getting a wife for Jusef, but a pregnant American wife, an instant family to prove this was no immigration scam. Yes sir, Jusef needed to provide for the American citizens in his life, a wife and little one. Donny Ray could smell the money and the waters of the Gulf of Mexico.

Merging back into traffic, he signaled a lane change and returned to American Express. Leaving Cassie asleep in the vehicle, he checked his status in the office. To his relief, Jusef had wired five thousand U.S. dollars with a message: "Sofitel Bellecour, reservations confirmed. Will call."

The clerk converted two thousand dollars to French francs, and the rest in travelers' checks. "You will need this money; I can tell you that," he said cheerfully. "Your hotel is 5-star – *trés cher*."

Pulling a map from a polished rack, the clerk unfolded it, marking the hotel's location. "You see, close to everything." He leaned in confidentially. "And laundry service for guests."

Upbeat, Donny Ray walked whistling to the van. Too bad he couldn't get Brigitta down here. Aw hell, why did he let himself think that? She couldn't go anywhere. He couldn't shake her loose from his mind. Like after his dad died, he'd think about calling him or telling him something, and it'd take a second to remember he'd already fed the sharks.

Donny Ray's stomach tightened. Gitta had a hard edge that he craved. If he hit her, she'd hit him back. They got into wall-rattling, dish-busting fights that would melt into bed-banging makeup sex every time. He missed it. Missed her. He needed to rethink that whole situation. They had the rest of their lives. That could be tomorrow or 10 years from now.

## CHAPTER THIRTY-TWO

### Genuine Pretense

Donny Ray pulled the van up to the hotel, congratulating himself on his good luck. Not a super big place, but still a fabulous accommodation overlooking the river. The doorman waved him away. "Service truck, back entrance," he pointed.

"No, no man, we're guests." He shouldn't have to explain himself, though it came as no surprise considering the shabby van. Still, it annoyed him. Whenever he and Gitta drove up somewhere in the Mercedes-Benz, valets treated them like Mick and Bianca.

Donny Ray left the van at the curb with Cassie sound asleep, her face pressed against the glass. He passed through the heavy revolving doors to register. Now this was more to his liking—gourmet restaurant, small shops, and bustling uniformed employees.

"*Oui, Monsieur Richard,*" the clerk said.

"English, please." Shit, he almost forgot he's *Monsieur Richard* now.

"I hope the suite pleases you."

Donny Ray reached for his wallet. "Do I pay upfront?"

"No, no, your assistant paid in advance." The clerk handed Donny Ray two keys. "Pleased to be of service."

Hmmm, that was a good surprise, he reckoned. "My assistant, yes, always effective."

The desk clerk summoned a bellman —a tall, slender, impressive guy with citrus aftershave and closely cropped hair. He followed Donny Ray to the van, now dotted with bug spatter and bird poop. Donny Ray knocked on the window and helped Cassie from the vehicle. "I've got a key for you."

Grimacing, she dropped it in her backpack and hobbled out, pulling the straps over her shoulders without comment. He figured she might be mad at him for any number of reasons, so he better make this good. He put his arm around her and pointed to the hotel—a boxy, modern building, rising eight floors above the ground. "Only the best for my baby," he said.

Tentatively, she took his hand and squeezed it.

"Let's see that pretty face." He found the softening in her eyes he'd been seeking. They ambled into the lobby, where trendies mingled with uniformed assistants, all acting important. "How about this? Better'n that crap-fest in Montreux, right?" Donny Ray cupped her cheeks in his hands and kissed her on each. "It's what you've been waiting for, kid."

## Pink Floored

Upon reaching the sixth-floor suite, the bellman opened double doors with a flourish, and drew the drapes to reveal the river scene below. Smiling, he gave a friendly salute before rolling out the baggage cart and closing the doors behind him.

"This is as big as my whole house!" Gaping at the furnishings, Cassie stumbled on the thick carpet but regained her balance in Donny Ray's arms.

He twirled her around and kissed her, then grabbed a ringing phone. "Jusef! Yes, we're settling in." He covered the receiver and pointed to another door. "Sweetheart, you've earned a nice bubble bath."

"All right!" she exclaimed. A far cry from her bathroom at home, where a spotted shower curtain spilled over chicken-wire tiling. Here, wow, gold faucets, porcelain fixtures, and a pink marble floor. The bathtub, on metal claw feet, stood on a lavish platform with mirrors all around. Hanging from the ceiling, a crystal chandelier reflected little rainbows all over the mirrored walls. Donny Ray had finally atoned for his travel sins, she thought—no kidding.

No matter how angry he made her, she couldn't stay cross. They always worked things out. The phone booth hang-up was a mistake, she decided. She didn't need a big apology, like Chuck's romantic pretenses. Donny Ray was genuine, she believed, the foundation of true love and devotion.

She opened a little bottle of jasmine bubble bath, poured it under running water, and climbed into the tub. Eyes closed, her thoughts drifted until she felt the water level creep over her shoulders. She turned off the faucet with her toes, cupped some suds in her hand, and blew bubbles into the air. They settled on her knees, which rose like promontories from the foam.

Donny Ray pushed open the door. "You ready for a real good dinner?"

"I sure am. Yeah, hold on."

She stepped out of the tub, wrapped herself in a thick cotton towel, and reached for her brush. Then she vomited into the bidet.

"Donny Ray, I need a doctor!" She flushed the water.

He helped her to the vanity chair and grabbed a washcloth to tidy her face. "I'll call downstairs," he said. "Let's get you dressed."

"Please hurry."

Donny Ray went down and talked to the bellman, then reported back to Cassie. "He's getting you an appointment with a guy up the street."

"Ah," she said weakly. "*Monsieur le Docteur.*"

## CHAPTER THIRTY-THREE

## Baby Needs New Shoes

Cassie leaned on Donny Ray as he escorted her wobbling into Dr. Jules Fortier's medical suite. The physician felt her pulse, listened to her heartbeat, and peered into her eyes. Then he pulled out his earpieces, letting his stethoscope hang from his neck. "First, you need a pregnancy test," he said.

"Why?"

Dr. Fortier put his hands in his lab coat pockets. "Your heartbeat is fast, your face is flushed, you complain of nausea and fatigue, constant urination, and – your eyes glisten. If you are at least three weeks along, the test will show."

He had that wrong, she thought. Glistening eyes meant fever. "I can't be pregnant. It's impossible." She twisted her silver token.

"Ah, mistakes happen," the doctor commented. "Condoms break."

"I've never used one of those in my life," she retorted. "I'm on the Pill."

"Eh, well, it isn't 100-percent effective, you know. Antibiotics, all manner of medications can interfere."

Antibiotics—shit, she thought, horrified. The Piggly Wiggly company doctor had given her antibiotics that would take down an elephant.

The doctor signed orders, and Cassie peed in a cup— that, she knew how to do. She handed it over, returned to the examining room, and dangled her feet off the table.

Shortly thereafter, Dr. Fortier breezed in with congratulatory news. "Hello, young mother."

"What?!" Cassie's jaw dropped, and an electric surge looped around her head. "Are you sure? When am I due?"

"Yes, I'm sure. Probably May or June. You can calculate for yourself, *oui?*"

Cassie dropped her face in her hands. She shouldn't dare wonder if the baby was Chuck's, but images of the *Kama Sutra* and the Moonrider Motel swirled through her mind.

Dr. Fortier quickly steadied her. "One moment while I call your companion."

Sauntering through the door, Donny Ray sidled up to her, eyebrows raised. "And?"

"Donny Ray, I'm pregnant!" Cassie forced a smile as disembodied voices melted in her ears.

"You heard what he said about the airport X-rays?" Donny Ray poked her arm. "The doc said be sure to stay away from them."

"I didn't hear anything after he called me a mother." Nothing made sense.

Stumbling out of the office door, Cassie rubbed her belly as they stepped back into the sunshine. "I sure wasn't expecting this," she gulped.

"Why not?"

"I've never missed a pill—not ever!" Cassie pressed her palms onto the office building's brick façade and touched the brass plate engraved *Docteur en Médecine Interne.*

"Oh Cassie!" He hugged her gently. "Baby makes three."

She brightened. After all, this is what she'd been wanting the whole time, marriage and a baby to stroll in the Marshall Mall. She and Donny Ray would make a home of their own, just as she'd always hoped. But dang, this baby better not come out looking like Chuck.

"When are we getting married?" she studied his shifting eyes. "You better say we are."

"Let's talk about it. Come on baby, I'm with you on this." He rubbed her temples. "You've got to trust me."

At a striped road crossing they stepped down dozens of stone pavers to the banks of the Rhône. Maybe he wouldn't marry her, Cassie fretted. Maybe he thought the baby was Chuck's. She stopped suddenly. "What a sorrowful sin!" she began to wail. "I've slipped up becaue of my ignorance and human weakness!"

"Goddamn it, Cassie, what are you talking about?" Donny Ray jerked his head back.

She sighed the huge sigh of a locomotive braking. When she was young, her daddy took her into railyards to inspect the pulpwood loads, and even into an old roundhouse, where twisted ropes secured machinery gasping with each load. Now here she was—gasping—with her Catholic guilt twisting on a Methodist rope.

## CHAPTER THIRTY-FOUR

## Immigration Man

Donny Ray patted an iron bench with curlicues on the legs and swirly vines on the back. "Sit down here, Cassie. Let's work some things out."

Cassie clutched her sides and rocked. She had to have a husband, and Chuck was out. "Are we getting married?"

His mouth tightened as he brushed hair from his eyes. "Let's wait a little while to decide."

"I can't be an unwed mother," she moaned, with visions of mysterious nurses giving her baby to missionaries in the far-flung Indies.

Donny Ray lit a cigarette and blew the smoke away from her. "Don't rush it. A lot is happening now to decide our future. Jusef is taking the train down today. We're going to talk some business."

"What kind?" Cassie cast her eyes downward, spying a gray pebble. She picked it up, rolling it between her fingers.

"Car parts. I already told you, Jusef wants to expand operations to the States—and Houston has the waterways and infrastructure. Me and him'll be partners."

He patted her cheek. "We'll have plenty of money—better than Torque & Power. You can live nice, never have to work again—just shop and have fun. And don't you want the best for the baby? None of that daycare stuff."

All right, that sounded pretty good to her. It showed he cared. Even if it wasn't his baby, simple finger-counting had introduced the question. So, Donny Ray would raise the child as his own, the same as on *One Life to Live*. Cassie warmed with a new sense of well-being.

"There's only one thing that could mess us up." Donny Ray put his hand on her shoulder.

"What's that?"

"We don't want Jusef getting home with us, and we're making all this money, then boom! Immigration swoops in."

She frowned and continued to rub the pebble. "I thought that was for Mexicans."

"No, these days, it's folks from the Middle East."

"Why?"

"Jimmy Carter's getting nervous on account of Iran—they had a revolution over there, and it's all messed up. There's about 50,000 Iranian students in the U.S., and now they're refugees because they don't want to go home. A lot of people are going to be deported." He squeezed her shoulder. "And Germans, too. Because of East Germany. Communists."

"What does that have to do with anything?"

"Jusef is half Iranian, half German, so it's a double whammy. Americans can tell who the Iranians are, what with those turbans and all, but they can't tell the difference between an East German and a West German. And folks might think Jusef's a Commie."

"Does this have anything to do with us running out of Basel?" Cassie looked hard at him. "Your secret East Germany mission?"

"No, I was kidding you about that. Point is, we need to get Jusef an American wife, on account of he's German and Iranian. Otherwise, we can't return to the States, and if Jusef don't go, I don't go."

Blood pulsed in her ears. "You mean you'd send me home alone?"

"No, you could stay here with us. You speak French, and just about everybody speaks English in Amsterdam."

Cassie closed her eyes and shuddered. Amsterdam.

"Help us out here," he said.

She thought a moment. Maybe one of the grocery cashiers at home would marry Jusef. "Let's say I found somebody for him. Would the marriage be legal?"

He scratched his ear and looked away for a moment. "Sure, the marriage would be fine—but keeping Jusef in the country is different. He can't just come in on a visa and get married for a green card."

"People do it, though." Cassie pitched the pebble and watched it bounce down the path.

"It's visa fraud if you don't do it right. Immigration smells that scam a mile away."

"That's not my problem." She worked her fingers into a church and steeple.

"Listen to yourself—it is your problem." He put his face close to hers. "You're pregnant. You need a husband. So, here's your solution."

True and true. But – "Wait a minute, what?" Cassie's fist came up. "You want *me* to marry Jusef?"

"Hold on, quiet now." He put his hand over hers and held it until she relaxed her fingers. "Hear me out. The baby needs a father, and Jusef needs a wife."

"You are out of your mind!" She rose from the bench, but he grabbed her arm and pulled her back.

"I'll be goddamned!" Donny Ray's nostrils flared. "Here I am, sacrificing my own interests, doing the best I can to make a good life for you and my baby. Think of somebody besides yourself for a change."

How did he always turn things around on her? "So, let me get this straight," she said. "The three of us go back home, and I marry him there?"

"No, no! We'd do common law marriage, starting here—so you'll be married before you go home. That way folks won't talk about you ugly."

She squinted at him. "Common law?"

"You know how that goes, right? It's easy. We could decide right now that we're married, and it would be 100-percent good in Texas if we went back and lived together."

She had trouble believing this. "So, that's all it takes—don't even need a marriage license or a church or anything?"

Donny Ray picked up a couple of pebbles of his own. "Well, you can file something at the courthouse to register the marriage—for legal protection, but you'd already be married, no question."

"If that's the case, I married Mikey Fowler by the Scout hut in the third grade."

"Okay, you're getting technical on me. It's true, you have to act like you're married for about seven years." Donny Ray rubbed his chin. "You know, I think that's the same time it takes to declare somebody dead if they run off."

Cassie's head throbbed, and her voice rose. "So, you can't be common law married until it's been seven years. Then what the hell are you talking about? I ain't putting up with this crap for any seven years."

"Look here, think of it as living in a rear-view mirror. You don't know where you've gone until you already passed it. And the law is, from the time you say you're married, everything from there on is legal marriage—community property, the good stuff, where you get half of everything."

Donny Ray's cigarette, drooping from his mouth, bobbed with every word. "So, see, if you'll agree to marry Jusef now, and say it out loud to each other, you and him'd be common law married before he applied for a green card."

Cassie's head tilted like a pinball machine. Round steel marbles clacked, bells whistled, and lights flashed in her mind.

"No! This baby is yours, and honest to God, if you don't marry me, I'll put your name on the birth certificate anyway and sue your ass. I'll send the law out after you."

A little vein popped out on Donny Ray's neck. "Okay, think about this." His voice went calm but somehow annoyed, each word taut. "You just pretend to marry him now. I mean, you don't have to fuck him or anything."

"Of course I'd have to, you idiot. We'd be sleeping in the same bed!"

Donny Ray shook his head. "Jusef don't want nothing but the green card."

"You're saying he's a homo?"

"I don't know, maybe. I mean, he never came on to me or anything, but I've never seen him out with anybody. He said he was buddies with Freddie Mercury, but he don't say nothing about sex to me. Ever."

Screwing up her mouth, Cassie shook her head. "Great. Just what I want: a man without a dick. All this sex business is what got me into this situation."

"You're making this more complicated than it is."

Cassie blew air into her closed lips and wiggled them before exhaling. "Jusef and I have to be legally married, or we can't get him a green card, right?"

"Uh, yeah."

"Then there's no pretending about it! For the plan to work, I'll have to marry the bozo." She tugged on Donny Ray's beard. "I'm not getting caught up in visa fraud. Anyway, Jusef could always bail, and then where would I be?"

She had heard plenty about unmarried mothers. The father runs off and doesn't pay child support, and everybody gets tied up with social workers and juvenile court. And after all that, the single mom works two jobs and leaves her baby in daycare, where impetigo and head lice run rampant. She was not having it.

"Jusef can fend for himself." Her voice escalated. "I don't want some crackass, green card, visa fraud bullshit. I want to marry a regular American citizen who'll honor court orders and show up for PTA meetings. I want a legal hold."

"Don't get hysterical. Good God." He frowned and put his arm over the back of the bench.

Cassie brought her left leg up and rested her foot on the seat, hugging her knee and watching the river. "Damn." She spilled tears down her pants.

Donny Ray fell silent for a moment. "I promise you, Cassie, someday we'll do a real ceremony, you and me and a priest." He threw a pebble, and they watched it bounce down to the riverbank.

"So, what's your answer?"

"I don't have one. This would be like a Third World marriage, where the girl has to marry a creepy rum-dum she's never even met."

"You're not a child bride, and Jusef ain't a creep. What's wrong with you?"

"I just... I just..." Her heart fluttered as she watched him. She didn't want to end up the way her mother finished, crazy and desperate, a bullet in her head. "All right, maybe I'll make a deal with you. One condition."

"Which is?"

"You and me, only us, we decide right now that we're married, like what you said a little while ago. And it would be good in Texas if we went back and lived together."

"But that would be bigamy if you carried things through with Jusef."

"Now you're worried about legalities? I'm telling you what, Donny Ray, I want to see your name in two places: on a marriage license and a birth certificate. You make a baby, you support it. You don't run off or weasel out, you got me?" She crossed her arms and settled back on the bench.

He cleared his throat. "But you are saying that you'll hold yourself out as Jusef's wife—and tell everybody the baby's his." A frown crossed his brow. "I mean, to get us going."

"I have to think about it. I'm not letting you out of this."

"Oh yeah, underestimate me, that's great." He took a final drag on his cigarette, flicked it onto the ground, and crushed it under his shoe. "And, uh, keep it secret about the immigration thing."

Cassie met his glower.

"You can keep a secret, can't you, Cassie?"

"Damn straight I can."

## CHAPTER THIRTY-FIVE

## Paging Dr. Zhivago!

Lounging on a striped sofa, Jusef looked up when Donny Ray and Cassie entered the hotel suite. His dark hair was tousled, and a thick mustache tickled his upper lip but it didn't obscure his wide smile and straight bright teeth. He clicked off the TV remote and rose to meet them. A room key dangled from his fingers. "The manager said to let myself in," he said.

Donny Ray reddened. "Sure. You're the one paying the bill, right?"

"You must be Cassie," Jusef met her eyes.

"Oh my, you're Dr. Zhivago!" Cassie gave him her hand. He kissed it with a tender caress to her knuckles.

"Hey baby, this is Jusef," Donny Ray pulled his mouth. "And he's no doctor. Don't embarrass yourself," he muttered.

"Not at all," Jusef said. "She means Omar Sharif, the actor. She compliments me." Jusef raised his chin.

Turning to Donny Ray, she pinched her lips together. "Don't you remember the *Dr. Zhivago* movie?"

"That one got past me."

"You took me to see it."

"Must have been the drive-in."

"Never mind," Cassie turned back to Jusef, relaxed her stance, and touched her hair. "Nice to meet you." Sure was! His right eyebrow wasn't exactly straight with the left one, but he was beautiful, especially with the crease in his chin.

"So, is anyone for an early dinner?" Jusef gestured with open palms.

Cassie's interest accelerated. "Sure, I'd like that," she said. And wouldn't she just, she thought.

Donny Ray wrinkled his forehead and looked from her to Jusef. "We didn't bring the right clothes. Not for dinner."

"Raymond, it's a weeknight." Jusef turned to Cassie. "More casual. Anyway, there's an informal bistro on the $2^{nd}$ floor. Old country food. Wear what you have. They'll be delighted to see us."

"Hold on," she said, "I'll be right back."

She changed into fresh denim jeans and a long-sleeved purple T-shirt, accessorizing with a gold-filled disco medallion. She had to dress for success. Jusef might make a good husband. There's nothing sinful about an arranged marriage, she thought. Whole countries do it that way. Her mother always said being in love was the worst possible reason for marrying somebody. You had to move beyond personal feelings for the best candidate. Just look what happened to Romeo and Juliet for not thinking straight.

The potato gratin and cassoulet melted in her mouth, reminding her of the country-style meal she had in Nancy. But Cassie's appetite was all about Jusef in his leather bomber jacket and turtleneck sweater. During the conversation, he looked at her intently, angling his head a bit, smiling at her every word, as though he found her fascinating. For her part, she imagined making love to this dreamboat and calling him "dear" at the dry cleaners on Saturdays.

This arranged marriage might be just what she needed. Unless Jusef was merely acting, he liked women fine. They would be a power couple in Houston and occasionally visit friends in Marshall to give them a thrill. She'd develop an accent to match his—and they'd be overheard at cocktail parties, conversing in French about art nouveau. The word would get out about her killer-handsome husband, and she'd get revenge on Sheree and Chuck.

Jusef signaled for coffee and dessert. So worldly, he knew something about everything—especially politics and power. He drew her into the conversation talking about Lufthansa Flight 181, which had been hijacked by Palestinians to force the release of certain Germans locked up in Stammheim Prison. "Only two years ago, you remember? German Autumn, they called it."

Now wait a minute. She'd heard of that, probably when flipping through newspaper articles, looking for commodity reports like her daddy taught her.

There'd been a big to-do about terrorists killing rich money types, and something about bad guys pushing a baby carriage across the road to make the cars stop before they sprayed them with gunfire. She definitely remembered the baby carriage part, but not much else. Headline news in 1977 wasn't on her mind at the time.

On impulse, Cassie feigned cluelessness to get Jusef talking, maybe gain more insight into this guy. She wanted to keep some cards up her sleeve, just in case. She shook her head and spooned *crème brulee*. "Why were they in prison?"

"Why are you even bringing that up?" Donny Ray cleared his throat. "It's not good dinner talk."

"I suggest Cassie wants to have a more informed view—if we are to enjoy each other's company, don't you agree?" Jusef turned to her.

"Sure." Cassie noted a stare-down between the two men. She found it unsettling. Donny Ray turned the subject to car parts and catalytic converters.

"They're full of platinum," he said. "Expensive as hell."

She'd heard about platinum jewelry and asked why it cost so much.

"It's dense," Donny Ray explained. "And rare. Used to be, American cars just powered up the exhaust and that's it. Now the law says you've got to have emission controls. And it's jacking up the price of cars. That's where we come in—after-market components."

Jusef called for the check. "I don't think she's interested in car parts."

"I'm really not." Cassie struggled to her feet. She'd have to take a little rest upstairs before going out on the town. Jusef had rented a super great BMW, and she was eager for a splendid ride through Lyon.

Once inside the suite, Donny Ray escorted Cassie to their bedroom—all swank and extravagant, thanks to Jusef. If she married him, she'd never need another travelers' check. Maybe Donny Ray had a fine idea about a husband for her after all, she thought.

"You've had a busy afternoon." With his arm around her, Donny Ray walked her to the bed, drew the covers, and flipped the control switches on a bedside radio. Violin strains wafted softly through the room.

Jusef appeared in the doorway. "Sleep well." He blew her a kiss. The men closed the door without a sound.

The hinges must be well-greased, she thought. She fluffed pillows and turned on her side. Jusef appeared gentle, and he had nice manners. He smelled good, too, and his hands were firm. No calluses. Clean fingernails. No sign of pulling engine blocks.

"Come with me to the Casbah," she murmured.

She sat up on her elbows. She could be the wife he wanted, she thought. She'd have to get past his peculiar ways—such as praising terrorists—but they could agree to disagree. Marry up, her mother had said, never down. And don't forget to put on a little lipstick.

## Lock and the Box

Mission almost accomplished.

Donny Ray dropped down on the sofa and propped his feet on the coffee table. "Take a load off, Jusef."

Smoothing his mustache, Jusef remained standing, arms folded. A deep frown wrinkled his forehead, his eyebrows knitting in the middle. "You managed to bollix things in Basel," he growled.

"Well, shit." Donny Ray had thought everything was cool. "I told you already, a poker game went south on me." He clicked the lighter and sucked on tobacco smoke. "Cops crawling all over the place. What was I supposed to do?"

"Not panic." Jusef glowered and parked his butt on an overstuffed chair. "And I told you to abandon the van. Instead, you drive it to France—fucking France!"

"That's where Cassie wanted to go."

Jusef sat forward and tapped his knuckles on the table. "That's an explanation. Not an excuse."

"You've made your point," Donny Ray said, rubbing his neck, avoiding Jusef's gaze. "At least I got us some French license plates."

"Did you now?" Jusef's face looked blank but for a twisted half smile.

Donny Ray reached for a lukewarm Coke on the table. He'd forgotten to call Jusef in Basel, big deal, he thought. Wasn't the telegram enough? Anyway, that was a long time ago in human crisis years. Better move to a tame topic. "So, what do you think of Cassie?"

"In truth, I resent your interrupting the conversation about the hijacked flight. Remember, we want to establish loyalty, pull her in. It's a process," Jusef narrowed his eyes. "And she's beautiful. I made it clear we wanted someone needy."

"Oh, she's needy now." Donny Ray patted his stomach. "She's pregnant!"

Jusef raised an eyebrow, weighing the news. "Indeed? I must think about that."

"Don't you see, that seals the deal. It's cool, right?" Donny Ray's confidence waned.

"Later." Jusef tapped his pocket. "We must return to Basel anyway. I bought diamonds in Antwerp. Drop them in the lockbox. Split the cash. Buy gold," he said.

Donny Ray pushed up his sleeves. "I only want cash."

"No. You want bullion bars. And Krugerrands. Keep them in the box with mine. This year, up-up-up, gold almost doubled value."

"But I'd have to come back for it. Ain't doing that."

"If you bring more than $10,000 cash through customs, the spotlight's on you, mate. Too risky." Jusef pressed his lips. "Put some cash into a savings account. Big banking in Texas, yes? Therefore, you get money wired in from Switzerland."

"Then I want my own secret bank account. Numbered, no name."

"You think anybody can walk into a Swiss bank and get such an account?" Jusef grinned.

"You've got one."

Jusef laughed, a broad hearty guffaw. "Ah, but much red tape. Only for established customers—which you are not. Unless you get a Swiss agent to represent you—which you cannot. But you may use my lockbox. Together we have the only two keys."

Donny Ray thought about the key nestled snugly in Cassie's duffel bag. "If I've got one, and you've got one, how did those Basel guys get that cash into there?"

"Third party exchange. I put it in."

Resentment and fear roiled Donny Ray's insides. "Then why the hell did you cancel on me? We could've gotten all the

Basel business done that day. This is the most screwed-up, crying-ass shit I ever heard."

"Don't be ridiculous. Think: they could have given you a dummy key. I had to keep eyes on them—and you. Anyway, transactions must be fragmented for security. It took all afternoon. And then a diamond exchange elsewhere. You think this is my only operation?"

Donny Ray's voice shook with anger. "But now you want me to share a lockbox with you, all my gold and cash stuffed in there with yours. Shithead!"

"Ah, settle down. You'll wake Cassie." Jusef's foot jiggled. "It's your buy-in. Your equity. The partnership must have a protected source of funds. Yours, mine, ours."

Donny Ray squinched his eyes, clenching his fists. "No way. I took all the risk, and I ain't giving you none of mine. Any kind of partnership funds go into Houston. I'm not leaving my money in Switzerland for you and your buddies to get into."

"Oh, well, you drive a hard bargain." Jusef's face betrayed genuine amusement. "All right, you keep half. But you still won't qualify for the unnumbered account. I'll help you get a private box, though. Simple." He laughed.

"It better be." He figured Jusef wanted that anyway.

"Your mail." Jusef pointed to a leather pouch on the dining table. "Not much."

A shrill jangle pierced the room. Donny Ray leaped up from the sofa and grabbed the phone on the third ring. Jusef stood and followed him, eyes narrowed, watching.

"Hello?" Silence. "Who is this?" Donny Ray shrugged.

The telephone operator's voice, clipped and cool, replied, "Call for Mr. Ahmadi from Mr. Aldo."

"Ahmadi?" Donny Ray repeated.

Jusef made a slicing motion across his neck. Donny Ray slammed down the receiver.

"Let's go," Jusef said. *"Now."*

Donny Ray darted into the bedroom and picked up Cassie's duffel bag from the floor. His hands trembling, he extracted the bank box key from its canvas nook. Turning fast, he stumbled slightly and palmed the bed to regain his balance. Cassie's head rose from the pillow.

"What's happening?" she mumbled.

"Change of plans—me and Jusef got to go somewhere. Be back tomorrow."

"Okay."

"You heard me?"

"Mm-hmmm."

"Good."

He shut the door and waved the key.

An hour out of Lyon, the shock of "Mr. Ahmadi's" call had not abated. It suggested a concerning gap in security, and Jusef's reaction hadn't helped. Donny Ray was more rattled than ever despite Jusef's explanation about obsolete RAF emergency warnings.

"You didn't get a call until I showed up," Jusef said. "They are looking for me, not you. But there's always the risk of collateral damage."

Steering the BMW through a mountain fog, Jusef appeared tense, frowning and fidgeting with the radio. "The caller had to know I was in your room or nearby, somehow connected with you. I must find out who knows my business. You haven't revealed your location?"

"No—of course not." Donny Ray felt hot under the collar. Annette had glanced at the telegram, but surely, she didn't have time to read it. Cassie got only a glance at it too, and he'd watched her the whole time in the hotel.

"When we finish in Basel," Jusef said, "I'll take the train north. You drive the car back to Lyon. Turn it in with keys, no problem. You have French license plates for the van? So, you did something right. Nobody will notice the old Volkswagen on rural roads. You need to leave the hotel ASAP."

"Cassie's going to blow up."

"Then make her think we're doing her a favor—move to a château in the Loire Valley. I'll take care of details. Be ready."

"How about Monaco instead?" Donny Ray lit a cigarette and lowered the window to exhale the smoke.

Jusef shot him a glare. "No gambling. Not after Basel. Anyway, money makes money with Escobar. And it gets better down the line." He said plans were sketchy, but they might also get involved with cells to burrow into the social fabric.

"We integrate the ordinary, blend in, and when the time is right, we strike. Sell our services to the highest bidder. No politics, no loyalties."

Donny Ray relished that idea. It rang of men's adventure magazines. His face relaxed, humming as Lake Geneva came into view. "Oh, say, did you bring the mail?"

"Damn," Jusef snapped his fingers.

## CHAPTER THIRTY-SIX

### Black Velvet Chances

Cassie awoke to a dark room with a surreal green light on the radio dial. Her heart beat fast. She called Donny Ray's name, but he didn't answer.

Was this another poker fiasco? she wondered. She switched on the bedside lamp and thought hard. She remembered he told her he was going somewhere, and Jusef blew a kiss, but otherwise, her memory was blank.

She rose from the bed, clutching her arms against the chill, and retrieved her rumpled jacket. She went through the suite, turning on lights, checking the doors. Hunger pangs gnawed. She couldn't call room service at that hour.

Cassie grabbed a bag of potato chips from the table. Those would do. Crumbs spilled as she contemplated her situation. When her daddy died, she got government benefit checks until she was 18, just for being his kid. Birth certificate, death certificate, and presto, Cassie was set. There had to be more to it than that, though.

Glancing at the clock, she figured it was almost midnight in Marshall. She would try again to call Beecher—he knew everything about those checks.

Things had looked good with Jusef last night, but anxiety set in. She doubted that she could commit to a half-Iranian character with "open sesame" mystics and veiled dancers. Maybe there were worse things than being unmarried with a baby. She should go home. She wanted Beecher to get her money from the closet and wire it in here. Their room was paid for several days—there would be time.

She rang up the hotel operator.

"Uh, can you get me a line to the States?" Cassie had a whole new skill set with the communications deal.

"With pleasure, *Mademoiselle*." The operator had a sweet voice. "You are third in the queue. Please hang up and stay by the telephone."

This was so much better than waiting in a phone booth, she thought, rifling through her duffel bag for the crumpled *Back to Godhead* magazine. It seemed a lifetime ago that she'd met those guys at the airport. She settled on the sofa to take another look.

Leafing through the pages, she recognized her handwriting: Rasonnati. Oh, yeah, the Krishna gal. From the transcendental plane. Cassie drew her legs under her to quiet her stomach as she reconsidered the articles and rattled crumbs out of the chip bag. Hunger made her edgy.

With a soft whizz, a folded newspaper slid underneath her hotel door. She put aside the magazine and retrieved the paper, placing it on the dining table. She stood tall, unfolding each section with a touch of ceremony, when a leather pouch on the table caught her eye. Picking it up, she studied the stitching, rubbing her fingers over hand-tooled shapes. She would rifle through it, she decided. Pregnant ladies had a right to know everybody's business.

Looked like a lot of nothing until a striped airmail envelope fell out—a letter from Sheree to Donny Ray! Written in blue ballpoint, Via Air Mail, to a post office box in Amstelveen? Cassie never knew that address, and the letter had been postmarked last month. Her breath rasping, she glared at the envelope and shifted her feet.

"Get thee behind me, Satan," she mumbled, letting Satan grip the envelope, pry open the corner, and break the seal in tiny motions to keep it from tearing. She removed a single sheet of paper, threw the envelope on the table, and focused.

*"Donny Ray, You sorry piece of shit. You left me hanging. You knew good and well I had to get rid of "our" little problem, not that you ever cared. Some nerve you've got, wanting me to come over there. When you get back, my boyfriend will kick your ass. —Sheree"*

Get rid of what little problem? Holy cow, did Sheree have an abortion? Cassie read the letter again, but the words didn't change. Donny Ray and Sheree, she thought, damn them to hell.

Molten lava coursed through Cassie's insides and lit her head on fire. She turned circles, round and round until she got dizzy, and then she plopped, dropped, sank to the floor, and cried. After she wore herself out, she reread the letter. He'd tried to get Sheree over there before he ever asked her. What a rat! She never wanted to see him, ever again, in her entire life.

Stop, she told herself. Get organized. She couldn't let him know she'd seen the letter; he'd realize she'd been meddling in his things. She crumpled it into the empty chip package and stuffed it in the trashcan. This wasn't just about her anymore. It was about her baby, too. Jusef and Donny Ray were a tag team; she shouldn't cut off ties with either of them. Not yet. She had to get home first. Her eyes moved left and right as her brain shifted gears.

Slumping in her chair, she twirled the silver token and began to relax as daylight sneaked under the drapes. The phone rang. She jumped. "Yes?"

"The line is open. Please stand by."

Breathless, Cassie counted the rings. One, two, three, four... twenty. The operator came back on the line.

"*Mademoiselle*, we do have a time limit. I must disconnect you."

Panic clutched Cassie's throat by the silver chain. "Can't we keep trying?"

"I am so sorry, *Mademoiselle*, there are others ahead of you now."

"But it didn't take that long to get through."

"You were lucky before 7:00 a.m. By mid-morning, European business takes the lines, and in early afternoon New York is awake. You must try again later. *Je regrette*."

### Basel Business

Donny Ray and Jusef entered a brass-bound vault of safe-deposit boxes. A gloved attendant carried Jusef's lockbox into a private room and closed a heavy door on the confidential transaction. The box was modest in size, and with some trepidation, Donny Ray watched Jusef lift the lid.

"Five hundred thousand dollars," Jusef said. "I have already verified."

They removed the half-inch stacks of one-hundred-dollar bills, flipping them carefully. "Ten thousand dollars in each stack," he said. "Twenty-five stacks apiece." They shuffled the stacks like playing cards and packed their currency into separate briefcases.

"Now downstairs, we make deposits, buy bullion, and..." Jusef removed a black velvet pouch from his inside pocket and dangled it in front of Donny Ray's eyes. "A game of chance? Fifty thousand dollars for double or nothing."

"You got diamonds in there?"

"Maybe." Jusef grinned.

"Well, let me feel." Donny Ray reached for the pouch, but Jusef pulled it away.

"It's not a gamble if you touch."

Crap, Jusef was playing him. Donny Ray's heart raced. Sweat beaded his forehead. Yet, for all he knew, the pouch held a few lousy ball bearings that Jusef always talked about. It felt like *The Price is Right.* He could either score big or get the booby prize behind Door #3.

"If there's good shit in there," Donny Ray said, "why would you let go of it?"

Jusef shrugged. "You're fun to watch when you're craving—forget about Monte Carlo. And even supposing they're diamonds, one way or another, I'll get them back."

"I don't know…"

"Yes or no? Pressure on, Raymond!" Jusef looked at his watch and grinned. "Thirty seconds, and…"

~~~

Downstairs, Donny Ray rented a lockbox, disappointed that it wasn't a numbered account. Even so, Jusef explained, banking privacy laws were sufficient to conceal holdings from prying eyes.

"Anyway, this is hardly enough to interest anyone besides you."

Outside of the bank, Donny Ray grinned and folded a thin stack of pink receipts. The smooth feel of the coins and heavy metal bars had given him a rush—all packed into his lockbox with the velvet pouch and the second key. He wouldn't risk carrying both keys on him. If he lost the first one, they could simply drill into the box—way cheaper with fewer repercussions.

Donny Ray had also opened a regular savings account into which he deposited cash for wiring home and to pay for the box rental on an annual basis. He kept some gold coins and sufficient francs for travel management.

Now behind the wheel of the rented BMW, he checked for oncoming traffic and pulled out of the parking lane on Freie Strasse. He glanced at Jusef. "Train station?"

"Right." Jusef checked his watch and scribbled marks on a leather-bound portfolio.

"And you want me and Cassie going where?"

"Saint-Étienne is good. For now, return to Lyon, and I'll call you with instructions. Then, once you're comfortable in the château, we can resume the Cassie romance and make the green card happen."

"Sure." Donny Ray adjusted his sunglasses, eyeing the bank in the rear-view mirror.

He wasn't a giddy kind of guy, but this was out of sight. Jusef doubled down on the bet. Heightened the tension—what gambling's all about. And then the sweet payoff. He couldn't risk smuggling anything into the States this go-around, though. He'd come back for them—and Brigitta. She hadn't seen the last of him, not yet. Now, with everything in order and Krugerrands jingling in his pocket, he wanted more.

## CHAPTER THIRTY-SEVEN

## Caught Together, Hanged Together

Room service arrived with beignets, cappuccino, sliced fruit, and a cheese omelet Cassie devoured every bite—eating for two, though now she felt sluggish and settled back on the sofa to watch morning TV, such as it was.

Dang, Benito Mussolini's widow Rachele had just died; lots of news coverage on that. She watched with interest. His widow had tolerated a lot about her husband's politics and his mistress. They were hanged together, but Mrs. Mussolini always honored the Italian dictator's memory and kept things together for the children until the end of her days. She'd even gotten part of the old boy's brain returned to her from the U.S. People admired that about her.

It occurred to Cassie that if Rachele Mussolini could always love Benito—hanging upside down dead with his mistress—then Della could have always loved Johnny Frank. Maybe a man really could love his children and different women at the same time.

Cassie found it odd that Mussolini would inspire her to have a more favorable disposition toward Johnny Frank. She needed to talk to Çois about it—to connect with him, let him know about the jam she was in. She reached for the phone and asked the operator to connect her.

The call rang through. An unfamiliar voice answered.

"*Bonjour. Camping,*" a woman with a lilting, musical voice responded.

"This is Cassie Tate. Uh... *puis-je parler avec Çois?*"

"Not here. *Désolé.*"

Cassie hesitated. "I have a question for him."

"Oh!" The woman's voice rose. She identified herself as Çois' wife Michaëlle. They exchanged quick hellos. She said Çois had gone for the day, out of town, but he left a note in case Cassie called.

Reaching for a pen and paper, Cassie poised to write the message details. She glanced at the doorway. Donny Ray better not come barging in. "What's it say?"

Papers rustled in the background, and Michaëlle read aloud. "Found your plates. We need to talk."

"He found my plates?" Cassie stiffened, confused.

"*Oui.*"

She twanged the telephone cord. "Anything else?"

"No, but Çois does want to talk to you. Very exciting, our new family."

"Yes, very much so." Our new family? This would take a lot of getting used to. It's far from the *The Brady Bunch*. "Please ask him to call me at the Sofitel-Bellecour as soon as possible."

"Yes, very good." A child cried in the background. "Oh, I must go," Michaëlle said. "Thank you."

Aw rats, she hung up the phone before Cassie could finish telling the information, but she supposed Çois could find the hotel number anyway after being a cop in town. Even so, she was frustrated. Çois' message didn't make sense, and she couldn't get an overseas phone line to Beecher. She dialed the front desk.

"What's the fastest way to get a message to Texas? In the United States." Cassie blinked. She felt funny saying that—she'd never thought of the U.S. as a foreign country before.

"Cablegram is fastest," said the clerk. "Is 125 francs to send, plus one franc per word. Cheaper at post office, but–"

"Thanks, I'll be right down." Cassie grabbed her traveler's checks and rushed to the lobby, where the clerk handed her a form to fill out. She said she was staying in a sixth floor suite and was expecting a call she didn't want to miss.

"Beecher," she wrote. "Pregnant. Need money wired. Call you later. Cassie."

"Here you go," she said, handing over the form and payment. As the clerk made change, Cassie jumped at a tap on her arm.

"You have a phone call," the concierge said.

Her hopes rose.

"You take it in the private booth, you see?" The man pointed. "House phone. *Troisième cabine.*"

"Oh, that's great. *Merci!*" She crossed the lobby to fancy wood and glass phone cabins with marble-topped writing tables. She entered the third cabin, sat in a plush chair, and grabbed the clunky phone as soon as it rang.

"*Allô, Cassie!*" Çois's voice sounded better to her than Johnny Hallyday's.

Her heart pounded. "You got my message?" She ran a finger along the edge of the upholstered chair; the textured pile rose and fell at her touch.

"Yes. Michaëlle told me. So, uh, I have your license plates. I found them in the Gypsy camp."

"But we've got license plates." Cassie shifted in the chair. "How could we be on the road without them?"

"The Gypsies said you have theirs."

She rubbed her pants. "Why would they want ours?"

"Useful currency."

So, for whatever reason, Donny Ray buddied up with the Gypsies to exchange license plates, and now, she had a gnawing fear that his green card project could be part of a criminal enterprise. She thought back to Jusef's interest in terrorists.

"Cassie, are you there?" Çois asked.

"Yes, sorry. I don't know what to do—I'm pregnant! And I'm almost afraid of Donny Ray now."

"What?" Çois' voice rose. "I work today in Besançon, so I cannot pick you up in Lyon. Take the train to Ambronay. Someone will get you there."

She clutched, still confused by a week's worth of trauma and crackpot announcements. If she simply up and left, Donny Ray would pitch a fit. But she'd probably be in Ambronay by the time he got back to the hotel. Çois could put her on the plane for home.

"Okay, I'll do it," she said, her voice quavering. "Just as you said. And Çois, I need you to call Beecher for me."

"*Certainement.*"

"You've got the number, right? Tell him I'm okay. I'm coming home. I'll call him."

Disconnecting the line, Cassie twirled her hair into a topknot and let it fall. She exited the booth and asked the hotel concierge about trains to Ambronay.

"Yes, schedule here." The concierge examined it. "You have missed the morning trains."

The next train didn't leave Lyon until 5:30 p.m. She had to gather her things and go straight to the railroad depot anyway. She couldn't risk Donny Ray catching her here.

## CHAPTER THIRTY-EIGHT

## Paper Tiger

Fingering her room key, Cassie watched the elevator floor needle moving down and around like a wall clock on the fritz. A hand gripped her shoulder and she jumped. "Donny Ray! Where've you been?" She played it as though she were glad to see him, hugging him and patting his back.

"I told you last night I had to take care of some business. And guess what," he whispered, "we're going to move into something extra lavish down the road."

"Now what?"

"Shhh, I'll tell you upstairs."

As they stumbled into the suite, she wondered how Mrs. Mussolini would have reacted. Cassie's fury had played out on the Sheree letter, but her head still felt like someone was pounding carpet tacks into her skull. Her cablegram to Beecher was hours away from delivery, and she couldn't be sure Çois would call him or when.

Donny Ray tossed folded papers onto the dining table, littered with snack wrappers and hotel receipts. He twirled his keys. "Let's pack up and get out of here."

She did a double take. "Now?"

"Yeah, Lyon is a big lot of nothing. We're moving on to Saint-Étienne. Jusef will meet us at a château there, plus, *plus*, they've got Roman ruins."

"So what? I don't want to leave!" Cassie's nerves fired electric bolts in her brain. She had to stall him. "Anyway, God knows you need a bath. I'm not going anywhere with you stinking to high heaven."

"What the fuck?" He sniffed his armpits, stalked out, and slammed the bathroom door. The shower soon cranked up, and water thundered through the pipes.

A swell of anxiety overwhelmed Cassie like a Six Flags ride of rings and corkscrews. Your stomach sinks, your stomach jumps, and your brain yells, "Get me off this thing!" There was still time to run out on him—she estimated three to four minutes. She'd risk it.

Spotting her passport on the table, she grabbed it along with her wallet and backpack. Money, she needed more money. Cassie sifted through Donny Ray's clutter and keys, then noted a small white envelope stamped Credit Suisse.

Unsnapping the closure and squeezing the envelope, she stuck her fingers in and gripped cool metal. Out fell a brass key. In the light through the curtains, she read the engraving: Credit Suisse. No mistake.

She compared it with her hotel room key—different cuttings but the same style, resembling skeleton keys with solid shanks and bits. What was Donny Ray doing with a Swiss bank key? She unfolded a set of pink papers, all carbon copies, with the bank logo printed at the tops of those, too.

Donny Ray was up to something, but Cassie had no time to wonder what. She switched her hotel room key for his lookalike bank key and stuck it back with his other stuff. Then she tossed the real bank key into her backpack, pulled a Credit Suisse page from the pink papers, and crammed it into her jeans pocket. Eventually, these could be her child support. Now to get the duffel bag and...

"Housekeeping!" A woman's voice called through the door with a series of knocks.

"Come on in!" Cassie yanked open the door and swept her hand in a welcoming gesture as a uniformed older lady wheeled in a cleaning cart.

Cassie dashed back to the bedroom to get her duffel. Suddenly the water stopped, and Donny Ray opened the bathroom door. "You coming in or what?"

She knew she was busted. She'd gotten his bank key.

"Yeah, wait a minute—I need to get something." She returned to the dining table to clutter it the same as before. On the other side of the room, the lady emptied the wastebasket into her cart and started wiping down counters.

Donny Ray's voice moved closer. "Leave my shit alone!" He stepped into the living area wearing a white terrycloth hotel bathrobe. Little gold embroidery threads and a crest glistened from the pocket.

"Sorry, *Monsieur*." The housekeeper blushed and stopped wiping.

"Not you!" Donny Ray pointed at Cassie. "Her."

"Excuse me. I'm trying to organize." Cassie made big gestures to hide her shaking hands. She held open Donny Ray's leather pouch and raked in the receipts, then slammed it down on the table.

He told the housekeeper to go. "Just leave. Thanks." Then he turned to Cassie. "What the hell is going on here?"

Cassie threw her shoulders back. "I'm not leaving."

"Don't tell me no." Donny Ray lit a cigarette.

"Too bad—that's what I'm saying. And you can put that in your Gauloise and smoke it. I'm staying here."

"And do what?"

"Go back to Ambronay. Çois's going to pick me up from the train."

"You're out of your mind!" Donny Ray pressed the heels of his hands into her temples. She jerked away.

"I can't let you do that," he said. "I won't. He's a pimp, and that old broad Annette, they'd sell you out."

"No, they wouldn't." Her cheeks burned hot. "He really is my half-brother."

"If you want to see him that bad, buy your own plane ticket and come back over here. But I'm not letting you out of my sight."

"Çois is expecting me."

"I don't give a shit."

"Then I need to call and cancel."

The phone rang with a terrible urgency. Donny Ray rushed to it. With a clutch in her throat, Cassie watched the red blinking light.

"Jusef? Hey man, did you fix-," Donny Ray started. His voice changed tone. "I get it." He ran his hands through his hair. "Yeah, yeah." After a short pause, he hung up the phone and turned to her. "Forget Saint-Étienne. We're going back to Amsterdam. Aldo was murdered."

"Who's Aldo?"

"An old man." Donny Ray paced, shaking his head. "He knew the wrong people."

"He was old! He probably knew lots of people."

"Don't argue."

"This again?" Cassie crumpled on the chaise and kneaded the back of her neck. She didn't believe Çois was a pimp, but a hundred violent scenarios played out on the movie spool between her ears. Maybe she'd told him too much after all. Beecher had warned her about foreigners and scams, and if she stayed with Donny Ray, he would get her home and support the baby. Later she could call off the Jusef thing, and the green card would be his problem.

"Hurry it up." Donny Ray grabbed the pouch and luggage, and they went bumping out the door, knocking chairs as they left.

In the lobby Donny Ray returned his room key to the desk clerk. "Where's yours?"

Cassie shrugged. "I must've left it upstairs. Want me to go see?"

"Aw hell, that maid might have picked it up already, and we ain't got time to screw around."

"I have to pee again."

He rolled his eyes. "Do it now, because we're not stopping for a long time."

Cassie walked quickly across the lobby, squeezed into a restroom stall, and pulled the pink receipt from her pocket. She sat on the toilet and read: Credit Suisse Bank, Hauptstrasse 49, Basel Switzerland, followed by a long telephone number.

She recognized the trademark loopy loops on Donny Ray's signature. Her heart raced. So, that's where he went last night. He got money from the Swiss bank. Maybe he paid off the poker thugs. There must be something left in that lockbox, she reasoned, or he wouldn't have kept the paperwork. She wound the pink receipt around the key and zipped it into an inside pocket.

She was tired of all this negativity with Jusef and their shadowy associates. The only murders she'd ever heard about at home involved whiskey and drug deals gone wrong. And the undertaker's son killed a couple of whores, hiding the bodies in other people's coffins.

"Cassie! Did you fall in the crapper?" Donny Ray's voice boomed through the washroom.

She jumped up, flushed the toilet, and sat back down. "Can't hear you!"

## CHAPTER THIRTY-NINE

## Ramping Up

Cassie sucked a breath mint as the hotel valet helped her into the van. All this drama, and ten-to-one the baby was Chuck's anyway, she thought.

"I've got the bags. *Merci.* Don't need any help here, thanks." Donny Ray nodded at the valet and climbed into the driver's seat.

"Okay, map girl, you ready?" He pulled the vehicle into the roadway.

"I guess. What's the plan?"

"Back to Amsterdam via Belgium and Luxembourg." He tapped his finger on the map. "See there?"

Cassie studied the map and drew her finger along the route. "Okay." She pointed. "We take that ramp." She folded the map in half. "Merge onto A6 for Mâcon. Hey, that reminds me of Macon, Georgia. You know, that's where the Allman Brothers band is from."

"Sure." He reached for his pack of cigarettes tucked into the sun visor. "But we ain't going there. We're going to Dijon. Don't get us all messed up."

"No, wait, what's–uh–no, it's still the A6."

"Damn it!" Donny Ray crossed several lanes of traffic with horns honking and fists pumping at him. "Pay attention. It's a map, not a rocket plan. Jesus."

"You want a co-pilot or not?" Cassie stuck out her chin. "You can pull on over and check the map yourself, then."

Donny Ray glared at the traffic, then at her. "What were all those charges on the phone bill?"

"What charges?" She combed her hand through her hair and wound a little pin curl.

"You call Beecher?"

"Yeah, but he didn't answer. There wasn't a charge for that, was it?" She stared straight ahead.

"Sure as shit was. Operator time ain't free. Neither are the lines. What were you going to tell him?"

"Nothing! I'm homesick, all right? I know you don't ever miss anybody, but I sure as hell do." She gathered her hair in a fat hank and let it fall down her back.

"You called Çois, too. I can't believe you let him con you." Donny Ray modulated his voice to a robot's calm. "So, I guess he knows we were at that hotel."

"It wasn't any big secret. Cool your jets." Cassie stroked her chin and pointed to a map symbol. "Okay, see it's this way—exit Dijon-Université. They have food places around there, shows them on the map. And I've got to pee again."

"We got to make this quick. First place we see."

"Over to your right, see there, it's a petrol station, has a little café."

Cassie caught herself saying "petrol station" with pride. That was the mark of European sophistication—like saying "the States" instead of "the U.S."

Donny Ray turned into the parking lot and pulled up to a pump. "We're almost out of fuel anyway." He dug in his pocket for some cash. "Where's my money?" His eyes widened. "Oh, wait. I left it on the table at the hotel. You got it, right?"

"I don't know. You wanted to hurry up and leave." She reached around the seat and pulled out the pouch. "Everything is in here."

Relief crossed his face. "Great. Give it here."

He rifled through the contents and held up a packet of francs, secured with a silver money clip. *"Wunderbar."* He opened the door and started to get out, but he stopped. "Let me see this bag again."

He stuck his hand into the sack, and paper receipts crinkled with junk mail. He brought out a fist full of litter and threw it on the seat. He looked through the pouch again, held it to the light, and stirred the contents. "Was there anything else on the table?" He stared intently at Cassie.

She shrugged one shoulder and reached for her backpack. She talked into the open flap so he couldn't read her face. "Not that I know of. The maid was in there, you know, maybe she got something by accident." Good thing she got Sheree's letter, anyway.

"Goddamn it!"

"Are you missing something?"

When a horn honked behind them, he jumped out of the van to fill the tank. Cassie jumped out too, waving as she ran inside the service station. She mimed to the clerk, pointed to the women's restroom door, and hurried inside.

"Phew," she held her nose. Stuffy and bad fumes in there. She pulled out the Bobtail's matchbook and struck one, then two. Blue flames jittered on the matchsticks, reminding her of the space heater at home on Burleson. Funny, she'd been hellbent to escape Marshall, and now all she wanted was to get back home.

She ambled out of the restroom, stopping to buy some cookies at the counter. From the window, she spotted Donny Ray at the pump, waving his arms like the captain of a sinking ship. Smoothing her hair, she edged past him.

"Just mind the van, that's all I want you to do," he griped. She watched him head for his turn in the loo. That gave her a minute, no more, and she didn't even know what she expected to find.

Crawling onto the floor of the vehicle, she jammed her hand about the seats. Nothing on, under, or in between. Inching over the console, she pulled up the mat beneath the steering wheel.

How did his glasses get under there? That couldn't be all he was upset about. Wriggling on her belly, she retrieved them, lowering her vision level with a white cloth stuck into a skinny gap under his seat.

Curious, she tugged on it, then gave a yank. A gold coin rolled out. She scrambled up from the floorboard to see if Donny Ray was coming. Not yet.

Gripping the coin with her thumb and index finger, she bent close to see a picture of a bearded man on one side and a horned animal on the other. "KRUGERRAND" 1979 and "FYNGOUD 1 OZ FINE GOLD."

Goosebumps traveled her scalp as she stuck it into her shoe. Surely the coin had something to do with that pink bank receipt. And the Credit Suisse key!

# CHAPTER FORTY

## Luxembourg

Cassie and Donny Ray made an early night of it and went downstairs the next morning for rolls, cheese, coffee—and chocolate croissants, a small slice of heaven wedged into her living hell. In a matter of weeks, everything she knew about her family had turned upside down, and in about nine months, she would add another character to the cast.

Donny Ray turned his spoon round and round in the coffee cup. He didn't say much, and he didn't drink much, either. He simply clinked that spoon and scowled.

"Can we go out for a while?" Cassie peeled apart delicate layers of flaky pastry and savored them one by one. "Hotel gal says Luxembourg was part of the Holy Roman Empire."

"All about you, isn't it?" Donny Ray lit a cigarette.

She nibbled a piece of cheese. "So, let me have some francs, then."

"Why?"

"I want to read a newspaper and get some chocolate. You're smothering me—holding me hostage or something."

"Don't ever say crap like that over here!" He lowered his voice to a whisper.

"You mean about hostages?"

This time he grabbed her wrist. "This ain't the States where you can say whatever you want. These people get real touchy about shit."

"Suit yourself. I want to buy a newspaper."

"You've gone all intellectual on me here lately." He flipped some franc notes to her. "This is all I owe you. A hundred Swiss francs."

"I had $200!"

"No, you didn't, you had eight travelers' checks worth $20 each. And you bought that jacket with my money, so I'm calling us even. I'm going back to the room."

"You are such a low life—you know that?" She tucked her hair behind her ears and shot him daggers, but he stood up, rammed his chair under the table, and walked away.

Marrying him might be a nightmare but she wouldn't have to stay married. Couples annulled and divorced all the time. There was honor in that, because it showed you made it down the aisle with somebody at least once.

A mirrored carousel twirled through her brain, offering doomsday visions and all Four Horsemen. If Donny Ray tried to dump her somewhere, she had to have money for a plane ticket home—or at least train fare for Ambronay.

She checked her cash. She needed more. She rubbed the silver token at her neck. She didn't want to turn loose of it, but silver prices were up, and she had to be ready to leave at a moment's notice. She'd check flights. Make a plan.

Wiping her mouth with a linen napkin, Cassie rose from the table, eyeing the cashier and the exit door.

# CHAPTER FORTY-ONE

## Sugar Time

While Donny Ray packed the van, Cassie picked up candy and a London newspaper from the front desk. Headlines emphasized trade unions and Margaret Thatcher, and a report on strained U.S.-Iranian relations. The Islamic regime's anti-American attitude had worsened with the deposed Shah's recent arrival in New York for medical treatment.

She climbed into the van, sat back, and flipped through the front section of the newspaper. Bold black print reported a demonstration in Tehran the day before, in which 3,000 demonstrators turned up outside the American embassy, some demanding the Shah's return, but most just mad about the U.S. generally—the Great Satan, they called it. No wonder Jimmy Carter was nervous, Cassie thought. "I am, too," she muttered, rubbing printer's ink from her fingertips.

Shuddering, Cassie returned to the newspaper, crinkling the pages as she found the financial section. Gold prices closed yesterday at $382 an ounce. Maybe she could sell the Krugerrand. But prices might go up even more and it would be hard to hide that much cash from Donny Ray.

Peeping over the newspaper, Cassie watched him go through the road-worthy checks before he slammed the hood and climbed into the van. He was handy, but she was still mad about Sheree. And the Aldo murder deal freaked her out. Was Donny Ray in danger? Was she? With Jusef being half-Iranian, things could blow up worse than Gorgeous U.

Departure from Luxembourg was relatively comfortable, as the van hugged the eastern border of Belgium in a less traveled route. The vehicle seemed to ride smoother than before, unless it was her imagination. Yet, she recalled a subtle change after Switzerland, so maybe it was altitude enhanced somehow. She scarfed down a raspberry-laced croissant and cast a glance at Donny Ray.

"How'd you pay the hotel bill?" She folded the newspaper and held it on her lap.

"In Lyon? Jusef paid the room in advance. I paid cash for your calls and shit. So now you owe me. How's that feel?"

"No, I meant the hotel here." Unwrapping a chocolate bar, she broke off squares, one by one. "They didn't want to cash my travelers' check."

He rolled his eyes. "Cassie, I carry cash for wherever I'm going. These little hotels aren't set up for nickel-and-diming foreign currency."

"Seems to me you've done a whole lot of traveling."

"I've been around some." He rested his arms on the steering wheel. "Hell, it's Europe."

She imagined Sheree draped over Donny Ray in the shadows of the Eiffel Tower. "Did Sheree come over here?"

"Forget Sheree!" He pulled out a cigarette and lit it with shaky hands.

"Then who's that woman you were talking to?" Cassie sat up straight.

"What woman?"

"The one you called from the campground. Çois said he heard you."

"Oh, Christ! Çois-boy heard me. That's great. And you believe everything he says, too."

"He said you were talking to a woman. And I want to know who, because I got your baby in me, and I've got a right to know if there's others out there." Cassie smacked the steering wheel for emphasis.

"There ain't no other babies out there."

"I don't mean babies, for God's sake, I mean women." Anger rose fast in her gullet, like a mallet-driven puck in a carnival strongman game.

"Okay, you got me dead to rights." He sighed. "I had a woman in Bremerhaven. Long time ago."

Ah ha! No way she'd feel guilty about Chuck when Donny Ray had been acting the fool. "What was her name?"

"Brigitta. There, are you happy?" He inhaled smoke with a grimace.

"Did you love her?"

"How could I?" He tickled her chin. "How much room does a man have in his heart? Only enough for one woman. Come here." Eyes still on the road, one hand on the wheel, he leaned over with a one-armed embrace and crooned *"In-A-Gadda-Da-Vida, baby."*

"Is she the one?"

"Forget it. Subject closed," he kissed her forehead.

Cassie nodded, ate every square of melting chocolate, and licked her fingers. He almost had her there with the Iron Butterfly thing—and memories of the glowing power button on his eight-track tape deck. Even so, she couldn't forget his messy history with other women. Donny Ray didn't deny Çois overheard him talking to the German gal.

Donny Ray cleared his throat. "So, you're still my co-pilot, right?"

She didn't reply, her anger at Sheree, and now Brigitta, still smoldering. She adjusted the sun visor and returned to the newspaper. "It says here there's a silver shortage." She fingered the token.

"That's what I've heard." His eyes searched the road signs. "Say, are you watching the map? We have to make sure we stay in Belgium."

Out of nowhere her ears started buzzing. She went cross-eyed and her head bobbed. Every few minutes, she struggled to see the map through her eyelashes, but damn, it was a sugar crash. All that chocolate. Sweet pastries. Croissants. "Take the Battice exit to E40," she mumbled.

"Are you sure?"

"Yeah." She closed her eyes, the engine hummed, and suddenly the van screeched to a halt.

Donny Ray's voice boomed. "What the fuck, Cassie? We're in Germany!"

## CHAPTER FORTY-TWO

## One Job

Cassie stirred, confused, and saw the maps had fallen onto the floor. "What happened?"

"You tell *me!*" Donny Ray pounded his fist on the steering wheel. "One job, that's all. You just had to read the damn map."

"Can't you turn around?"

"No!" He looked in the rear-view mirror as cars came up behind him. "Cassie, I told you a hundred times, we wanted to go straight through. No stopping. Now you've blown it!"

"Why are you so mad?"

He sneered. "Do I have to spell it out? Instead of going right into Holland, now we've got a shitload of border stops."

"But the–"

"I don't want to hear it." Donny Ray's jaws tightened, and his fists clenched. "Now sit there, and don't say another word, or next stop, you're *out.*"

The van moved into line at the checkpoint. She gulped. He wouldn't throw her out, would he? Frowning, she turned her attention to the "wanted" posters on the guard booth beside them. She'd try to lighten the mood.

"Hey, Donny Ray, German terrorists. And looks like some Dutch ones, too." She stared out the window as they approached the border station. "I thought terrorists were frowny Palestinians, hijacking planes and all that—the way Jusef said."

His face stony, he didn't reply. Instead, as he eased the vehicle into position, Donny Ray braked and studied the posters. Two small dots of sweat beaded his forehead. He wouldn't even look at her. Rubbing his hands and cracking his knuckles, he took a deep breath and blew it out slowly. Adjusting his eyeglasses he ruffled his beard, shifting around in his seat.

"Did you ever see any of those guys?" Cassie sat forward and took a closer look at the photos, some standard mugshots, and others were grainy images from security cameras or maybe spy devices. "They wear a lot of black."

"Shut up. Be quiet."

"Well dang, man, I'm the one having the baby. You're just Paul Anka."

"Sorry. *Sorry.* There's a lot to being a father," he said. "I'm starting to feel the pressure." He coughed and gave her a side-eye. "Maybe you don't want to have it."

"*Not have it?* You're crazy!" She slapped the seat.

"All right, all right, it was just an idea," he bristled. "Forget I said anything."

"And you better not try to kick me in the stomach or something," she scowled.

"Calm down. Nobody's kicking anybody. We'll get through this."

As they took their turn for inspection, Donny Ray held out both passports and nodded stiffly. The officer turned the passports sideways and back, checked the photos, and asked for a driver's license. Donny Ray wriggled his billfold out of his jeans and produced it.

"Hmmm, ok." The officer stamped both passports and handed them back. "Welcome to Germany," he said and waved them through.

"That wasn't anything," Cassie said. "I don't know why you were so jacked up about it."

He pulled the van into a parking area. "Let me see that map." He bent over it and talked to himself, thinking outloud while running his fingers along the route.

"Okay, back into Holland, Heerlen to Amsterdam. Three hours." He put the vehicle into gear.

## CHAPTER FORTY-THREE

## Love is Blue

Donny Ray turned to Cassie and pursed his lips in an air kiss. "After we get things sorted with Jusef, you'll like Amsterdam. I'll get us a room at this hotel I know on Keizersgracht."

"Oh, super." Cassie's voice was flat. She sighed, pulled out her crossword puzzle, and paid little attention to the scenery crawl until the van slowed again.

"The border traffic is backed up worse than I expected." He shot Cassie a scold. "Now see why I wanted to stay in Belgium?"

"Yes. And I guess we'll have to get over it, won't we?" She pulled down the visor, licked her finger, and wiped mascara from her lower lid. Casting a glance at Donny Ray, she followed his gaze. "Dang, they've got the same people posted on the Dutch wall, too."

This time, she could study them a while longer. In four languages, the black-inked headlines repeated the same urgent message. The English version made clear these were killers and co-conspirators, armed and dangerous.

She noticed his eyes tracked to a police mugshot that showed a bug-eyed, dark-headed woman staring into the camera. Next to it, a blurry photo showed a man wearing a dog collar. Cassie couldn't read the names.

The uniformed border guard leaned into the vehicle window. "*Paspoorten?*"

With a slight tremor, Donny Ray handed over their blue passports. The guard walked to the back of the van and lingered before calling someone else over. Momentarily, the first one returned to the driver's window. "Please exit your vehicle and come with me," he said.

"Are they talking to us?" Cassie's skin prickled.

"Shit," Donny Ray gripped the steering wheel.

Uniformed officers in crisp white shirts and jaunty visors opened her door. "Get out," one commanded. Cassie's hands shook as she grabbed at the striped peppermints spilling onto the floorboard.

"Hurry up!" Border police trained machine guns on them as they climbed from the vehicle. Cassie flinched, gripping her backpack and Donny Ray's sweaty hand.

"Don't panic," he said under his breath. "This is a mistake." His chin quivered.

They followed the officials into a security zone, where working dogs paced at the ready. Cassie stood with her arms straight out from her sides, the backpack at her feet. Two dogs took turns, circling her, and sniffing her privates, same as any other mutts, she thought. But these dogs were all about business, and her fear was rising like onion fumes. They could probably smell it. "Holy Mother," she prayed, "reach out and pinch their noses."

"It was a miracle," she breathed. Neither the backpack nor her sweaty running shoes impressed the dogs, so they repeated the drill with Donny Ray. Tiny beads of perspiration glistened over his eyes, but otherwise, he was stone-faced.

The animals didn't alert, so their handlers left the concrete pad with them and headed for the van. Cassie watched the dogs jump in, flexing hind legs, heads bowed, doing some serious panting and sniffing.

"This way," said an officer. He urged Cassie and Donny Ray into the guard station.

She tugged on Donny Ray's sleeve, whispering, "What kind of dogs are those?"

"Belgian Malinois."

"Why do they need two?"

"One for drugs, one for explosives. Shhh. Zip it."

Donny Ray nudged Cassie forward to a cluttered desk with clunky black telephones. Man, she hadn't seen that style phone since 1962.

After studying the passports, one of the officers approached them—a short, round fellow. His salt-and-pepper mustache peeped over a lined mouth, and piercing blue eyes betrayed a profound weariness. A plastic nametag clipped to his pocket said Kpt. Voorhees.

"I am *Kapitein* Voorhees. You are American, yes? Do you speak Dutch or German?"

"Some German," Donny Ray said. "No Dutch."

"Okay," the officer launched into Dutch with his colleagues. Donny Ray's face went blank. Cassie sweated from every pore, or else she had wet her pants. She couldn't tell.

Three phones jangled on the desk, and three officers answered them. All frowning, they jabbered into the receivers, eyebrows furrowed. One by one, they hung up and checked a clipboard, pointing at a line of interest.

Kpt. Voorhees folded his arms and looked hard at Donny Ray. "Your license plates are questioned. Perhaps lost or stolen. Mr. Richard, do you have anything to declare?"

There's that Mr. Richard again, Cassie thought. She gritted her teeth. Donny Ray cut his eyes at her.

"No sir." Donny Ray kept his poker face.

"Mr. Richard, where are you coming from?"

"France. My fiancée and I are taking a vacation together." He squeezed Cassie's shoulder. She trembled.

"And where are you going?"

"Amsterdam," he said.

"Why?"

"End of our holiday. We're going back to the States." Cassie wrinkled her brow.

The officer examined both passports again, inspecting them with a magnifying glass. "You are from Texas?"

"Yes sir." Donny Ray stood straight. Cassie nodded.

"So now a few questions, okay? We look at Texas and see how much you know." The officer pulled a weathered reference book from his shelf. "Sometimes people say they are from one place, but they come from another, you know?"

"We're proud Texans from the Lone Star State." Donny Ray held his shoulders back in an Army parade stance.

"That's good. The Lone Star. But let's do a little harder." Kpt. Voorhees thumbed some pages. "Okay, so tell me, who was Sam Houston?"

"Big war hero. Won Texas War of Independence, 1836. He said to remember the Alamo." Now relaxed, Donny Ray looked Kpt. Voorhees directly in the eyes. "The city of Houston is named after him."

"And the state capital?"

"Austin."

"Very well," the officer said. "Tell me, where did you get your vehicle?"

"Bought it from a guy on the street. In Lyon."

"Were you not concerned it could be stolen?"

"No, sir. The title looked good to me."

"Young lady, where are you from?" the officer asked.

"Marshall, Texas, sir." She sank into an aluminum-framed chair.

"Why are you so far away?"

She put her hands over her face and shook her head, thinking she should have stayed at the Piggly Wiggly.

"Now, dear, please don't cry!" Donny Ray put a protective arm around her and met the official's eyes. "She is with child." He patted her tummy.

An agent appeared at the door with an empty butane tank and a Colt .45 wrapped in a striped dishcloth. He held them out. "Explain."

Cassie's heart sank, her head felt light, and her stomach rumbled. That was Donny Ray's service revolver, the one he strapped around his ankle at the campsite—have gun, will travel. Now with his fake passport and bad license plates, they were going to get hauled in.

Her cheekbones ached. She knew exactly what would happen if she didn't keep her wits about her. She'd have the baby in a foreign prison, and she'd lose it to an orphanage serving gruel and castor oil. In a flash, she vomited into the officer's trash can.

Donny Ray went to his knees beside her, putting one hand on her shoulder, the other on her chin. Kpt. Voorhees' assistant brought water and a damp cloth. Cassie sipped slowly and straightened her back.

"She is sick, and now we have trouble here?" Donny Ray frowned and tried to support her as she sank into the chair. Her shoulders lurched, and she threw up again, narrowly missing the officer's desk. Remnants of croissant and jam puddled on the scuffed linoleum floor.

Kpt. Voorhees snapped his fingers, blew a whistle, and called for a mop. As personnel scurried about, the officer put on gloves and inspected the Colt .45. He removed the magazine, looked down the well, and checked the chamber. A round popped out. Donny Ray's face went pale.

Clutching her sides, Cassie's breath burst in and out. "I need more water!"

"It's okay. It's okay," Donny Ray said, then whispered in her ear, "I got this." Turning to address the officer, he noted, "That food down in Belgium upset her stomach."

Hmmm, exactly what had he "got"? He'd suckered her into something she might forever regret. Her stomach lurched. She swayed.

"My sympathies for your illness." Kpt. Voorhees redirected his attention to Donny Ray. "Still, you must explain. The vehicle is yours, so you are presumed to own and control these things. Explosive material and a loaded gun. Talk." He clenched his fists.

"Yes, sir. I bought the butane to warm the van and heat water." Color returned to Donny Ray's cheeks. He kept his voice level and eyes straight, no wavering or looking around. "We were camping."

Kpt. Voorhees lifted an eyebrow. "Campgrounds are closed for the season."

"Not this one." He rubbed his palms on his jeans.

"And the gun?"

"I don't know how it got there."

Cassie did a double take. That gun had been under the driver's seat, in the little compartment, where the Krugerrand had rolled out. Who else would've put it there?

Fingering his beard, Donny Ray maintained voice control, but his bottom eyelid quivered slightly. "The gun belongs to the campground owner. She had me shoot a snake. But I'm sure I gave it back to her."

Donny Ray was a lying dog, Cassie thought. She clenched her teeth.

Kpt. Voorhees returned his attention to the barrel. "U.S. Army issue. Odd. Registration number scratched out."

Cassie spoke up. "There were a lot of Gypsies at the campsite. Maybe they stole it and put it in our van."

"Why would they do that?" the officer asked.

"Because they didn't want to get caught with it." Her ears grew warm with a flush.

"Hmmm, unlikely." Kpt. Voorhees turned the gun over in his hands. "So, if I call the campsite, this owner will say yes, this is her gun."

Donny Ray chewed a cuticle. "I don't know how I wound up with it."

The *Kapitein* put down the Colt and folded his arms. "So how do we find this place, which is open when all other campgrounds are closed?"

Donny Ray balked. "Uh..."

"I can tell you! Give me that backpack." Cassie fingered the straps, pulled it up, and reached inside. She met Donny Ray's stare while she rooted around the contents. His brow relaxed when she withdrew a blank invoice and waved it.

"Let me see." Kpt. Voorhees studied it. "*L'Amour est Bleu*, the Love is Blue campsite near Ambronay. Okay." He reached for a phone and dialed the numbers shown.

Cassie's hand went to the sawmill token and rubbed it hard between her fingers.

"*Hallo? Bonjour?*" Kpt. Voorhees looked up at the ceiling and shifted his eyes.

Annette's tinny voice rang through the line, and Cassie thought Kpt. Voorhees did a decent job with French. He verified an open campground with Gypsies, and he asked about a Colt .45 and an American couple in a van. That last part struck a nerve somehow, and he held the phone out from his ear for a moment. "*Très bien, oui,*" he said.

Disconnecting the line, Kpt. Voorhees turned back to them. "The *Madame* confirmed your story about camping, but she said it was not her gun."

"Look, sir, I'm begging you to believe me, it's not my gun, either. I swear, it belonged to her. That's all I know."

With his hands behind his back, the *Kapitein* listened and nodded, but his face showed no emotion.

Maybe he was trying to see if Donny Ray would crack, Cassie guessed. She could tell by the mild change in his voice that Donny Ray was unraveling a little. He'd always thought he was King Kong, powering his way through anything, but now a short Dutchman had him by the balls.

Clearing his throat, Donny Ray glanced at her and lifted his chin. She knew that look—he needed some help.

Holding a cold cloth to her forehead, Cassie piped up. "Sir, there were some Swedes on the campground singing protest songs."

"Protest songs?" Kpt. Voorhees raised both eyebrows. "Swedish have nothing to protest."

"Maybe they weren't really Swedes," she said. "They had an 'S' on their car, but they could have been something else. They looked like hippies, and I smelled marijuana smoke. Maybe they stashed the gun in our car so they wouldn't get caught with it."

"I see." Kpt. Voorhees cleared his throat. "Gypsies and Swedes—tracking them down to compare stories. It's not worth our resources. The fact is, you possess the gun. Illegally."

"It's not my gun," Donny Ray said. "I don't want it."

Kpt. Voorhees clasped his hands and gestured toward them. "But you don't deny the butane is yours. The cylinders are highly explosive, also illegal to bring over the border. Surely you know of their use in making bombs."

"Bombs?" Color drained from Donny Ray's face.

The officer gestured to the same set of terrorist posters. "And it happens you've come up from France. Perhaps you were in hiding?"

"No sir, no sir." Donny Ray's chest rose. "We're simple Americans. On vacation. Off-season on the cheap."

A clipboard of "wanted" photos was within reach, and Kpt. Voorhees flipped through them, comparing the women to Cassie and the men to Donny Ray. He paused at the picture of a man with a dog collar, looked up, and stared across the desk.

Evidently, Kpt. Voorhees could not make a good match, and he returned the clipboard to his desk.

"So, you still have charges," the Dutchman said. With ballpoint pen heavy in hand, he checked boxes and wrote a few sentences, then handed a citation and summons to Donny Ray.

"Mr. Richard, you may go to jail until next Tuesday and plead your case, or you may pay a fine now. Four hundred Dutch Guilder. Cash."

"Swiss francs, that's all I've got." Even Donny Ray's eyebrows were sweating.

"Okay. Two hundred francs." Kpt. Voorhees folded his arms. "You understand, this covers the cost of our investigation. I will dispose of the butane and keep the gun."

Donny Ray's face contorted as he dug into his pouch, removed a short stack of bills, and handed them over. And that, Cassie thought, is exactly why she kept the silver token around her neck, and now a gold coin in her shoe. Her daddy was right. Sometimes you had to buy your way out of a jam.

## CHAPTER FORTY-FOUR

### Tired Tires and Fan Belts

Still backed up in line, autos spewed exhaust and more than a few curses as their drivers waited for passport checks. Some heads turned to watch Cassie and Donny Ray, as he helped her into the disheveled vehicle. Apparently, the dogs had alerted on the gun locker, because it was forced open, the lid ajar, and the lock dangling.

"What's this about?" she asked. "I didn't know you had a cabinet under there."

"Later." He turned on the ignition and put the van into motion. Cassie's eyes narrowed, and she reached for a pack of Malabar chewing gum.

"You're so full of shit, *Mr. Richard*. Let me see your passport." She snatched it and read his name aloud. "Raymond Richard. Why not Scooby Doo? And what's the deal with the license plates?"

"Some mix-up is all. New registration—plates weren't in the system."

She cocked her head. "Quit lying. These new ones are French plates, and you had Dutch before. Blue and yellow with a big NL sticker. Don't try to tell me any different. And that was *your* damn gun."

"I only did what I had to do." Guiding the van through the exit, he reached for another cigarette. "Where'd you come up with the Swedes? What kind of a random–"

"Just came to me. I knew you caved. I saved your butt, you know that?"

"You did not! Annette vouched for me."

Leaning forward, Cassie knuckled his arm. "Listen, mister, you didn't even know the name of the campground—where do think you'd be if I didn't get that for you? I had the good sense to vomit into the man's trashcan. I could've held it back for a bathroom, but I've seen the detective shows. Got to have a distraction."

Slamming on the brakes, Donny Ray pulled over to the side of the road. "But it's your fault we got stopped in the first place!" His left hand on the steering wheel, he slammed the back of the seat with his right. "You fucked us with a blowtorch! We wouldn't of got stopped if you'd done the one thing I asked you to do!"

"And why the hell did I fall asleep, big guy?" She slammed the seat the same way that he did. "On account of I'm pregnant with your baby. And," she shrugged, "I'd like to know how you call Annette vouching for you. Whole time we were there, she had little bluebirds tying ribbons over your head. And when we left out of there, you wouldn't even tell her bye."

Donny Ray grimaced. "That's enough, okay?"

"Not yet. The woman said it wasn't her gun! Maybe she'd have covered for you if you hadn't treated her like shit. I bet she stashed it in the van herself to get you caught."

Cassie couldn't believe she was gigging him that way. "Revenge, baby, revenge. What goes around, comes around. You better have a damn good reason to dump a woman, or she will bite your ass."

"They would have jailed you too, you know."

"For what?"

"Conspiracy."

"I didn't conspire for nothing." Cassie chomped a stick of gum, balled up the paper wrapper, and threw it at him.

"Caught together, hanged together," he scowled.

She closed her eyes and envisioned the black Kit Kat clock. Her mother had told her Donny Ray was trouble, from that very first 7-Eleven night, when *M*A*S*H* was on TV, playing the "Suicide is Painless" theme music while the credits scrolled. Cassie should open the van door and throw herself out in the mountains, roll down the rocks, and smother herself in the snow.

Too bad the landscape was as flat as a sheet of cardboard now, she thought. Canals, barges, and warehouses stretched for miles in a gray scape of concrete and asphalt. She had no sense of being anywhere but in a black-and-white picture until splashes of color crept into view.

Buildings rose higher, and windows multiplied magically. So did the Amsterdam traffic, which slowed to a big city crawl. Bicyclists made better time than autos crossing ramps and bridges.

Donny Ray inched the van through a commercial district. Sleek modern brick-and-glass structures shone next to grim old buildings with graffiti painted on dirty brick.

Slinking down on the seat, she had a fluttery feeling in her chest. She needed to channel her daddy's disposition, she thought. Despite his own anxieties and sense of loss, he carried on. He managed. He faked a lot.

For her part, she should lighten up and fake it for a while, too. She still needed to get Donny Ray's name on the baby's birth certificate. Everybody knew the husband was always presumed to be the father of the baby unless somebody challenged paternity. She knew Chuck sure wouldn't.

Within minutes they pulled up to a two-story, red brick building with a single window on the street. Donny Ray jumped out and pressed a buzzer mounted on the garage door frame. The rolling door rose, and he drove into the garage.

## CASSIE'S COMET

Cassie watched heavy springs judder as the door panels closed behind them. In the adjacent parking space, Donny Ray's prized Mercedes coupe shone brightly. Jusef emerged from an interior door with a drilled peephole and yellow warning decals. He helped Cassie out of her seat.

"This way. Mind the step. Are you bringing the backpack? Here, let me help you." He put his arm around her shoulders and escorted her into the service bay and shop, the backpack dangling from his elbow.

Her nerves shot Black Cat bottle rockets. So much for the Johnny Frank School of Mood Management. She grimaced and sidestepped a tire. Maybe some familiarity would calm her down. She remembered Donny Ray's old shop with pride. She delighted in a nostalgia-laden bouquet of hydraulic fluid and motor oil.

Industrial lights, suspended from the ceiling, revealed a car on a lift and spare parts lining the walls. A rack of tires, shelved cables and batteries stood by a glass-blocked window. Underneath a workbench, tabby cats darted among power strips and tools.

"I see you've got that roller door at the back for the customers," Cassie said. "Does it open onto a street?"

"No, it's a wide alley." Donny Ray pulled a Zippo lighter from his pocket.

Cassie turned to the men. "How do you make any money here? I mean, your old shop at home was more than three times this big."

"Lot less overhead now." Donny Ray patted a fender. "Custom jobs."

"Just looks like a chop shop to me." Cassie's tone carried a sting.

Nobody spoke.

"Well, is it?" She put her hands on her hips.

"Now Cassie," Donny Ray began, "things aren't always what they appear."

"Y'all are spies, aren't you?" She clenched her fists and suppressed the urge to throw a can of brake fluid at him.

Donny Ray pulled a face. "Yeah, sure, we got microfilm in our shoes."

"So, that's why we got stopped at the border!"

Jusef's eyes narrowed, and he stepped toward them. "What border?"

"Heerlen." Donny Ray lit a cigarette.

"What was the problem?"

"License plates." Donny Ray chewed a cuticle and looked the other way.

Jusef pounded his fist on a worktable, and three screwdrivers bounced off. He glared at Donny Ray.

Cassie had a sudden inclination to stir things up. "They didn't find the gun until later," she said.

"What?!" Jusef's face turned red.

"Don't be mad at him." Cassie touched Jusef's arm. "They didn't see it until after they already stopped us. Isn't that right?" She glanced at Donny Ray as though she sought approval, while inexplicably seeking to ignite Jusef's fuse.

Jusef scoffed. "My dear, no such searches are unplanned—license plates, routine traffic stops, all are pretext. Police already know what they'll find because confidential informants alert them. You weren't stopped going into Germany, were you?"

Cassie shook her head.

"Because the Germans didn't know to look. The Dutch did. And why was that?" Jusef raised his voice and circled back to Donny Ray, who blinked rapidly.

"Maybe he doesn't know!" Cassie took Donny Ray's hand in a show of solidarity.

"Oh, he knows," Jusef's lips curled. "Because the informant knew he would not risk entering Germany. He would go through Holland. Therefore, the Dutch police were alerted. Who would know that?"

Donny Ray studied the floor.

Jusef shouted at him. "Brigitta!" He threw a wrench, which clanged on a radiator pipe.

"Your old girlfriend?" Slack-jawed, Cassie jerked her hand from Donny Ray's.

"What did he tell you about her?" Jusef asked, pinching Cassie's chin.

She blinked and drew away, now regretting her passive-aggressive setup. She hadn't anticipated this twist.

"That's all she knows." Donny Ray cleared his throat. "Just girlfriend."

"Leave me out of this," she said. "I don't have anything to do with any of it."

"Oh, but you do," Jusef smirked.

She recoiled, then turned to Donny Ray. "What the devil is he talking about?"

"Yeah, uh, remember those calls from the phone booth last month? All of them were monitored." He blew a stream of blue smoke from the corner of his mouth.

"Why? We only talked mess!" Cassie stepped forward.

"I didn't even know for a while. I was told to use this or that number, it's free, and I didn't question it." Donny Ray stuck his cigarette in a cup full of sand. "Turns out, these kinds of numbers go through official channels."

"Dozens of call logs," Jusef said, "some with your number on them. If it came down to it, you'd have a hard time explaining that to a magistrate."

"You set me up?" Tears welled in her eyes.

"All in the game," Jusef said. "Anyway, who has a free phone from Western Europe? Not enlisted men, I assure you!"

Cassie rose on her toes and put her face in Donny Ray's. "Now! You mean to say you screwed me over to get that jackass an American wife? You crazy sons-of-bitches! I don't know what's going on, but it ain't about tires and fan belts. Gimme my backpack. I'm out of here." She started for the door.

"Ah-ah-ah," Jusef blocked her way, crossing his arms. "There's another matter you must consider."

# CHAPTER FORTY-FIVE

## Bubbling Bouillon

Jusef touched Cassie's cheek, "You're in with us."

"Wrong." She jutted out her chin.

"Ah, but you made a weapons run to Switzerland."

She turned to Donny Ray. "What weapons? You got knives in your boots?"

Leaning against the door, Jusef worked his palms like a weak bongo drummer. "Tell her, Raymond."

"Well, we, uh, delivered some guns to a contact in Basel." Donny Ray looked down and smoothed his hair, his voice trailing off. "You and me."

"You dirty dog bastard!" Cassie swept her forearm across the worktable, knocking cans and tools to the ground. "No. 5" screws tinkled across the concrete floor.

"Settle down. I can explain." Donny Ray attempted to take her hand.

"My hind foot!"

"Enough! You must contain your temper," Jusef's voice grated. "Please relax. Go upstairs and freshen up. Raymond and I have matters to discuss."

She stomped the floor. "I am not going to shrink back while you make plans that mess up my life even more. So, say it all, right here in front of me."

Donny Ray put his hands on her shoulders. "You've got to quit carrying on." He arched his eyebrow toward Jusef.

"I'm calm. I'm calm." She'd heard pregnant women could miscarry if they get their blood pressure up. Taking a deep breath, she counted to 10 and exhaled. "Now tell me what you're going to decide here."

"We'll save your part for supper. Okay?" Donny Ray stroked her hair. "Right now, we want to talk about money and car parts and the Houston setup. I swear, we'll wait to talk about anything concerns you. Now you go on up—" He gestured toward concrete steps running up the far wall, with an iron railing and another heavy door at the top.

"Yeah, all right." She had to pee anyway, but acting agreeable might benefit her. "Can I get my duffel bag? I want something clean to put on."

"Not now," Jusef said. "You can wear something of mine. Clothes are in the closet."

"Oh, never mind." With the backpack over her shoulders, Cassie clomped up the steps and glanced at the shop below. With his hands outstretched, Donny Ray looked up at her with a quizzical expression, as though he didn't know what was going on. "Bullshit," she muttered.

She grabbed the heavy chrome door lever and shoved her way into a dimly lit apartment. She looked right and left, inspecting the Spartan rooms and furnishings, narrow hallway, kitchen—not much to it. The bathroom was no place to relax. The tub had been reglazed, but this place hadn't been painted in 40 years. And with rusted iron fixtures, mottled chrome, and silver coating peeled from the back of the mirror, it was exactly what she'd expect from a chop shop in an iffy neighborhood.

She opened a cabinet and fingered through the medicines. Nothing beyond the usual aspirin, floss, and razor blades. She closed it and looked in the streaked mirror. In her reflection, she saw a pale girl with blue smudges beneath her eyes. And dirty hair.

"You dumbass."

Slow, big tears plopped on the discolored sink. Lord, she couldn't remember ever being such a crybaby. She opened the cabinet again and touched a razor blade. Maybe this.

No, that wouldn't work, she figured. The guys would find her bleeding out, dump her in an ER, and leave the country. She'd wake up alive and be worse off. Suicide wasn't painless like the *M*A*S*H* theme song said. Besides, it was a mortal sin.

She couldn't simply get a taxicab to the airport and fly off without an airline ticket and money. So how? She didn't know a solitary soul.

Soul. The word struck a chord, no, more like a gong. The Krishnas. Yes.

Rasonnati mentioned a temple here. Cassie could hide out and make a break later. Right, right, she could put on one of those jangly outfits and abscond with airport magazine money, if necessary.

Comfortable with a possible escape plan, she unzipped her jacket, pulled off her T-shirt, and dropped her pants on the tile floor. She slid the Krugerrand into the toe of a dirty sock and stuffed it into her shoe. Then she draped a towel on the side of the bathtub and sat down to run the water. Turning to reach the faucet, she bent over the tile and heard voices. A radio? When she stood, they stopped. "What th–?"

The pipes. She heard voices coming up the old pipes. She climbed into the bathtub and curled up on her side, ear to the porcelain. Jusef's voice came through clear as a bell.

"Enough of the license plates."

"Maybe the Gypsies called them in," Donny Ray said.

"Impossible! Gypsies do not call police. France deports them at every turn."

"It must have been that damn Çois."

"Love is blind, eh Raymond? Brigitta talks from jail. She is still in the network—she knows where you went, where you are. And she'll keep talking when she's released. End of story. As for Cassie–"

"I can't let you kill her," Donny Ray's voice wobbled. "I love her."

"That makes you a liability too."

"Oh, my God!" Cassie covered her mouth. Did they mean her or that other woman? Seconds ticked away. Too quiet down there, she thought. Did Jusef have a gun? She struggled to hear. Donny Ray's voice broke, "Okay. Pull the trigger, clip the brakes, whatever."

"Smart."

Something metallic clanged on the garage floor. Cassie kept her head down. Curled up like a doodlebug, naked in the tub, she strained to listen.

Jusef said something about soup. Bouillon. No, that's gold bullion, she realized. "In a few years, worth a million dollars," he said.

Cassie gulped. A million dollars?

"I'm fucked." That was Donny Ray's voice. "I lost the lockbox receipt."

"How?"

"I don't know. I've got the other receipts. I think the hotel maid threw it out."

"Another blunder," Jusef said. "Do not travel with the paperwork. Mail it to a trusted friend in the States. Surely you have such a contact."

"Got a cousin," Donny Ray said. "In Houston."

That would be jug-eared Mark, Cassie thought.

"Maybe Cassie has it," Jusef said.

Cringing, she kicked the side of the tub.

Donny Ray continued, "She hasn't let go of the backpack except at Heerlen."

"Get it now. And check the duffel bag when you bring it in. Anyway, you've got the key, right?"

"Sweet Jesus!" Her heart racing, she stepped out of the tub and removed the pink-wrapped key. She stuck it up a sleeve and tucked it under to appear that she'd simply tossed the shirt on the floor. Then she flushed the toilet, ran water into the sink, and cranked the faucet knobs on the tub. She climbed in, sat down, rubbed a little, and hustled out. She'd barely covered herself when Donny Ray barged in.

"Here's your duffel bag." Donny Ray stepped inside and dropped it on the tile with an amplified thud. "Mind if I get some gum from your backpack?"

As she reached for it, he batted her hand out of the way. "I can find it," he said.

He closed the door, then she heard four or five steps. Another door closed. She figured he took it to his bedroom.

She knelt on the tile and rolled up her jeans with the bank key and the Krugerrand sock, tucking them into the bottom of the duffel. Standing up, she opened the bathroom door and came face to face with Donny Ray.

"You scared me!" She clutched her chest and gripped the towel to keep it closed around her.

"How long you gonna be?" His eyes traveled her torso.

"A little while. I need to fix my hair." She rocked back and forth on her bare heels.

"Right. We'll be waiting." He turned and left.

Breathe. Breathe deep, she told herself. Jusef had threatened him because of her—would she make it home? "Who were these people?" she mumbled. No regard for life. And now she had a gun at her back. She had to think of a way out of this.

Banging the bags through the doorway into Donny Ray's room, she threw them on the bed, now littered with cookie crumbs, melting chocolate squares, and stray sticks of chewing gum. At least he saved her the trouble of cleaning out the backpack, she thought.

She retrieved the Krugerrand sock, put it back on, then tucked the key inside her underwire bra. God, this was killing her nerves. But tomorrow she'd bolt for the Krishna temple.

The towel dropped as she rummaged through the backpack. Swiss francs intact. "Where's the passport?"

Her breath came in gasps, and her muscles stiffened. She turned the backpack inside out, unzipping every pocket and patting every stitch. A cold realization washed over her. Donny Ray had swiped it.

Cassie reappeared downstairs in the service bay—hair combed, face shiny, and a sweet smile masking boiling fury.

Head tilted, Jusef evaluated her. "You're all set."

"Where's Donny Ray?"

"Out there." He pointed to the exit door, just beyond the service bay. "Ready for supper?" He checked his watch.

"I want to see if I left anything in the van." Cassie stepped toward the garage door.

"Looking for your passport? Don't worry, I've got it. Best to keep all three together." Jusef turned up the corners of his mouth and showed some teeth.

Dang, this place redefined the Iron Curtain. "I want to keep my passport," she faced him, arms folded.

"No." He toyed with the ends of his mustache like a cartoon villain. He must have known she'd try to bolt.

"Why can't I have it?"

"We leave soon, and we need to be organized. We'll talk at supper, right?"

"If you say so." She had no choice. "I want to go in the garage and take a look inside Donny Ray's Mercedes."

"Mercedes-Benz." He rubbed his palms and sniggered. "One last fling, is that it? Suit yourself. But tell him to make it quick. I'm hungry."

What a jackass, she thought, heading for the exit.

The steel door was heavier than she expected. As she shoved the crash bar, motion detectors immediately lit up the bay. The door slammed behind her, and exhaust fumes assaulted her nostrils. Her eyes burned. Coughing, she smacked the wall controls, and one of the garage doors lifted. Cold, damp air rushed in.

She ran to the outside perimeter and inhaled deep, grateful breaths. She turned and saw the parked Mercedes-Benz spewing clouds of white vapors into the night.

"Donny Ray!" Her breath burst with unspeakable fear. She bolted to the driver's side and yanked open the door. With his head against the steering wheel, he sat unmoved in the driver's seat, his right hand gripping a bottle of Scotch. She forced him aside and turned off the ignition. Both the engine and the Grateful Dead went silent.

"Can you hear me?" She pinched his face and pulled on his shoulder. He opened bloodshot eyes, acknowledged her, and closed them again.

"Shut the damn door," he mumbled. Still alive, still rude, but still better than a corpse, she thought.

Cassie returned to the wall controls, pressed a button, and the galvanized steel curtain rumbled its descent. Her head hurt, and so did her heart. She scuttled to the coupe, her emotions flaming. "Open up!" She rapped on the passenger door window.

Donny Ray unlocked it and turned away. He put the Macallan bottle to his mouth, took a pull, and sprawled in the seat. Gasping, Cassie grabbed his upper arm. "You could have killed yourself!"

"No, I couldn't." He bumped the bottle against the steering wheel. "The bay's too big. I'd run out of gas first."

"Then what are you doing here?"

"Just grooving." Tears streamed down his cheeks. Cassie had never seen Donny Ray cry. She had to get that Scotch away from him. She knew he'd get mean in a minute.

"Can I have some?" She reached for the bottle, and his fingers went limp. She pretended to take a swig and tucked it on the side of her seat.

"Shit, my head." He palmed his temples and wagged his head from side to side. "Everything got away from me, girl."

"What do you mean?"

"It started out, just a little cash, that's all. Some car repairs with Aldo. And Brigitta." He slurred his words. "I love her. Go ahead and hit me."

This was taking a turn into deep shit. "I'm not going to hit you, for God's sake."

He lit a cigarette and pulled open the ashtray.

"Hey, what's in there?" Cassie wiggled her fingers.

"Ashes!" He slapped at her hand. "What else do you think it would it be?"

"Don't hit me!" She slapped back, retrieving a green cardboard square, singed, and torn. "This is, uh, your military ID." She turned it over in her hands. "Why'd you burn it?"

"Didn't need it anymore." He pulled a face. "Throw it out. Nothing matters." He put his hands on his face, and his upper body shuddered. "God, I want to puke."

He cracked open the door and bent his head, but only a few yellow drops trickled out with a choke. He wiped his face on his sleeve and tilted his seat back. "Jusef played Brigitta. And me. He screwed the pooch."

Donny Ray whimpered. She sighed. He'd been Mr. Big Stuff in Marshall, now look at him—no match for someone as sinister as Jusef, reeling him in with ego strokes and the promise of big money. As a result, everybody got the shaft—especially her.

Cassie squeezed the leather armrest remembering this was the luxury car she'd hoped for—but somehow, like everything else on this godforsaken trip, the anticipation paled compared to reality.

"Okay, now think," she whispered, rubbing the silver pendant between her fingers and thumb. Jusef had her passport, but they would be leaving anyway, so that might be no harm, no foul. Then there's Donny Ray, crying about that Brigitta woman. If he had half a chance, he'd probably disappear with her.

## CHAPTER FORTY-SIX

## A Standup Couple

Cassie couldn't get over it: Donny Ray had cried. That was more than enough to make her duck for cover. He'd cried for Brigitta, without a word about Cassie's horrific mess. The "wanted" posters at the Dutch border gave her pause. Crap, Cassie could be shaking jail bars right now if she hadn't proved they were camping down south.

The more she considered it, the more likely it seemed that Çois had reported them. After all, he'd been a cop in Lyon, home of the Interpol, and she had told him Donny Ray's real name and Army details. Maybe Çois had also seen the butane tank—with its simple warning decal: danger, cartoon man falling into flames.

She followed the guys up the sidewalk, muscle-twitching nerves clutching her in the damp night air. "Your Krishna temple is up this way," Donny Ray quipped. "Watch out for dogshit." Jusef laughed as a tram whirred past. Cassie stepped up her pace, her mind in full rotation. Rasonnati's man at JFK airport said the Hare Krishnas have priests who can marry people.

Now we're cooking, she thought. Donny Ray would make a ton of money with the foreign cars. That gold in Switzerland would be community property, half hers, but only if she could prove he acquired it during their marriage. *People* magazine had schooled her on that, with all the celebrities' financial issues.

It also meant their riverside conversation in Lyon had to be their common law starting point. Good thing he didn't buy the gold until the next day.

Of course, he hadn't officially agreed to the marriage. He'd blubbered in the car back there, then got all cocky again. It would be his word against hers, and if Brigitta showed up, that's all she wrote.

She stomped the ground, marching, then her heart skipped a beat. A white, two-story clapboard house lay ahead, with a sign and lighted pictures of the Vedi people. That must be the touristy tearoom, but surely Krishnas lived inside, she reasoned, as she couldn't imagine they'd waste all that upstairs space. Well-lighted, it appeared to be open. Her mind raced. If the Krishnas gave them a wedding certificate, it would prove Donny Ray meant to marry her common law.

Heads ducked, they walked through the freezing mist, stopping outside a tavern. "This here's a brown café," Donny Ray said. Fresh oxygen must have done him some good, she thought. He didn't smell like Scotch anymore, and his eyes were clear. Maybe he needed another drink to keep him mellow. She had a hard-sell job coming up.

He grunted and opened a heavy door into the dark and noisy interior. They sat in a booth and the guys ordered dark, bitter ale. She asked for Seven-Up. The server brought baked fish with horseradish sauce and sides of pea soup.

The men fell silent, clinking spoons in their pea soup, alternating bites of trout. "Oh, the smells, ugh," she winced. She placed her right hand against her cheek, lightly stroking her skin with her silver token and its soothing cool.

Background voices and laughter melded into a drone, rising and falling in waves. To bend them to her will would take all the courage Johnny Frank could radio-wave from heaven.

Except for perfume samples at Dillard's in Shreveport, she'd never negotiated anything in her life.

"Earth to Cassie," Donny Ray snapped, poking her elbow until it gave way.

"What you looking at me for?"

"Marry Jusef."

She sipped some Seven-Up. "I told you before, I'll make you a deal."

"Don't get testy here, Cassie."

"I'm not. You know it's a good offer."

Jusef made fists with his thumbs tucked inside. He pounded lightly on the table. "Let's hear it."

"We've been over this already." She swept her hair from her eyes. "Jusef, you need a wife, and I need a husband—mainly, I need a father for the baby," she eyeballed Donny Ray, "who happens to be him."

"And?" Donny Ray watched her over his stein.

"You also said we could be common law married, as of two days ago, by the river in Lyon."

"You said that?" Jusef frowned at him.

"I just said we *could!*" Donny Ray adjusted his drink on the coaster. "It was hypothetical."

"News flash: you said it." Cassie snapped her fingers. "Well—you didn't disagree. And I've got to have a husband with the same last name as the baby's on the birth certificate."

She shifted her view. "Sorry, Jusef, but you might decide you don't want to stay in America, and then what happens to me? I'll tell you what, I want my baby to know family and jump in a bouncy castle at home."

"This isn't a deal at all," Jusef crossed his arms.

"Yeah, it is. I'm willing to pretend me and you are married, and we'll untangle it later." She glanced around for eavesdroppers. "You'll get the front you want, and the neighbors will say how cute we are, and they'll sign affidavits saying we're a standup couple."

Sliding his chair closer, Jusef thumbed his ear. "Let me get this straight. You want to marry Raymond first, your *Donny Ray*, to get what you want for the baby. But you only pretend to marry me so it'll look good to the neighbors? That's absurd."

She toyed with the salt and pepper shakers, rearranging them on the table. "Not really."

"Yes, really. So, call yourself common law with Raymond if you like, but you and I will go to a Texas courthouse, get a license, and get married legally. We must have documentation. A paper trail."

"Doesn't anybody want to know what I think?" Donny Ray thumped his fist on the table.

Jusef cleared his throat. "No. You never said this woman would be pregnant."

"How the hell was I supposed to know?" Donny Ray lit a cigarette and blew out short breaths. "Anyway, it makes your marriage look legit. Why don't you see that?"

Taking a sip from the beer stein, Jusef had a know-it-all look on his face—sneering with the half-cocked head. "Because it changes the whole picture. Now we've got a cost-benefit analysis—all this time and trouble setting things up, and I do not want legal responsibility for your baby. So, I agree with Cassie in this respect."

Leaning into the conversation with renewed enthusiasm, Cassie brightened. "Yeah, because I don't want folks counting backwards on their fingers and figuring out this child was conceived out of wedlock."

Jusef did a double take. "Who cares?"

"Nice people do," Cassie flapped her hand. She didn't want to oversell.

The men exchanged glances. Donny Ray shrugged, "Shotgun wedding, I guess."

"Whatever that means," Jusef clasped his hands on the table directing his attention to Cassie. "Of course, if you don't agree to my plan, we take you down if something goes wrong. Not everyone in prison is guilty of something, you know?"

"Uh, sure." She'd been so focused on the baby that she forgot they were holding the conspiracy card against her. "Don't forget, that Krishna place is on the way back. Let's stop in and get married there, Donny Ray."

"What? I've got to piss." Donny Ray stood up, bumped his chair under the table, and stalked off, heading for the lavatories at the back. Jusef and Cassie studied each other until she broke the silence.

"I thought you'd take sides with Donny Ray."

"Ah," he reached for a roll, broke it, and spread butter in thin stripes. "Think pragmatism if you will. Strategy. My operations require it."

"So, those guns we took to Switzerland, what was all that about?" Cassie asked.

Jusef raised his eyebrows and buttered another roll. "You know what you know. Everyone gets a clue to the puzzle, but nobody gets them all."

# CHAPTER FORTY-SEVEN

## Hare Rama, Hare Rama

Cassie squinted in the halo of streetlamps, mist swirling in the tungsten aura. She'd heard about spousal privilege years back when catechism went off the rails. The privilege attached to spousal communications wasn't absolute, unless the spouse wanted to use it.

Donny Ray didn't seem to know about that. She clamped her lips like a toothless woman in the town square. He would marry her only if he thought it protected him from prosecution.

Cassie slowed at the Krishna house crosswalk. "Okay, that's it y'all. Up ahead, see to the right." The porch light beckoned them.

"This is bullshit," Donny Ray muttered. "They probably won't even let us in."

"I bet they will if we pay something." Dang, just then she realized she left the backpack at the shop. "You've got some money don't you, Jusef?"

"Hey, this is your party. I don't get involved."

Donny Ray crossed his arms, straightening his back against a street sign. "Your problem, Cassie."

"Figure it out," Jusef said. "I'll meet you across the street in an hour." He pointed to a bookshop, its lighted displays of classics and contemporaries glowing beneath striped awnings.

Cassie turned to Donny Ray. "Come on, you really won't help? We only just fell out of bed, and already you're dodging child support."

"Hold on. Where's he going?" Donny Ray pulled out a cigarette and stuck it in his mouth. They watched Jusef dodge some cars and lope past the bookshop awnings.

"See here, Cassie," he dug into his pockets. "Swiss francs, coins, it's all I've got." He closed them in her hand and said he'd be right back. He sprinted past pedestrians and caught up to Jusef. They stopped. They talked. This was her chance, but the Krishnas' porch light went out.

She turned and ran as hard as she could, down the pavement, across the grass, up to the doorway. She rang the bell, banging on the door, peering through the curtains.

A man dressed in Krishna garb turned on the light and cracked open the door, the safety chain still fastened. "May I help you?"

"Yes! I want to get married! Will you do the ceremony for me?"

He hesitated before admitting her. "We just finished prayers," he said, as a lady stepped out of an anteroom.

"Please sit down," he said. Dressed in a swirl of tangerine silks, the slight man had a skinny braid streaming down his back. "My name is Dhuma. This is my wife, Mayra. Some herbal tea for our guest?"

Mayra nodded, disappearing behind a counter where she rattled a few pans, put a teakettle on to boil, and promptly served chamomile brew in a delicate china cup.

Dhuma examined Cassie's face. "And whom do you want to marry?"

"Well, he's gone up the street for a minute, so I came down here to see about it. We're leaving for the States tomorrow. And I'm pregnant."

"Are you Krishnas?"

Cassie sipped her tea, studying him over the china rim. "I'm working on it. I want our baby to be at least half-Krishna."

"Half-Krishna? This is irregular, of course," Dhuma explained. "A Hare Krishna wedding ceremony is spiritual, with families present, and holy fire. Both bride and groom must vow to serve the Supreme Personality of Godhead and to stay together always."

"Isn't it enough for me to serve Lord Krishna?"

Dhuma exchanged glances with his wife, who bowed out of the room.

Cassie stuck her tongue to the side of her mouth. "I know you think I'm crazy, wandering to your door this way."

"Not unusual. We welcome stragglers from the night," he said. "But there are those who pretend without commitment in their hearts. What interests you about our precious Godhead?"

Recalling the airport magazine, Cassie said the karma and the Vedic viewpoint were her primary concerns. "Eternal travelers wandering from one body to the next."

Dhuma raised his eyebrows. "Tell me more."

Clasping her hands in a church-and-steeple, Cassie took a deep breath. "First, allow me to ask, do you know a lady named Rasonnati? I met her in New York."

"I do know her!" Laughing, he threw back his head, streaming the braid down his back.

"She's the one who talked to me about it." Cassie slowed her speech to accommodate creative thinking. "She seemed so wise, and I got a magazine, so if you won't marry my fiancé and me, I'd appreciate staying with y'all if I could."

"You would not return to America with your fiancé?"

Aw hell, now she'd painted herself into a corner.

Cassie studied her teacup and tilted her head, hoping to appear wise and spiritual while she thought of something else.

"I meant to say, we would like to stay with y'all, that is, if you can't marry us tonight, we could be Lord Krishna's servants. And all that." Gracious. All she wanted was to get the man to document a wedding.

Dhuma frowned. "Oh, we have a waiting list—no room for you now. Very sorry. Maybe in a month or two? Anyway, you cannot stay here without a visa." He pulled his braid over his shoulder. "Immigration authorities frequently stop in. We cannot let anyone overstay a welcome."

Immigration, again? She wondered why so many people wanted to change countries all the time.

Wide-eyed Hare Krishna devotees, lining the stairs, distracted her with a call-and-response chant. Yards of multicolored silks and rayons ruffled through the banister spindles. Cassie tippy-tipped her fingers in a shy greeting and returned her attention to Dhuma.

"So, you'll marry us," she said.

"This isn't a sacred temple," he said. I am not a priest."

"But I'll pay you."

"Ah. Well, we may be interested. How much money do you have?"

Cassie pulled the coins from her pocket and counted them out. "Twenty Swiss francs. That's, uh–"

"About fifteen American dollars," he shook his head. "No good. Sorry. Fifty dollars minimum." His eyes traveled to her chest. "What is that around your neck?"

"Uh," she shuddered. "Do you want to see?"

"Yes, please," he said, extending his fingers to touch the silver token.

Cassie's chest tightened, as a rush of thoughts cascaded through her brain. Why didn't she bring her money? She was risking the token now. And where was Donny Ray? The Krishna boys might hit her in the head and dump her in a canal. Nobody would ever know, especially if Donny Ray was getting knocked off somewhere, too. She shuddered.

Dhuma examined the sawmill token. "Very interesting. Come with me."

Cassie followed him into an old-style cloakroom. He reached for digital scales underneath a counter.

"Let's see. Neck chain included? Good chain!" Smiling, he scanned the numbers. "Very lucky for you. Fifty-one grams, 1.8 ounces."

"Wow, how much is that worth?"

"Ummm, silver is at fifteen to twenty U.S. dollars an ounce now."

Cassie frowned. "And this is worth..."

"Thirty-five dollars. Firm."

"That's all? But this is an antique!" Cassie's heart sank. It was supposed to buy her way to freedom. Thirty-five dollars would hardly pay for cab fare to Schiphol.

"I sure thought it was worth more," she said.

"But this is sterling—not pure silver. It appears alloyed with some nickel, maybe copper. I'm doing you a favor to pay on the high side."

"There's a silver shortage, though." Her pulse quickened in a bad way.

"Eh, before the shortage, it was three dollars an ounce. So, you see it is very valuable now. And combined with your Swiss francs, it is fifty dollars. Congratulations. Now where is your groom?"

"He's coming. May I have this back? Only to wear at the wedding, if you don't mind."

"Time grows short," Dhuma raised his eyebrows.

"And I want an official certificate to show you married us in a legal ceremony."

"Anything else?"

"On the certificate, I want it to say–"

"You write it out, and one of the members will copy in calligraphy." He clapped his hands. A young man quickly appeared with pen, ink, and official Hare Krishna parchment with gold leaf swirls in the margins.

Cassie bent over a table in the cloakroom with him, as others prepared the tearoom for the wedding. They pulled out a wooden pallet, moved furniture, and screeched tables across the floors.

"My wife will help you get ready for the ceremony. We will explain," Dhuma clapped his hands for his wife, but she was distracted by someone banging on the door.

"Yes?" Mayra nudged the curtains and peered out. She called to Cassie. "Is this the groom?"

She rushed to see. "Yes, yes, that's my fiancé!"

The door opened to a disheveled Donny Ray, concealed anger seeping through his pores. Cassie could smell it. She introduced him to Dhuma, who carefully explained the basics of the ceremony.

"We will do short version, very fast," the Krishna said.

Dhuma's wife draped a saree around Cassie and a cloth around Donny Ray's neck. "This is a dupatta," she said. "Very important." She gestured to the pallet. "You stand on the platform. When we're at the temple, we use a mandap, but this will suffice."

Cassie pointed at a lighted candelabra in the middle of the room. "What's this for?"

"Traditional ceremony has open fire, but safety rules forbid us to have it here," Dhuma said. "Candles must do. You circle them seven times, the man leading for four rounds, then you lead for three. You tell each other of love and happiness, similar to a Christian vow, so you can make that up as you go. Then you exchange garlands, and we are done."

Cassie and Donny Ray circled the candelabra, with him reciting song lyrics, and Cassie recalling Bible verses and love poems ("I run! I run! I am gathered to thy heart!"). They exchanged garlands, and the followers sang the Hare Krishna mantra with clapping and more swirling of garments.

Once Dhuma declared them married, his assistant presented the calligraphy. Cassie examined it carefully. "Yes, good, this is what we wanted."

Dhuma read it aloud, as Cassie and Donny Ray held hands in front of him. "We the parties agree that Cassandra Jean Tate and Donny Raymond Duggan Richard entered into marriage on October 30, 1979, by the banks of the River Rhône in Lyon, France, solemnized by the most holy Hare Krishna wedding ceremony."

"Beautiful!" Dhuma declared.

"Your assistant helped me with it," Cassie beamed. They signed it and Dhuma affixed his special seal. He rolled it up and his assistant tied it with a purple ribbon.

"You'll keep a copy, too? In case I lose this?"

"Inscribed in our holy book." He gestured.

She unfastened the silver chain around her neck and kissed the silver token. Shivering, an upswell of emotion triggered cascading images of Johnny Frank and Jean François, *The Umbrellas of Cherbourg*, and the double tragedy of Della and Éliane. She touched Donny Ray's cheek and for a fleeting moment, she saw affection in his eyes.

# CHAPTER FORTY-EIGHT

## Ipana Fangs

Cassie clutched the marriage certificate. She'd done it—the first step to securing the baby's future. Even so, she wanted to run back into the Krishna house and reclaim the sawmill token. She'd always had it around her neck, always, and it was almost as much a part of her as Johnny Frank himself. But she had to buy her way out of a jam.

Her dad would be okay with it. Nonetheless, its surrender crushed her spirits. Her chest heaved as she sputtered with silent rebukes.

She put her arm through Donny Ray's. "Aren't we going to meet Jusef at the bookshop?"

"Nah. Just keep walking."

He pulled out another cigarette, lit it, and turned them back on course. "He had to mail a couple of letters, get things sorted. Here's the plan: Jusef will be traveling as a German graduate student at the University of Houston. Political science. You'll be his American wife."

"I thought he was Iranian."

"Nah, I told you already, Jimmy Carter is kicking them out. Don't worry about it, all part of a deal."

"I wish I knew more about these deals of yours." She blew foggy breath into the chilly night air.

"If I told you, I'd have to kill you." He squeezed both of her shoulders.

Shuffling her feet, Cassie wasn't amused. She tugged on his sleeve. "Tell me again about the Switzerland thing. Where'd y'all get the weapons from?"

Donny Ray checked over his shoulder and lowered his voice. "The Russians. Commies—hammer and sickle crowd."

"I mean, was it a consignment or something?"

Slowing his steps, Donny Ray guided her to a pastry shop window, where ginger buns, sugar bread, and kolaches beckoned from rotating platters. He looked around, pulled her close, and whispered into her ear. "Soviets sold them to Jusef, and Jusef sold them to Iranians. All Russian-made. Not a thing American about them."

She studied a bear claw. "So, explain how we got tied up in this?"

"Jusef paid me to drive the guns to Switzerland." Donny Ray turned his head toward her. "And you rode with me. And that's all there is to it."

Ah, that's where he got the money to buy the bullion. Therefore, she had a rightful claim to the gold anyway because she was riding shotgun at the time. She was part of the operation, and she deserved to be paid for it. Not that she'd want to argue that point with anyone, but at least she didn't need to feel guilty about swiping the Krugerrand.

"I think this is a lot of noise about nothing," she said. "All the big drama didn't involve you any more than me—and God knows, I had no idea." She huffed breath on the window and drew a circle on the tiny patch of fog. "What happened to the German man?"

"Aldo? Don't know." He hugged her shoulders. "He was a Nazi honcho, though, chief mechanic. There's a lot of people still pissed about all that. You remember what Jusef was saying about the German terrorists? They're trying to wipe out the leftover Nazis. No telling who all was trying to get to him."

Donny Ray was either lying or leaving out a lot of stuff, she thought. All that crying in the garage and carrying on, running in and out of Europe. He had a million reasons to protect Jusef, and they were all in the Swiss bank.

Jusef joined Cassie and Donny Ray back at the mechanic shop. He pulled a stool from underneath a counter. "So, we're on countdown." He checked his watch.

"This is a great opportunity. Houston gets us the ship channel and ports. The street scene is as good as Amsterdam." Donny Ray nudged Cassie. "Don't forget spousal privilege."

She wrinkled her nose. "You mean sex?"

"No, the immunity thing," Donny Ray pointed his finger. "A wife don't testify against her husband. And you got two—me and him. On account of that's how you want it to be."

"That's like the priest-penitent privilege," she said.

"Yeah, but with husband-wife stuff, it's so they don't upset the household. So, if somebody asked about you running guns to Switzerland, I'd just say 'no comment,' and they couldn't make me talk about you."

Cassie scowled and reached for a tire gauge.

"What's fair's fair," Donny Ray said. "You can't talk about either one of us."

Jusef nodded with a scoff.

She flipped the tire gauge and pressed her finger on the silver pin that made the marker move up and down. "I could talk about you if I wanted to, though."

"But you won't, or your dominos fall. You ain't no angel. We could make a good case against you. A good lawyer can do any kind of thing and make it stick."

Cassie slumped in her chair. When Donny Ray grinned, she saw fangs where an Ipana smile once had been.

## CHAPTER FORTY-NINE

### Dateline Schiphol: 11/03/1979

Donny Ray poked Cassie in the arm. "The damn flight's delayed for maintenance."

She looked up from a crossword puzzle. "How long?"

"Don't know."

Cassie said nothing, but her stomach roiled. Her nerves weren't so good anyway, and now a delay. She reached to touch her silver token. "Not there, *mercy*."

At least she passed the security check. She'd stuck the Credit Suisse key in the backpack so it wouldn't ping when she walked through the metal detector. The lady with the X-ray machine let it slip by. Merely a key, right? But at the first opportunity, she dashed into the bathroom and stuck it back into her bra. She couldn't trust anybody now, even the guy sweeping the floor. Anyone might steal that backpack.

She walked to the window overlooking the tarmac.

Only a glass wall separated her from the planes, so she passed time watching them taxi to their gates. The 747 resembled a giant shark, from the tail end rudder to a double deck hump. Little windows appeared to be beady eyes mounted on top behind its snout. She nosed up to the glass for a closer look. The plane moved, and it seemed to kiss the windowpane. She jumped.

Donny Ray put his hand on her shoulder. "Go sit down." He sounded like a cranky nun, she thought. "I can't look away from you for a minute."

She poked around in her bag and pulled out a French comic book. She noticed mustard stains, right off the dinner plate at the campground.

Jusef nudged her. "I bought you a bottle of mineral water and, here—a Dramamine."

"Thank you for the water." Cassie half-smiled. Maybe the pill packet was tainted. "So, let me ask–"

"And I have something else for you." He pulled a diamond ring from his pocket.

She gasped. Imagine reaching up grocery shelves with that rock, she thought. It must be a carat and a half! She knew. She'd priced them. And if it's real, it could pay for a year's worth of groceries, diapers, and even Ward's Cafe.

"This makes it official, yes? Put it on before we board."

Her fingers were a little swollen, but the ring fit fine. Maybe this is how Mafia wives started out. A little gilt for the guilt, she thought.

"What were you going to ask me?" He looked at her with those Dr. Zhivago eyes, and she forgot what she was going to say. Oh, those eyes so beautiful, but he still had a proverbial gun in her back. Now, instead of hearing "Lara's Theme," she saw flashes of *Gunsmoke*.

After an hour, the Braniff lady called the flight. They boarded, sitting three across with Cassie trapped in the middle. Light was coming through the airplane window, making a pie-plate halo around Donny Ray's head—of all the people to have a saintly glow.

## CHAPTER FIFTY

## Two Out of Three Ain't Bad

The intercom announced the approach to JFK International Airport. Donny Ray stirred and opened the window shade. Mid-afternoon sunlight beamed into the row, and Cassie realized that in a few minutes, the plane would be landing on U.S. soil. God, such a relief, she thought. She wiped her eyes.

"What's wrong?" Donny Ray asked.

"I'm just so happy we got across the ocean, and the baby is safe." She leaned over him to see the Manhattan skyline. Jusef stirred, his right elbow encroaching on her armrest. Cassie nudged it off. She planned to fix his wagon and keep the diamond ring.

Donny Ray checked his watch, "I can't figure out if we'll be on time for the Houston flight." The plane dipped and circled, then rose with the pilot's announcement that they would keep circling until the tower cleared them for landing.

"Why the hell can't they set it down in New Jersey?" Donny Ray bit his cuticle.

"Cool it, Raymond," Jusef clasped his hands, returning his elbow to the armrest. "Don't draw attention to us."

Cassie looked at him sideways. Yeah, you'll get yours, she thought. She wasn't about to get stuck with New York City detectives and Brooklyn accents. She'd wait until Houston before she told anyone. She wished Beecher could meet the plane there, give her a ride home.

Tapping her fingers and twiddling her thumbs, she exhaled slowly. Questions, she had questions. Did Beecher get the cablegram she sent him? Did he talk to Çois?

She'd phone Beecher from JFK, she decided. Closing her eyes, Cassie practiced deep relaxation techniques featured in the airline's flight magazine. Only a few months ago, the height of danger was a beauty school fire.

By the time they cleared Customs, they'd have missed their connection to Houston. Not another direct flight until the next day—Sunday afternoon. "No good," Jusef said.

"I wouldn't mind taking a bus into the city to kill some time," Cassie said. "Or let's spend the night in Times Square."

Jusef glared at her. "Absolutely not."

"Why? I heard the city never sleeps."

"We have people in place," Jusef snapped. "We go to Houston tonight."

People in place? She got a bad vibe.

Jusef scrutinized the flight monitors overhead. "Best option is Dallas, then Houston."

They trooped to the ticket counter, where exasperated reservation clerks rebooked travelers. JFK to Dallas was four hours, non-stop. With the time change they'd get in about 11:00 p.m. They could try connecting to Houston on a red-eye flight from there.

Examining the new ticket, Cassie's nerve endings stung with anxiety. "I need to use the bathroom."

"Who's stopping you?" Donny Ray rubbed the back of his neck.

"Just thought I'd say, because you're always wondering where I'm at. And I've got to get some dimes." She stuck out her lip. "For the pay toilet."

"I thought they'd outlawed pay toilets."

Cassie knew they had, but she needed dimes for the phone. "Well, in case they've still got them here."

"I don't have any change," he said. "We need to find a currency exchange anyway."

Cassie could hardly contain her excitement, as they exchanged francs for dollars and a roll of dimes. "There, that ought to hold you," Donny Ray said. He pointed across the wide corridor, crowded with travelers. "Don't take all afternoon. We'll wait here for you."

## Beecher, Don't Lose That Number

Trough sinks with faucets and soap dispensers anchored the center of the restroom facility, with counters lining walls and mirrors at every turn. Women and children crowded the stalls, along with hand dryers, and diaper-changing shelves. But no pay phones!

Cassie spotted an exit on the far wall and stooped to blend in with a group of ladies in long black robes, their eyes peeping out from slits in their headdresses. Then she caught a pack of older folks in nubby wool sweaters squeezing into a pancake house, pay phones lining its walls. She ducked in with them and went to the phone farthest from the door.

With a slight shiver, she inserted a dime into the slot and dialed the operator.

"Yes ma'am," she said, "I want to make a collect call to anyone at this number." She stammered. "It's from Cassie."

She shifted her feet on the smooth vinyl floor, and her throat tightened. A husky voice answered after several rings. TV noise blared in the background.

"Beecher here." He accepted the call, and Cassie swelled with joy.

"Beecher!" Holding the receiver to her ear, she ran her fingers up and down the armored phone cord.

"What in the world is going on?"

"Did you get my cable?" She stuck her little finger in her free ear.

"Yeah, I got it. You're pregnant? Oh my God, Cassie! Is the shithead going to marry you or what?"

Cassie raised her voice to hear herself talk. "We're married already. No time to tell it. I'm at JFK, in New York. We're flying to Dallas from here. DFW. Can you come get us?"

"When are you getting in?"

"About eleven o'clock tonight," she checked her ticket. "Braniff Airways, Flight 4033."

"So, it's you and Donny Ray?"

Cassie's voice escalated in pitch. "Yeah, him and an Iranian Communist guy."

"An Iranian Communist?"

"Yeah, except he's traveling as a German so Jimmy Carter won't kick him out. It's a big mess with a green card and they want to go to Houston, and I'm supposed to be the Iranian's wife for show."

Beecher's voice rose, "What the hell have you gotten yourself into?"

She glanced toward the door to make sure Donny Ray wasn't sneaking a look. "I'll explain later. I've got to go now. Just remember I love you."

## CHAPTER FIFTY-ONE

## Braniff Stitched in Blue

Finally on board, Cassie thanked God for old man Braniff, rest in peace—one of his planes was taking her home. Her hands resting on the tray table, Cassie fingered church-and-steeple, three times, four times. She'd tell the stewardess about Jusef. Turn him in. The pilot could radio the ground. She frowned. But then Donny Ray, and possibly Cassie, might get in the mix as co-conspirators or something.

It would be okay. They would use their spousal privileges and come out clean, while nailing Jusef to the wall. He'd cooked up these schemes, running in and out of terrorist dens and hanging out with war criminals. Now she was embarrassed that she'd found him so handsome. She still wondered why he never made a move, but it didn't matter now. He'd be locked up.

The plane hit a little air pocket, sloshing ginger ale over her tray. The "Fasten Seatbelt" and "No Smoking" signs lit up as flight attendants hurried to their jump seats. "Ladies and gentlemen, ordinary turbulence here, nothing to worry about," the pilot said over the intercom.

Cassie felt some turbulence of her own. She clutched the armrests with a sensation of sunburn from the inside out. Her teeth locked in place.

Falling however many feet—thirty, forty? The plane jerked, then corrected. She loosened her grip on the armrests and sneaked a look at Donny Ray, who sat erect, gripping a Marlboro flip-top box. All this craziness, and he didn't do anything—they didn't do anything, except drive guns to Switzerland. They stayed out of Germany the whole time.

So yeah, she'd play this card. No telling what Jusef and his contacts were up to. The idea that a car parts business had such a strict deadline—we must be in Houston Saturday—was nuts. Something else, something big was going on.

Actually, she'd be doing Donny Ray a favor—not that she owed him one. Get him out of this mess. The worst that could happen would be a short stay in a federal lockup—which meant a golf course and steak dinners on Fridays. He'd bond out, plead down, get a suspended sentence, and be home for Christmas. Smart tradeoff. She had it all figured out.

The second the seatbelt and no-smoking signs blinked off, Donny Ray shook a cigarette out of the red box. "I've got to use the bathroom," she said to his eyerolls and groans. Jusef stood up to let her by. Cassie wobbled down the airplane aisle to the flight attendants' galley, where they stood ready to resume service.

She stopped in front of a stewardess wearing a snappy apron with Braniff stitched in blue across the front. Cassie ducked into the kitchenette alcove.

"Ma'am, I need your help."

The woman placed a tray of cold drinks on the beverage cart and raised her eyebrows. "Yes?"

Butterflies swirled in Cassie's stomach. "I'm with a foreign criminal. A fugitive. I need you to tell the pilot so he can radio the ground and get him arrested." She flattened her palms against the walls to support herself.

"Show me." The stewardess looked down the aisle.

"Row 21–on the right," her voice quivered. "I don't want them to see us staring."

"There's more than one?"

"See the man on the aisle?" Cassie jerked her head. "He's Iranian, posing as a German so he can get into the country. He's dangerous. He might have a weapon in his shoe." It was possible, she reasoned. Jusef wore steel-toed boots. Maybe the metal detectors hadn't caught a knife.

Cassie bobbed her ring finger. "The other man is my husband. I'm sitting between them."

The stewardess studied Cassie's face. "It's a federal offense to file a false report. You understand?"

Heartburn surging through her chest, Cassie nodded.

"I need you to give me names—yours, theirs, everything helps. An Iranian? This is a big deal."

Cassie flinched. "But they'll see me writing stuff."

"Here, take these," she handed Cassie paper napkins and a ballpoint pen. "In the lavatory. Go."

Cassie locked the lavatory door and began scribbling on the napkin with a shaky hand: "Jusef Ali. 'Mr. Big.' Iranian. German. Fake passport. Gun Runner. Visa fraud. Donny Ray Duggan. U.S. Army vet. Cassie Tate Duggan. American. Donny Ray's wife."

Hey now, Donny Ray's wife. That's me.

The plane dipped, and the fasten seat belts sign came back on. Now her palms were sweating. Calm down, she thought. Don't give yourself away. Passing the napkin to the flight attendant, she returned to her seat. While most of the other passengers napped in the dim cabin lights, Cassie sat stiff and envied their ability to relax.

The stewardess pushed the beverage cart down the aisle, nodding and smiling at passengers. She picked up Jusef's peanut wrapper and plastic cup, making fleeting eye contact with Cassie—a barely perceptible wink. Cassie clenched her fists for a moment, then slowly relaxed. Her left thumb stroked the inside of her wedding finger and the thin metallic bump of a new gold ring.

Finally, the lights of Dallas-Fort Worth twinkled in the dark beneath them. She wondered if she could ever explain what happened so that people would understand. Maybe this was how Chuck and Beecher felt when they tried to tell her about Vietnam—recollections from a distant place and time, which nobody else could comprehend if they weren't there.

"Ladies and gentlemen, we are approaching Dallas-Fort Worth." The pilot's voice, deep and reassuring, elated her. Cassie's thumb twisted the diamond to the inside of her hand, and she made another fist. The sharp edges of the stone provided an odd sense of relief, as somehow it distracted her from fears.

"Please extinguish smoking materials and return tray tables and seats to the upright position," a stewardess announced. "Stand by for landing."

Donny Ray gripped the armrests. Jusef lifted an eyebrow. Cassie squeezed the diamond. The plane touched down. Bump. Bump. No explosion. Yet.

# CHAPTER FIFTY-TWO

## Dateline Dallas: 11/04/1979

Now past midnight, passengers grumbled as the plane remained on the tarmac after a delayed landing. The captain dryly explained that maintenance personnel had to install a new jetway due to mechanical problems at the gate. He apologized for the delay.

Donny Ray cupped his hands over the window to see past his reflection. "They ain't doing a thing. Just standing around is all."

Even Jusef appeared restless, pulling on his shirt collar, "I don't like this."

Cassie pointed to baggage handlers stacking bags and suitcases on carts. "At least they're getting our stuff unloaded. That'll save some time." She instinctively reached for her silver sawmill token. Gone, she agonized. She began to shake, a nervous full-body shudder.

"What's wrong with you?" Donny Ray ran his fingers across her forehead. "You got a fever? Man, you're sweating. It's that panic thing, ain't it?" He put his arms around her. "Breathe deep. Let's get a barf bag out of that seat pocket."

"I'm okay," she mopped her forehead. Suspense poured sweat over her brow. Was Beecher at the Braniff gate? God, would they get Jusef? What if...

"Ladies and gentlemen," the intercom sounded, "our apologies for the delay. Please remain seated as we approach the gate."

Applause rippled through the cabin as the captain continued. "Do not crowd the aisles. Please unload in orderly fashion by section."

Donny Ray glared at a flight attendant. "I've got a sick wife here."

"It's my sick wife," Jusef said.

Cassie stuck out her chin. "Hey, it's your sick ass, Bucko," she muttered.

A wave of adrenaline carried Cassie into the terminal. "Welcome to Dallas-Fort Worth" hung in huge letters across the waiting area. She wanted to kiss the floor, but as her eyes adjusted to the bright lights, her joy fell.

No Beecher, she thought. Holy Mother, did he have a wreck? The place was just about empty except for stragglers and the pilots walking behind her. No FBI, no cops, no nothing. She failed. Oh God, the plan failed.

"Hurry up, hurry up, follow me," Jusef angled through flight attendants breezing past with their shoulder bags. A trickle of airport personnel and a few cleaning people with mops and buckets, stymied Jusef's pace.

A Coca-Cola vendor carting a load of soda bumped Cassie. "Excuse me," he said, quietly hustling her to a nearby counter. "For your safety, Miss." He held her arms tight.

Dropping buckets and mops, the cleaners swarmed Donny Ray and Jusef. "Undercover agents!" they blurted.

Mouth agape, Cassie watched the collection of crewcut uniformed officers jump in with revolvers drawn. The angry mass of bodies erupted like oatmeal boiling over. Her pulse racing, Cassie's breath came fast, as the undercover officer held her still.

"Let up! Let up!" Donny Ray yelped, his face mashed to the tile. In the blur of arms and legs, he broke free and ran, leaping onto the moving walkway. His old football speed kicked in, but when someone hit the safety stop, he fell to the wide rubber belt, the comb-plate strafing his face. Shouts and clangs drew her attention to Jusef, lurching through mop pails, kicking them into the wall.

With turns and sways, the officers dumped both men on their stomachs, hands twisted behind their backs, their fingers splayed and wiggling in handcuffs. Jusef twisted his head around to Cassie, his eyes bulging under the strain of capture. The cops cracked knuckles, pulling him up by the handcuffs, and jerking him around like a dog's rag toy. Then they dragged him out.

Blood pooled on the floor beneath Donny Ray's face. He looked up, his nose misshapen and bleeding. "He needs me!" Cassie cried, her brain exploding with the lights of truck stops, Swiss trams, and an old 7-Eleven sign.

She squirmed in the officer's grip as two military policemen held Donny Ray in custody, pulling him to a vestibule. Men in gray dungarees followed them like geese to market. He met her eyes.

"Cassie! I love you!" he wailed, disappearing.

Sick with fear, her knees buckled. An official-looking blonde lady in a dark suit propped her up.

"There you go. You're okay. Come with us," she said. "We need to ask you some questions."

"Am I under arrest?" Cassie's lips quivered, looking behind her, where suddenly Beecher appeared like a silent movie star, the images flashing in herky-jerky fashion. "That's my brother—Beecher!" She turned to the officials. "Can he get my bag for me?"

"We've already got it." The lady gripped Cassie's arm. A man in a suit with an ID badge stood alongside.

Beecher approached, out of breath. "Where are you taking her?"

"Stand back, sir," the man in the suit showed his palms.

Holy Mother, they're gonna lock me up, she thought, her chin trembling.

His face ashen, Beecher stormed ahead. "I've got a right to know!"

"Airport security, the interrogation room, downstairs." Touching Cassie's shoulder, the lady strode past him. "Keep your distance, sir." The officer talked into a Motorola radio. "Need escort."

## CHAPTER FIFTY-THREE

### All the Federales Say...

The lady in the dark suit showed her FBI badge—Margaret Ross. "Would you like something to drink? You've had a long flight." Agent Ross poured herself a cup of coffee from the decaf pot.

"Water, please." Cassie wiped her face with a tissue.

Agent Ross introduced her partner, who handed over Cassie's duffel bag and then filled a paper cup from a cooler in the room. Cassie knew how this was going to go—good cop and bad cop. She wouldn't be suckered into that.

"Where's Donny Ray?" she asked.

"Somebody else is talking to him. I have a few questions for you here." Agent Ross shuffled papers and settled on one page. "You're the informant?"

Informant? The truth sank in. "Yes ma'am."

The agent smiled in that terse, official-business way of school principals whenever a lunchroom felon got busted for a food fight. "You have identification?"

"My passport." Cassie unzipped the backpack and gripped the little blue booklet.

Agent Ross inspected it, writing down the passport number and personal information. She checked the photo and examined the visa stamps. "Nice trip you took. And what is your relationship to the men in question?"

"I'm Donny Ray Duggan's wife." Cassie held up her left hand with the sparkly diamond ring.

"All right, been married for a while?"

"Uh—yeah—common law. Six or seven years. And now I'm pregnant, so we've made it official. Do you want to see the wedding certificate? All signed. I've got it right here." Cassie reached into her backpack and withdrew the crumpled paper, the ribbon raveled and loose.

"Maybe later. First, tell me why you were traveling with the other man. Coming from," she checked the paperwork, "Amsterdam via New York, I see."

Cassie smelled a rat. "Do I need a lawyer?"

"At some point down the line. Right now, I'm trying to get the cast of characters here, how you know each other."

"Donny Ray is innocent. I'm claiming my spousal privilege on him."

"I understand."

"Jusef Ali is a crook, and he's all tied up with Soviets and Iranians—some East German Communists, too, I think."

"Tell me about the Iranians," Agent Ross clasped her hands on the desk.

"He was selling them Russian guns. And I'll tell you right up front. I didn't know about *any* of this. I went over there for Donny Ray. Next thing I knew, Jusef wanted a green card wife."

"Okay. Does Jusef have another name?"

"Jusef Ali. That's the only one I know."

Cassie picked up a marble paperweight from the desk and moved it from one hand to the other.

"So how did Donny Ray get over there?"

"He was in the Army. West Germany."

Agent Ross shuffled through the papers again and turned down a corner on one. "We seem to be missing some documentation." Her partner cleared his throat.

"Will you excuse us a moment?" They bowed their heads in whispers by the water cooler before resuming their places at the table.

"There's some question about his term of service," Agent Ross nodded at her partner, who clicked his ballpoint pen and watched them.

Didn't they believe her? Cassie wondered. "I can show you his picture from the military ID," Cassie said.

"Sure, let's get a look. Army veterans deserve special consideration." Agent Ross held out her hand.

Cassie put down the paperweight and plucked Donny Ray's photo from her wallet.

"This is interesting," the agent commented. "Handsome man, your husband. And I see the signature underneath, with just a few words here. What does that say?" she pointed. "I can't read it."

"Geneva Conventions Identification Card," Cassie blushed. "He took me to Lake Geneva."

"Very good. May we keep this?"

"Sure, but please make me a copy." She figured Donny Ray would catch a break for veterans' preference.

The agent put her elbows on the table and clasped her hands. "Where was he based?"

"Bremerhaven. North Sea."

"He stayed over there instead of coming home after he left the Army?" her eyes locked on Cassie.

"That's right," Cassie lowered her voice. "He had another girlfriend for a little while, so there was that."

"Interesting. Do you remember her name?"

"Brigitta."

"Affairs of the heart, yes. So, let's get back to Jusef Ali." The agent reached for a pencil and tapped it on the table. "Do you know that Iranian extremists took over the American embassy in Tehran today?"

Cassie's mouth fell open. "When?"

"About three hours ago—6:30 a.m. their time. Armed with American weaponry. They took 66 hostages."

Cold chills ran up and down Cassie's arms. "Hostages?" Oh shit. She wondered if Jusef had anything to do with that. She and Donny Ray drove Russian-made guns to Switzerland, not American-made. That kept them in the clear.

Agent Ross studied her. "So, you see why we are very interested in what Mr. Ali can tell us. We may need to keep him as a bargaining chip for the hostages."

"Yeah, sure." Cassie's head grew light, and she bounced both knees. "I never would have thought. Oh man."

The FBI agent kept her there for several hours asking a million questions, over and over, leaving the room and returning with still more. She wanted to know everything about the trip through Europe, whom they met, and where they stayed. Finally, the agent relaxed, tapping an ever-growing file.

This was more trouble than Cassie ever expected. She had stopped shaking hours ago, but a deeper worry set in: what was Jusef telling investigators? He might try to pin everything on her and Donny Ray.

"Anything you remember will help. Even the smallest detail is important." Agent Ross stood up. "You're free to go now, but we'll need to question you again. The passport information is still good—address and phone number?"

Cassie nodded.

"We appreciate your cooperation," Agent Ross shook her hand. "Next time we meet, you'll need a lawyer. Do not, under any circumstances, speak to reporters about this. They'll get the story soon enough, but remember, you're a person of interest."

"Person of interest?" That's what law enforcement always said about people they were looking to arrest and send to the electric chair.

"Don't worry—but do get a lawyer. Here's my card if you have any questions. Your brother is ready to take you home."

# CHAPTER FIFTY-FOUR

## Culture Shock

Cassie's eyelids fluttered in the late morning sun. All night, she'd fought jet lag and anxiety, and now a blanket of depression swathed her in generalized pain, with a creeping sense of nausea. Only hours before, tearful reckonings and disbelief had driven her back to Marshall with Beecher, who told her about Chuck's latest overdose. So, nothing had changed with him, not even the zip code.

Hunger soon overcame inertia, and as she padded through the kitchen, everything seemed to shine a spotlight on her gullibility—especially that stupid coffee mug, *Willkommen in Bremerhaven*. Beecher had left her a plate of biscuits, now stale, but she washed them down with coffee and considered her new reality: culture shock. She needed to escape the silence and reorient herself.

Grabbing the car keys from a brass hook, she opened the back door, its broken spring still twanging. Yep, she was back and headed for her personal ground zero—Highway 59, right through town.

Cassie parked the Comet on a dusty lot—all that remained of Gorgeous U. Construction workers in hard hats worked on a rebuild, a sort of Phoenix rising from the ashes with convenient Port-O-Lets. Even if stinky, they had actual sit-down pots, a welcome sign of home. Then a construction guy pointed to a "no trespassing" sign and motioned her off.

The car engine restarted quickly, of course, as the battery was practically new. She winced at the fleeting realization that she was married and pregnant. Be careful what you wish for, her mother always said. But Keepsake diamond commercials painted an entirely different picture. Nobody ever mentioned terrorists and green cards.

She headed for Ward's Café, then braked to make a U-turn. Some of her old classmates might be there, or somebody else she knew. Reports about Donny Ray's arrest had already been on the radio, and they'd ask her questions. Now she understood why movie characters always turned off the TV whenever they heard news about themselves. "No comment," she practiced, in case reporters showed up at her door.

## Low Profile

One week after the airport takedown, Cassie sat stone-faced in the little den on Burleson Street. The DFW airport operation—with the fake mechanical delays and cops in janitor coveralls—ran on a continuous loop in her head. The Marshall and Shreveport newspapers and television stations exploited the local angle for the Iranian hostages' story. Even a Dallas radio outlet asked her for an interview. But no way was Cassie going to open her mouth. She was keeping a low profile.

Jar lids banging and mayonnaise slapping white bread got her attention. Beecher called from the kitchen. "Want a baloney sandwich?"

"Sure. Thanks." She rubbed her middle, still not showing yet, but the waistband in her pants pinched a little. She'd made doctor and lawyer appointments—a whole support staff. Yet in all of this, she hadn't heard from Donny Ray or Çois. She was gripped by an uncertain sensation that she'd never hear from either one of them again.

Yet, Çois did call Beecher when Cassie left Lyon, just as he'd promised. Beecher thought it was a crank call and hung up. Donny Ray, however, must have broken his dialing finger.

"Why doesn't he phone me?" A frown line etched between Cassie's eyebrows. She took a bite of Wonder Bread.

Beecher turned on college football and sat down beside her. "The cops don't let them make a call unless it's for a bail bondsman or a lawyer." He popped an olive into his mouth.

"Nobody can even tell me where he is." She shook her sandwich at him.

"You tried calling that FBI lady?"

"Margaret Ross? She doesn't know. Or she isn't telling." Cassie chewed slowly, focusing on the TV commentators, their faces overlaid by football action. She took a final bite, touched her lips with a napkin, and slapped the crumbs from the palms of her hand.

She nudged his arm. "Wonder how Chuck's doing?"

Beecher held up a finger for silence until the play clock ran out on the TV screen, then he turned down the volume for a commercial break. "I talked to him today. He's all right."

"Did you tell him I'm pregnant?"

Beecher tilted his head and scratched his ear. "Not the right time for that."

"Dang." She heard a muffled thunk outside the front door and saw the postman's silhouette move past the curtains. She retrieved a manila envelope with multiple postmarks and a dazzling display of multicolored French stamps.

"Whoah, Beecher, look at this. I got something from Çois!" Relief massaged her shoulders as she tore open the envelope and read the letter aloud. "Dear Cassie, I know our news shocked you, so here are pictures of Johnny Frank with Mama, and a certified, true copy of my birth certificate."

Trembling, Cassie examined the document, stamped with an official seal, verifying it as the real thing. She waved it in Beecher's face. Still chewing, he grabbed it, inspected it, brushed away a few breadcrumbs, and handed it back.

"Now Cassie, I'm going to tell you one more time. There's no sure way you can prove any of this. So even though Daddy took the credit—or the blame..."

"Don't you believe me?"

"I believe you believe it," Beecher sighed.

"I want to call Çois—right now."

"Are you nuts?" Beecher lurched on the couch. "Do you know how much that costs?"

"But it's weekend rates!" She reached for the phone. "International operator, please."

### Wrong place, wrong time

"*Allô*, Cassie?" Çois's voice rose in pitch. "How are you? I sent some things."

"They came today!" She fanned herself with a year-old *TV Guide*.

"Excellent! I wanted to prove everything to you and Beecher. We should do blood types, too."

"Good idea, yeah. But listen—Donny Ray got arrested." Cassie made eye contact with Beecher and frowned.

Çois' voice faded. "I told you he was a bad guy."

"We even got stopped at the Dutch border." Talking on the wall phone, stretching out the coiled cord, Cassie took tiny steps around the kitchen. "Stopped and searched. They found Donny Ray's gun, I'm sure it was. But did he give it to Annette? Like, I'm not saying you, but did somebody frame him?"

"No frame. It was his gun, not Aunt Annette's."

Holy Mother, she thought. Leaning against the drainboard, she steadied herself. "The border police pitched a fit about the license plates, too."

"Yes, those. A mix-up. I checked into it. Police stopped some Gypsies for speeding. The license plates didn't match, so the Gypsies told police Donny Ray stole theirs. They gave up the numbers."

"So, you didn't turn us in?" She stretched the telephone cord to the kitchen table.

"No, but I followed up with the Dutch police. They were on alert for a van of your description and French license plates, associated with Dutch radicals—pro-Moluccans, nothing to do with you. Wrong place, wrong time I'm afraid."

As for Aldo's murder, Çois explained, former colleagues informed him the Red Army Faction had unsuccessfully sought a ransom for the old German. Evidence indicated he was executed because he'd outlived his usefulness—and of course, he was still a Nazi. Jusef had provided the Lyon hotel information to ensure confirmation of the kill.

"So, that emergency stuff was a scam?" Cassie studied the tops of her shoes. "Why did Jusef pull us out of there?"

"He couldn't be certain what the RAF would do next."

Beecher stood over Cassie, mouthing "wind it up, wind it up" and pretending to twirl a lasso in the air.

"Oh, Çois, I need to get off the phone now. But I do want to know more. I meet with a lawyer next week. I'll let you know how it goes."

Cassie staggered back to the den and collapsed on the couch next to Beecher as he raised a nacho chip, stopping halfway to his mouth.

"Well?" he groaned.

She stared vacantly at the TV screen. "I'm screwed."

## CHAPTER FIFTY-FIVE

## All Spent

Cassie stepped into the lawyer's office in a rehabbed storefront on the Marshall town square. The workplace, awash in taupe and trimmed in dark wood, had burgundy drapes that opened onto views of the federal courthouse and the Department of Veteran Affairs. Military memorabilia decorated the walls, along with Texas state bar association certificates and a special commendation from the Judge Advocate General's Corps.

"Please sit down," Jud Allbright gestured to an upholstered chair. "Can we get you something? Coffee? Soda?"

"No, thank you." Lawyers and detectives always offered cold drinks and coffee, as though that would relax someone whose life was in shambles. She'd already sold the Krugerrand to raise money for this consultation. It better be worth it.

"Well, let's get to the point." He gestured to the framed documents on the wall, a relaxed smile of pride crossing his face. "I'm a former JAG officer, separated from service, and licensed to practice in Texas. So here we are."

"Yes, sir."

"Call me Jud." A box of Kleenex perched on the corner of his glass-topped desk—probably because everyone who came in was miserable and wanted to cry about it.

She slumped in the chair, her jingly holiday sweater contrasting with the vanilla suede cushions. "I want to know what happened to Donny Ray. Nobody will tell me a thing. About him, about me, about anybody."

Jud clasped his hands on the desk. "To start with, Margaret Ross is the Special Agent who interviewed you initially. I've talked with her at length. First, the good news: you did a valuable service in tipping off the FBI to Jusef Ali—a dangerous character who Interpol wanted pretty badly."

My goodness, she thought. She puffed up, setting her shoulders straight.

"And please verify for me—your original destination was Houston, correct?"

"Yes, sir."

"It's fortunate that you didn't make it. Information develops as we speak, but it appears that it was planned to be a hit on Jusef and Donny Ray."

Cassie's back arched. Struggling to breathe, she listened as Jud explained how they tried to move in on drug kingpin Pablo Escobar's territory. Escobar would have none of it and planned a double cross in Houston. "From what I understand, a car was scheduled to pick you up from the Houston airport for delivery to the Ship Channel. *You* would have been collateral damage. As it is now, you're a material witness."

Fatigue gripped her. She slumped to eye level with a fountain pen desk set. The bells on her sweater tinkled as she shifted uncomfortably.

Jud rapped his knuckles on the desk. "You're not out of the woods here. The U.S. Attorney might also want to file charges against you. It's highly unlikely, but not impossible."

"I see. Would I go to prison?" Her breath came out in short spurts.

"Not if you cooperate. Your value is in your testimony. Anyway, the government always overcharges to get some bargaining room. We'd work a deal."

Cassie took a deep breath. "But where's Donny Ray?"

"Stuttgart. West Germany."

"*What?*" She jerked her head back. "How did he get from Dallas to Stuttgart?"

Jud made prayer hands and touched them to his lips. "First, Donny Ray deserted his Bremerhaven post. Are you aware of that?"

"No. You can't be serious." Cassie squeezed her eyes shut and opened them to Jud's shining gold cufflinks, reflecting off the glass tabletop.

"Think about it. If he had been discharged from the Army under ordinary terms, he would have returned to the States and processed out."

Nodding, Cassie twisted her diamond ring, tugging it over her knuckle and back.

"Now, you gave names to the airline stewardess, am I right? The captain called them in, and agents at the airport ran them through databases. They got hits on both men."

Cassie pinched her nostrils to stave off another nosebleed. She reached for the tissue box on Jud's maple desk. "Just tell me about Donny Ray."

"His passport was bogus, under his deceased father's name, but the fingerprints matched a partial they got from you." Jud examined a paper on his desk. "According to the agent's report, you voluntarily surrendered his military ID, sufficiently intact to confirm it was him."

"The bitch tricked me!" Cassie pounded the table.

"Watch it now. You'll crack the glass." He frowned.

Cassie rotated in the chair and rubbed her neck. "But why is he back in Germany?"

"U.S. Army-Europe still has jurisdiction over him because he deserted a German base. He had a security clearance, dealt with weapons, and associated with a foreign national. He's their guy. They want him for debriefing and court martial." Jud told about Donny Ray allegedly stealing weapons from the Army installation and Jusef funneling them via German terrorists to Iran.

"I thought Jusef bought the guns from the Russians."

"No, they were American weapons—almost certainly Donny Ray's contribution to the enterprise. Where did you get the idea they were Soviet arms?"

"I don't know. They're just always the bad guys. And that's what Donny Ray said."

The lawyer fiddled with his cufflinks, explaining a laundry list of bad shit Donny Ray could face—treason, espionage, death penalty. "It's all here in the Military Code," Jud said, thumping a volume on his desk.

"M-may, may I have that glass of water, please?" Cassie's voice wavered.

"Now we're talking *worst* case." Jud stood and walked over to a cowboy bronze on a pedestal in the corner. He patted the cowboy's hat while he talked.

"The feds need Donny Ray's testimony to build their case against Jusef. That could help him down the way. Of course, the United States will have to get in line for Jusef. West Germany would hang the son-of-a-bitch if they had a death penalty. You're aware of his connection to the Red Army Faction?"

Cassie sat up straight. She could feel her face reddening. "No, I never heard anything about a Red Army! And I had no idea Donny Ray was AWOL or deserting, or anything illegal, I mean at first." Cassie squeezed her eyelids together, and tiny tears forced their way out.

Patting the bronze pedestal, Jud looked up. "Relax. This isn't my first rodeo."

He strolled back to his desk and sat down. "Anyway, Donny Ray wasn't holding that much cash on him—about $5,000 in francs and Krugerrands, that's it. So maybe he wasn't in that deep after all—unless he stashed it in Switzerland. It's generally impossible to get past banker-client privilege there."

Cassie twisted strands of hair around her fingers, still thinking about the lockbox and whatever that held. "Can we still be common law married if Donny Ray's in jail?"

"Sure, but we need to file a Declaration of Informal Marriage to get it recognized for the record," Jud said. "Good thing you got the marriage certificate from those hippie-dippies in Amsterdam. But the flip side is that investigators were able to match the signature to his military ID, and anything else he signed. Hotel registry, such as that."

Questions, she had more questions, and Jud had the answers. But results were mixed. If convicted on major felony charges, Donny Ray would go to Fort Leavenworth, the military lockup. A jailhouse wedding was possible, but marriage applications came strung with red tape. "And I'm curious," Jud said. "When did he give you that ring?"

Slow moment. "Does it matter?"

"A lot," Jud explained. "If he bought it with ill-gotten gains, the government could seize it in partial satisfaction of what he owes them. That'll be part of their case—considered repayment for the weapons he stole." Jud steepled his fingers. "But if it's a family piece, for example, you could get a pass. Did you see him buy it?"

She blinked. Her voice cracked. "He didn't buy it. Jusef gave it to me."

"Put it away for now. Don't wear it in public."

"What do we tell the FBI lady?"

"Nothing—unless she asks." Jud paused. "She's not the one I'm worried about."

# CHAPTER FIFTY-SIX

## School of Hard Coughs

### 1992

Twelve and a half years had elapsed since Cassie's flight home from Amsterdam. Now, for the first time, she rode in first-class. Boeing 747. Leather seats. Dinner menu. Free champagne. Wow.

Cassie wiped her fingers on a warm, damp cloth provided with peanuts on a tray—none of those foil packets and antiseptic wipes you get in the back of the plane. True, she wouldn't get to Switzerland any sooner than the rabble behind the economy curtain, but she wouldn't mind. This luxury would be short-lived.

Resting her head against the plush pillow, Cassie eyeballed Jud's tray table. He'd fanned out certified copies of Donny Ray's identification papers—birth certificate, Social Security card, fake passport, international driver's license, and military mugshot. She inched forward and tapped the tray.

"Mind letting me see those?" Her copies were at home for safekeeping, along with an unopened cigarette pack and a half dozen copies of *Sports Illustrated*, the remnants of his life in lockup.

She occasionally read the magazines, rubbing the pages, pretending to be an inmate, trading cigarettes for a new issue.

Somehow, making herself hurt for Donny Ray helped relieve her burning regrets.

Because of him, she kept the Comet under a tarp in her carport. She drove a shiny Dodge Caravan now, but she couldn't give up the old car. Donny Ray had babied it, souping it up for the quarter-mile while "Kung Fu Fighting" blasted from the AM radio speakers. He swore it'd be worth a lot to auto collectors, so she'd been reluctant to part with it. Besides, it symbolized their relationship. Worth hanging onto, if only to keep Donny Ray in her life—for reasons she would never fully understand.

Cassie stirred in her seat. If she hadn't squealed on him, he wouldn't have been arrested. On the other hand, if she hadn't alerted the stewardess, their corpses would have fed the fishes in Galveston Bay. That was one of the first things Jud told her when they consulted a few weeks after the big brouhaha in the Dallas airport.

The jet engines whined, returning her to the present. The plane gained altitude, and Jud poked Cassie's elbow. His argyle sweater was right out of old Archie comics, but he was still a distinguished gentleman. "Are you about finished looking at Donny Ray's stuff?" he asked. "I want to keep everything together. No mistakes."

"Sure, yes. I'm a little distracted."

It wasn't air travel or even the DFW airport that revved up her pulse. The thought of returning to Basel, and that terrifying race through the city, sucker-punched her at every turn. And yes, please, she'd take a cocktail. Some glazed almonds, too.

She sipped, stirring with a little plastic straw nudging the square ice cubes. The past decade or so had wrung her out. Post-traumatic stress disorder could happen to regular people. She knew the PTSD drill from Educational Psychology. She hit a lot of diagnostic points. Sometimes she experienced nervous, hyphenated breathing along with intrusive recollections.

Her daughter Francie's parentage weighed heavily on Cassie's mind through the years. The little girl's earlobes and funky little pinkie toes couldn't have come from anyone but Chuck. When Sheree dug up some old medical records, his rare blood type confirmed what Cassie had always known. She told him so, and Chuck blew a gasket.

"You're after my money! Don't deny it!" He'd thrown a cypress knee across the room and busted up some liquor bottles, amber liquids streaming off the bar top and puddling on the parquet floor.

"I don't want it for me," she insisted. "I want it for Francie. You pay to play."

"No, *you* pay to play!"

He stayed high and mad for a week. Then he talked to his lawyer, who pointed out that the trust fund would terminate at Chuck's death. The remaining money would go to the Oklahoma Sooners athletic department. A hell of a deal. Chuck hated the Sooners.

Cassie drained the glass, aware of Jud talking low into a hand-held Dictaphone. He told about Cassie and Donny Ray's marriage, telling the common law chronology, and how they got married all over again when he was an inmate. No chapel, no cake, just a telephone ceremony with a priest and a lawyer. She sighed and leaned her seat back a little farther, plagued with rock-solid Catholic guilt.

Ginning and sinning in a graveyard, getting pregnant out of wedlock, betraying Donny Ray—she cringed to think of how many Commandments she'd broken. Getting into Chuck's business worsened everything, but she'd wanted to do right by Francie. At least she'd tried.

Thirty-five was not old, but she would turn 36 in late fall and Cassie didn't have the energy she'd had as a new teacher.

Maybe professional athletes could retain their vitality in their 30s, but they didn't eat lunch in a school cafeteria, where hair-netted servers plop mashed potatoes onto plates with ice cream scoops. And she always took two rolls.

She and Çois patched together a family relationship—awkward but getting better over time. When he came to visit her in Marshall, a writer for the *Shreveport Times* did a big feature on them.

That brought Donny Ray's mother out of the woodwork, claiming grandma privileges, but Cassie got rid of her, and the old girl slunk back to the Bossier Strip where she called herself a den mother. No wonder Donny Ray never acknowledged her. The old mare had been "rode hard and put up wet," as they like to say in Texas.

Cassie had to let go of all that and focus on the present. Nighttime over the Atlantic Ocean. Dim cabin lights. Pitch black beyond the windows. She tried to sleep, but an air pocket jostled the plane. She grabbed the armrest, wide awake now. They sure better not crash after all this, she thought.

Breathing deeply to recapture the sense of Hare Krishna calm, she envisioned herself on that first flight into Amsterdam—so guileless, anticipating Donny Ray waiting at the gate, desperate to swoop her up in his arms. Desperate was the only thing she got right about that scenario. What a pitiful job she'd done of reading men. Della was right about every guy who walked through their screen door. Cassie glanced over at Jud, snoozing on, wondering what Della might make of him.

Jud was divorced when he took on her case. There'd been a spark, but he wasn't inclined to remarry, and she didn't want to divorce Donny Ray—not after all the trouble to get married in the first place. She and Jud eased into a comfortable relationship, though. Early on, before she got her teaching degree, he hired her part-time at his firm to answer phones and run files to the courthouses. She pictured them as Perry Mason and Della Street, engaging in the steamy action off-camera.

Plus, proving entitlement to Donny Ray's lockbox for a possible community property settlement could be problematic. "Don't let's stir anything up," Jud cautioned. She risked losing everything to the feds for payback on Donny Ray's offenses.

Anyway, Cassie wasn't hurting too much financially. After Jud worked lawyer magic, she avoided testifying against Donny Ray and was limited to depositions only about Jusef. Her information was not compelling in the big picture, but useful enough to escape the net on a conspiracy charge.

After all that dust settled, she retrieved the diamond ring Jusef had given her, which turned out to be of startlingly good quality. Jud insisted that she consult diamond expert Camp Flournoy at Flournoy Jewelers in Shreveport. He declared the stone near-flawless. So, Jusef did some good after all, as it paid a lot of bills, including her college tuition at East Texas Baptist University in Marshall.

Lucky for her. However, Donny Ray wasn't so lucky. Neither was Brigitta. As predicted, his court martial got ugly, and based in part on her testimony, they put him away for 20 years. Subsequently, she had a fatal encounter with a runaway bread truck, which Jud found suspicious, but it didn't bother Cassie a bit. Anyway, parole was still a possibility for Donny Ray because he was sentenced before 1987. Otherwise, Cassie tuned out the Sentencing Reform Act particulars. She wasn't so sure she wanted him home anyway.

Even so, on her first visit to Fort Leavenworth, the sheer size of the facility both intimidated and thrilled her, rising from the Kansas plains with its dome, massive castle walls, and rows of triple razor wire.

It gave Cassie the jitters, but she'd settled into the visitors' room—large, well-lighted, with at least a hundred sets of sturdy tables and chairs; a school cafeteria arrangement, except for the barred windows.

That's where she waited for her husband.

Donny Ray strode in, dark brown shirt tucked into belted brown work pants. He'd put on weight and was super clean-shaven. Her man. That was her man, and she'd stand by him like Tammy Wynette, at least until she could figure out what to do about that lockbox.

As guards watched, they exchanged a quick hug, holding hands for an instant, but not above the elbows. The rules were fine with her. She hadn't seen him in almost three years, and her mind was reeling.

"Well, you look really good," she said, her stomach churning with excitement.

"Thanks. You too," he cocked his head and studied her. "How's life on the outside?"

"It's fine. The baby is great," her eyelids fluttered.

He shot a lopsided smile. "We did good, didn't we?"

"We sure did!" Grin and bear it, she thought.

"Got her a French accent yet?"

Cassie laughed softly, "Well sure, to go with her name and all."

"None of that calling her Françoise bullshit, I told you already." He drummed his fingers on the table.

"I know, I know. We call her Francie."

"Who calls her Francie? You better not tell me you have a boyfriend."

"No, no—me and Beecher. Sheree. Everybody." Cassie looked down at the table, a stranger's initials inked on the varnished edge. She wrestled with telling Donny Ray the truth about Francie's biological father.

Donny Ray shook his head. "Now that's messed up, Beecher and Sheree. Married. Good God. But let's move forward. Tell me something. Anything," he gazed into her eyes. "You're so beautiful."

Ah, the old magic. "I'll always love you," she stammered. An awkward moment passed, then she clapped her hands lightly. "I'll finish my teaching degree next winter."

"Congratulations," he smiled, flashing yellowed teeth.

She fidgeted with her top button. "Anyway, I guess you're keeping busy."

"Damn straight! Screen printing—T-shirts, wallpaper, you name it." He beamed. "The other day, the rotary press broke down in the middle of a big run. I jumped right in and fixed it."

"That's great, Donny Ray. I'm so proud!" And surprisingly, she really was.

"They let us smoke in the yard," he said. "But we're so regimented. It's still the Army, just all locked up."

"Do the prisoners bang their spoons in the mess hall?" She lightly bounced her fists on the table.

"No, nothing like that," he laughed softly. "You always cracked me up."

They talked as long as allowed, at least an hour, and she returned the next day. He had banked a lot of visiting time since no one else came to see him. He talked some about prison life, but mostly about his old football heroics and adventures with his cousin Mark, now in lockup, too, at the Texas state pen.

"He was a baby-faced con artist, let me tell you. What a little smartass!" Donny Ray couldn't stop laughing, but with a sort of crying sound. When he leaned back, she noticed slight tears at the corners of his eyes and the now-faded scar. Laughter turned to coughing and he wheezed his way through the next little while.

"You okay?" Cassie thought of Ratso Rizzo in *Midnight Cowboy*, hacking to death in the back of a Greyhound bus. "You shouldn't keep smoking."

"Blah, blah, blah. It's only in the yard. Just a couple a day. That don't hurt nothing." He regained his breath. "Hey, you still got that old Comet? Great car."

"Oh yeah, I can't part with it," she half smiled.

"Sometimes, when this place gets to me, I imagine cruising downtown Marshall. You by my side. Comet humming." His gaze fell, then quickly resumed his upbeat composure. "Listen, I've been wanting to tell you. There's this oldies station out of Kansas City. One of the songs makes me think of you."

"Which one?"

"Elvis. 'You Were Always on My Mind.' Remember?" Donny Ray leaned forward and tucked a lock of hair behind her ear. "It's how I feel about you now."

She hugged her arms, feeling the old warmth just looking at him. "You know," she said, "Elvis recorded that after he and Priscilla separated, and they had poor little Lisa Marie, just four years old, and Priscilla cried for him, same as us."

"We had a good time together. Until you screwed it up." He twisted his mouth. "Kidding. It was some of my fault."

Silence draped their shoulders like an old quilt. The Devil works his ways, she thought. "I got something to tell you."

"You divorcing me?" His face hardened.

"Divorce? Uh, no. Something else," she winced. "Chuck died. The sniper. He overdosed."

"Hah! Good riddance!" Donny Ray slapped the table and tilted back his chair.

She frowned, "That's not nice! He up and killed himself on purpose."

"Who cares?"

"Well," she clenched her teeth, "fact is, Chuck was Francie's father."

Donny Ray grimaced. His voice went low, and his glare scorched her eyelids. "I knew that all along—big fat baby couldn't have been premature. Who did you think you were kidding? I was just waiting for you to come out and admit it."

A cold stillness oozed into Cassie's soul. "Why didn't you say anything before now?"

"I liked watching you squirm. Told you a long time ago, you've got the face of a thousand tells. Anyway, it wouldn't have changed anything." He lowered his head, fixing his eyes up on her. "If I could change anything, I wouldn't be here."

## CHAPTER FIFTY-SEVEN

## Ribbon and Threads

Five pairs of hands riffled, stamped, and passed documents around the horseshoe curve at a sleek conference table. Cassie took a deep breath beneath shimmering chandeliers, where two attorneys, including Jud, and three officers of the Credit Suisse bank checked, rechecked, and initialed pages stamped with enough official seals to fill a book.

Looking over his half-glasses, the white-haired bank officer thumped the stack of documents on the table. "All is in order," he said.

Everyone rose. Jud fastened the top button of his suit jacket as administrators reached across the polished mahogany to shake hands. Hardly containing her excitement, Cassie smoothed her palms against her pleated skirt. Good vibrations and exultations rang in her head.

But did the lockbox contain anything of value? Donny Ray never made clear exactly what was in there, what with his telephone calls being monitored, and his letters censored.

By the time he made deathbed confessions, he was pretty loony on a morphine drip, thin cotton gowns draping his frail body. Asbestosis from being around brake linings and insulation, exhaust fumes, and two packs of cigarettes a day killed his lungs. Cars, cigarettes, cancer. They conspired to kill, and they did.

Cassie had hoped to catch him during a lucid interval, but he was always tripping out, mumbling, and humming a little pirate song about gold doubloons and pieces of eight. She couldn't figure out if he was trying to tell her about the lockbox or merely nostalgic about the Mickey Mouse Club and *The Mystery of the Applegate Treasure.*

Question marks hovered over Donny Ray's bed along with choirs of angels. And angles. He worked the angles until the end.

Proving ownership of the lockbox contents was expensive, and she was still bleeding cash. Jud put a Swiss attorney on the case, and it took months to get foreign authorities to enforce U.S. court judgments recognizing Cassie's rights. By the time she paid off advances and loans, she would need a hell of a lot of bullion just to break even.

Despite overwhelming stress, she had a daughter to think about and her own future—the story of her life, it seemed. Mixed emotions swung like pendulums, still loving Donny Ray while hating his duplicity.

Escorted into an atrium, Cassie blinked in the bright sunlight, adjusting her purse straps and clenching the lockbox key. "Only one person may accompany you," the banker said. He paused. "Security, you understand."

Jud winked and adjusted his silk necktie. Cassie touched his hand, "I want him, please." His Swiss counterpart, snappy in a French cut suit, remained in the anteroom.

"This way," one of the bankers gestured, solemn as a funeral director. Cassie and Jud followed his lanky strides down a cavernous hall, past armed guards and heavy steel doors swinging over crimson carpet, then into a room lined with brass boxes gleaming with promise.

Finally, he stopped, stock-still, before box number 230825, and turned his palm face up. "Your key, please."

She handed him the envelope, frayed and damp from her nervous clutch, bulging with a key inside. Momentary panic struck: could it be the old hotel key, after all? Of course not, she'd checked it over and over again. Would it fit? She held her breath, grasped Jud's hand, and watched the banker turn his master key with hers.

Tumblers clicked into place. Then the banker, escorted by a guard, carried the box into a private room with a glass-topped table. "Press the bell when you are done," he said, and with a muted thud, he locked Cassie and Jud inside.

She eyed the box, smaller than what she'd expected, but Krugerrands don't occupy much space. Cassie snapped open the latch. Holding her breath, she tried to suppress her anxiety, even as her heart pounded in and out of her chest. Steeling herself for the big reveal, she raised the lid and gripped a black container about the size of a tool kit, compartments molded in its sides.

"It's heavy," she smiled, setting the case down before them. She removed a honeycomb of short, fat tubes. Jud gripped one, pried off the security cap, and tilted it to reveal a prancing South African springbok antelope engraved on a Kruggerand—the first of 10 shining coins that trickled out, clinking across the glass.

Her eyes wide, Cassie shrieked, grabbing another tube. Jud opened another and another. Dozens of gold coins spilled through their fingers.

"It's true, it's true!" Catching her breath, she gaped at the bounty, eyeing the empty containers. Then suddenly, her insides crashed.

Even at $375 an ounce, this was hardly enough gold to cover legal fees and travel expenses.

"It's worth the same as in 1979, so you haven't lost value," Jud said. "It's more than you had before. Hold on long enough and it'll increase with the changing political winds."

"Yeah, but still." She rubbed the pockets of her new tweed outfit, bought on credit at Neiman Marcus. "I don't have time to wait for gold prices to go up. Everybody wants to be paid now." She sighed and flicked a coin, watching it spin to a stop. "Let's cash in downstairs, I guess."

Cassie's heart sank. If her life was a train, a drunk switchman had taken the controls. She thought for sure there'd be more gold. Donny Ray's savings account had been depleted by lockbox rent and service charges, so this whole trip was a bust. At least they'd join Çois and his wife for a short holiday in Spain, but it would be a lousy vacation, considering.

She gathered the coins while Jud refilled the tubes. "Wait a second," she said, looking hard at the box, cocking her head like a robin.

A sliver of frayed black ribbon peeped from inside the bottom. She pinched it, raveling threads between her thumb and forefinger. Resting her chin on the edge of the table, she slowly pulled the chest closer, drawing an imaginary vertical line on it.

"This thing is deeper than that tray," she observed. "Let's get up under that ribbon."

Jud patted his pockets, retrieved a pocketknife, and jabbed the blade between the layers of plastic, gliding it up and down to separate them. After a long half-minute, he jarred the upper tray loose to show a bottom compartment.

They peered in together. Silver bars gleamed through plastic covers.

"*Silver?*" Cassie held her head in her hands. "The dumbass bought silver? Those prices are in the gutter now." Damn that Donny Ray—all hat and no cattle. Bragging big over a dribble of coins. All he ever gave her was disappointment.

"Bars are sealed tight, aren't they?" She gripped one and peeled away its cover. She blinked, turned the bar over, and blinked again. Her pulse raced as she pulled out more bars, more wrappings, more covers.

"Jud!" she cried. "This is platinum!" She stacked the bars on the table. "Anything else in here?"

She peered into the box, running her fingers around the sides, retrieving a small black velvet pouch. Her fingers trembled as she loosened the drawstring, releasing dozens of small diamonds onto the table. "Holy Mother!" She grabbed Jud's arm.

Unnerved, he cleared his throat, taking quick breaths.

Pulling a tissue from her purse, Cassie dabbed her upper lip. Fear prickled the back of her neck. "You know Jusef will hunt me down."

"No, no. Jusef stays in Stammheim prison. For life." Jud touched her shoulder, meeting her eyes. "This is all yours."

Cassie trickled the diamonds into her palm, playing them into the lights. It called up her trembling hands back in November 1979, as she scribbled on a napkin: "Jusef Ali. Mr. Big," before slipping it to a stewardess aboard an aircraft bound for Dallas. Odd, how one bold act of faith catapulted her into a dynamic she never expected, like a comet, out of nowhere, streaking across the sky.

"Goodness, what a trip," Cassie murmured, as swirling images surfaced like old Polaroid snapshots in a gust of wind—gear shifts and fenders, screen doors, cold Cokes and beer, guns, diamonds, gold coins, and a little silver token, dangling. The thought struck her, right there, twinkling amidst loose diamonds, that Donny Ray finally came through. The no-account that Della warned her about had somehow, even if by accident, provided for her and Francie. And that's all Cassie ever wanted.

## *The End*

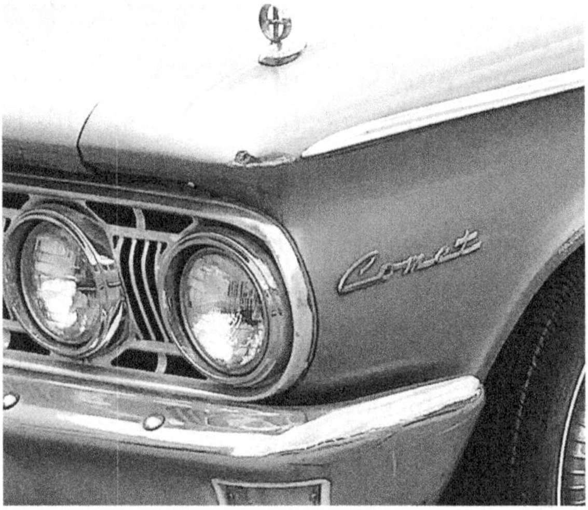
Comet

## ABOUT THE AUTHOR

Scotty Comegys grew up in Shreveport, Louisiana, with close connections to the East Texas towns featured in *Cassie's Comet*. Her depictions of Europe reflect adventures abroad during her 20s, with backpacks and bicycles, a VW bus, and colorful characters who inspired her novel. She taught high school English in Shreveport before spending a decade in the Midwest, where she attended graduate school in Indiana and worked in the Chicago news scene. She returned home in 1985 to practice law and morphed from big city single to married with children, juggling business law with hometown PTA, while dabbling in fiction writing. Over the years, her flair for capturing Southern characters and conflicts in her short stories earned awards and praise among local and small press publications. An attorney for a federal agency, her narrative voice bears little resemblance to her published work on legal topics. For Scotty, this, her debut novel, represents a new leap.

Made in the USA
Las Vegas, NV
15 September 2023